ANOTHER KIND

CAIT MAY & TREVOR BREAM

HARPER alley

An Imprint of HarperCollins Publishers

CHAPTER ONE

WE KNOW WHAT YOU ARE

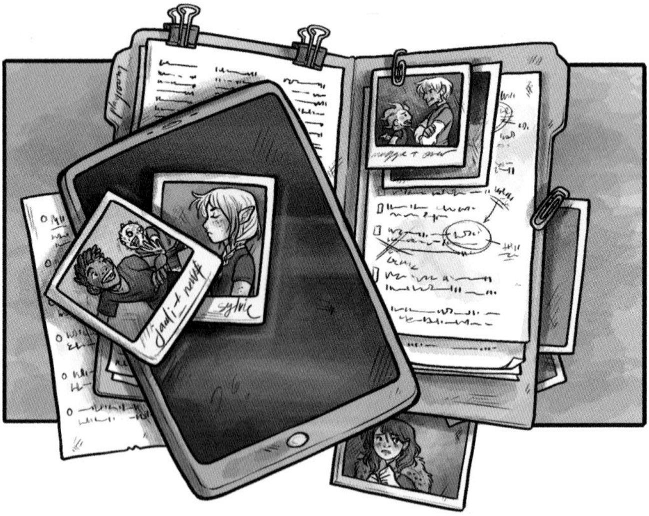

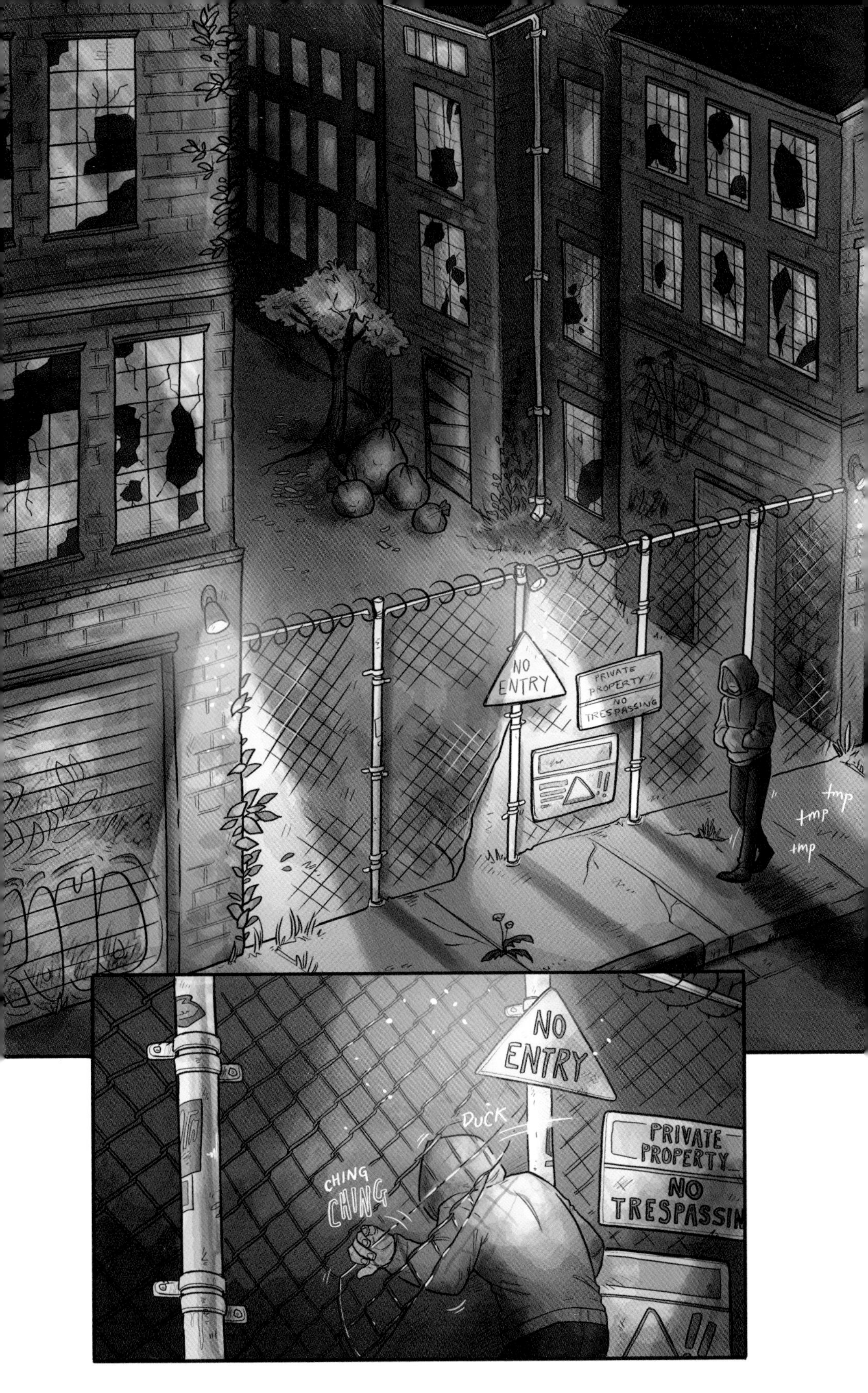
NO ENTRY
PRIVATE PROPERTY
NO TRESPASSING
tmp
tmp
tmp
NO ENTRY
DUCK
PRIVATE PROPERTY
NO TRESPASSIN
CHING
CHING

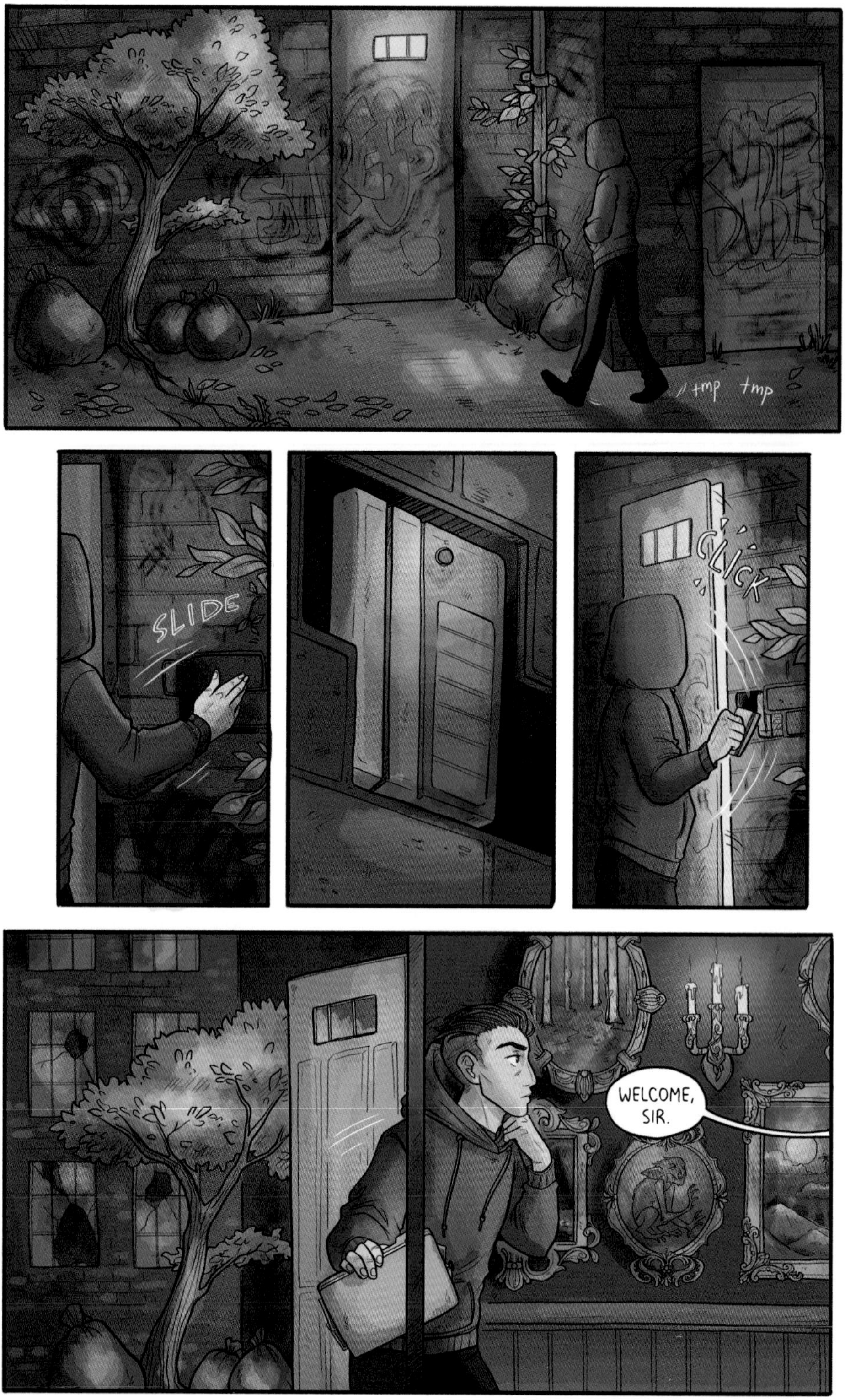
tmp tmp
SLIDE
CLICK
WELCOME, SIR.

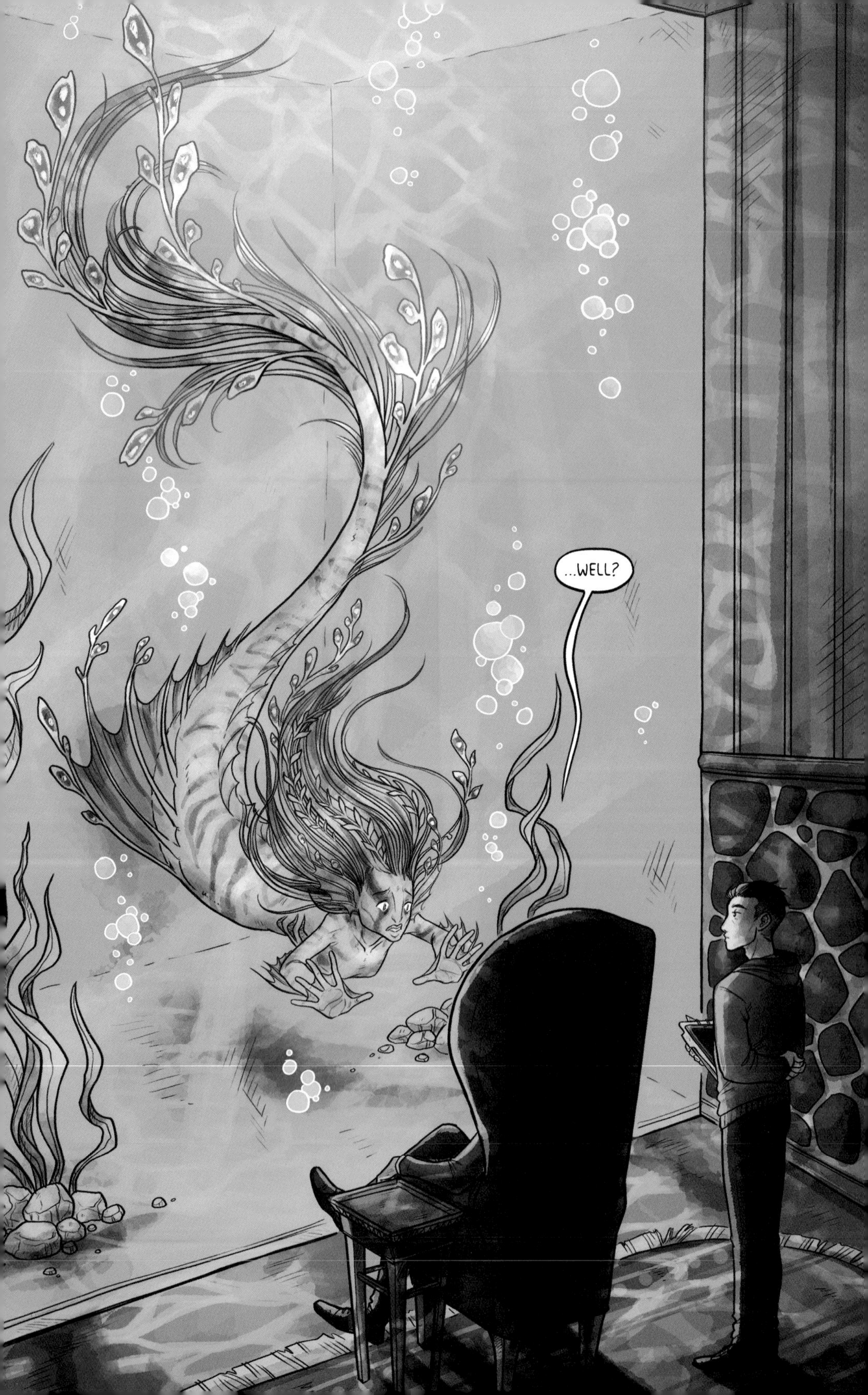
...WELL?

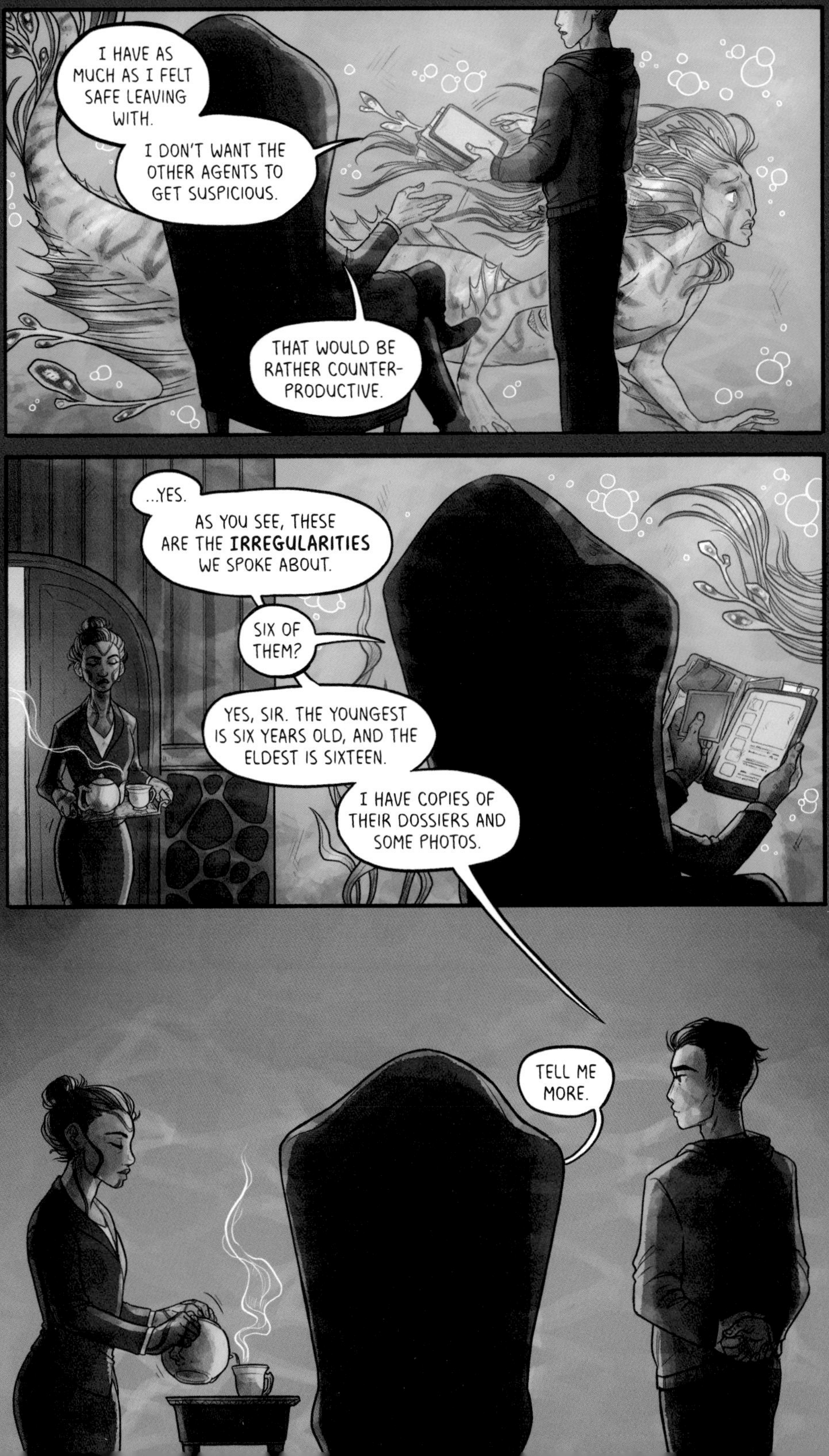
I HAVE AS MUCH AS I FELT SAFE LEAVING WITH.
I DON'T WANT THE OTHER AGENTS TO GET SUSPICIOUS.
THAT WOULD BE RATHER COUNTER-PRODUCTIVE.
...YES.
AS YOU SEE, THESE ARE THE **IRREGULARITIES** WE SPOKE ABOUT.
SIX OF THEM?
YES, SIR. THE YOUNGEST IS SIX YEARS OLD, AND THE ELDEST IS SIXTEEN.
I HAVE COPIES OF THEIR DOSSIERS AND SOME PHOTOS.
TELL ME MORE.

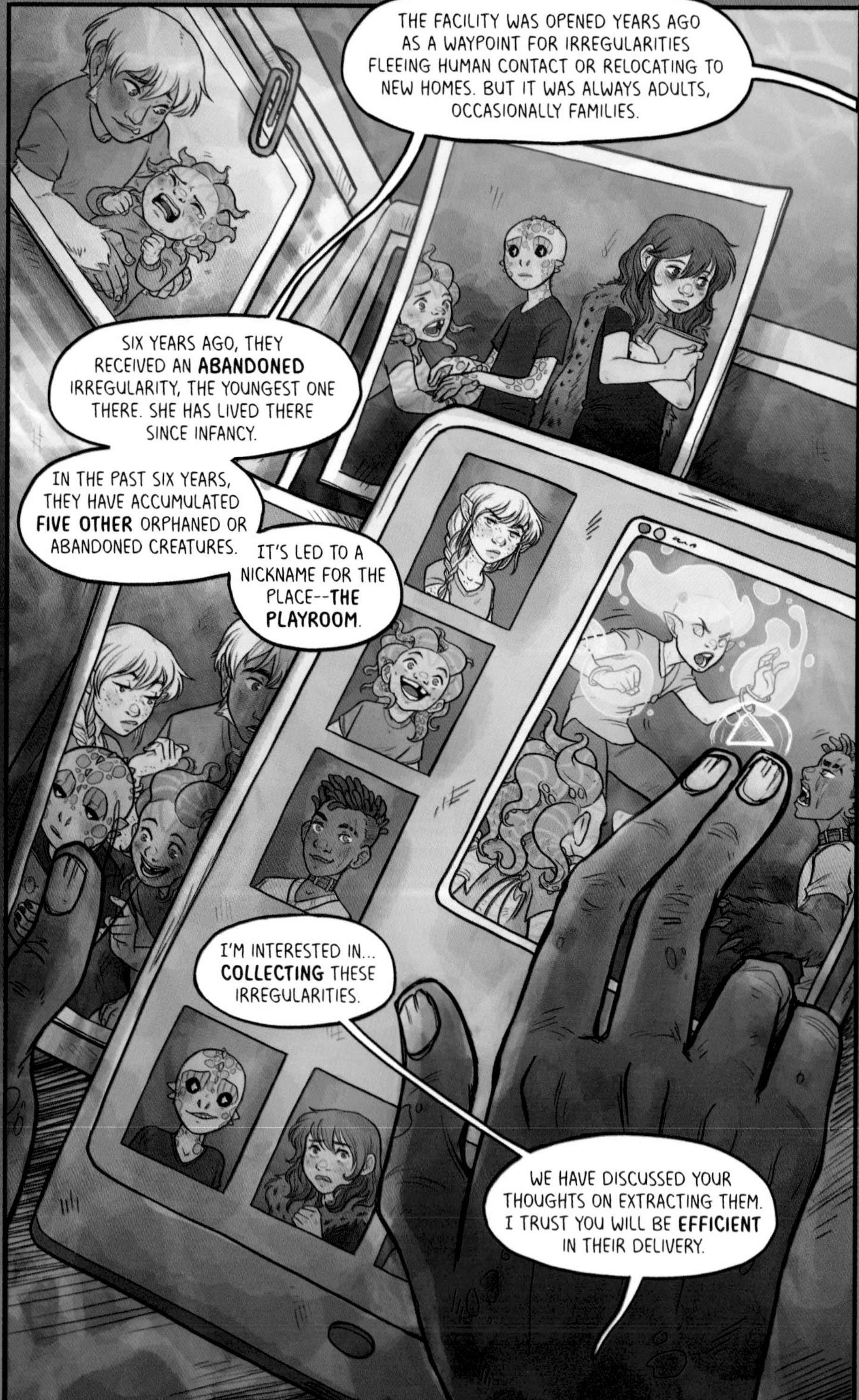
THE FACILITY WAS OPENED YEARS AGO AS A WAYPOINT FOR IRREGULARITIES FLEEING HUMAN CONTACT OR RELOCATING TO NEW HOMES. BUT IT WAS ALWAYS ADULTS, OCCASIONALLY FAMILIES.
SIX YEARS AGO, THEY RECEIVED AN **ABANDONED** IRREGULARITY, THE YOUNGEST ONE THERE. SHE HAS LIVED THERE SINCE INFANCY.
IN THE PAST SIX YEARS, THEY HAVE ACCUMULATED **FIVE OTHER** ORPHANED OR ABANDONED CREATURES.
IT'S LED TO A NICKNAME FOR THE PLACE--**THE PLAYROOM**.
I'M INTERESTED IN... **COLLECTING** THESE IRREGULARITIES.
WE HAVE DISCUSSED YOUR THOUGHTS ON EXTRACTING THEM. I TRUST YOU WILL BE **EFFICIENT** IN THEIR DELIVERY.

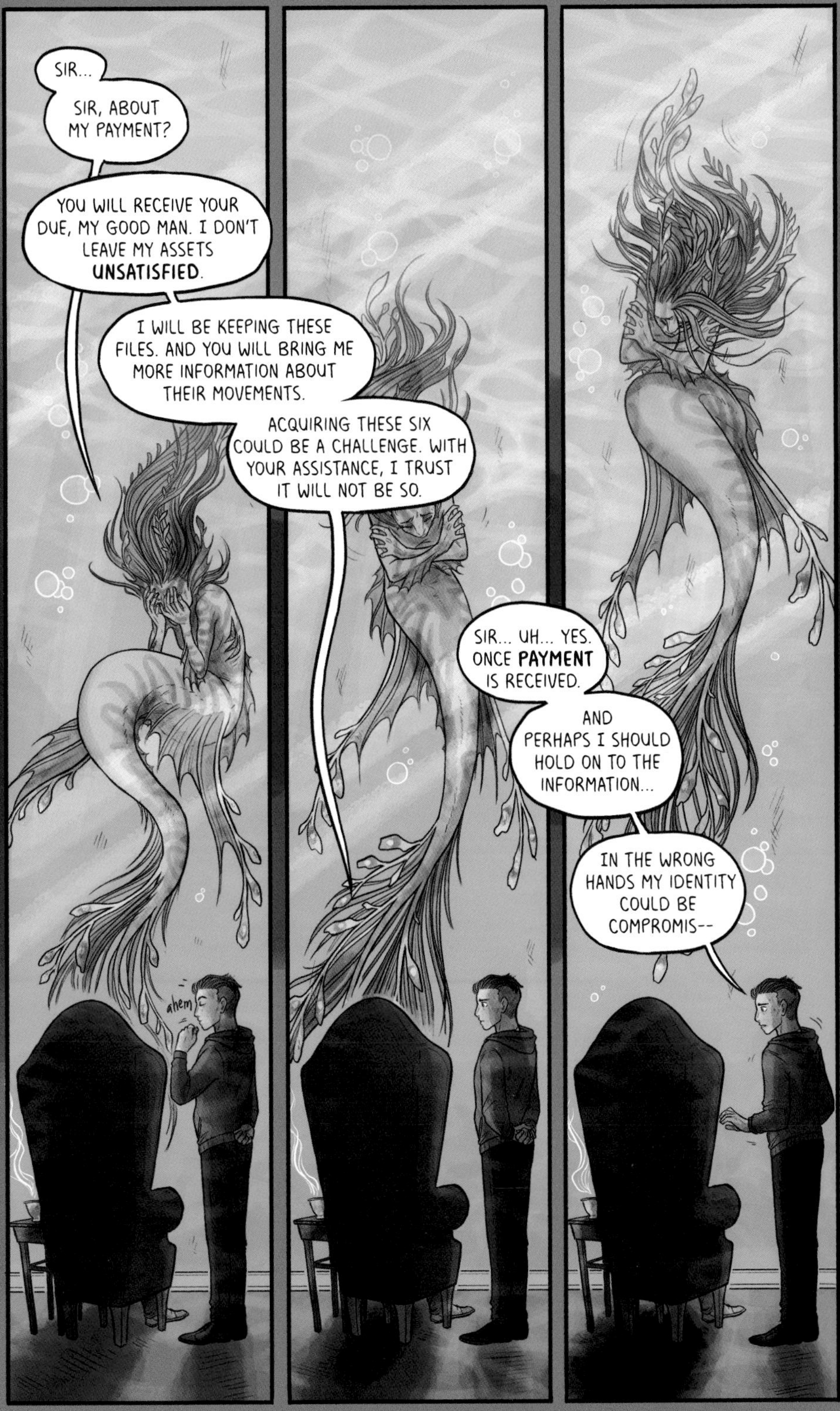
SIR...
SIR, ABOUT MY PAYMENT?
YOU WILL RECEIVE YOUR DUE, MY GOOD MAN. I DON'T LEAVE MY ASSETS **UNSATISFIED**.
I WILL BE KEEPING THESE FILES. AND YOU WILL BRING ME MORE INFORMATION ABOUT THEIR MOVEMENTS.
ahem
ACQUIRING THESE SIX COULD BE A CHALLENGE. WITH YOUR ASSISTANCE, I TRUST IT WILL NOT BE SO.
SIR... UH... YES. ONCE **PAYMENT** IS RECEIVED.
AND PERHAPS I SHOULD HOLD ON TO THE INFORMATION...
IN THE WRONG HANDS MY IDENTITY COULD BE COMPROMIS--

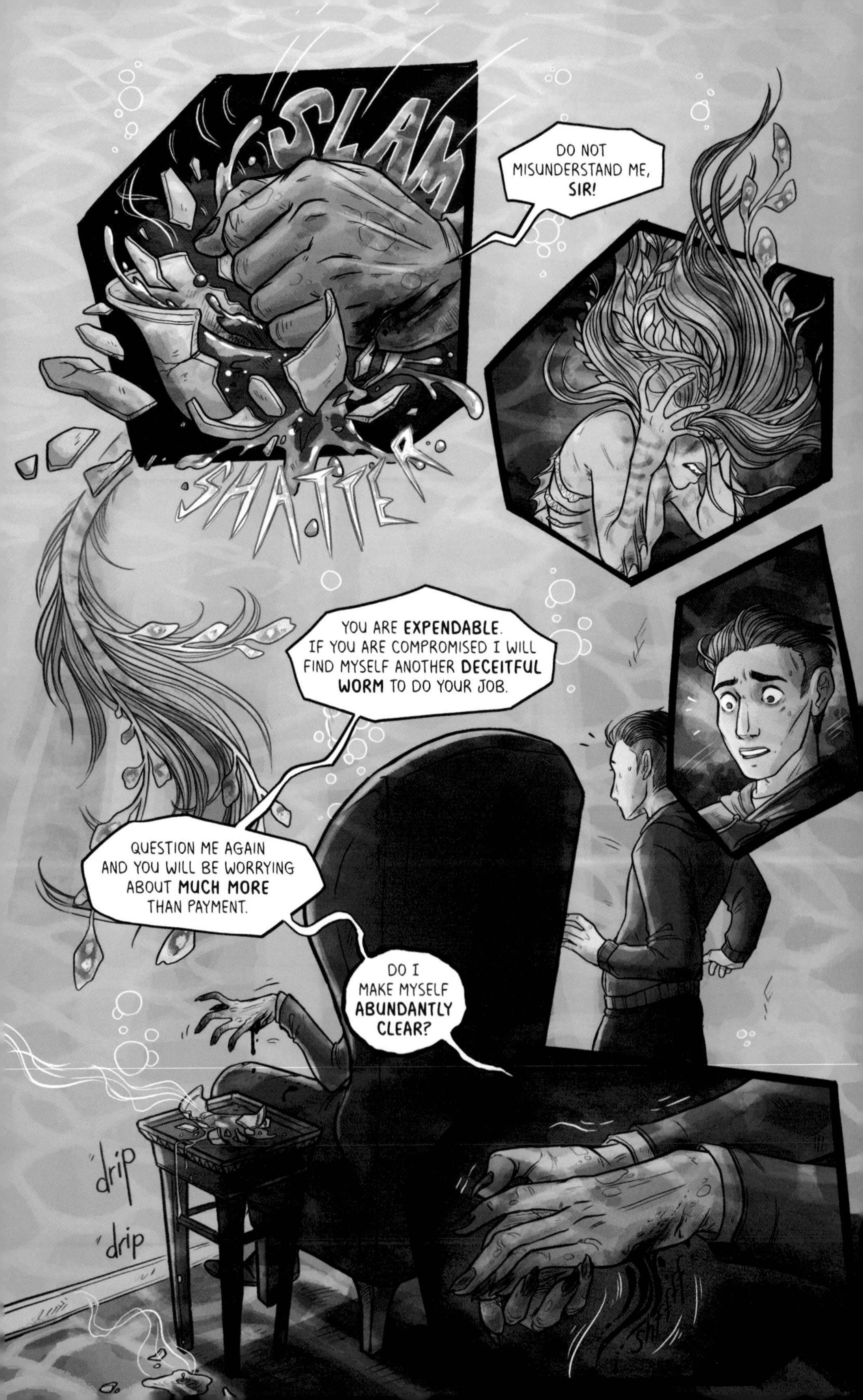
SLAM
SHATTER
DO NOT MISUNDERSTAND ME, SIR!
YOU ARE EXPENDABLE. IF YOU ARE COMPROMISED I WILL FIND MYSELF ANOTHER DECEITFUL WORM TO DO YOUR JOB.
QUESTION ME AGAIN AND YOU WILL BE WORRYING ABOUT MUCH MORE THAN PAYMENT.
DO I MAKE MYSELF ABUNDANTLY CLEAR?
drip
drip
shfff

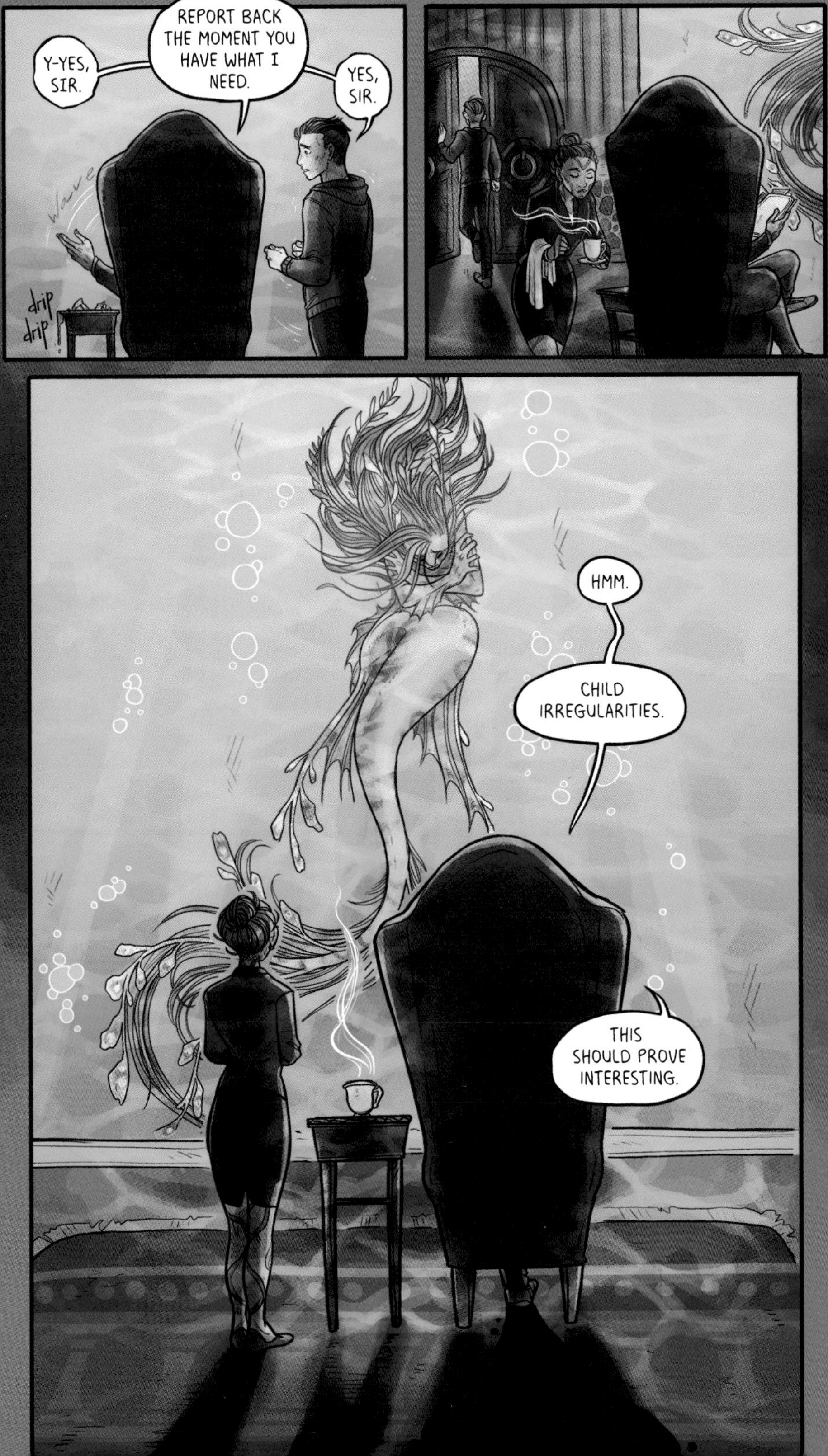
REPORT BACK THE MOMENT YOU HAVE WHAT I NEED.
Y-YES, SIR.
YES, SIR.
wave
drip drip
HMM.
CHILD IRREGULARITIES.
THIS SHOULD PROVE INTERESTING.

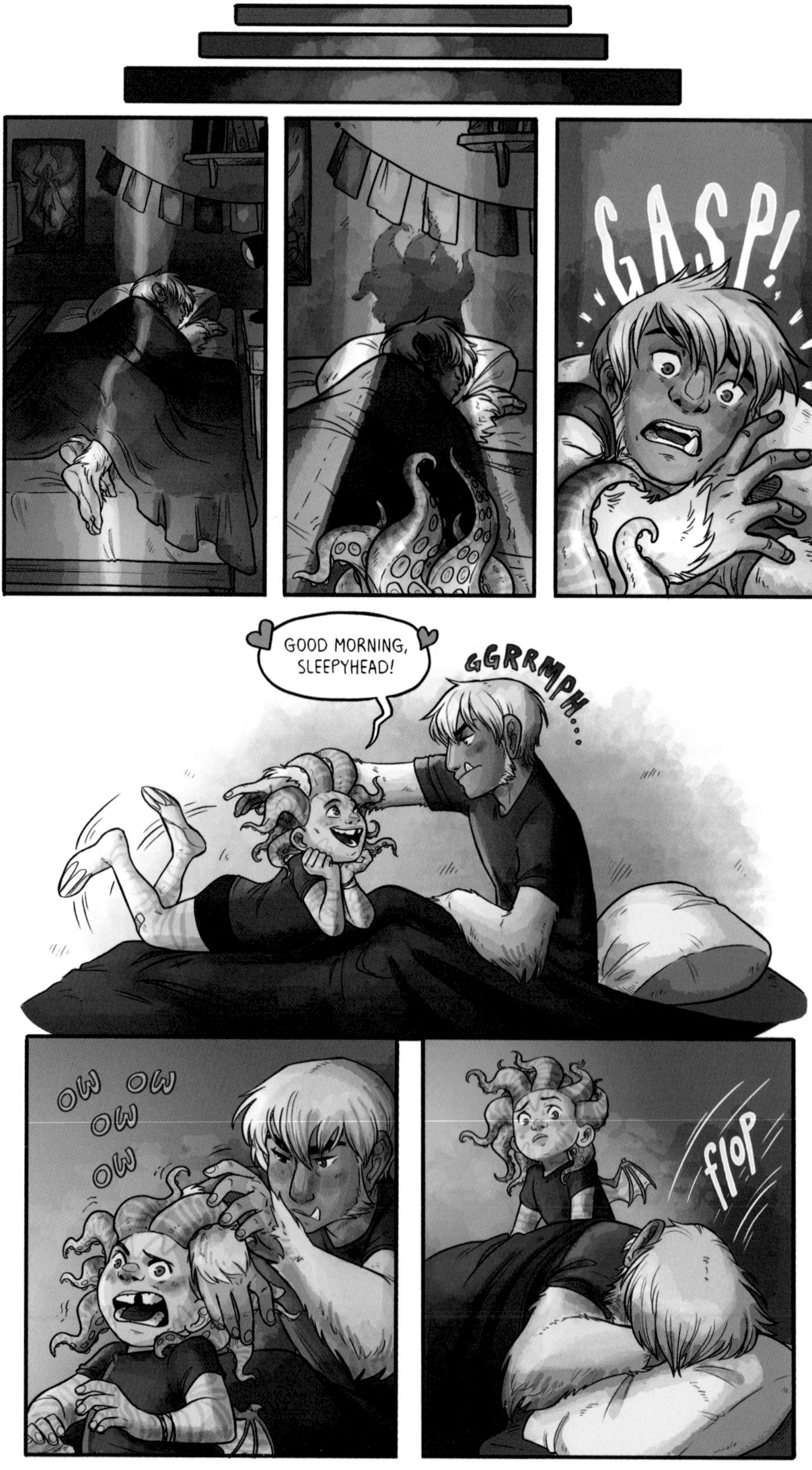
GASP!
GOOD MORNING, SLEEPYHEAD!
GGRRMPH...
OW OW OW OW
FLOP

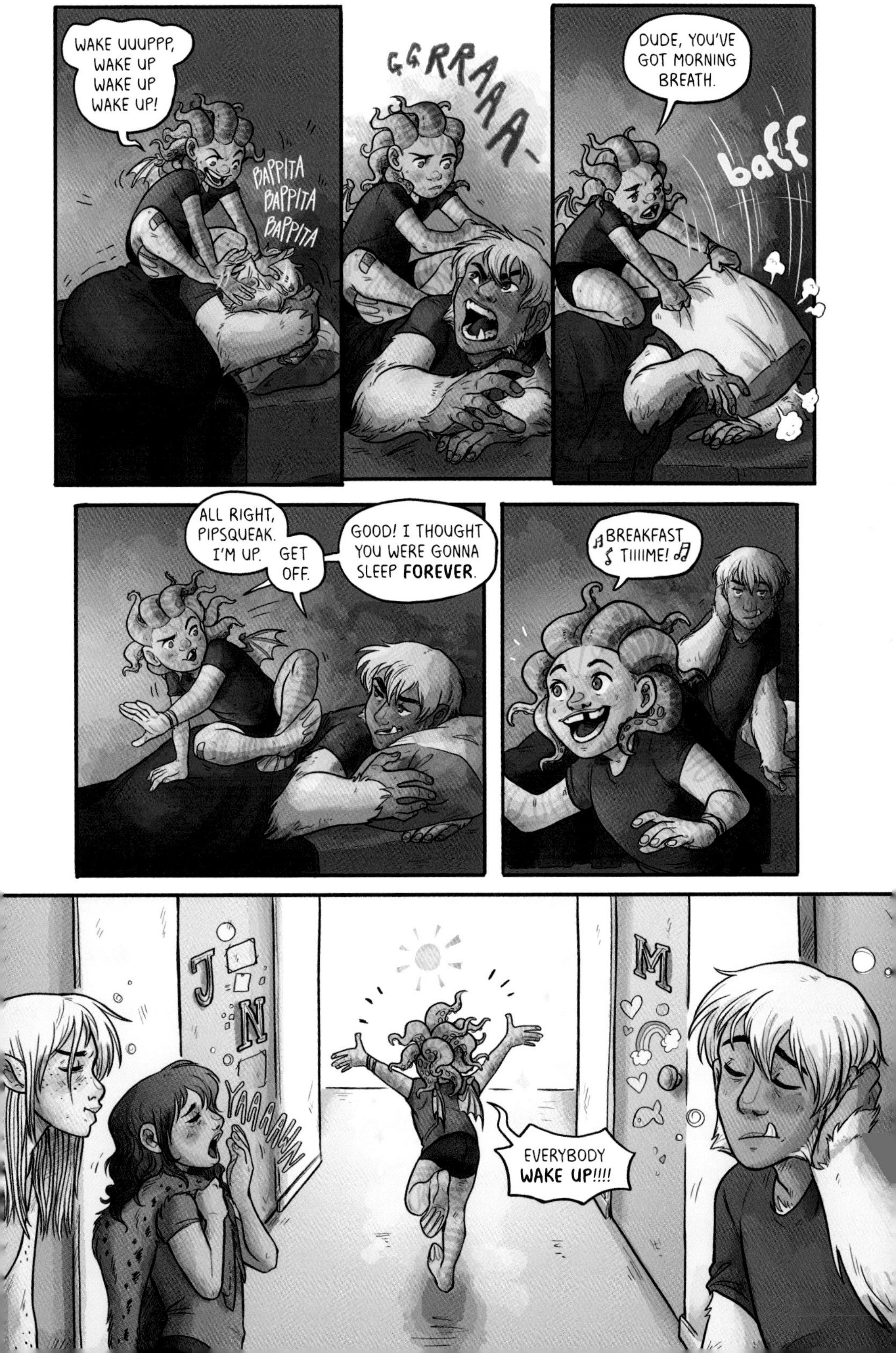
WAKE UUUPPP, WAKE UP WAKE UP WAKE UP!
BAPPITA BAPPITA BAPPITA
GGRRAAA-
DUDE, YOU'VE GOT MORNING BREATH.
baff
ALL RIGHT, PIPSQUEAK. I'M UP.
GET OFF.
GOOD! I THOUGHT YOU WERE GONNA SLEEP FOREVER.
BREAKFAST TIIIIME!
J
N
M
YAAAAAWN
EVERYBODY WAKE UP!!!!

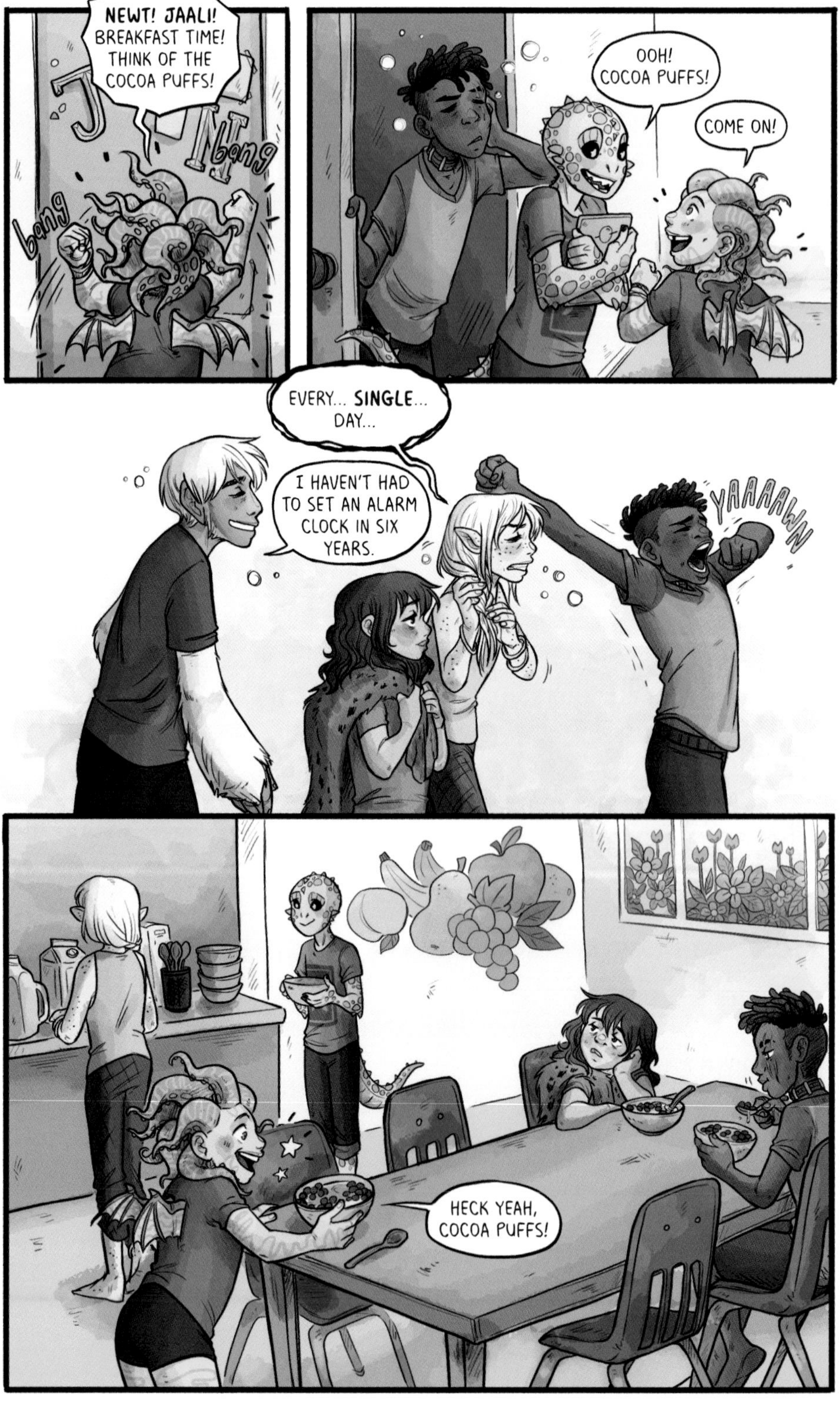
NEWT! JAALI! BREAKFAST TIME! THINK OF THE COCOA PUFFS!
bang
bang
OOH! COCOA PUFFS!
COME ON!
EVERY... SINGLE... DAY...
I HAVEN'T HAD TO SET AN ALARM CLOCK IN SIX YEARS.
YAAAAAWN
HECK YEAH, COCOA PUFFS!

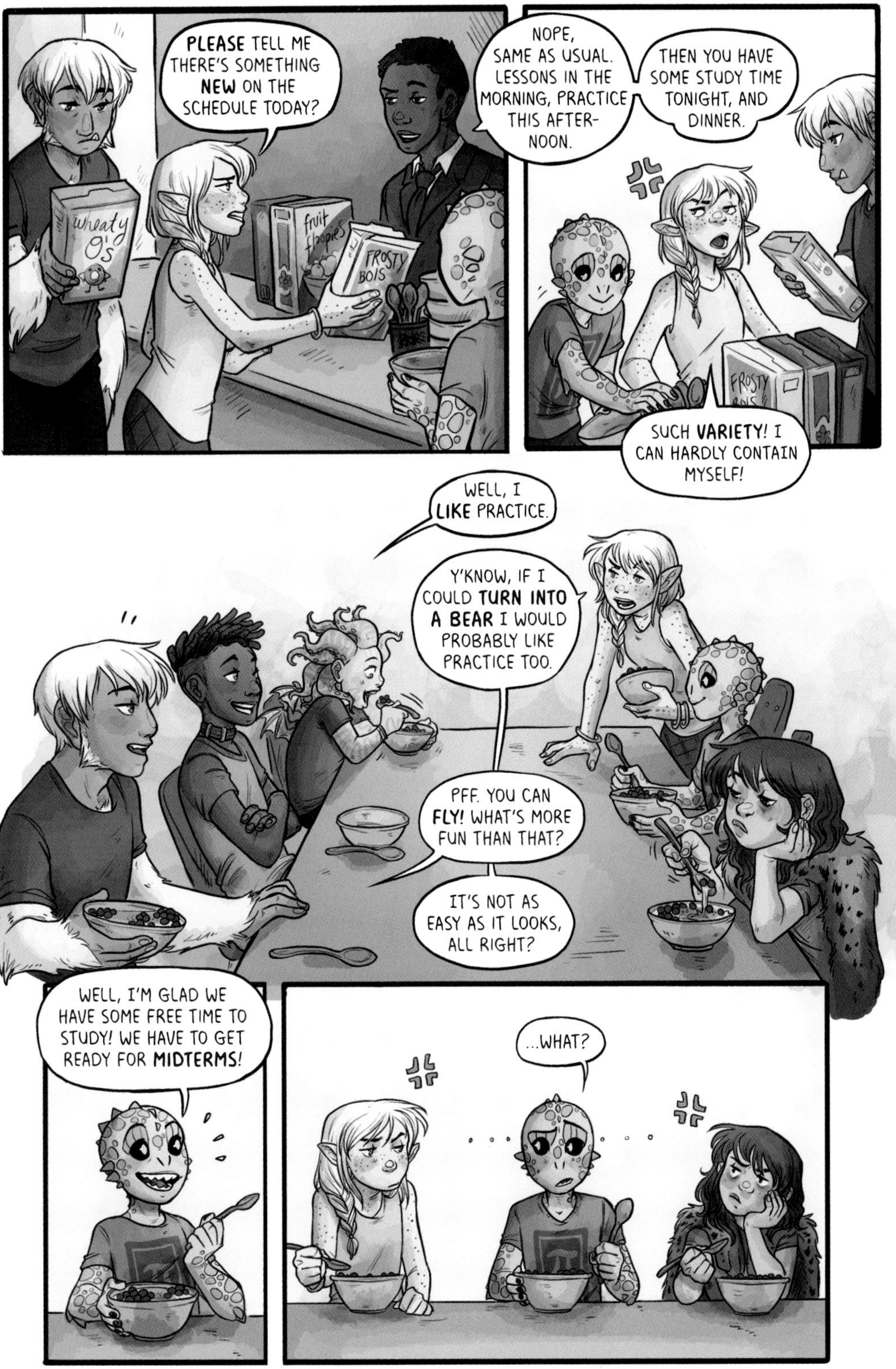
PLEASE TELL ME THERE'S SOMETHING NEW ON THE SCHEDULE TODAY?
wheaty O's
fruit floopies
FROSTY BOIS
NOPE, SAME AS USUAL. LESSONS IN THE MORNING, PRACTICE THIS AFTER-NOON.
THEN YOU HAVE SOME STUDY TIME TONIGHT, AND DINNER.
SUCH VARIETY! I CAN HARDLY CONTAIN MYSELF!
WELL, I LIKE PRACTICE.
Y'KNOW, IF I COULD TURN INTO A BEAR I WOULD PROBABLY LIKE PRACTICE TOO.
PFF. YOU CAN FLY! WHAT'S MORE FUN THAN THAT?
IT'S NOT AS EASY AS IT LOOKS, ALL RIGHT?
WELL, I'M GLAD WE HAVE SOME FREE TIME TO STUDY! WE HAVE TO GET READY FOR MIDTERMS!
...WHAT?

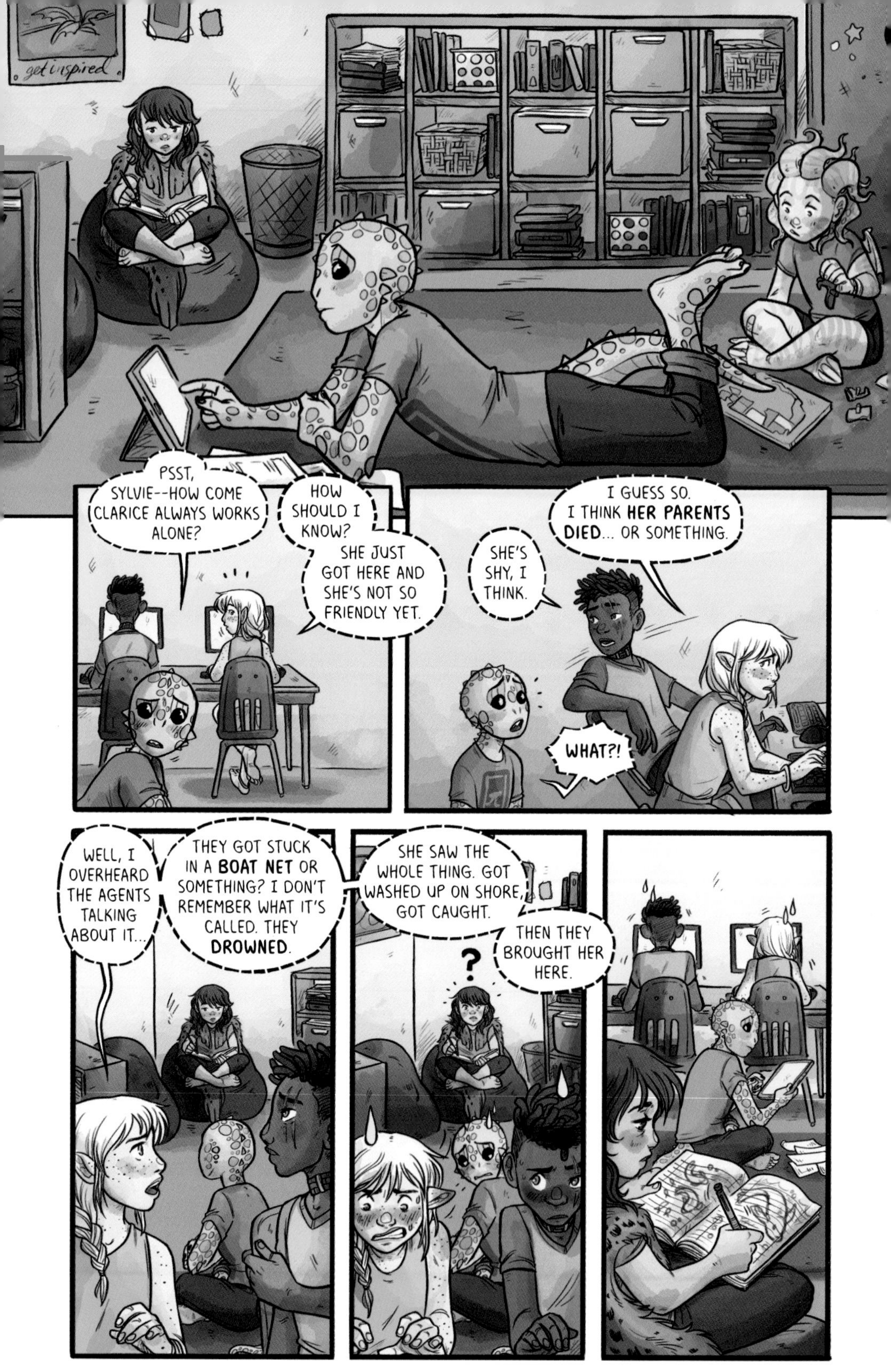

get inspired
PSST, SYLVIE--HOW COME CLARICE ALWAYS WORKS ALONE?
HOW SHOULD I KNOW?
SHE JUST GOT HERE AND SHE'S NOT SO FRIENDLY YET.
SHE'S SHY, I THINK.
I GUESS SO. I THINK **HER PARENTS DIED**... OR SOMETHING.
WHAT?!
WELL, I OVERHEARD THE AGENTS TALKING ABOUT IT...
THEY GOT STUCK IN A **BOAT NET** OR SOMETHING? I DON'T REMEMBER WHAT IT'S CALLED. THEY **DROWNED**.
SHE SAW THE WHOLE THING. GOT WASHED UP ON SHORE, GOT CAUGHT.
THEN THEY BROUGHT HER HERE.
?

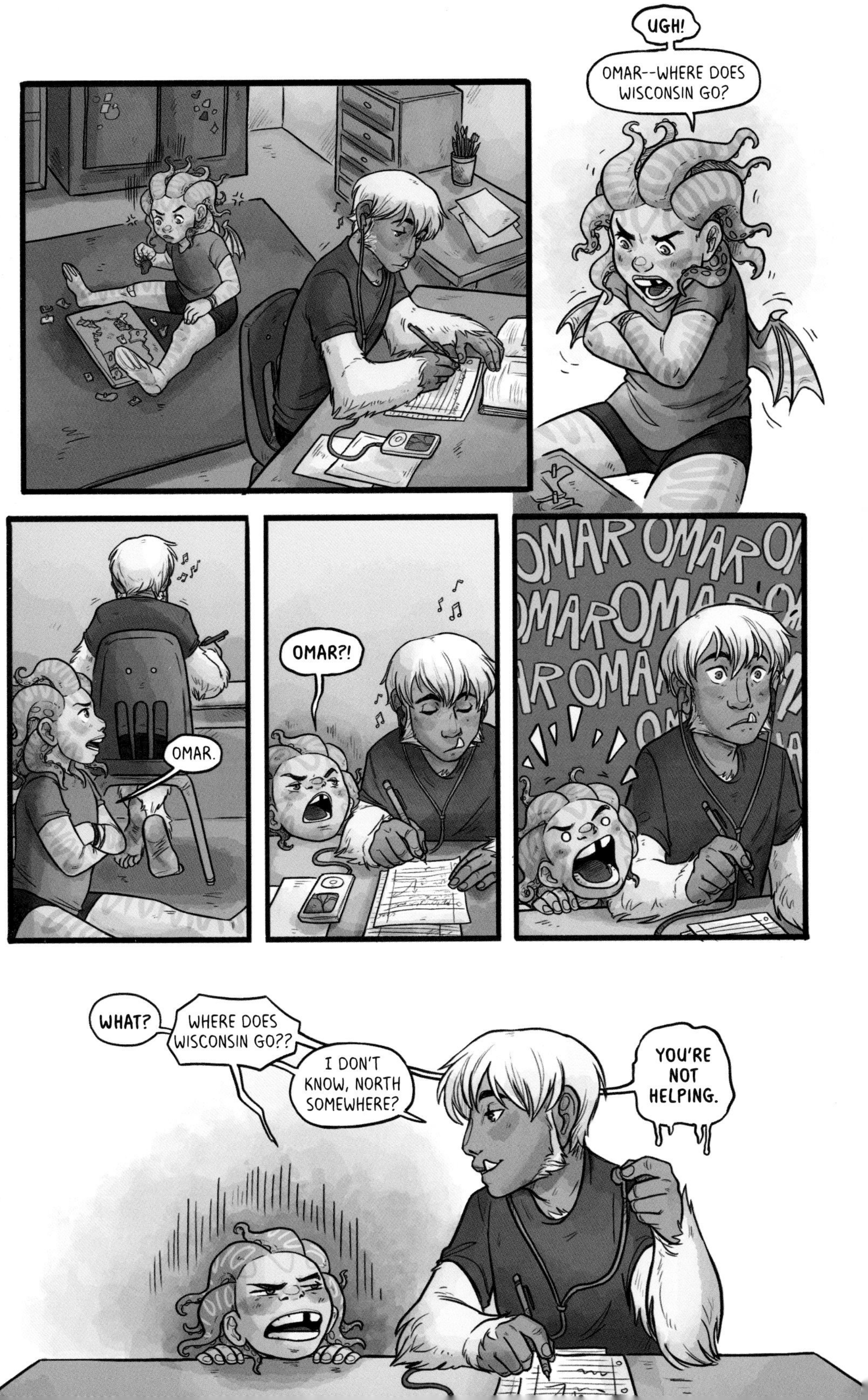
UGH!
OMAR--WHERE DOES WISCONSIN GO?
OMAR.
OMAR?!
OMAR OMAR OMAR OMAR OMAR
WHAT?
WHERE DOES WISCONSIN GO??
I DON'T KNOW, NORTH SOMEWHERE?
YOU'RE NOT HELPING.

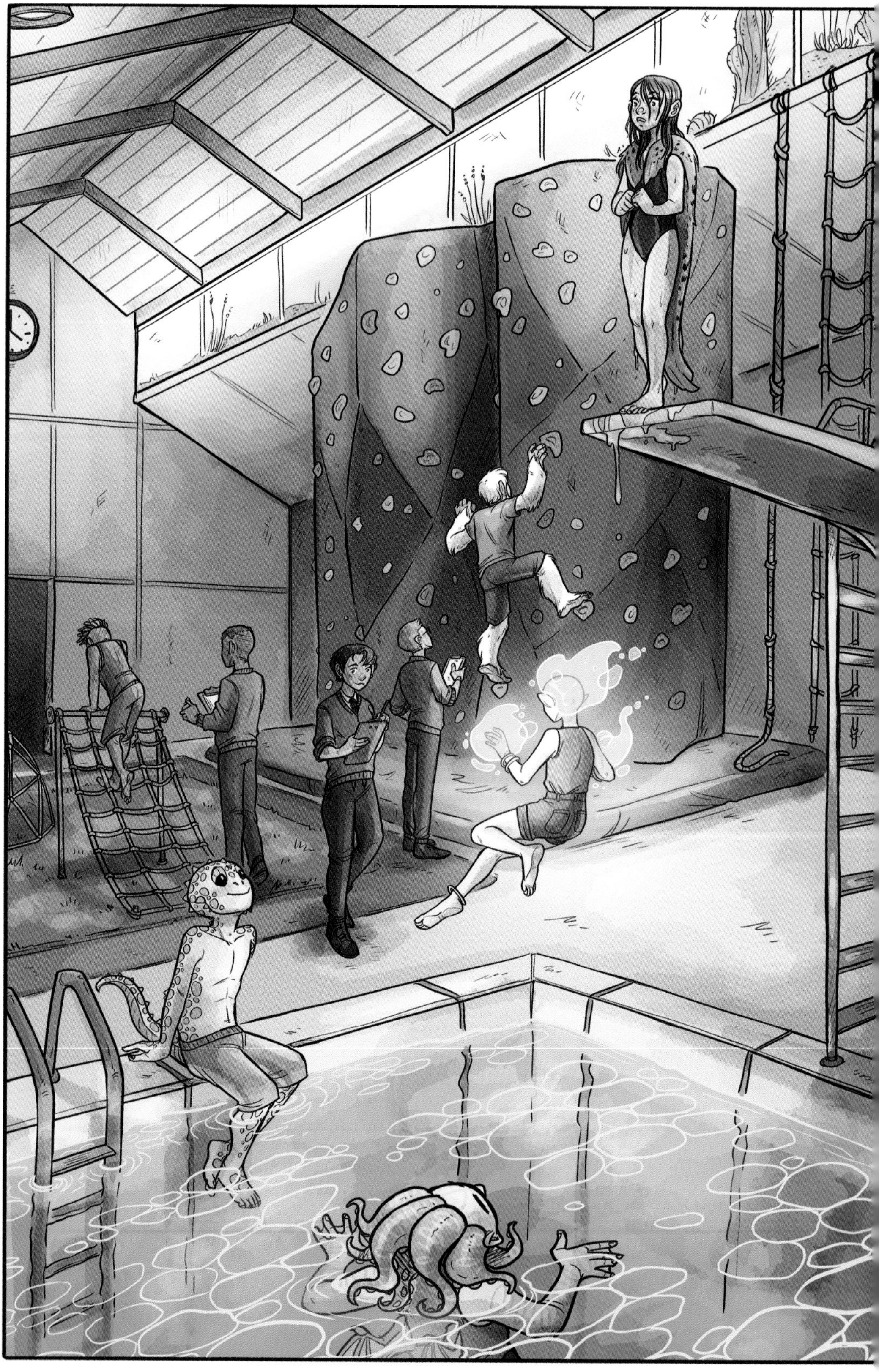

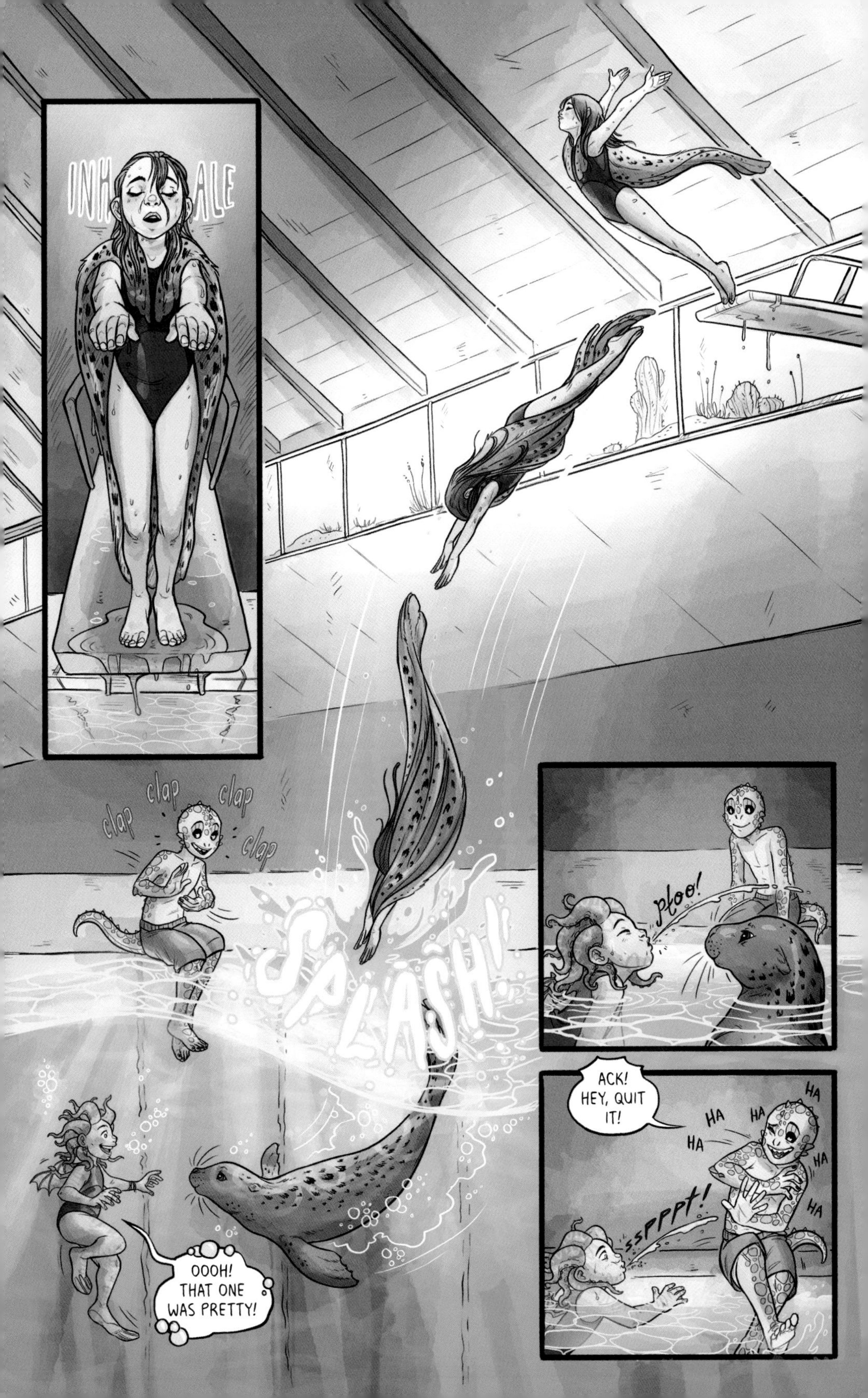
INHALE
clap clap clap clap
SPLASH!
OOOH! THAT ONE WAS PRETTY!
ptoo!
ACK! HEY, QUIT IT!
HA HA HA HA HA HA
ssPPPt!

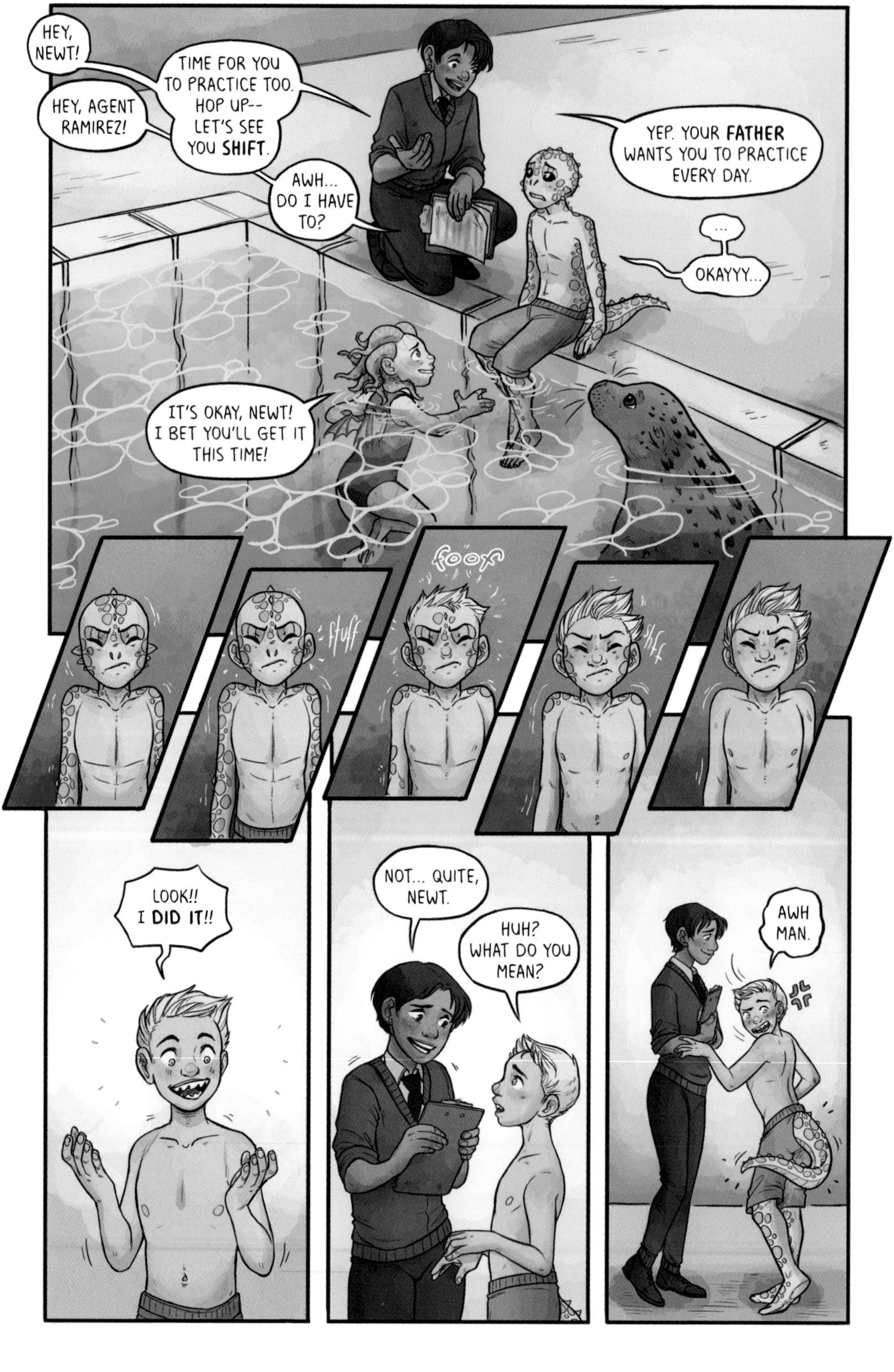
HEY, NEWT!
HEY, AGENT RAMIREZ!
TIME FOR YOU TO PRACTICE TOO. HOP UP-- LET'S SEE YOU **SHIFT**.
AWH... DO I HAVE TO?
YEP. YOUR **FATHER** WANTS YOU TO PRACTICE EVERY DAY.
...
OKAYYY...
IT'S OKAY, NEWT! I BET YOU'LL GET IT THIS TIME!
stuff
foof
shff
LOOK!! I **DID IT**!!
NOT... QUITE, NEWT.
HUH? WHAT DO YOU MEAN?
AWH MAN.

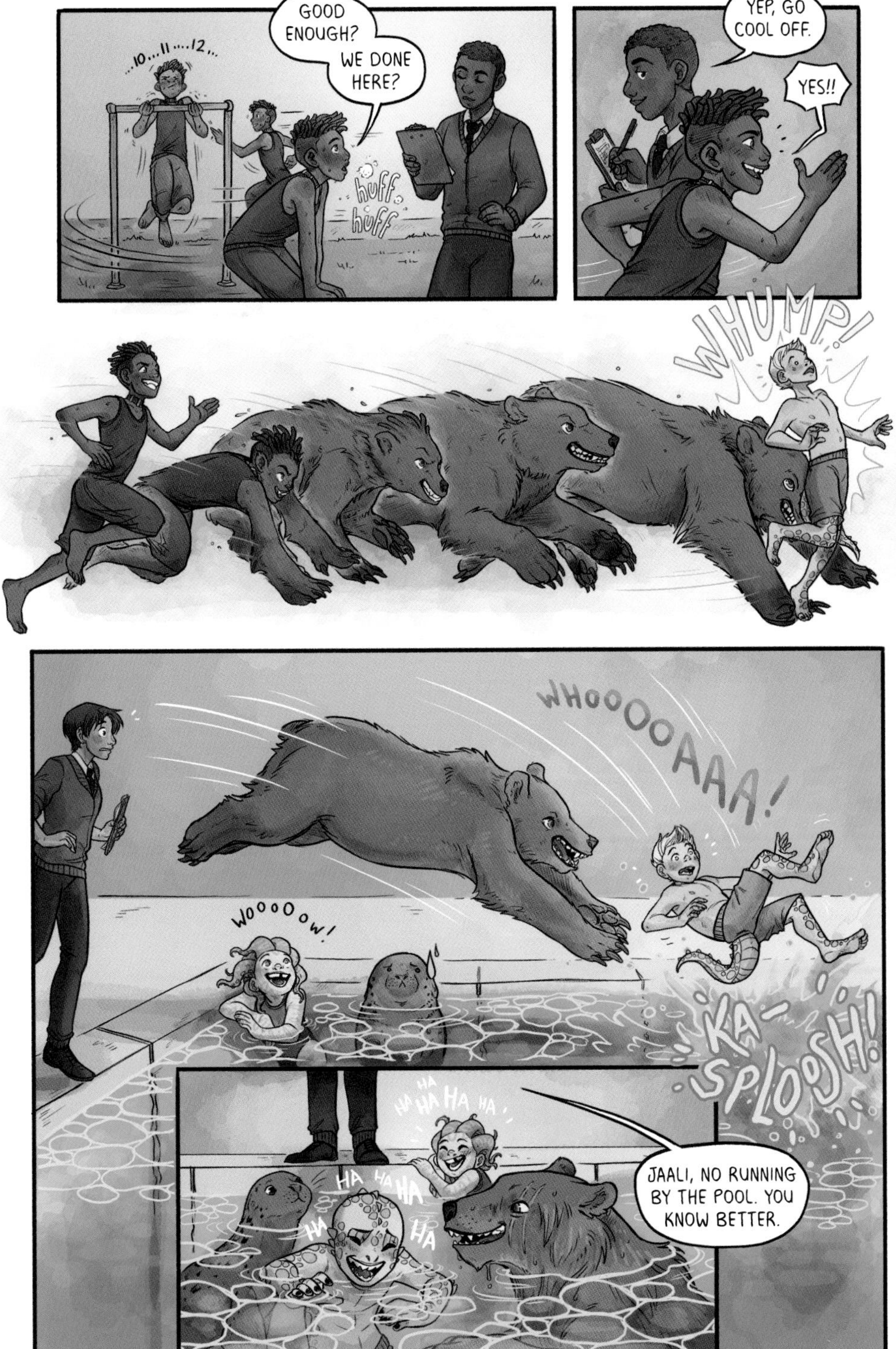
...10...11....12...
GOOD ENOUGH?
WE DONE HERE?
huff huff
YEP, GO COOL OFF.
YES!!
WHUMP!
WHOOOOAAA!
WOOOOow!
KA-SPLOOSH!
HA HA HA HA HA
HA HA HA HA HA HA
JAALI, NO RUNNING BY THE POOL. YOU KNOW BETTER.

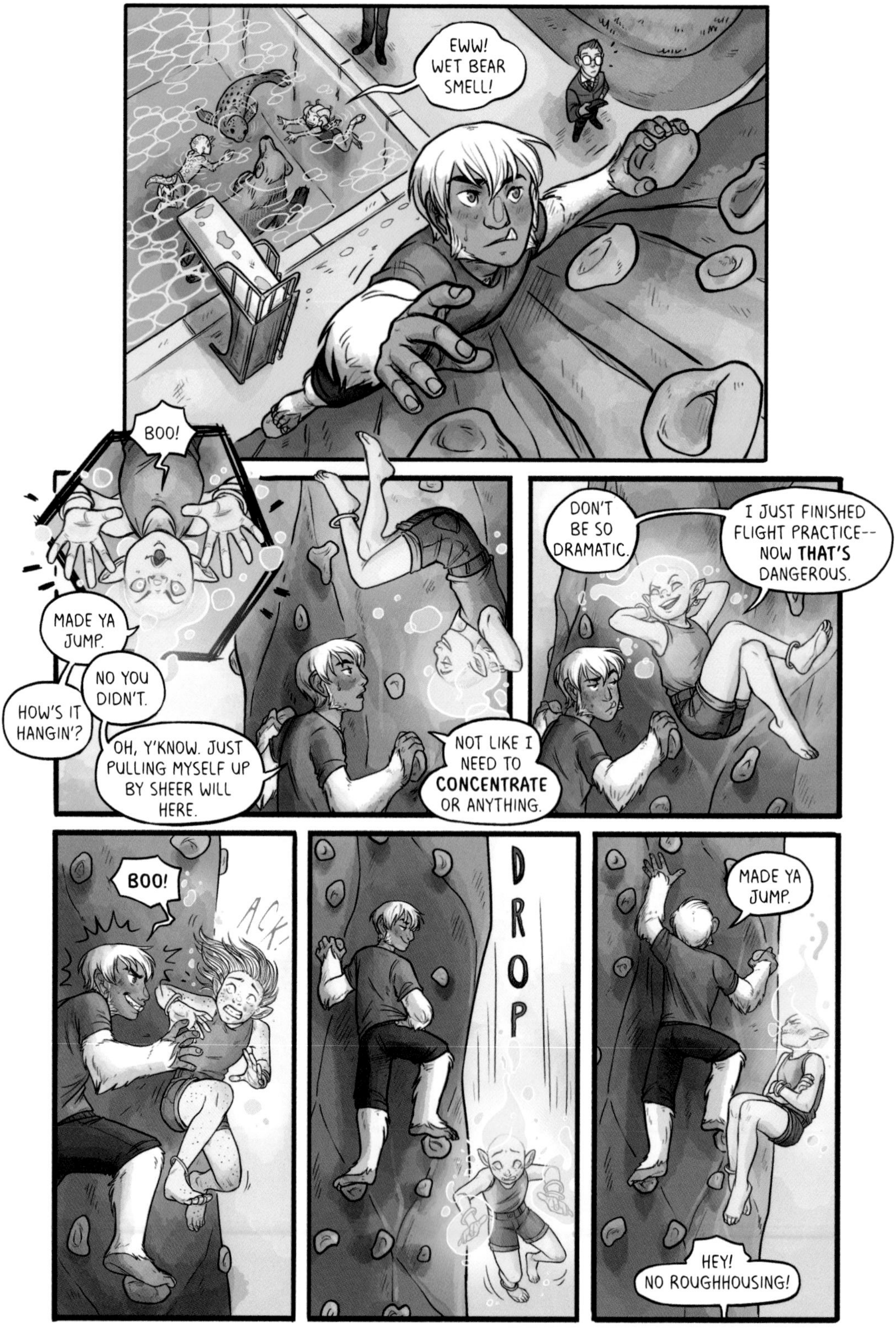
EWW! WET BEAR SMELL!
BOO!
MADE YA JUMP.
NO YOU DIDN'T.
HOW'S IT HANGIN'?
OH, Y'KNOW. JUST PULLING MYSELF UP BY SHEER WILL HERE.
NOT LIKE I NEED TO **CONCENTRATE** OR ANYTHING.
DON'T BE SO DRAMATIC.
I JUST FINISHED FLIGHT PRACTICE-- NOW **THAT'S** DANGEROUS.
BOO!
ACK!
DROP
MADE YA JUMP.
HEY! NO ROUGHHOUSING!

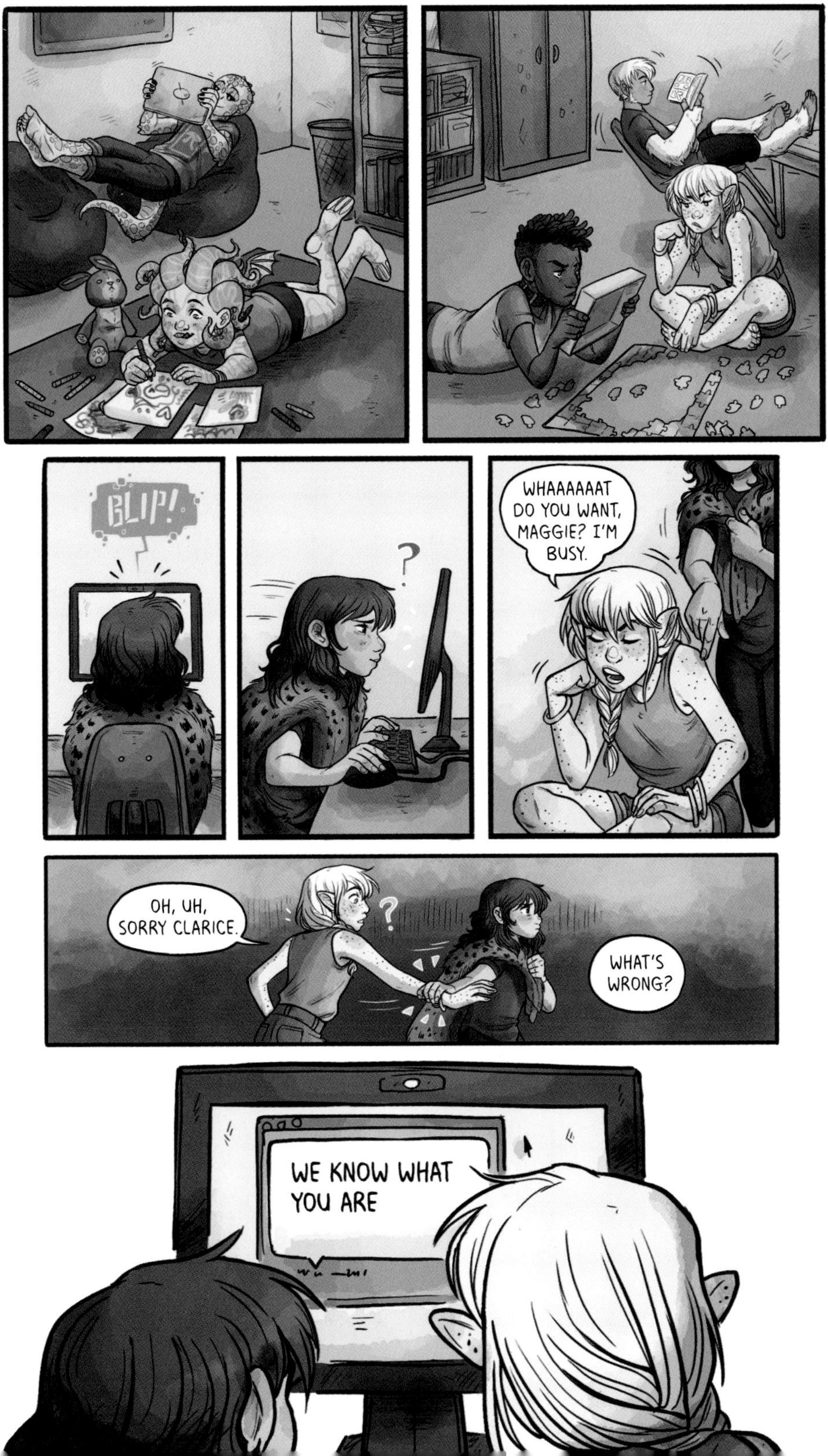

BLIP!
?
WHAAAAAAT DO YOU WANT, MAGGIE? I'M BUSY.
OH, UH, SORRY CLARICE.
?
WHAT'S WRONG?
WE KNOW WHAT YOU ARE

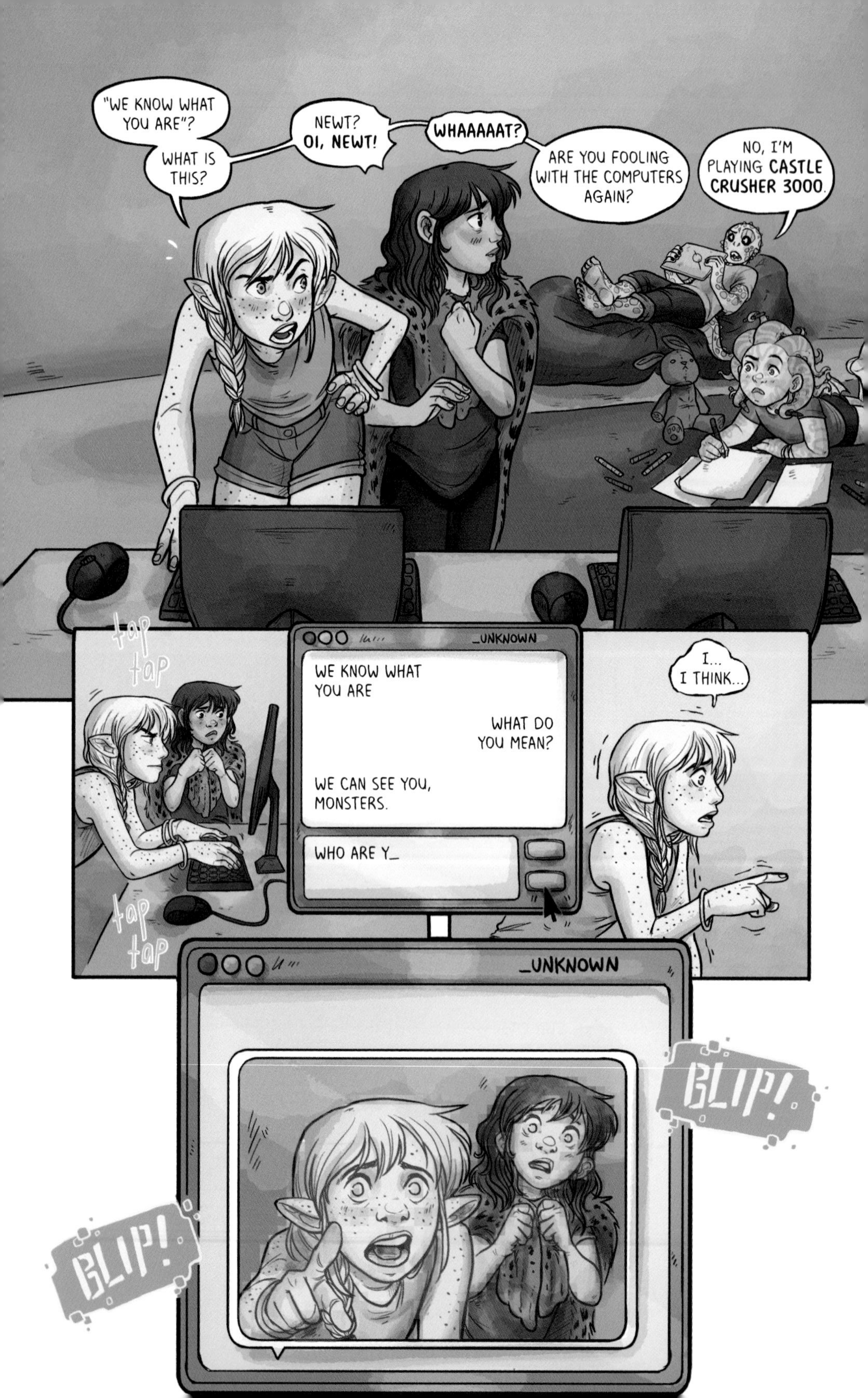
"WE KNOW WHAT YOU ARE"?
WHAT IS THIS?
NEWT? OI, NEWT!
WHAAAAAT?
ARE YOU FOOLING WITH THE COMPUTERS AGAIN?
NO, I'M PLAYING CASTLE CRUSHER 3000.
tap tap
_UNKNOWN
WE KNOW WHAT YOU ARE
WHAT DO YOU MEAN?
WE CAN SEE YOU, MONSTERS.
WHO ARE Y_
I... I THINK...
tap tap
_UNKNOWN
BLIP!
BLIP!

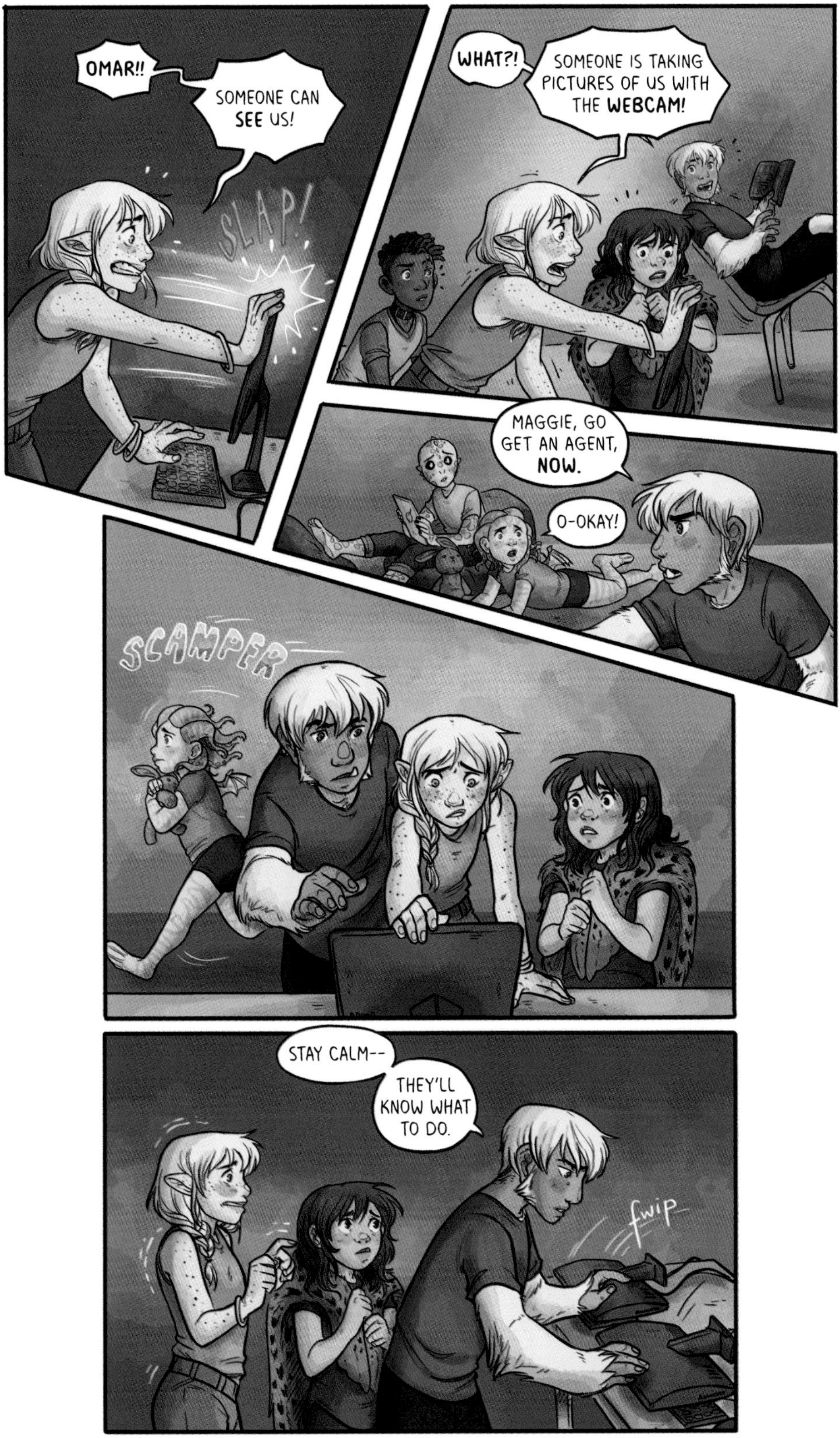
OMAR!!
SOMEONE CAN SEE US!
SLAP!
WHAT?!
SOMEONE IS TAKING PICTURES OF US WITH THE WEBCAM!
MAGGIE, GO GET AN AGENT, NOW.
O-OKAY!
SCAMPER
STAY CALM--
THEY'LL KNOW WHAT TO DO.
fwip

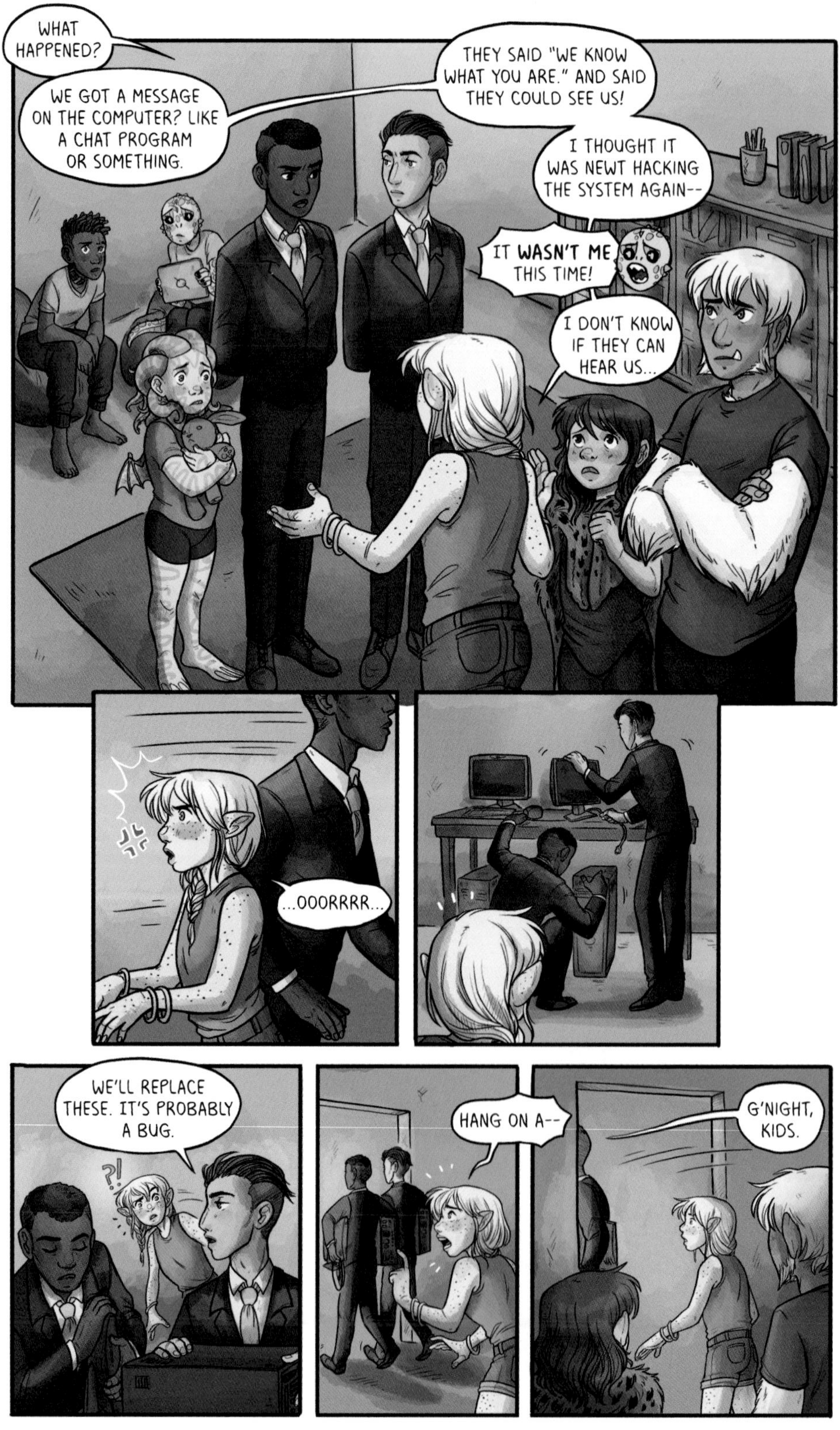
WHAT HAPPENED?
WE GOT A MESSAGE ON THE COMPUTER? LIKE A CHAT PROGRAM OR SOMETHING.
THEY SAID "WE KNOW WHAT YOU ARE." AND SAID THEY COULD SEE US!
I THOUGHT IT WAS NEWT HACKING THE SYSTEM AGAIN--
IT **WASN'T ME** THIS TIME!
I DON'T KNOW IF THEY CAN HEAR US...
...OOORRRR...
WE'LL REPLACE THESE. IT'S PROBABLY A BUG.
?!
HANG ON A--
G'NIGHT, KIDS.

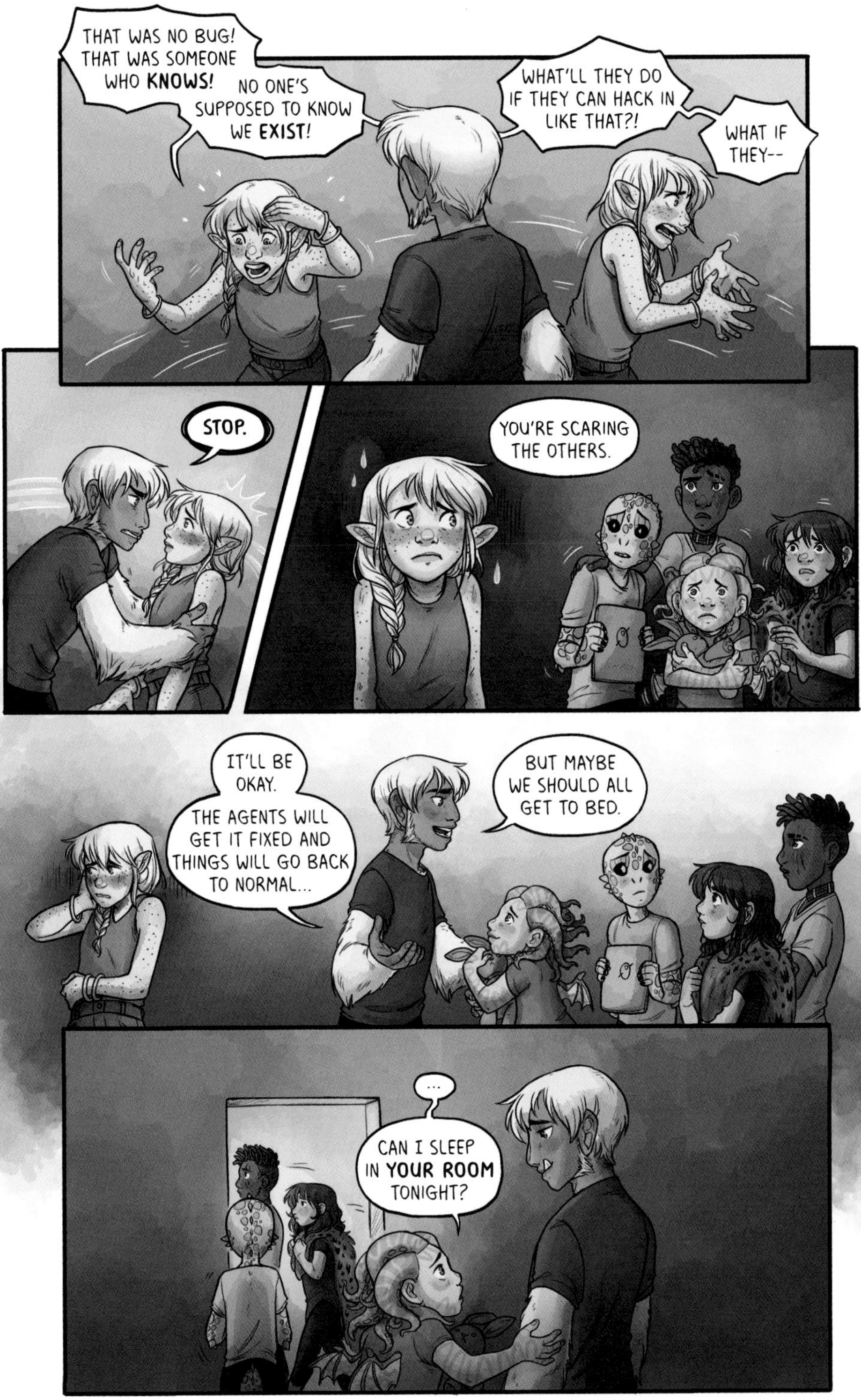
THAT WAS NO BUG! THAT WAS SOMEONE WHO KNOWS!
NO ONE'S SUPPOSED TO KNOW WE EXIST!
WHAT'LL THEY DO IF THEY CAN HACK IN LIKE THAT?!
WHAT IF THEY--
STOP.
YOU'RE SCARING THE OTHERS.
IT'LL BE OKAY.
THE AGENTS WILL GET IT FIXED AND THINGS WILL GO BACK TO NORMAL...
BUT MAYBE WE SHOULD ALL GET TO BED.
...
CAN I SLEEP IN YOUR ROOM TONIGHT?

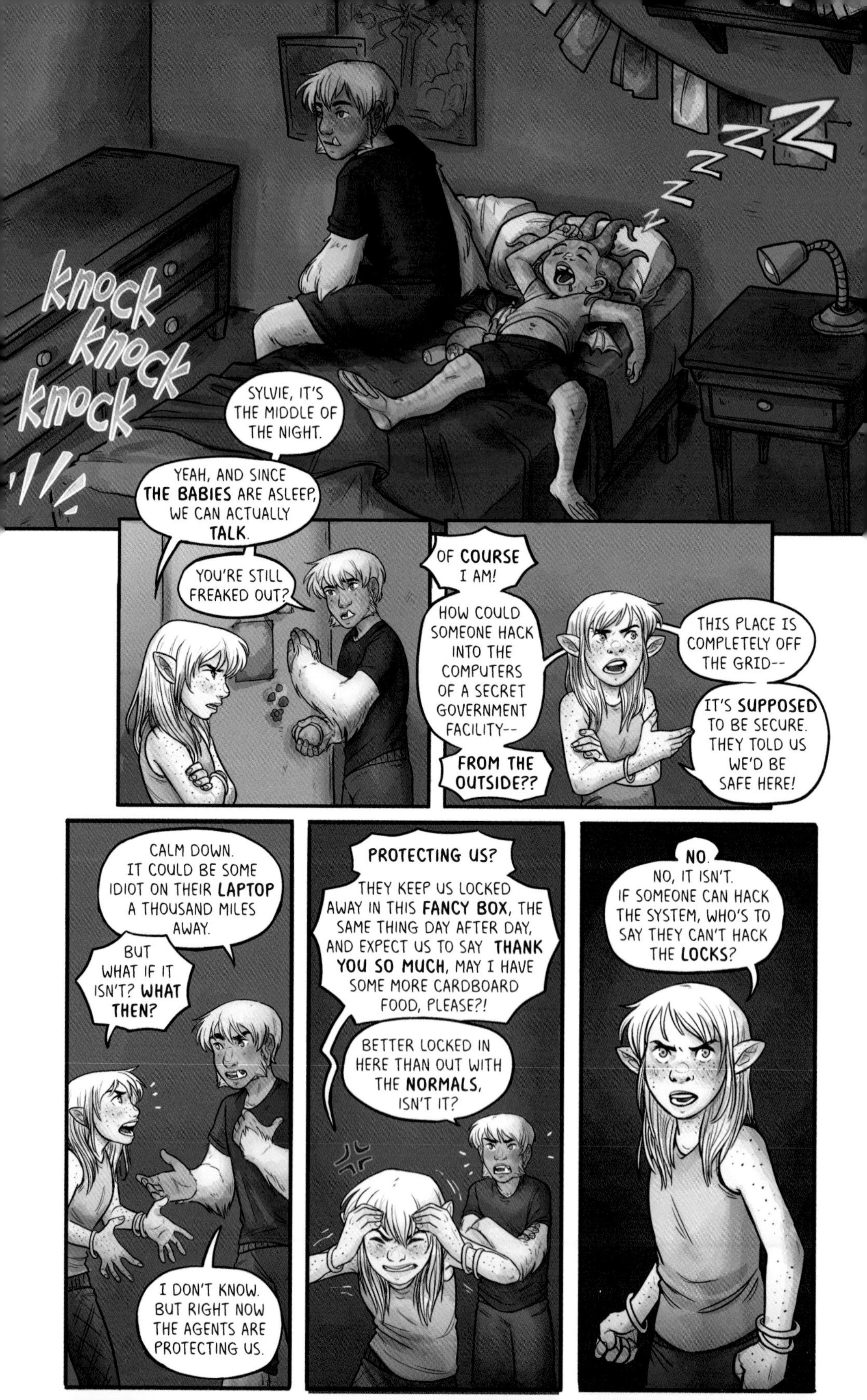
knock knock knock
SYLVIE, IT'S THE MIDDLE OF THE NIGHT.
YEAH, AND SINCE **THE BABIES** ARE ASLEEP, WE CAN ACTUALLY **TALK**.
YOU'RE STILL FREAKED OUT?
OF **COURSE** I AM!
HOW COULD SOMEONE HACK INTO THE COMPUTERS OF A SECRET GOVERNMENT FACILITY--
FROM THE OUTSIDE??
THIS PLACE IS COMPLETELY OFF THE GRID--
IT'S **SUPPOSED** TO BE SECURE. THEY TOLD US WE'D BE SAFE HERE!
CALM DOWN. IT COULD BE SOME IDIOT ON THEIR **LAPTOP** A THOUSAND MILES AWAY.
BUT WHAT IF IT ISN'T? **WHAT THEN?**
I DON'T KNOW. BUT RIGHT NOW THE AGENTS ARE PROTECTING US.
PROTECTING US?
THEY KEEP US LOCKED AWAY IN THIS **FANCY BOX**, THE SAME THING DAY AFTER DAY, AND EXPECT US TO SAY **THANK YOU SO MUCH**, MAY I HAVE SOME MORE CARDBOARD FOOD, PLEASE?!
BETTER LOCKED IN HERE THAN OUT WITH THE **NORMALS**, ISN'T IT?
NO.
NO, IT ISN'T. IF SOMEONE CAN HACK THE SYSTEM, WHO'S TO SAY THEY CAN'T HACK THE **LOCKS**?

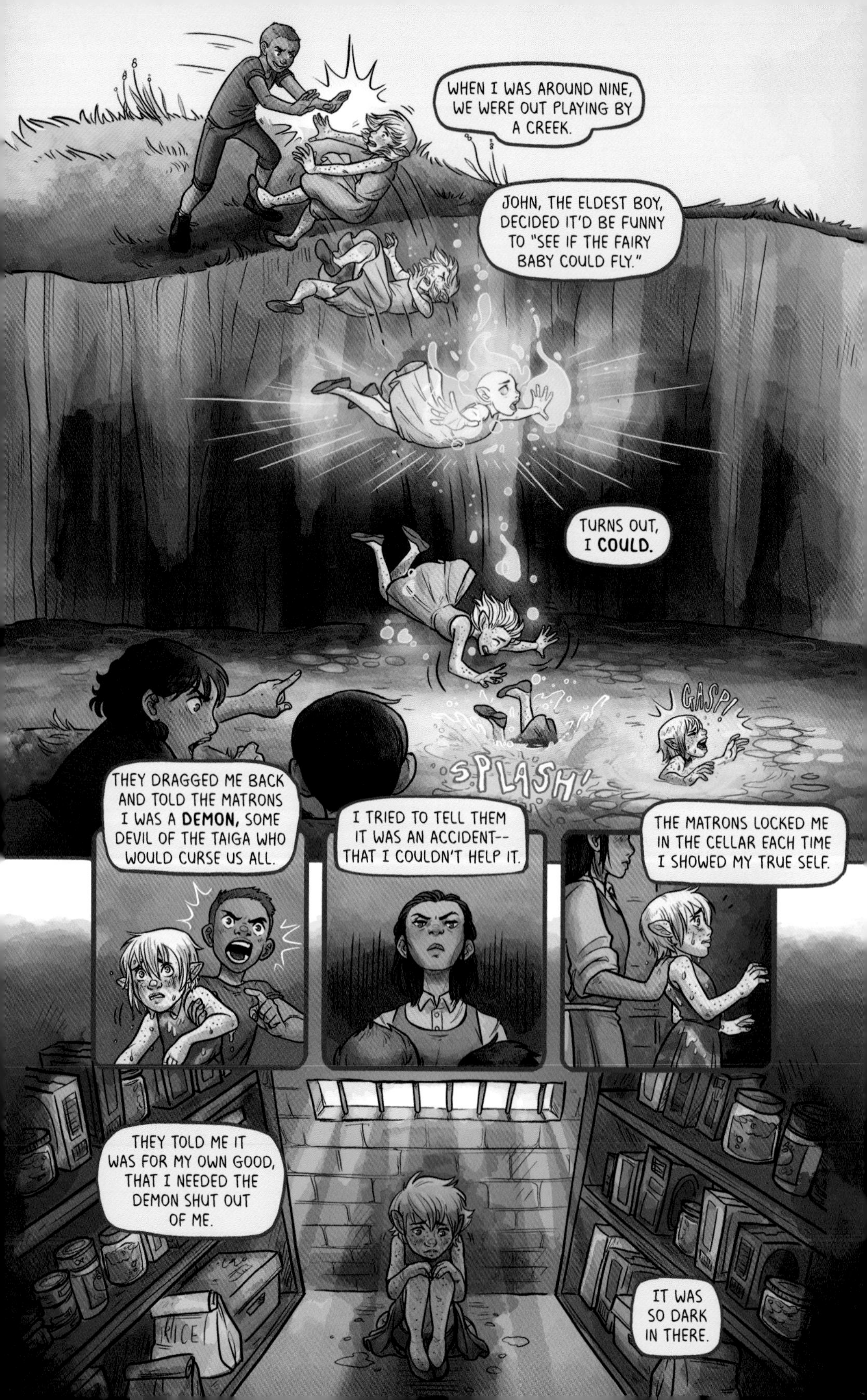
WHEN I WAS AROUND NINE, WE WERE OUT PLAYING BY A CREEK.
JOHN, THE ELDEST BOY, DECIDED IT'D BE FUNNY TO "SEE IF THE FAIRY BABY COULD FLY."
TURNS OUT, I **COULD.**
GASP!
SPLASH!
THEY DRAGGED ME BACK AND TOLD THE MATRONS I WAS A **DEMON,** SOME DEVIL OF THE TAIGA WHO WOULD CURSE US ALL.
I TRIED TO TELL THEM IT WAS AN ACCIDENT--THAT I COULDN'T HELP IT.
THE MATRONS LOCKED ME IN THE CELLAR EACH TIME I SHOWED MY TRUE SELF.
THEY TOLD ME IT WAS FOR MY OWN GOOD, THAT I NEEDED THE DEMON SHUT OUT OF ME.
RICE
IT WAS SO DARK IN THERE.

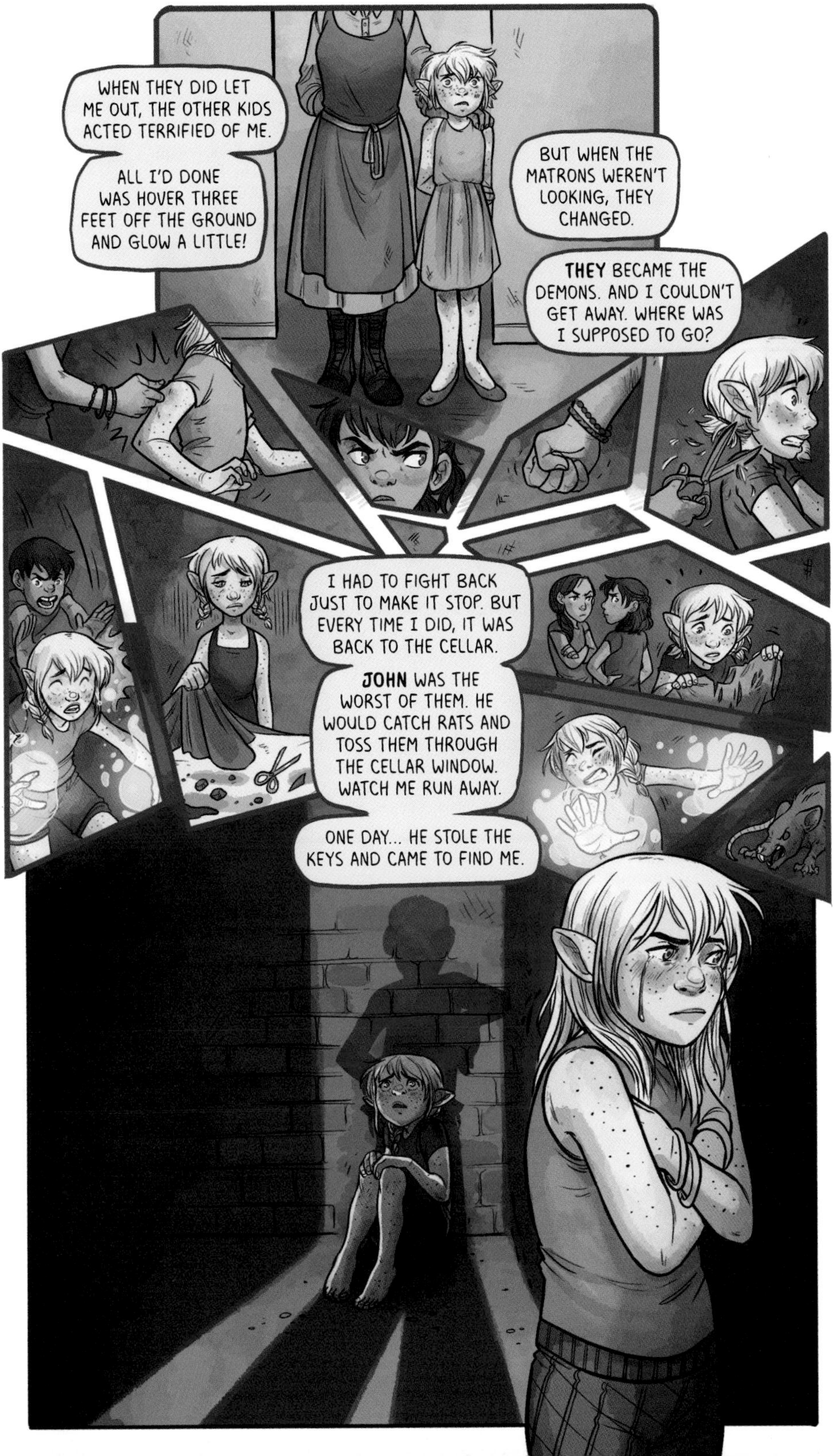
WHEN THEY DID LET ME OUT, THE OTHER KIDS ACTED TERRIFIED OF ME.
ALL I'D DONE WAS HOVER THREE FEET OFF THE GROUND AND GLOW A LITTLE!
BUT WHEN THE MATRONS WEREN'T LOOKING, THEY CHANGED.
THEY BECAME THE DEMONS. AND I COULDN'T GET AWAY. WHERE WAS I SUPPOSED TO GO?
I HAD TO FIGHT BACK JUST TO MAKE IT STOP. BUT EVERY TIME I DID, IT WAS BACK TO THE CELLAR.
JOHN WAS THE WORST OF THEM. HE WOULD CATCH RATS AND TOSS THEM THROUGH THE CELLAR WINDOW. WATCH ME RUN AWAY.
ONE DAY... HE STOLE THE KEYS AND CAME TO FIND ME.

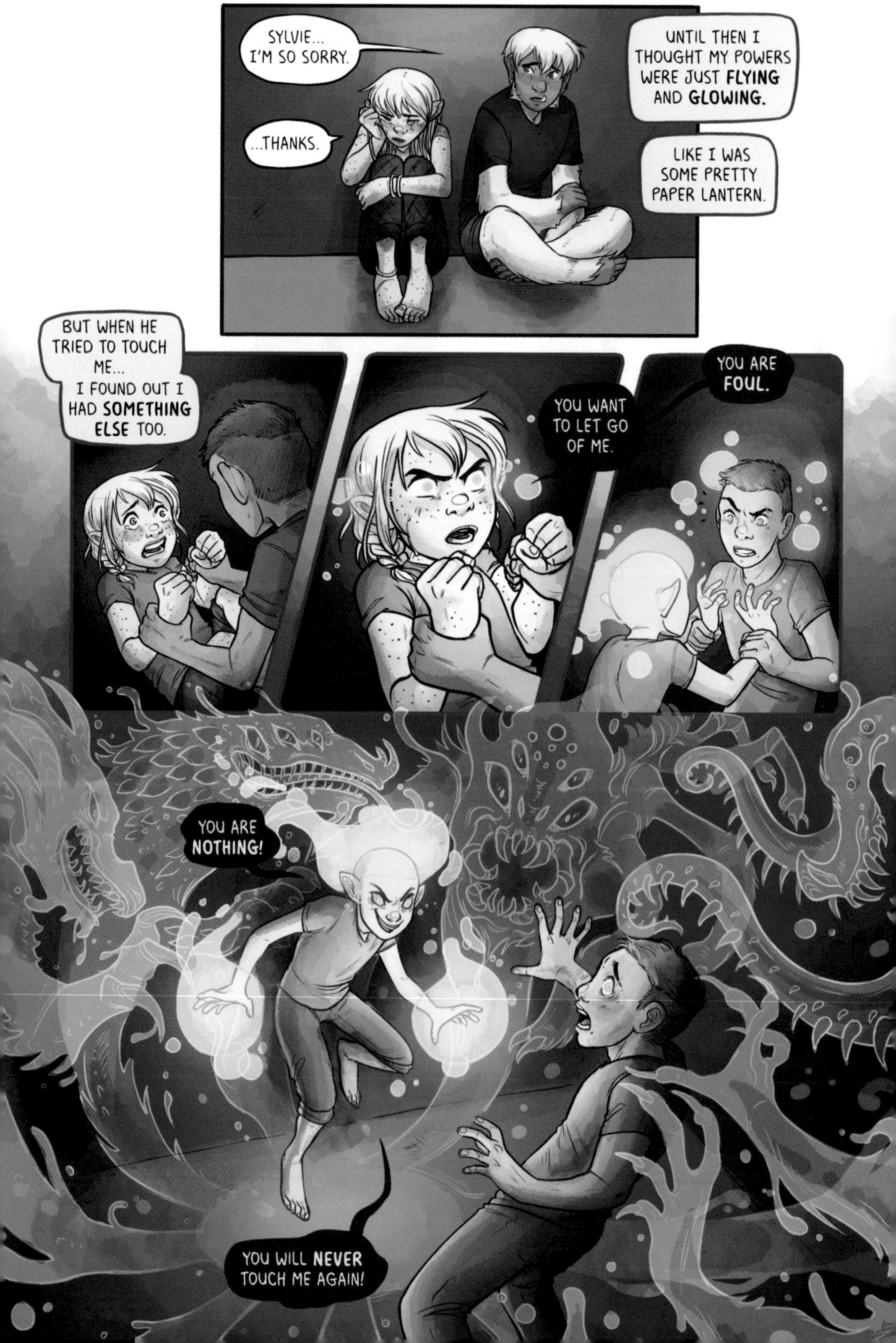
SYLVIE...
I'M SO SORRY.
...THANKS.
UNTIL THEN I THOUGHT MY POWERS WERE JUST **FLYING** AND **GLOWING.**
LIKE I WAS SOME PRETTY PAPER LANTERN.
BUT WHEN HE TRIED TO TOUCH ME...
I FOUND OUT I HAD **SOMETHING ELSE** TOO.
YOU WANT TO LET GO OF ME.
YOU ARE **FOUL.**
YOU ARE **NOTHING!**
YOU WILL **NEVER** TOUCH ME AGAIN!

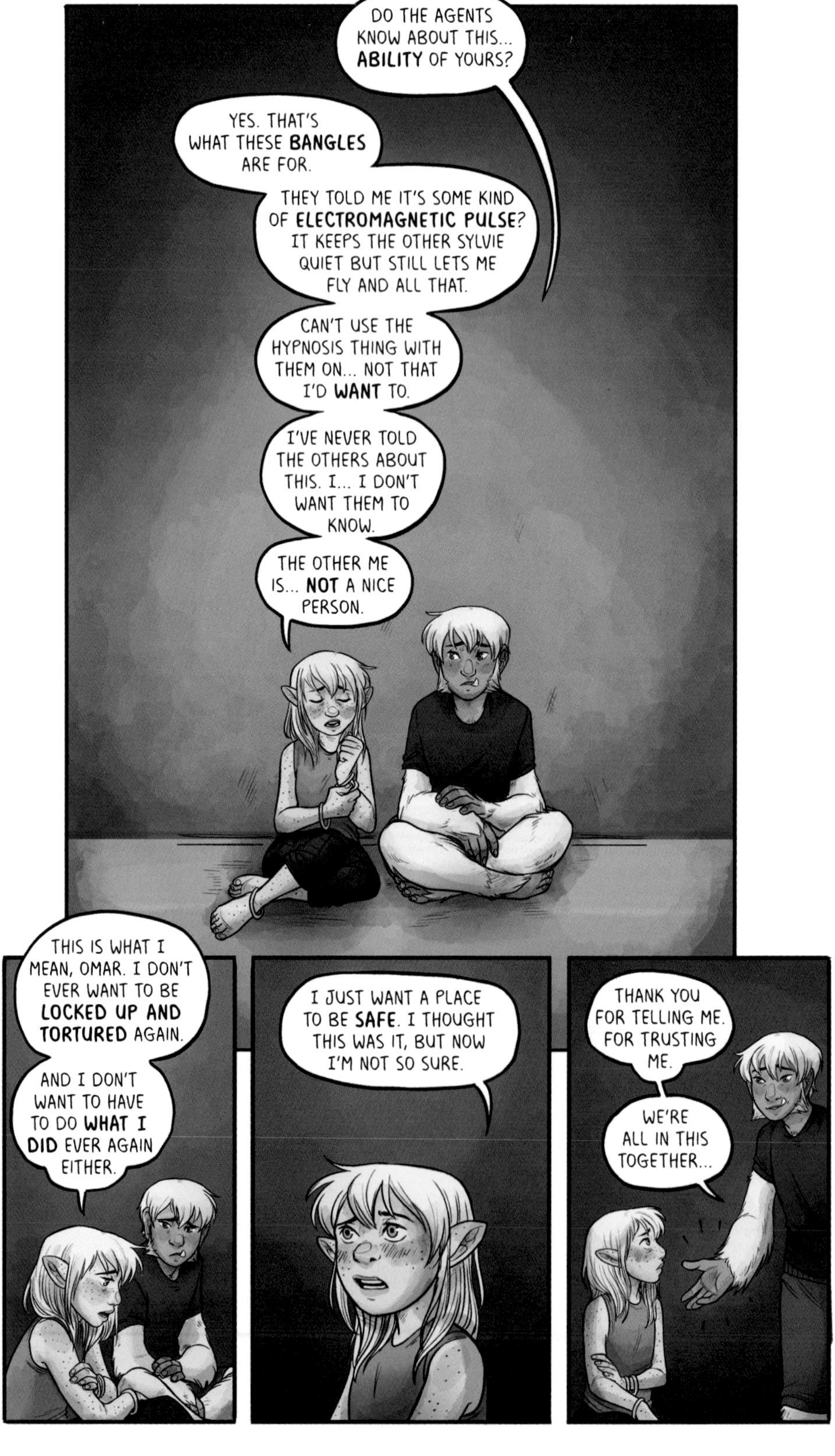
DO THE AGENTS KNOW ABOUT THIS... ABILITY OF YOURS?
YES. THAT'S WHAT THESE BANGLES ARE FOR.
THEY TOLD ME IT'S SOME KIND OF ELECTROMAGNETIC PULSE? IT KEEPS THE OTHER SYLVIE QUIET BUT STILL LETS ME FLY AND ALL THAT.
CAN'T USE THE HYPNOSIS THING WITH THEM ON... NOT THAT I'D WANT TO.
I'VE NEVER TOLD THE OTHERS ABOUT THIS. I... I DON'T WANT THEM TO KNOW.
THE OTHER ME IS... NOT A NICE PERSON.
THIS IS WHAT I MEAN, OMAR. I DON'T EVER WANT TO BE LOCKED UP AND TORTURED AGAIN.
AND I DON'T WANT TO HAVE TO DO WHAT I DID EVER AGAIN EITHER.
I JUST WANT A PLACE TO BE SAFE. I THOUGHT THIS WAS IT, BUT NOW I'M NOT SO SURE.
THANK YOU FOR TELLING ME. FOR TRUSTING ME.
WE'RE ALL IN THIS TOGETHER...

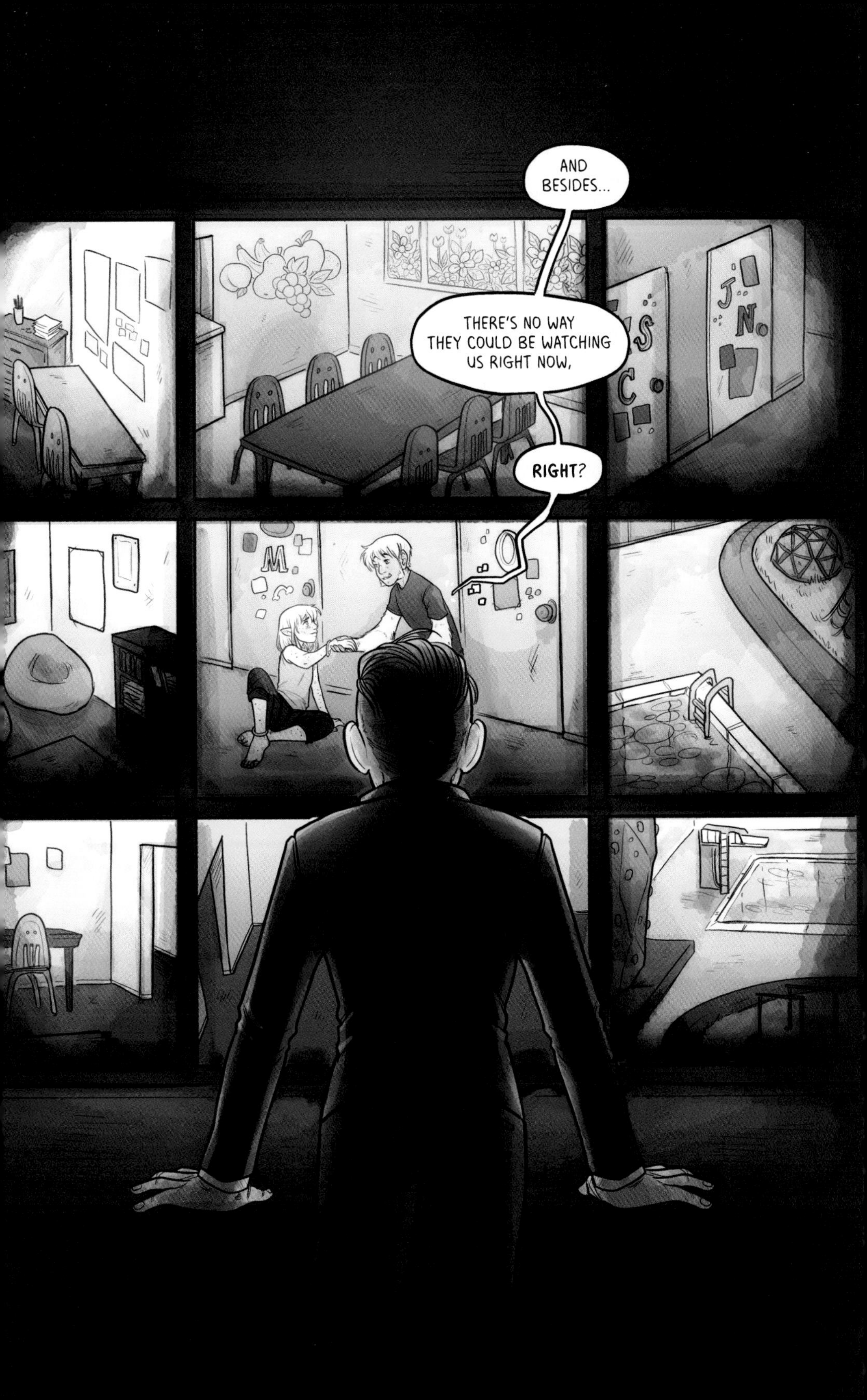
AND BESIDES...
THERE'S NO WAY THEY COULD BE WATCHING US RIGHT NOW,
RIGHT?

CHAPTER TWO

YOU CAN RUN BUT YOU CAN'T HIDE

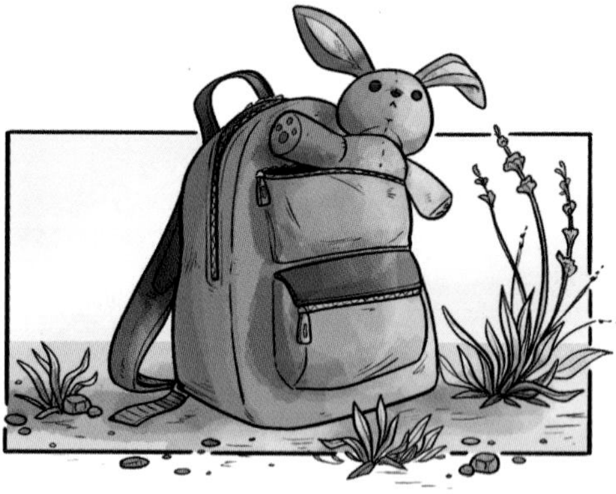

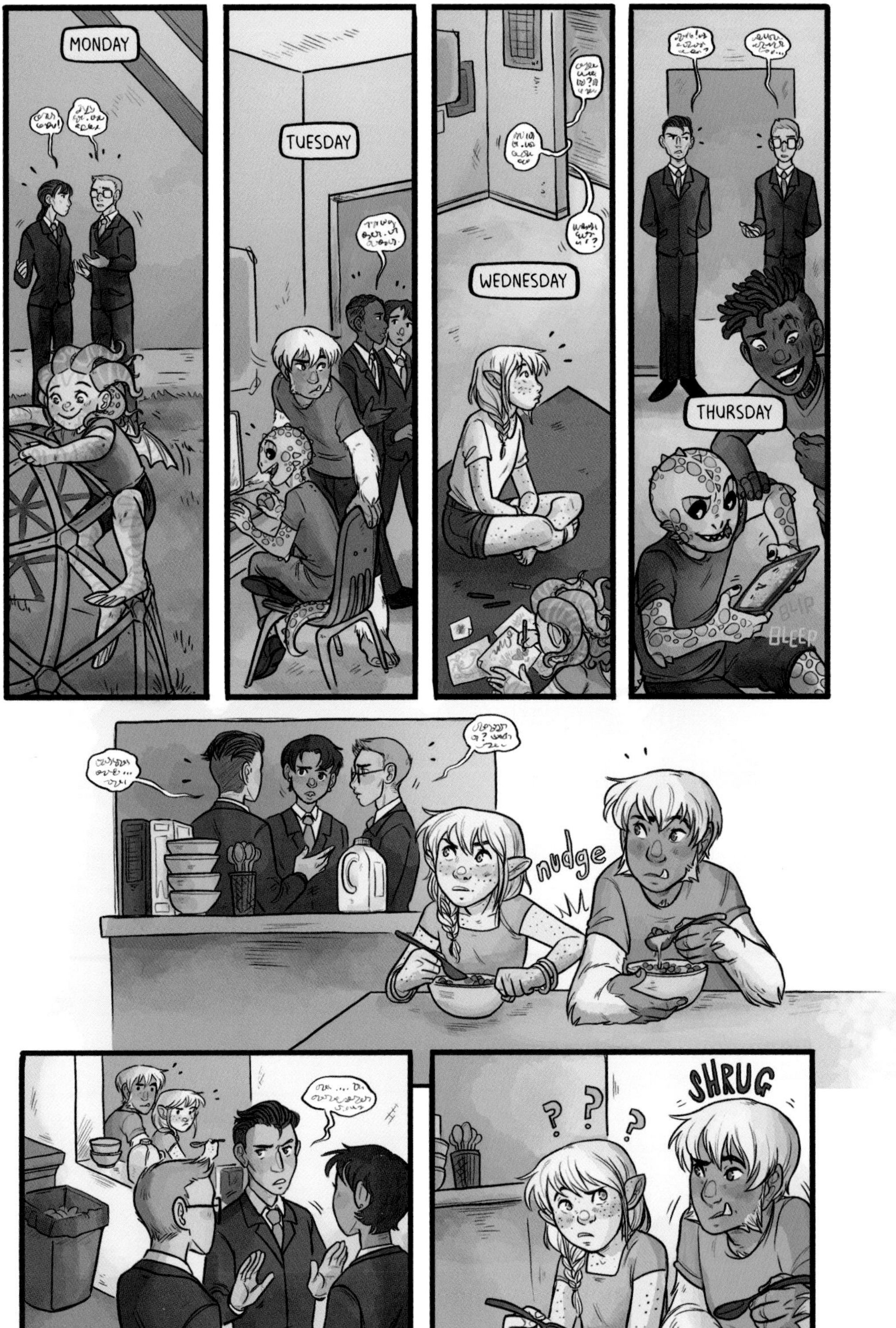
MONDAY
TUESDAY
WEDNESDAY
THURSDAY
BLIP BLEEP
nudge
? ? ?
SHRUG

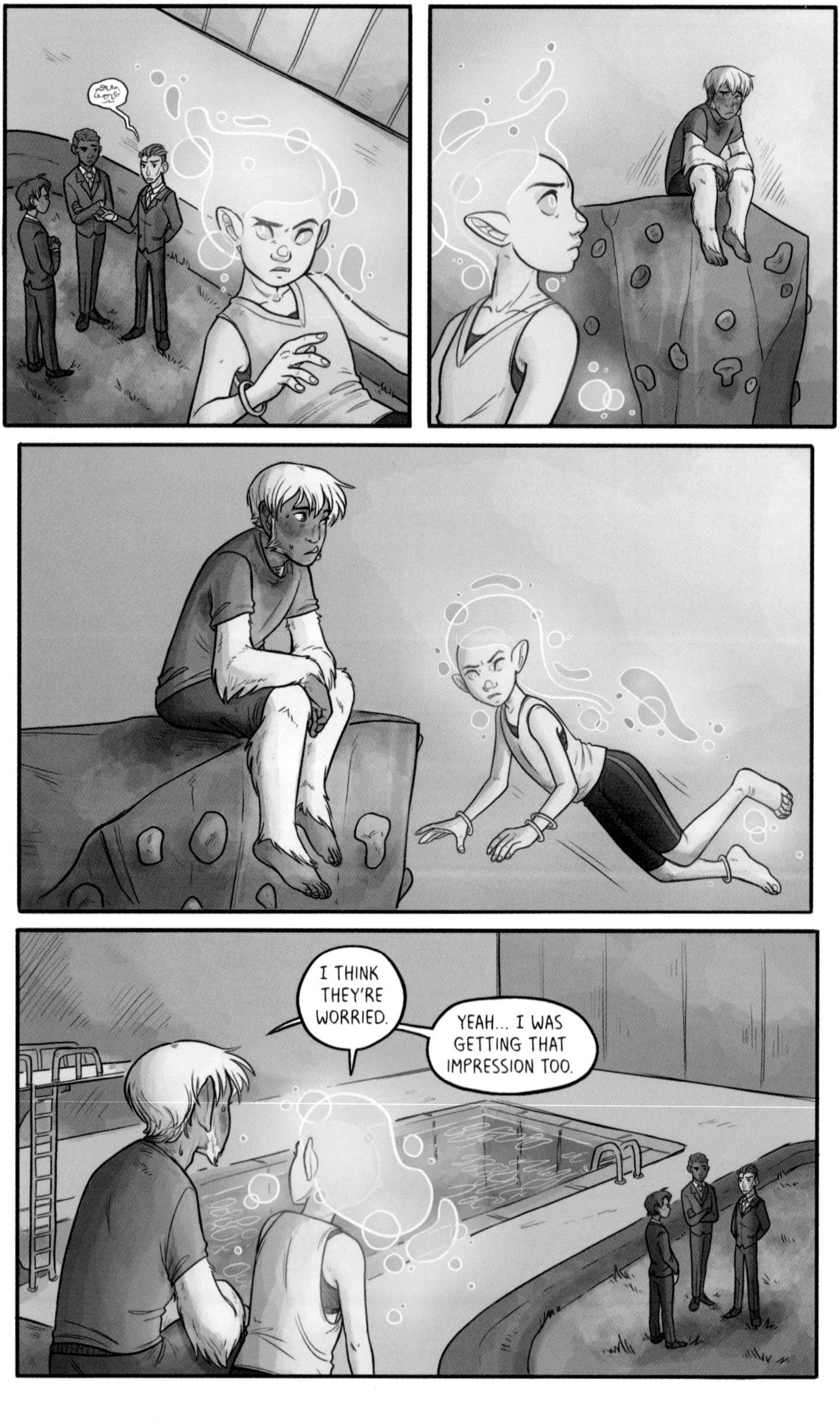
I THINK THEY'RE WORRIED.
YEAH... I WAS GETTING THAT IMPRESSION TOO.

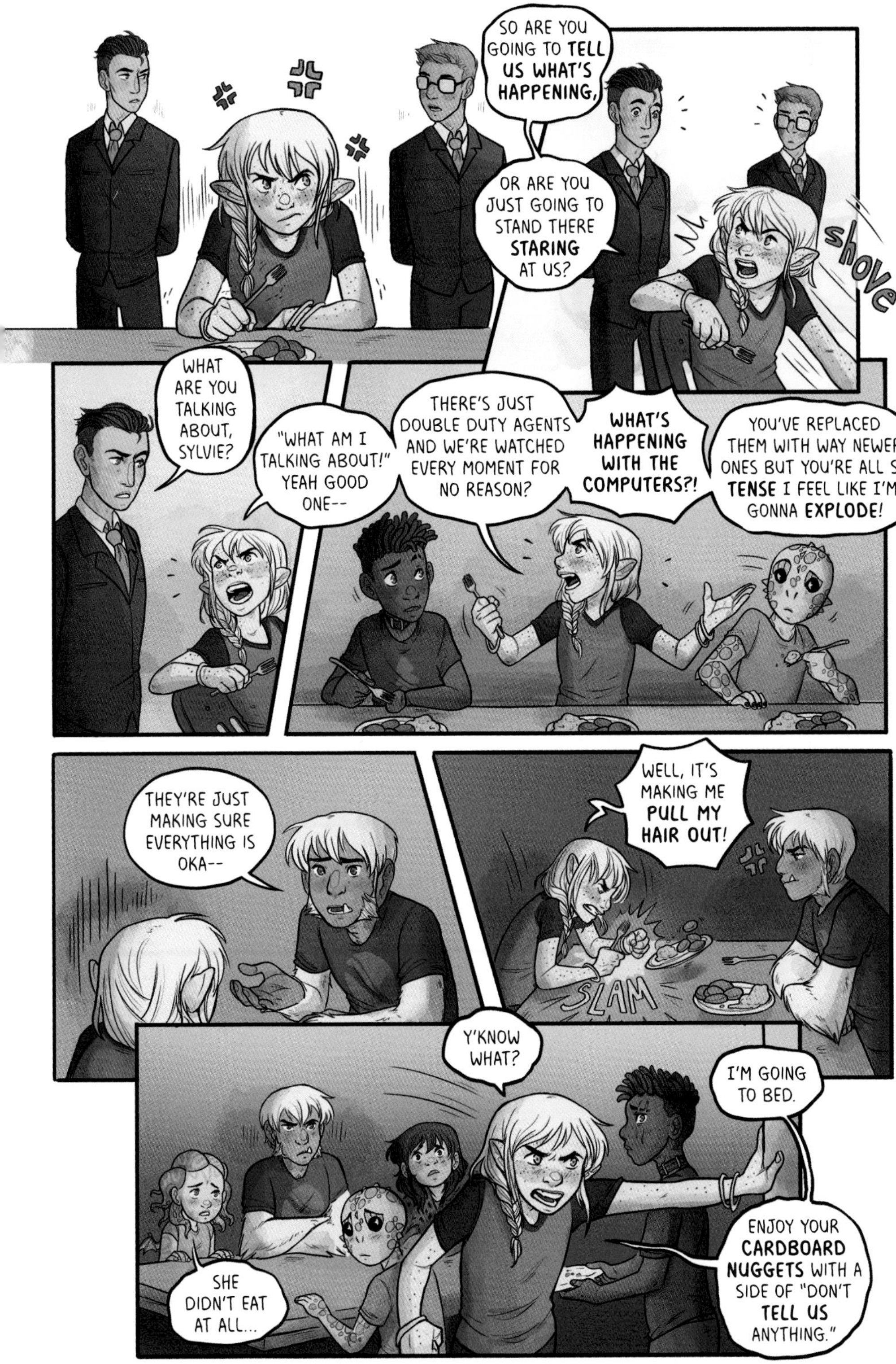
SO ARE YOU GOING TO **TELL US WHAT'S HAPPENING,**
OR ARE YOU JUST GOING TO STAND THERE **STARING** AT US?
shove
WHAT ARE YOU TALKING ABOUT, SYLVIE?
"WHAT AM I TALKING ABOUT!" YEAH GOOD ONE--
THERE'S JUST DOUBLE DUTY AGENTS AND WE'RE WATCHED EVERY MOMENT FOR NO REASON?
WHAT'S HAPPENING WITH THE COMPUTERS?!
YOU'VE REPLACED THEM WITH WAY NEWER ONES BUT YOU'RE ALL SO **TENSE** I FEEL LIKE I'M, GONNA **EXPLODE!**
THEY'RE JUST MAKING SURE EVERYTHING IS OKA--
WELL, IT'S MAKING ME **PULL MY HAIR OUT!**
SLAM
Y'KNOW WHAT?
I'M GOING TO BED.
ENJOY YOUR **CARDBOARD NUGGETS** WITH A SIDE OF "DON'T **TELL US** ANYTHING."
SHE DIDN'T EAT AT ALL...

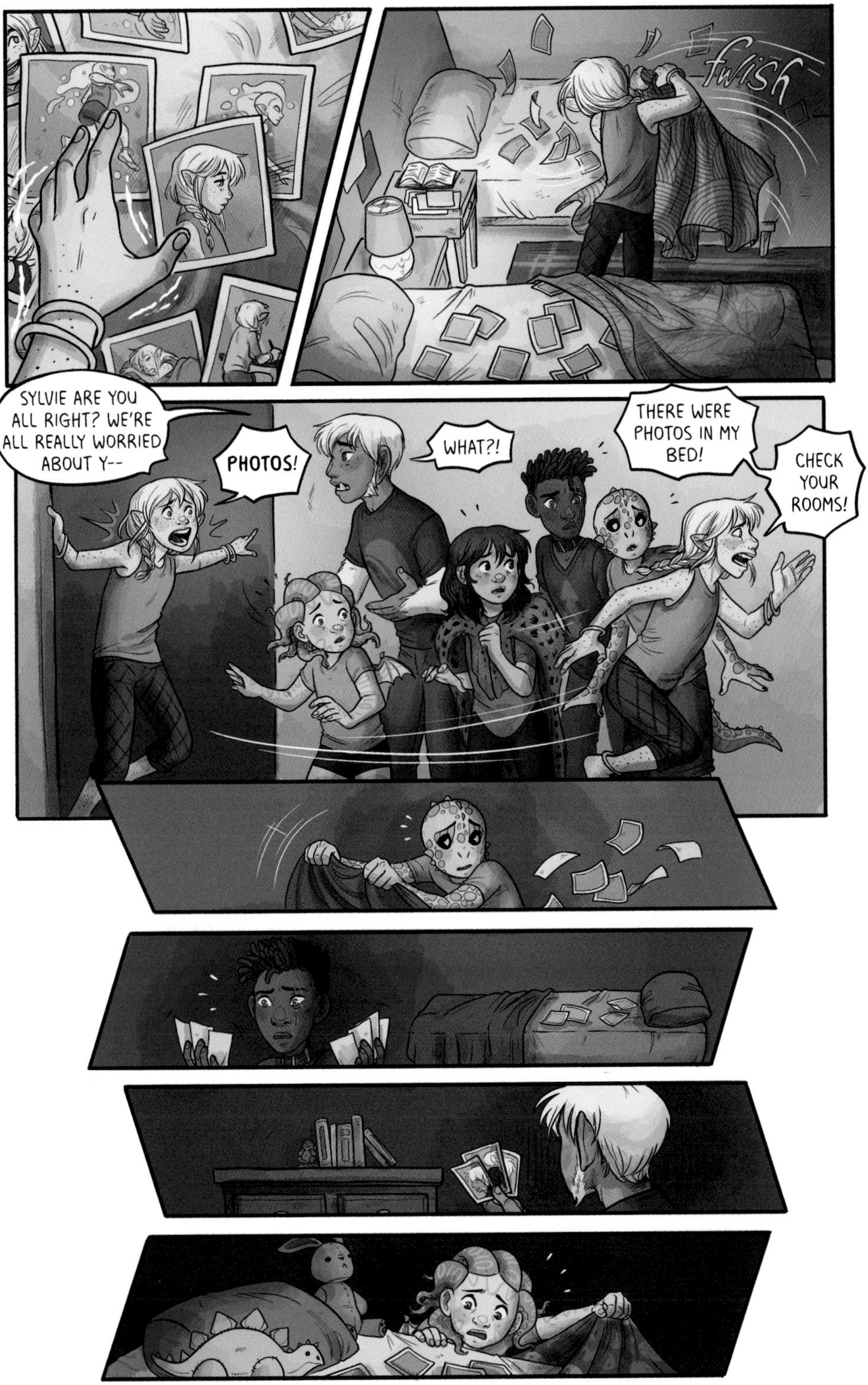
FWISH
SYLVIE ARE YOU ALL RIGHT? WE'RE ALL REALLY WORRIED ABOUT Y--
PHOTOS!
WHAT?!
THERE WERE PHOTOS IN MY BED!
CHECK YOUR ROOMS!

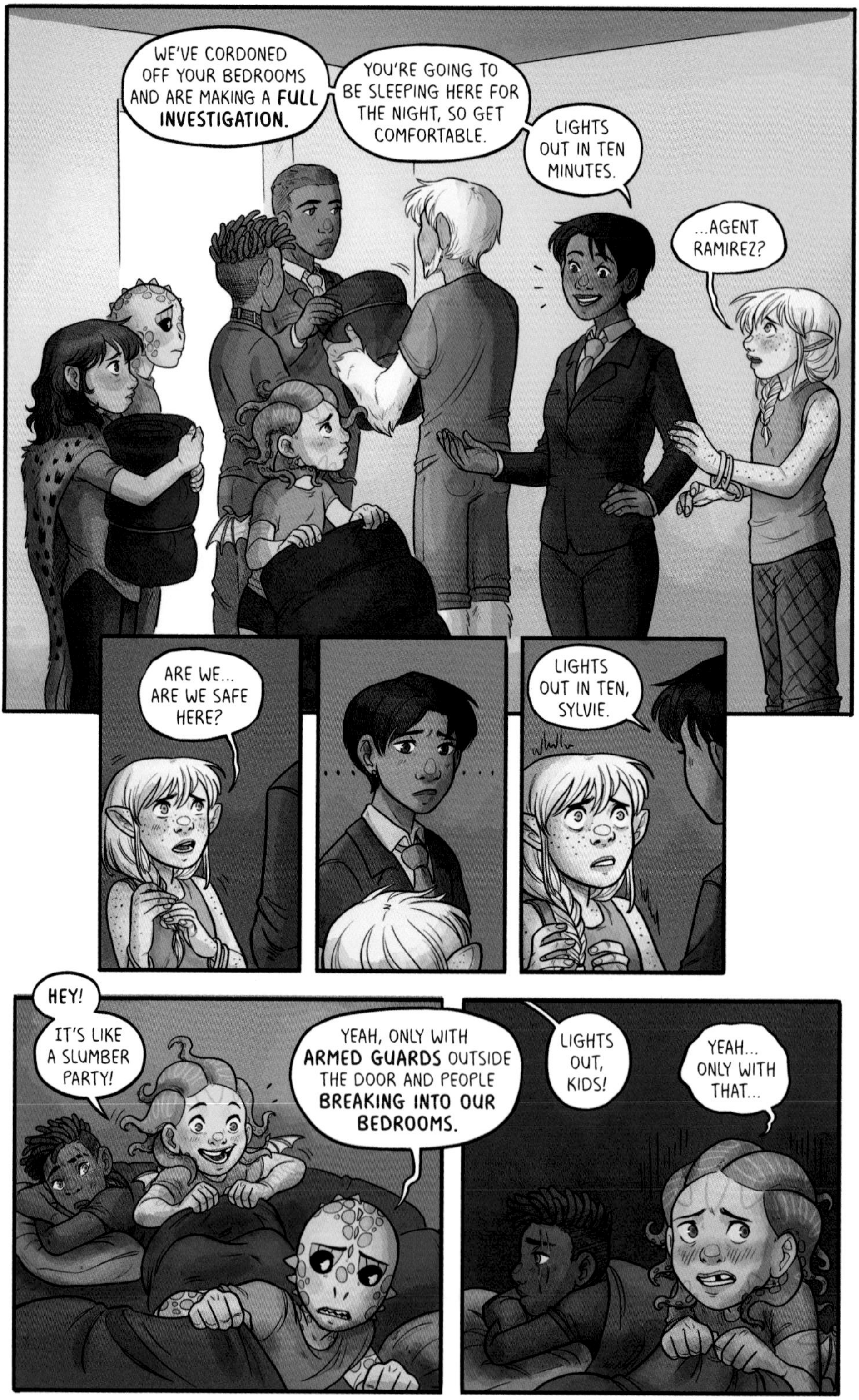
WE'VE CORDONED OFF YOUR BEDROOMS AND ARE MAKING A **FULL INVESTIGATION.**
YOU'RE GOING TO BE SLEEPING HERE FOR THE NIGHT, SO GET COMFORTABLE.
LIGHTS OUT IN TEN MINUTES.
...AGENT RAMIREZ?
ARE WE... ARE WE SAFE HERE?
LIGHTS OUT IN TEN, SYLVIE.
HEY!
IT'S LIKE A SLUMBER PARTY!
YEAH, ONLY WITH **ARMED GUARDS** OUTSIDE THE DOOR AND PEOPLE **BREAKING INTO OUR BEDROOMS.**
LIGHTS OUT, KIDS!
YEAH... ONLY WITH THAT...

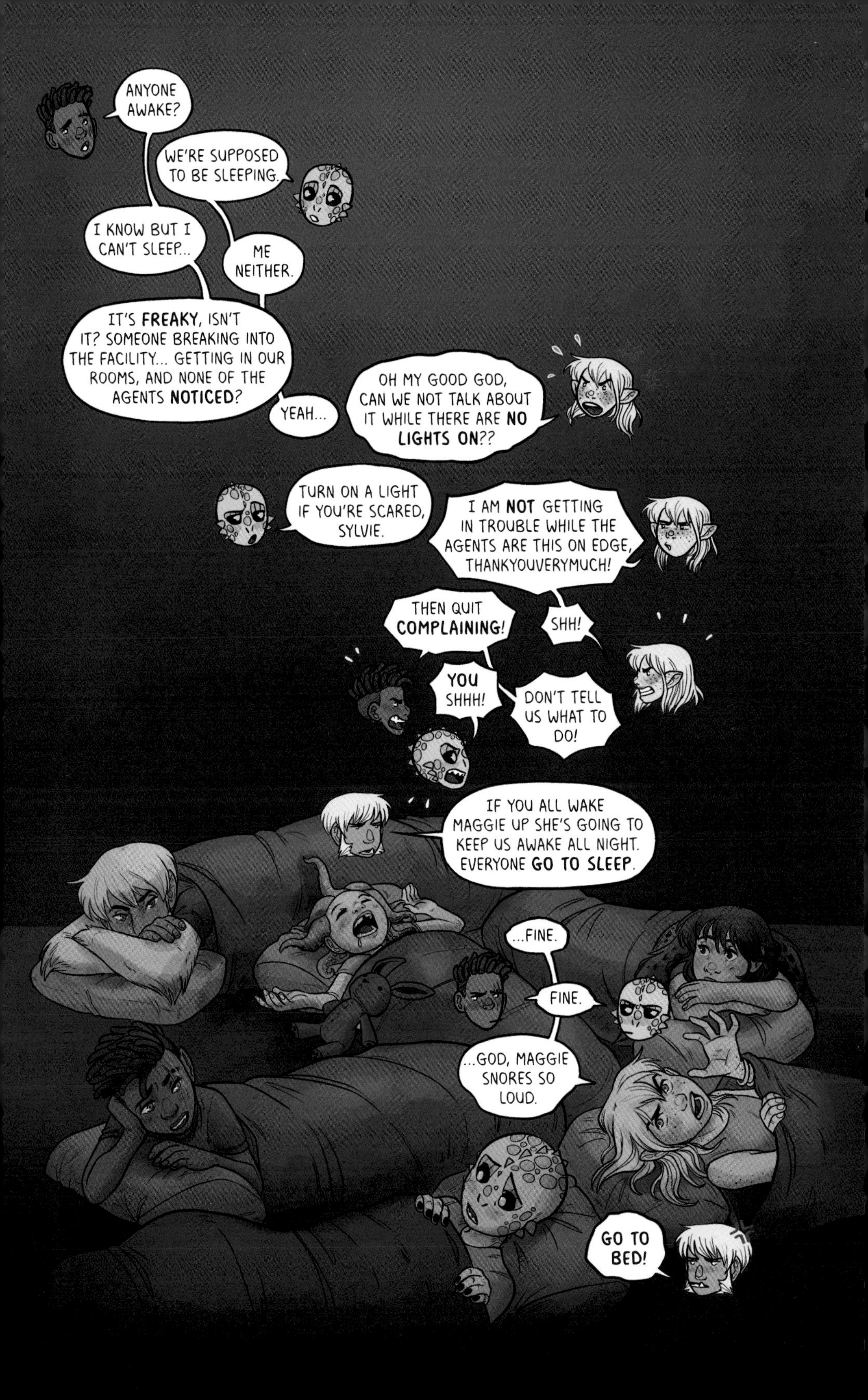
ANYONE AWAKE?
WE'RE SUPPOSED TO BE SLEEPING.
I KNOW BUT I CAN'T SLEEP...
ME NEITHER.
IT'S **FREAKY**, ISN'T IT? SOMEONE BREAKING INTO THE FACILITY... GETTING IN OUR ROOMS, AND NONE OF THE AGENTS **NOTICED**?
YEAH...
OH MY GOOD GOD, CAN WE NOT TALK ABOUT IT WHILE THERE ARE **NO LIGHTS ON**??
TURN ON A LIGHT IF YOU'RE SCARED, SYLVIE.
I AM **NOT** GETTING IN TROUBLE WHILE THE AGENTS ARE THIS ON EDGE, THANKYOUVERYMUCH!
THEN QUIT **COMPLAINING**!
SHH!
YOU SHHH!
DON'T TELL US WHAT TO DO!
IF YOU ALL WAKE MAGGIE UP SHE'S GOING TO KEEP US AWAKE ALL NIGHT. EVERYONE **GO TO SLEEP**.
...FINE.
FINE.
...GOD, MAGGIE SNORES SO LOUD.
GO TO BED!

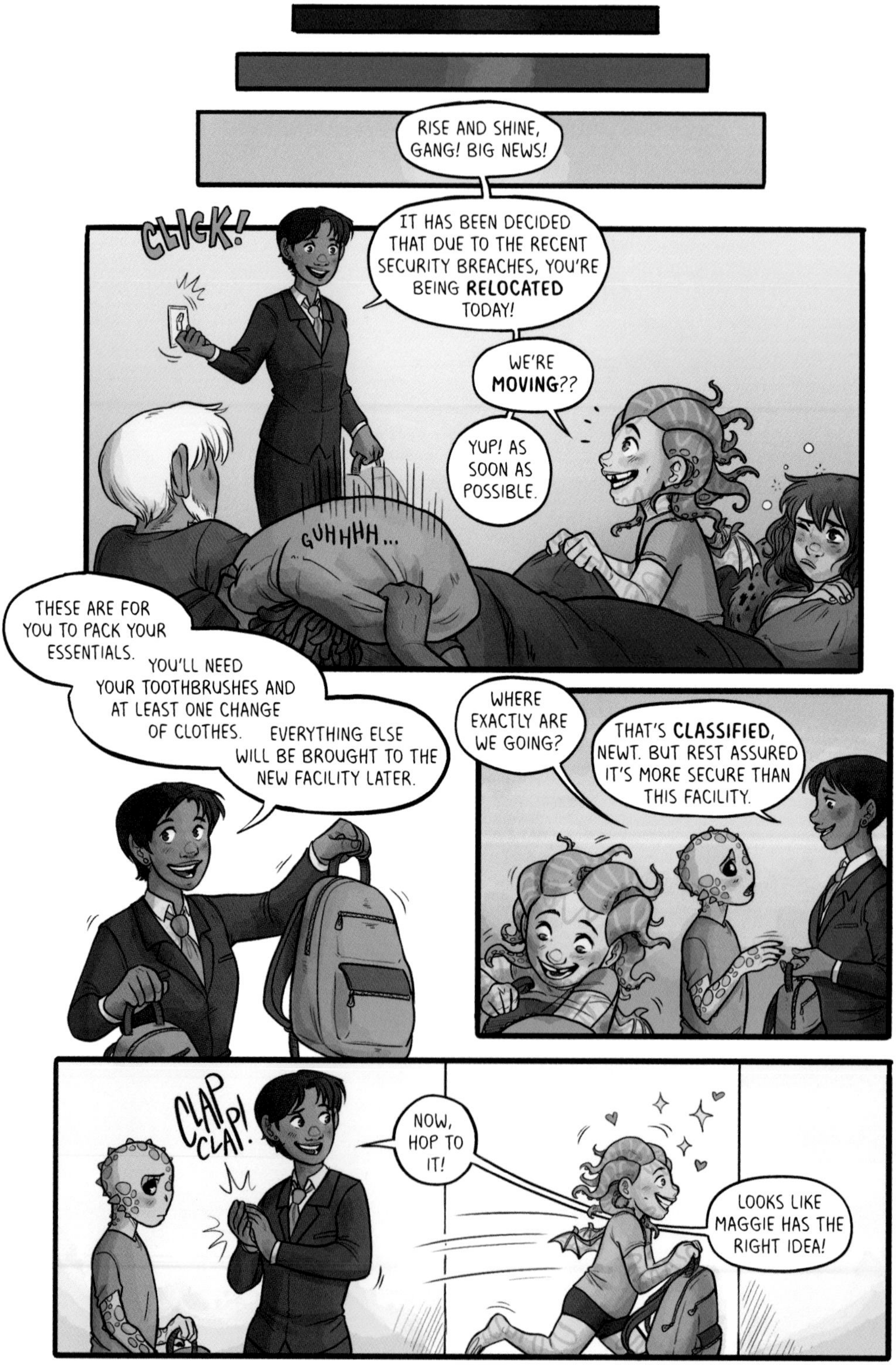
RISE AND SHINE, GANG! BIG NEWS!
CLICK!
IT HAS BEEN DECIDED THAT DUE TO THE RECENT SECURITY BREACHES, YOU'RE BEING **RELOCATED** TODAY!
WE'RE **MOVING**??
YUP! AS SOON AS POSSIBLE.
GUHHHH...
THESE ARE FOR YOU TO PACK YOUR ESSENTIALS.
YOU'LL NEED YOUR TOOTHBRUSHES AND AT LEAST ONE CHANGE OF CLOTHES.
EVERYTHING ELSE WILL BE BROUGHT TO THE NEW FACILITY LATER.
WHERE EXACTLY ARE WE GOING?
THAT'S **CLASSIFIED**, NEWT. BUT REST ASSURED IT'S MORE SECURE THAN THIS FACILITY.
CLAP CLAP!
NOW, HOP TO IT!
LOOKS LIKE MAGGIE HAS THE RIGHT IDEA!

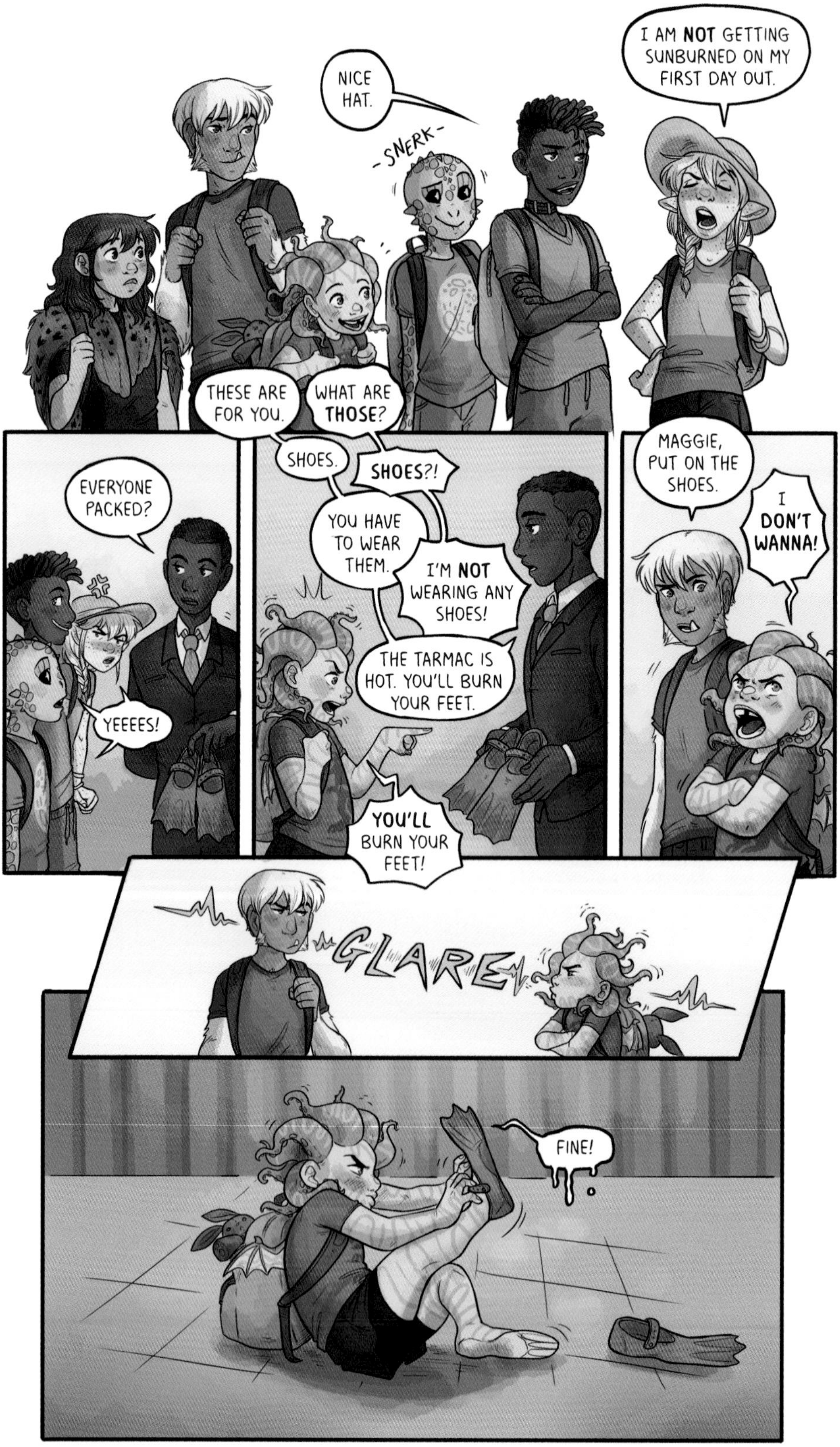
NICE HAT.
I AM NOT GETTING SUNBURNED ON MY FIRST DAY OUT.
-SNERK-
EVERYONE PACKED?
YEEEES!
THESE ARE FOR YOU.
WHAT ARE THOSE?
SHOES.
SHOES?!
YOU HAVE TO WEAR THEM.
I'M NOT WEARING ANY SHOES!
THE TARMAC IS HOT. YOU'LL BURN YOUR FEET.
YOU'LL BURN YOUR FEET!
MAGGIE, PUT ON THE SHOES.
I DON'T WANNA!
GLARE
FINE!

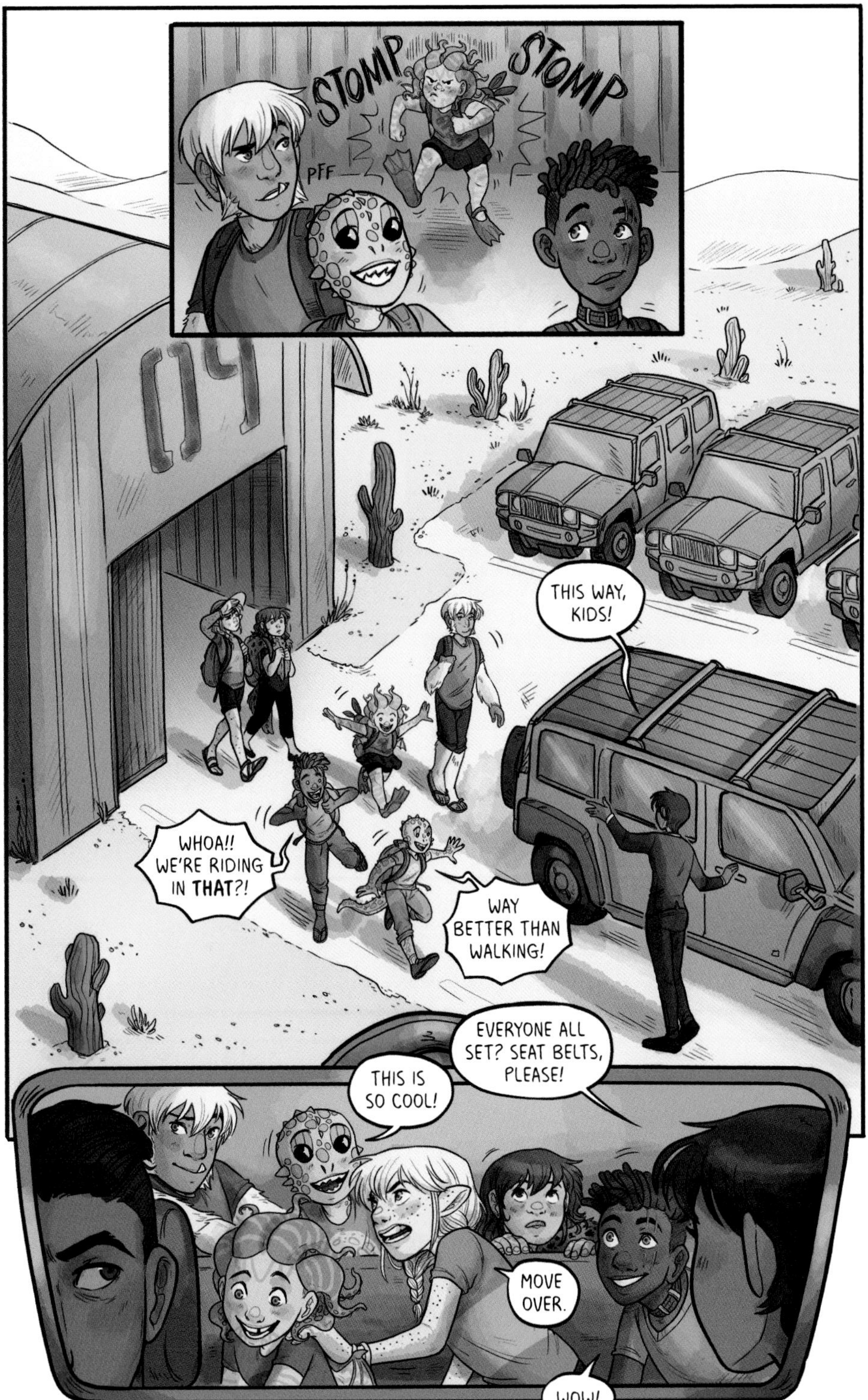
STOMP
STOMP
PFF
THIS WAY, KIDS!
WHOA!! WE'RE RIDING IN THAT?!
WAY BETTER THAN WALKING!
EVERYONE ALL SET? SEAT BELTS, PLEASE!
THIS IS SO COOL!
MOVE OVER.
WOW!

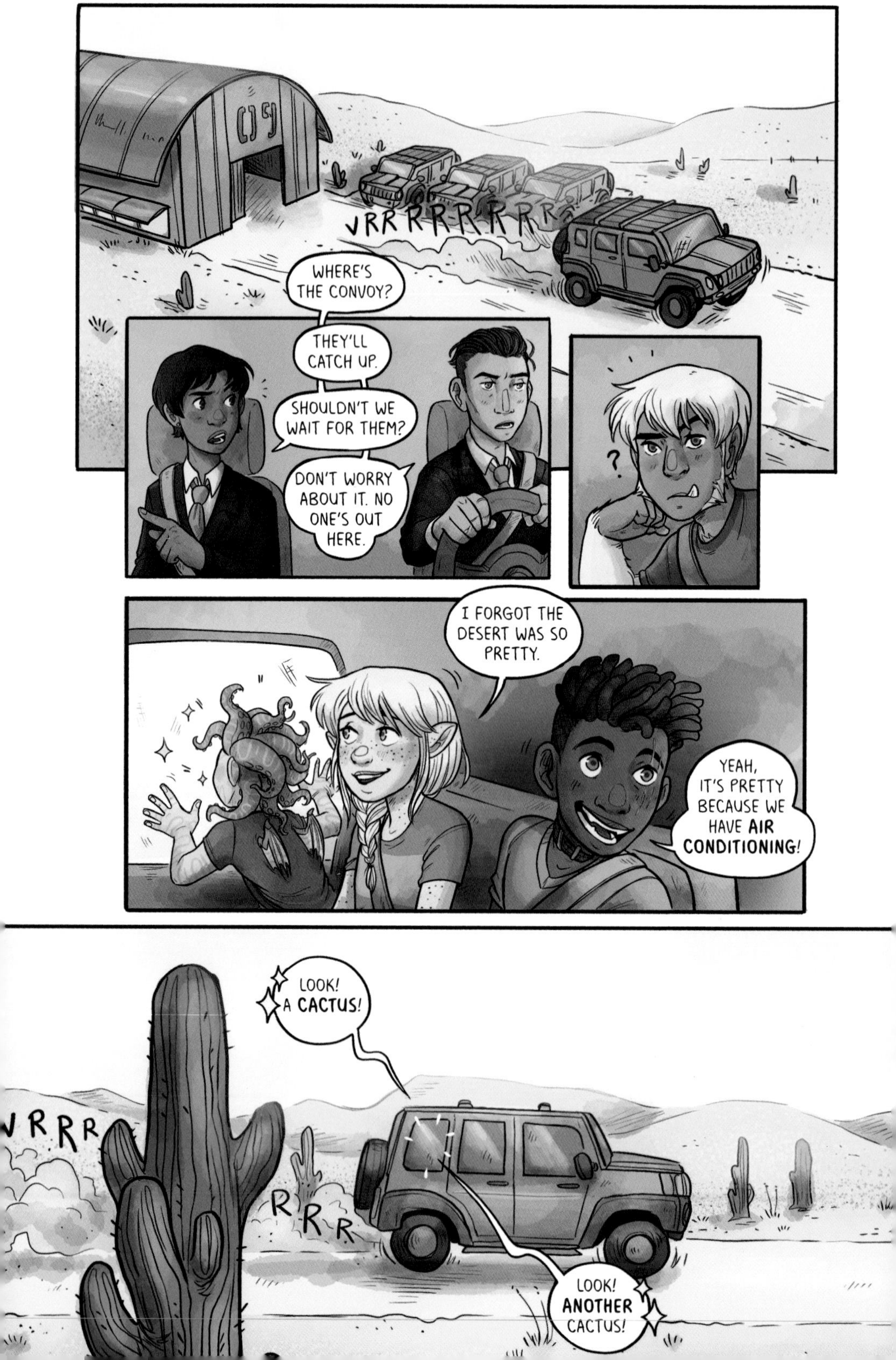

VRRRRRRRRRR
WHERE'S THE CONVOY?
THEY'LL CATCH UP.
SHOULDN'T WE WAIT FOR THEM?
DON'T WORRY ABOUT IT. NO ONE'S OUT HERE.
?
I FORGOT THE DESERT WAS SO PRETTY.
YEAH, IT'S PRETTY BECAUSE WE HAVE **AIR CONDITIONING**!
LOOK! A **CACTUS**!
VRRR
RRR
LOOK! **ANOTHER** CACTUS!

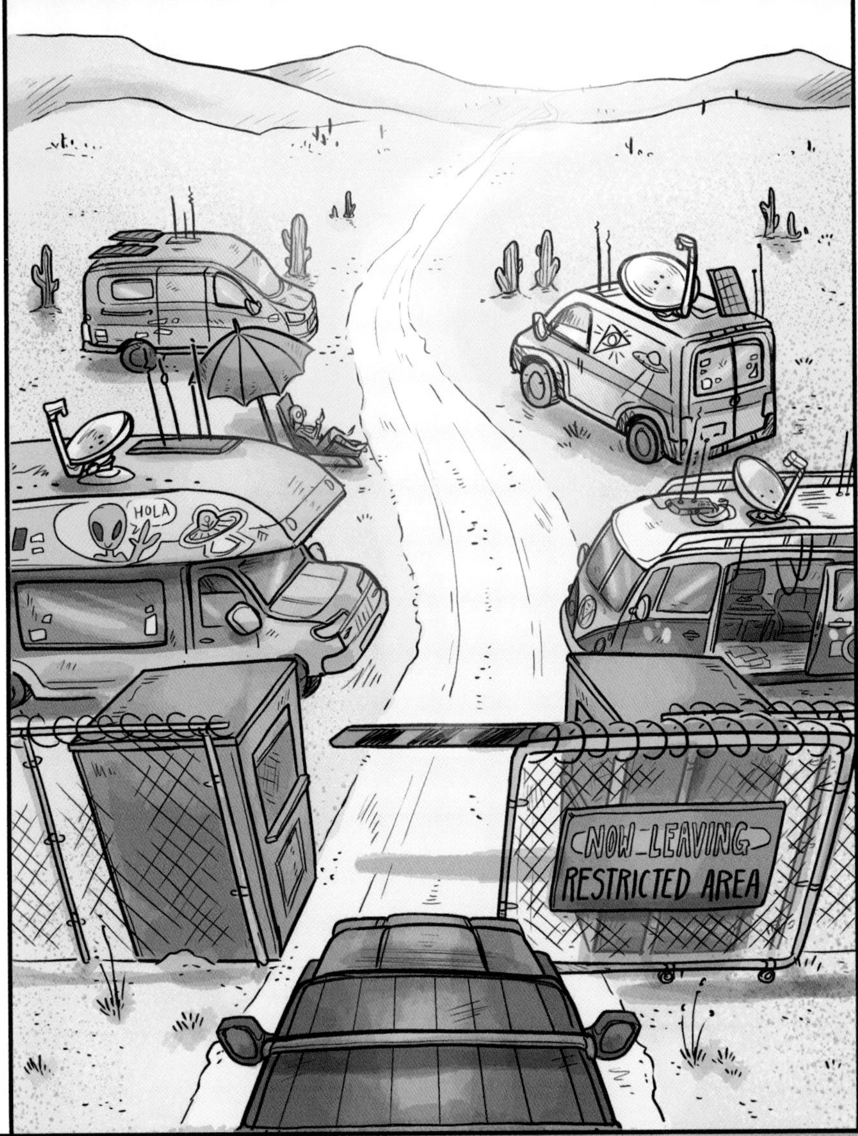
HOLA
NOW LEAVING
RESTRICTED AREA

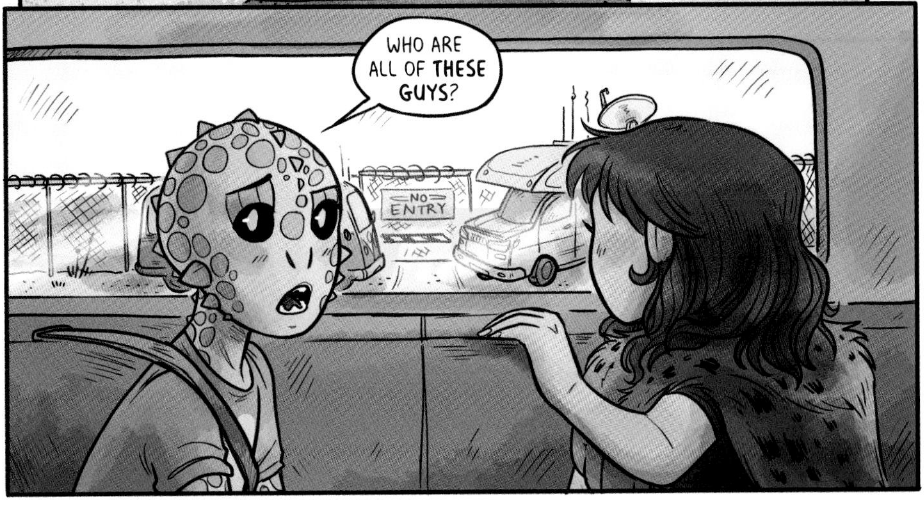
WHO ARE ALL OF **THESE GUYS**?
NO ENTRY

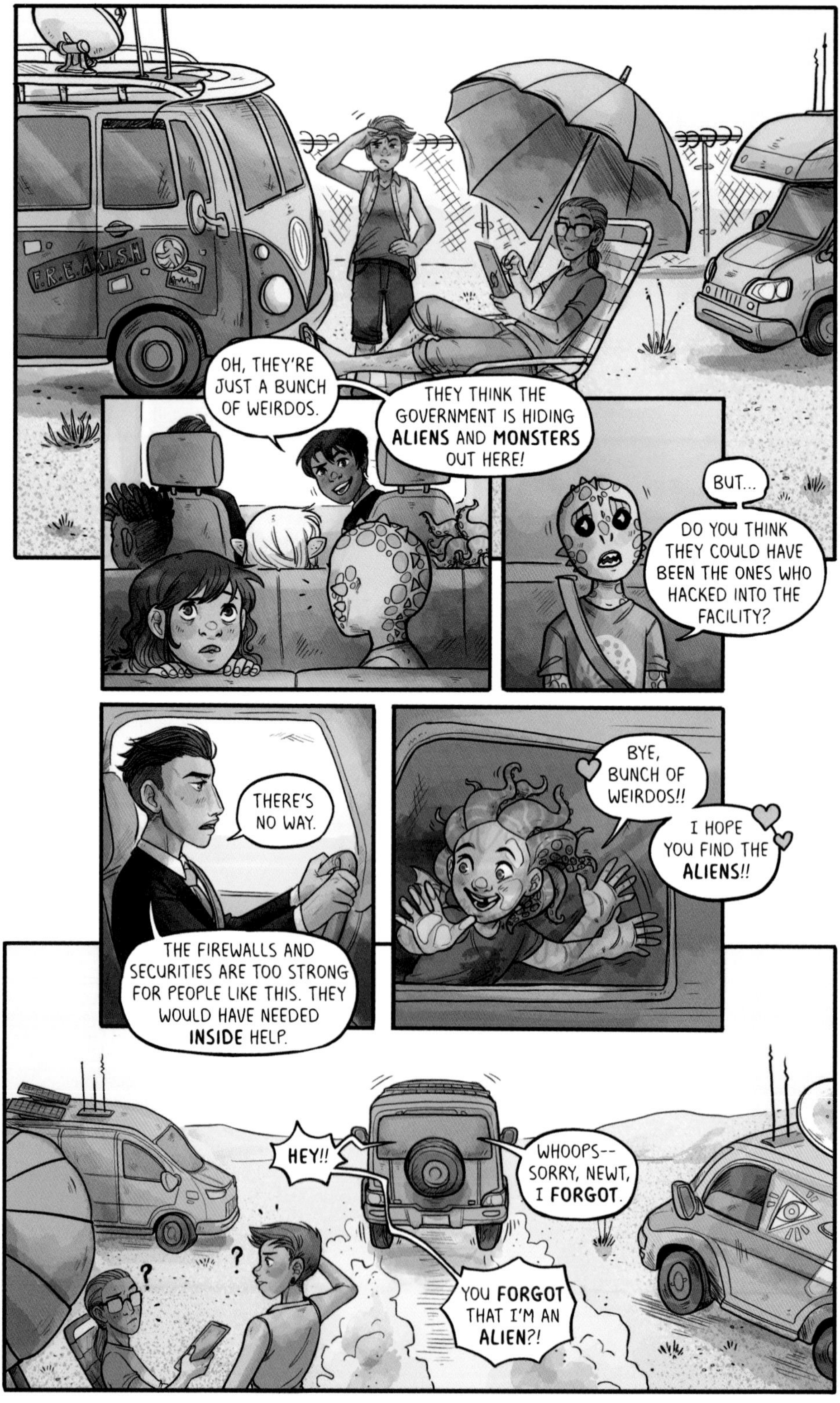

OH, THEY'RE JUST A BUNCH OF WEIRDOS.
THEY THINK THE GOVERNMENT IS HIDING **ALIENS** AND **MONSTERS** OUT HERE!
F.R.E.A.K.I.S.H
BUT...
DO YOU THINK THEY COULD HAVE BEEN THE ONES WHO HACKED INTO THE FACILITY?
THERE'S NO WAY.
THE FIREWALLS AND SECURITIES ARE TOO STRONG FOR PEOPLE LIKE THIS. THEY WOULD HAVE NEEDED **INSIDE** HELP.
BYE, BUNCH OF WEIRDOS!!
I HOPE YOU FIND THE **ALIENS**!!
HEY!!
WHOOPS-- SORRY, NEWT, I **FORGOT**.
YOU **FORGOT** THAT I'M AN **ALIEN**?!

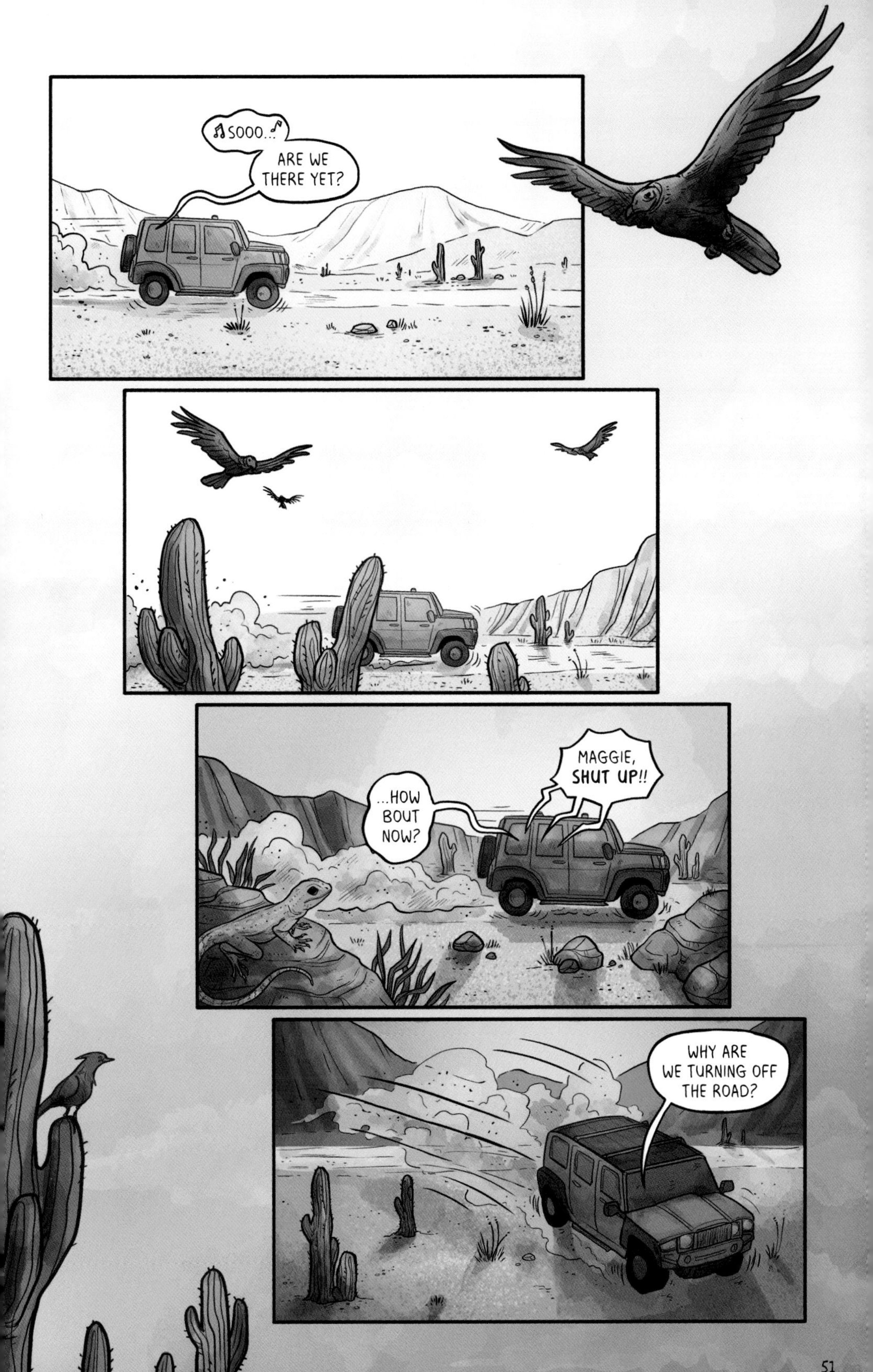
♫SOOO..♪
ARE WE THERE YET?
...HOW BOUT NOW?
MAGGIE, **SHUT UP!!**
WHY ARE WE TURNING OFF THE ROAD?

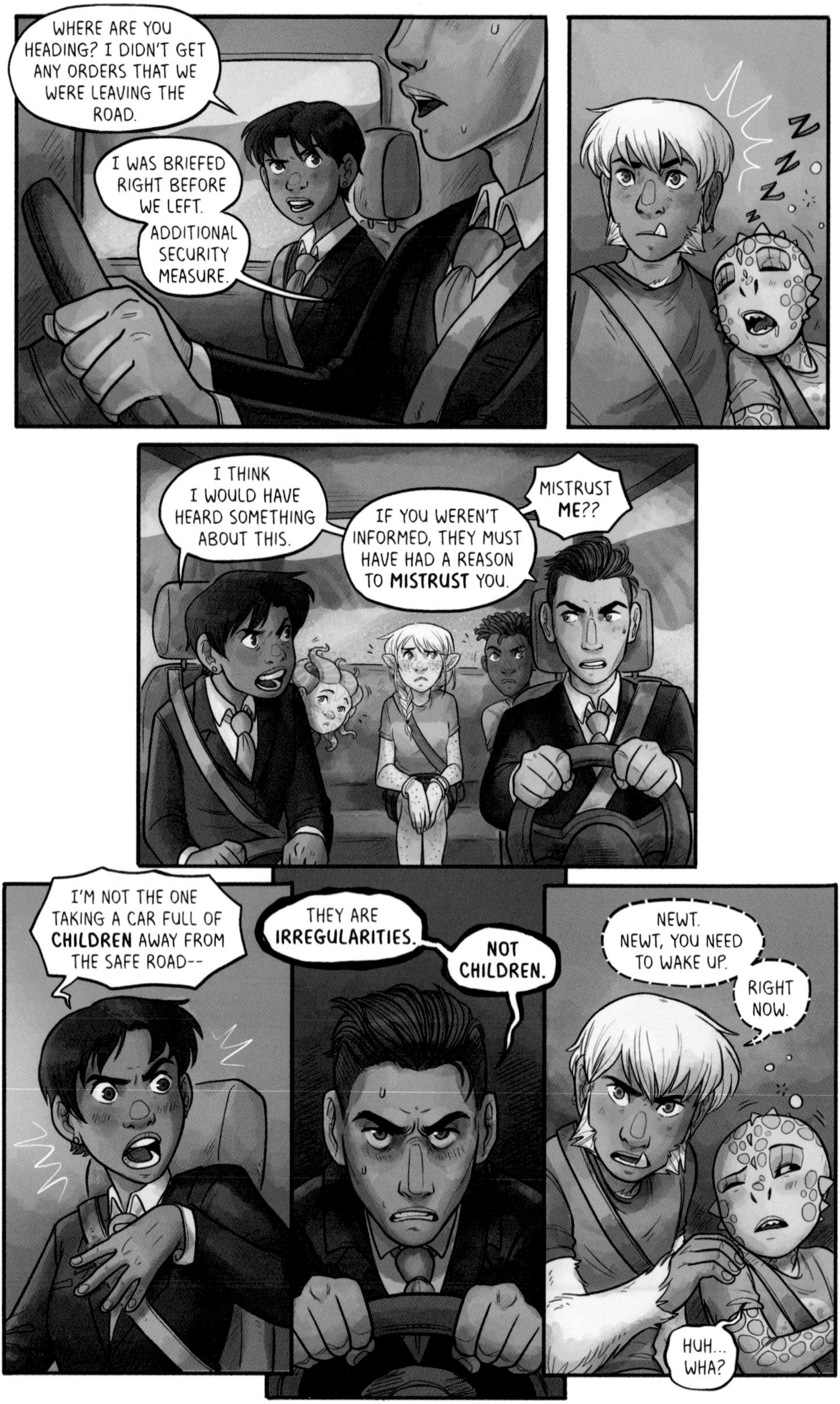
WHERE ARE YOU HEADING? I DIDN'T GET ANY ORDERS THAT WE WERE LEAVING THE ROAD.
I WAS BRIEFED RIGHT BEFORE WE LEFT.
ADDITIONAL SECURITY MEASURE.
Z Z Z Z
I THINK I WOULD HAVE HEARD SOMETHING ABOUT THIS.
IF YOU WEREN'T INFORMED, THEY MUST HAVE HAD A REASON TO **MISTRUST** YOU.
MISTRUST **ME**??
I'M NOT THE ONE TAKING A CAR FULL OF **CHILDREN** AWAY FROM THE SAFE ROAD--
THEY ARE **IRREGULARITIES.**
NOT CHILDREN.
NEWT. NEWT, YOU NEED TO WAKE UP.
RIGHT NOW.
HUH... WHA?

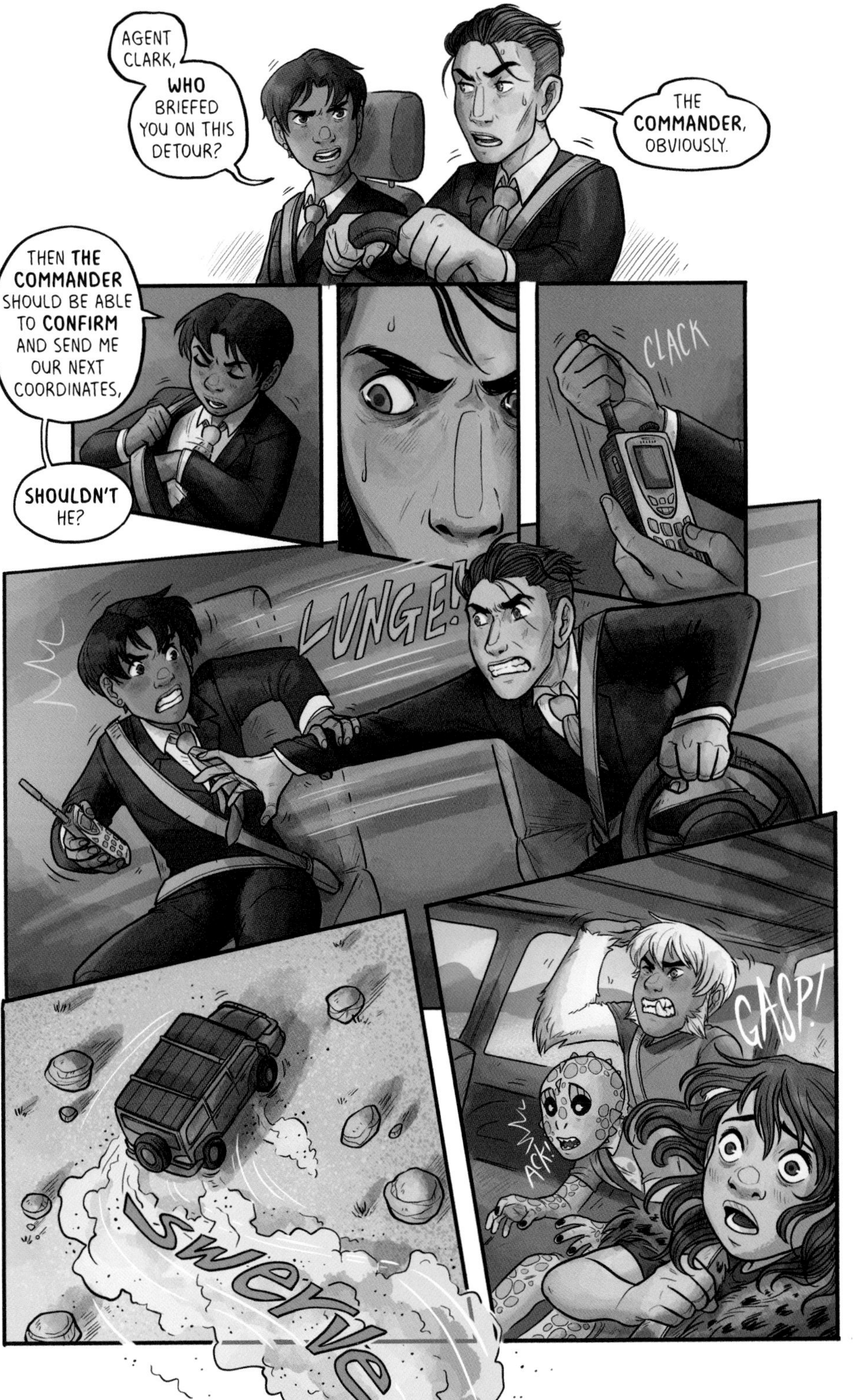

AGENT CLARK, **WHO** BRIEFED YOU ON THIS DETOUR?
THE **COMMANDER**, OBVIOUSLY.
THEN **THE COMMANDER** SHOULD BE ABLE TO **CONFIRM** AND SEND ME OUR NEXT COORDINATES,
SHOULDN'T HE?
CLACK
LUNGE!
swerve
GASP!
ACK!

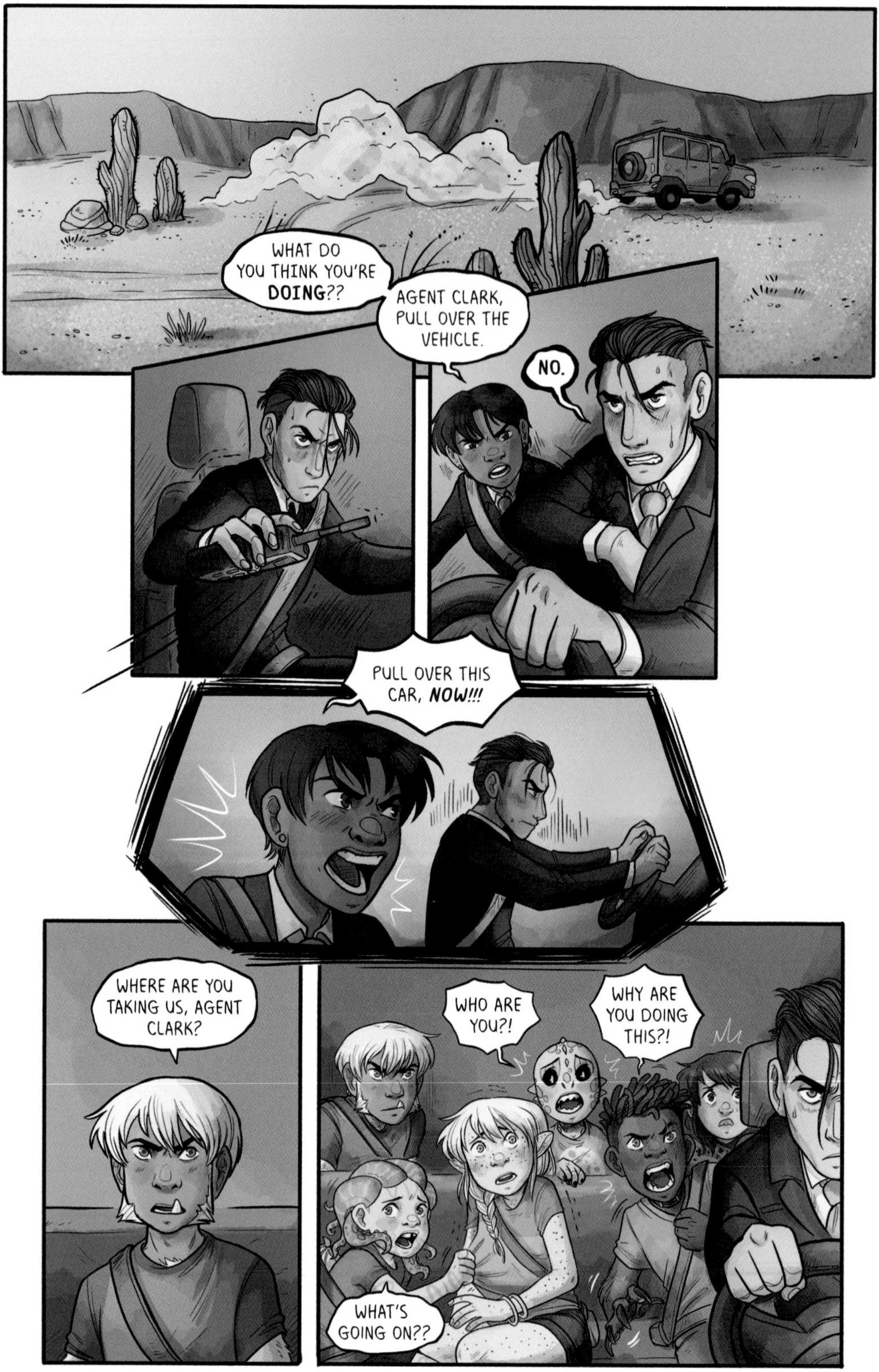

WHAT DO YOU THINK YOU'RE **DOING**??
AGENT CLARK, PULL OVER THE VEHICLE.
NO.
PULL OVER THIS CAR, ***NOW!!!***
WHERE ARE YOU TAKING US, AGENT CLARK?
WHO ARE YOU?!
WHY ARE YOU DOING THIS?!
WHAT'S GOING ON??

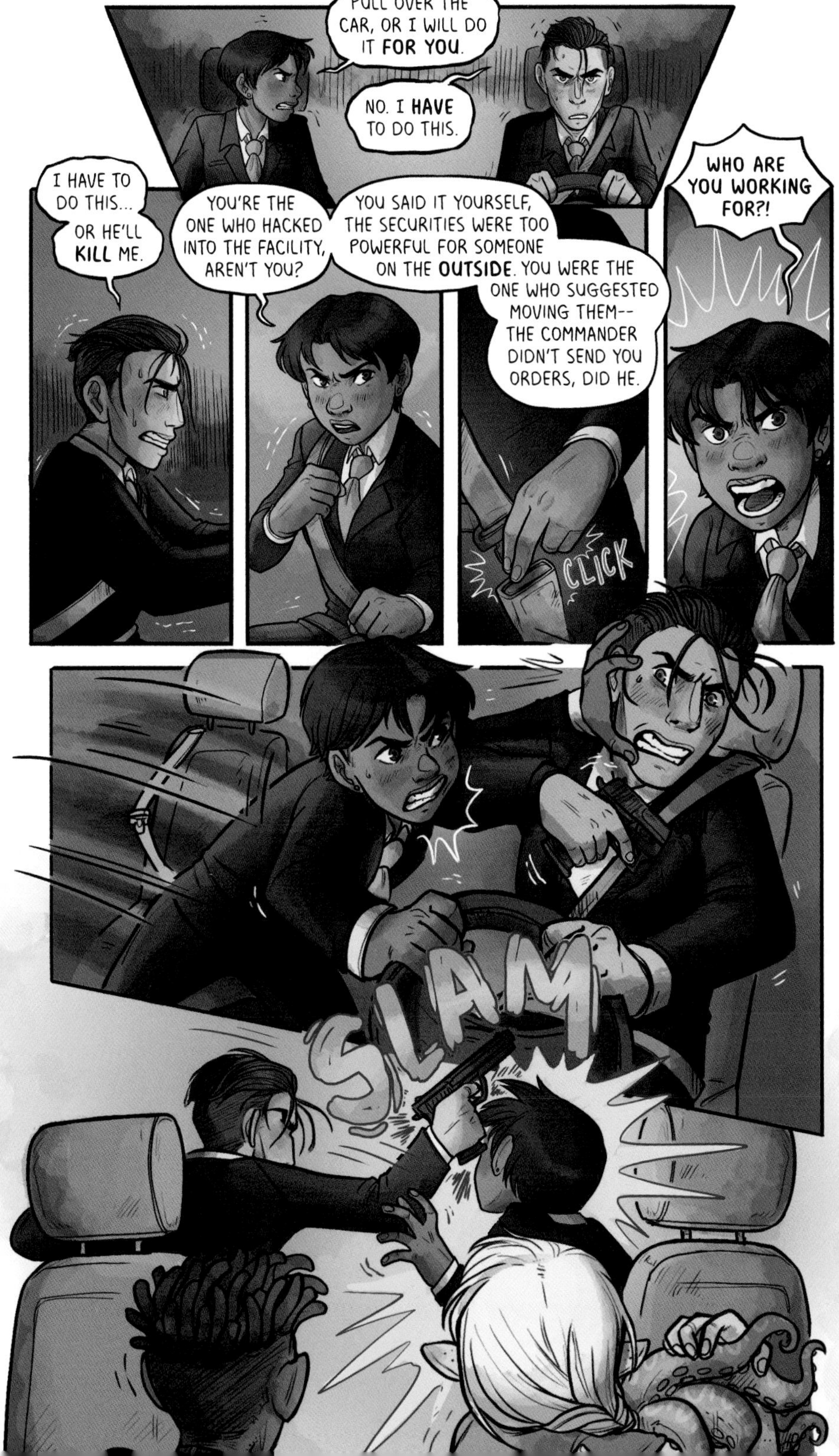
PULL OVER THE CAR, OR I WILL DO IT **FOR YOU**.
NO. I **HAVE** TO DO THIS.
I HAVE TO DO THIS...
OR HE'LL **KILL** ME.
YOU'RE THE ONE WHO HACKED INTO THE FACILITY, AREN'T YOU?
YOU SAID IT YOURSELF, THE SECURITIES WERE TOO POWERFUL FOR SOMEONE ON THE **OUTSIDE**. YOU WERE THE ONE WHO SUGGESTED MOVING THEM-- THE COMMANDER DIDN'T SEND YOU ORDERS, DID HE.
CLICK
WHO ARE YOU WORKING FOR?!
SLAM

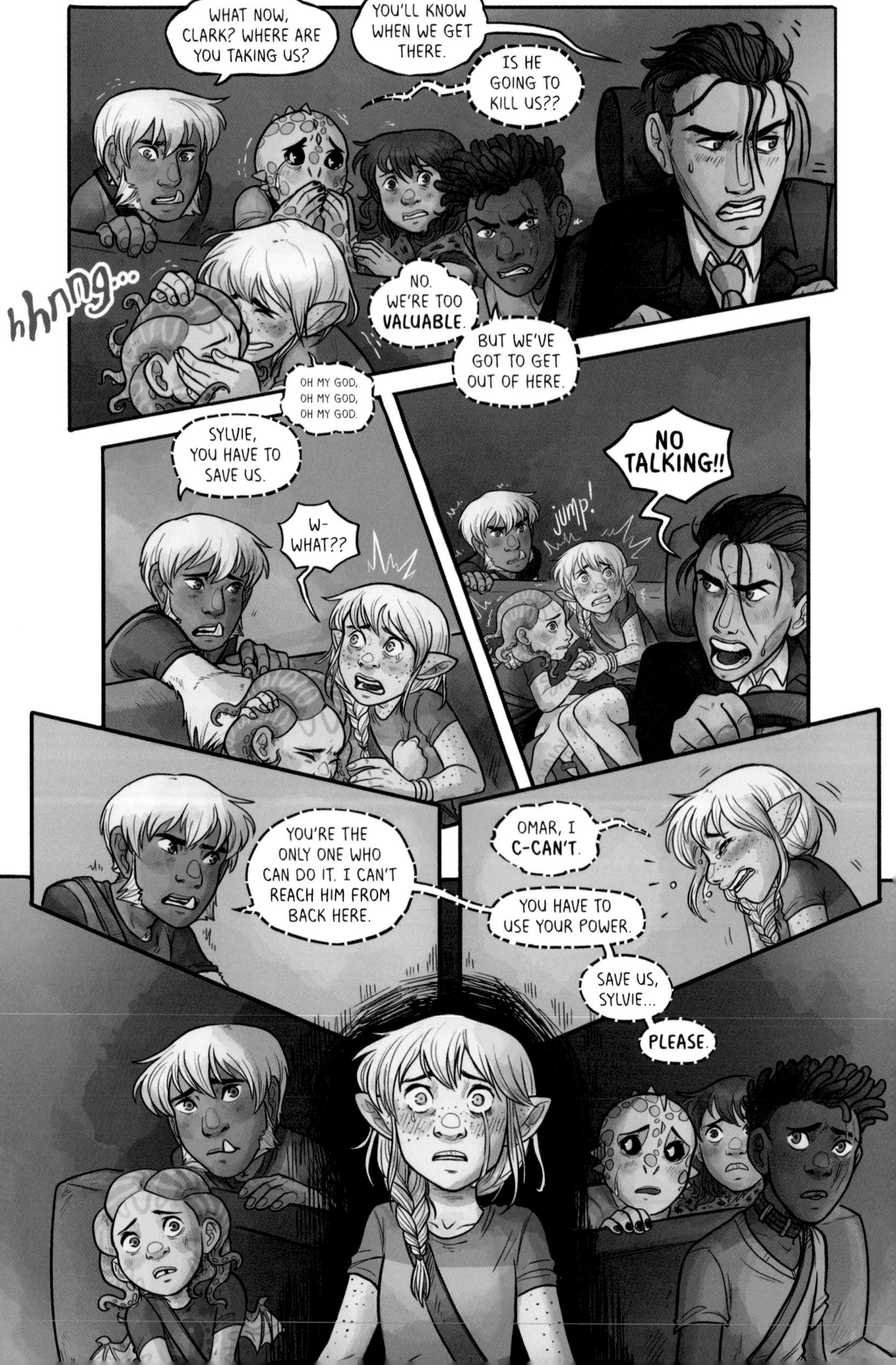
WHAT NOW, CLARK? WHERE ARE YOU TAKING US?
YOU'LL KNOW WHEN WE GET THERE.
IS HE GOING TO KILL US??
hhnng...
NO. WE'RE TOO **VALUABLE**.
BUT WE'VE GOT TO GET OUT OF HERE.
OH MY GOD, OH MY GOD, OH MY GOD.
SYLVIE, YOU HAVE TO SAVE US.
W- WHAT??
NO TALKING!!
jump!
YOU'RE THE ONLY ONE WHO CAN DO IT. I CAN'T REACH HIM FROM BACK HERE.
OMAR, I **C-CAN'T**.
YOU HAVE TO USE YOUR POWER.
SAVE US, SYLVIE...
PLEASE.

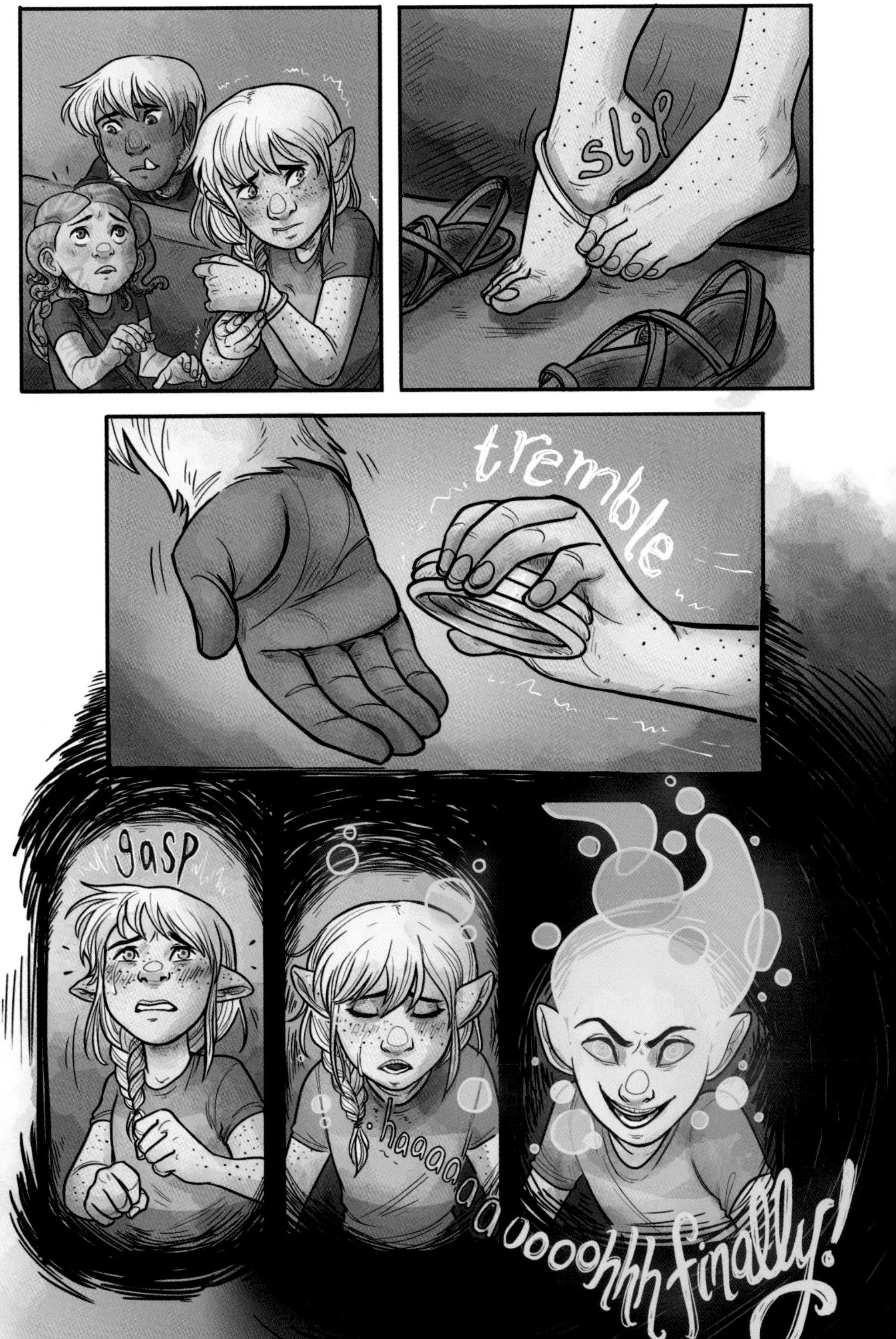
slip
tremble
gasp
haaaaaaaooooohhh finally!

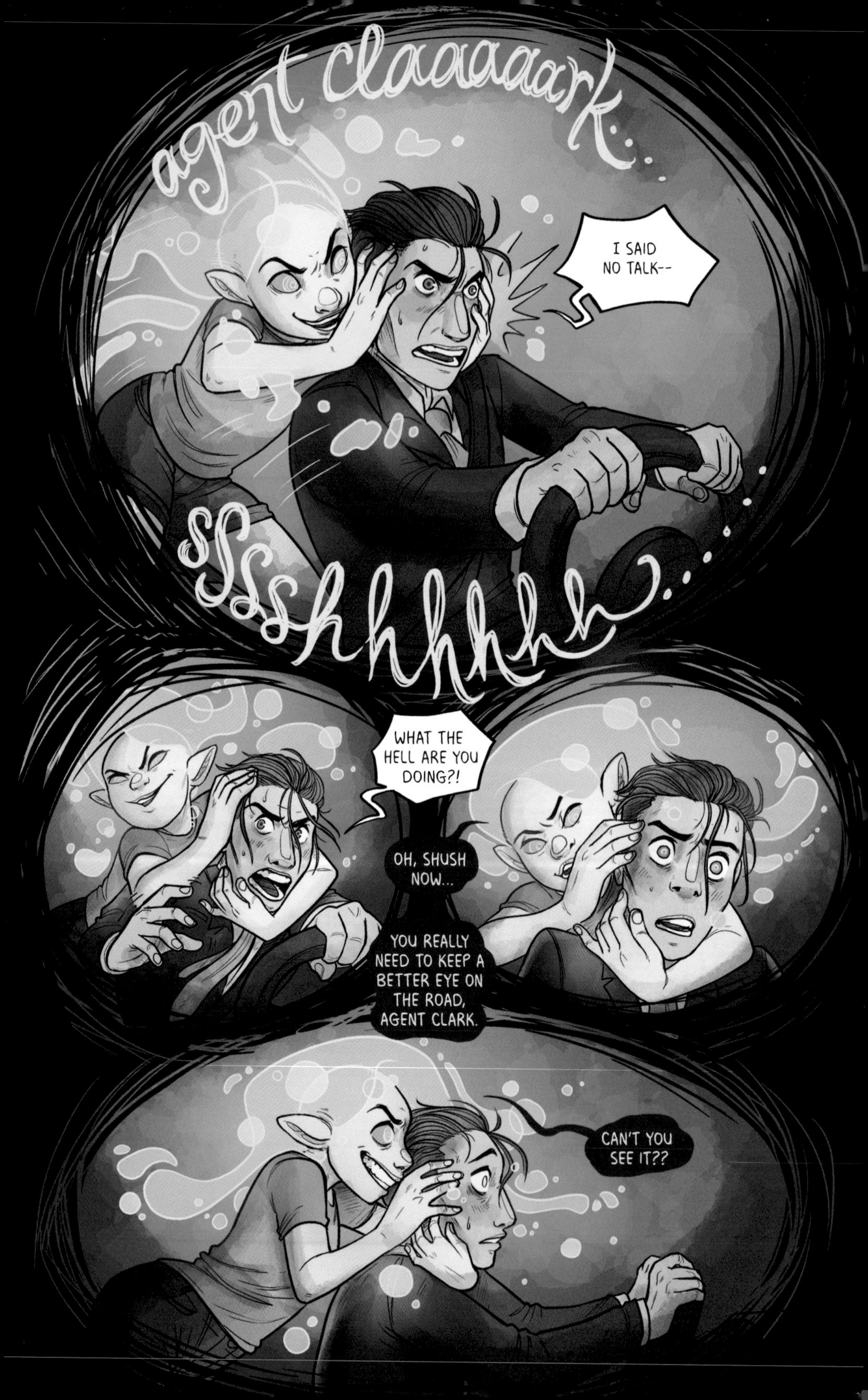
agent claaaaark
I SAID NO TALK--
sssshhhhhh.....
WHAT THE HELL ARE YOU DOING?!
OH, SHUSH NOW...
YOU REALLY NEED TO KEEP A BETTER EYE ON THE ROAD, AGENT CLARK.
CAN'T YOU SEE IT??

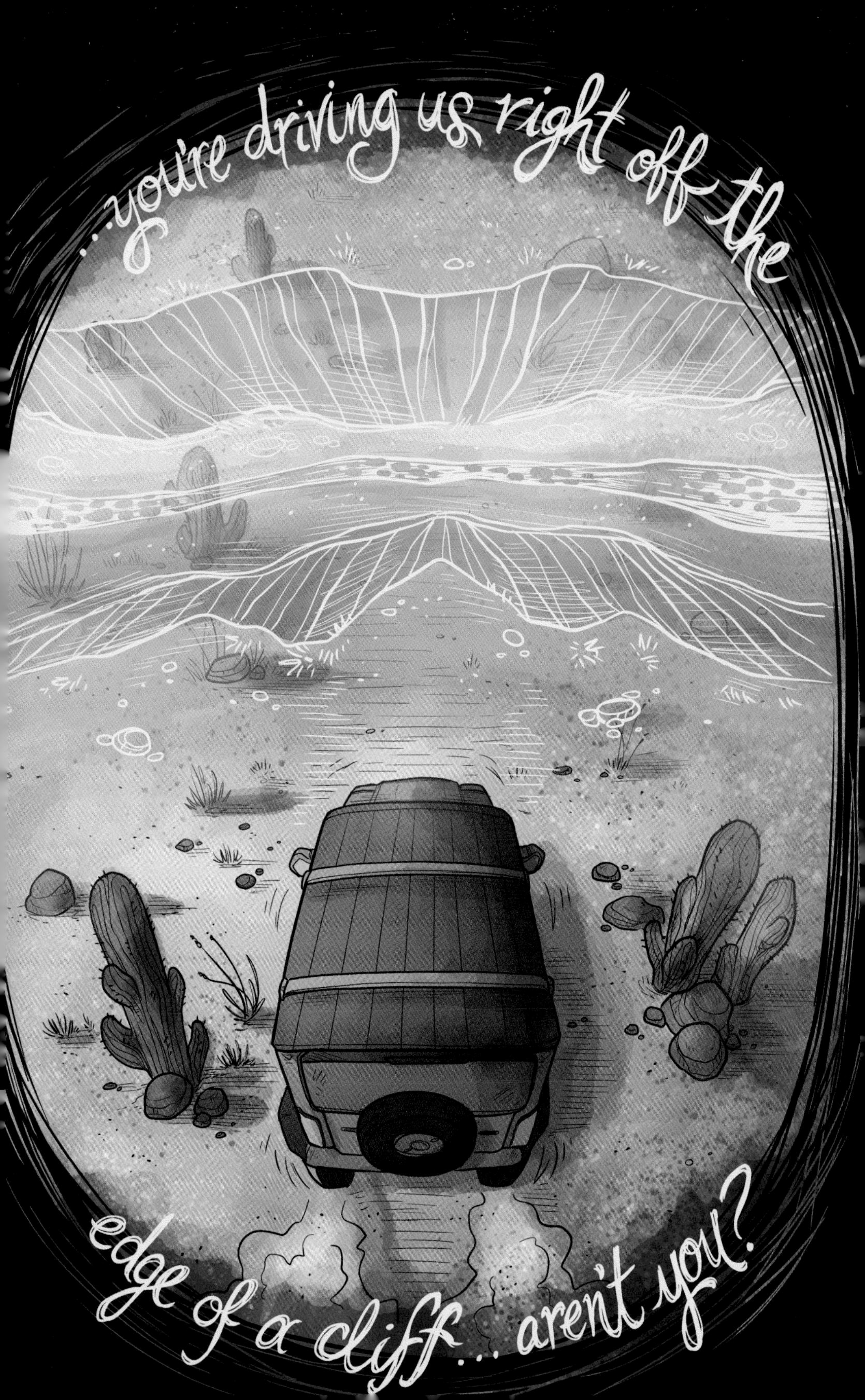
...you're driving us right off the
edge of a cliff... aren't you?

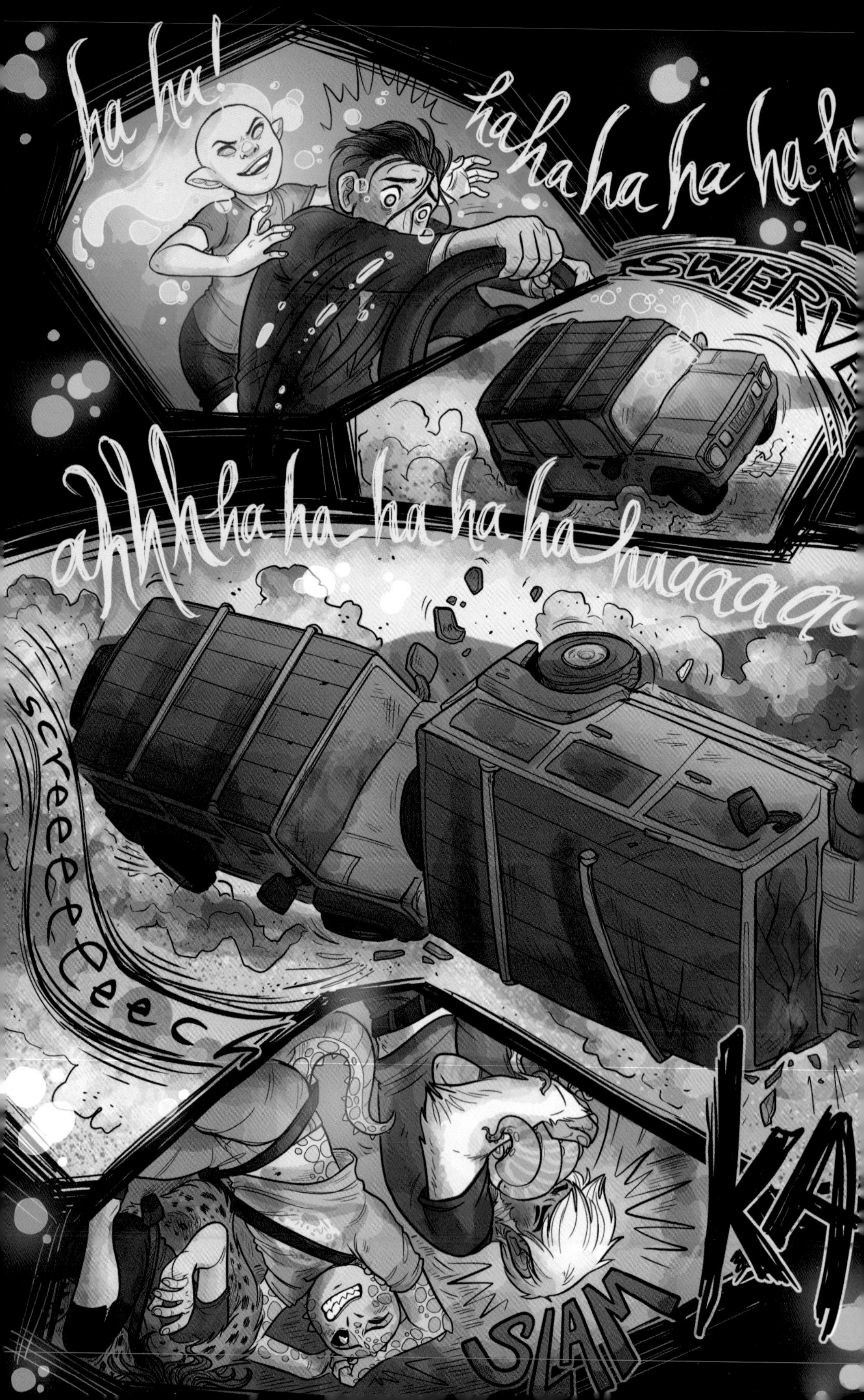
ha ha!
ha ha ha ha ha ha
SWERVE
ahhh ha ha ha ha ha haaaaaa
screeeeeeech
SLAM
KA

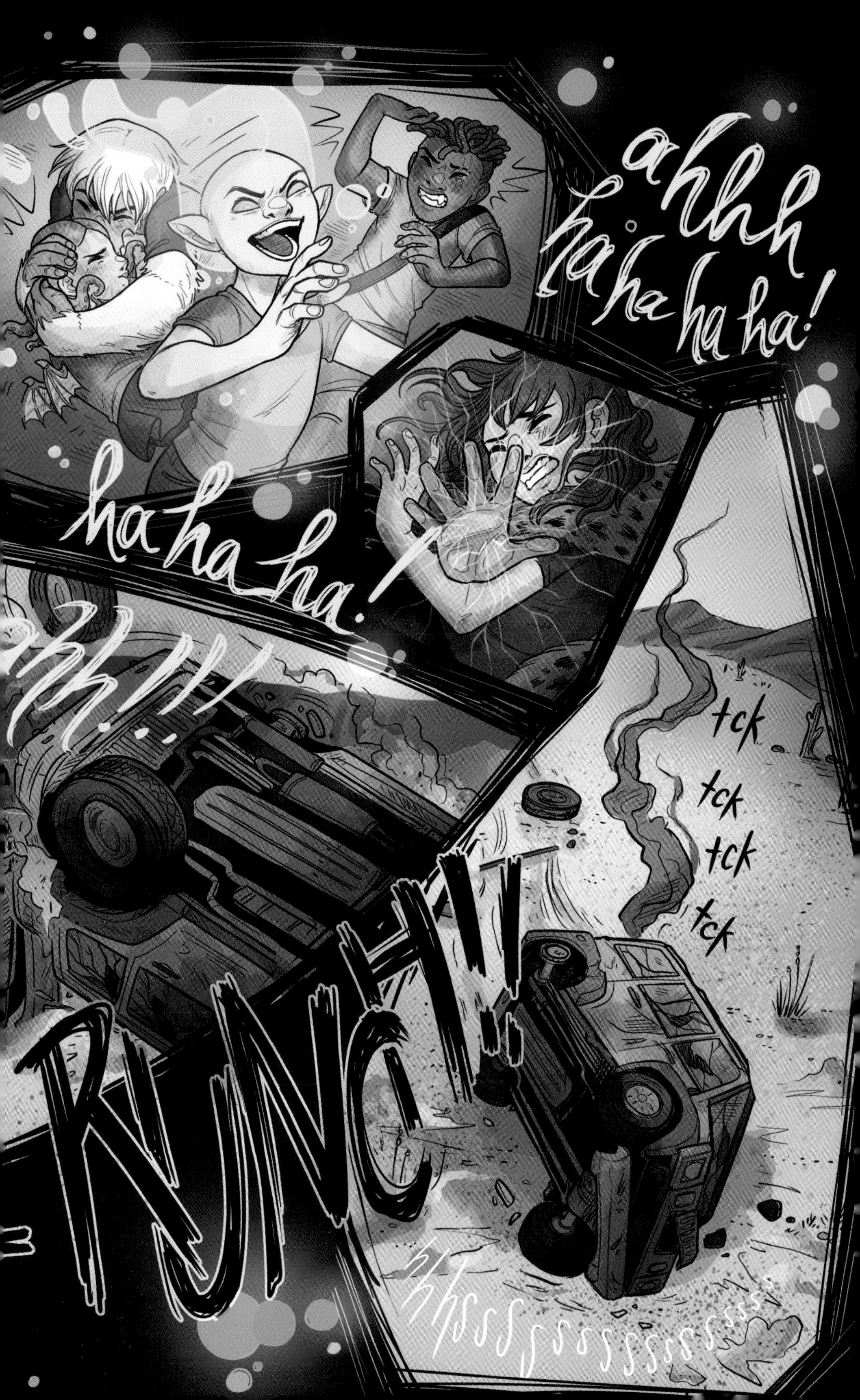

ahhh ha ha ha ha!
ha ha ha ha!
ahh!!
tck
tck
tck
tck
KRUNCH!!
hhsssssssssssss

CHAPTER THREE

WHITEOUT

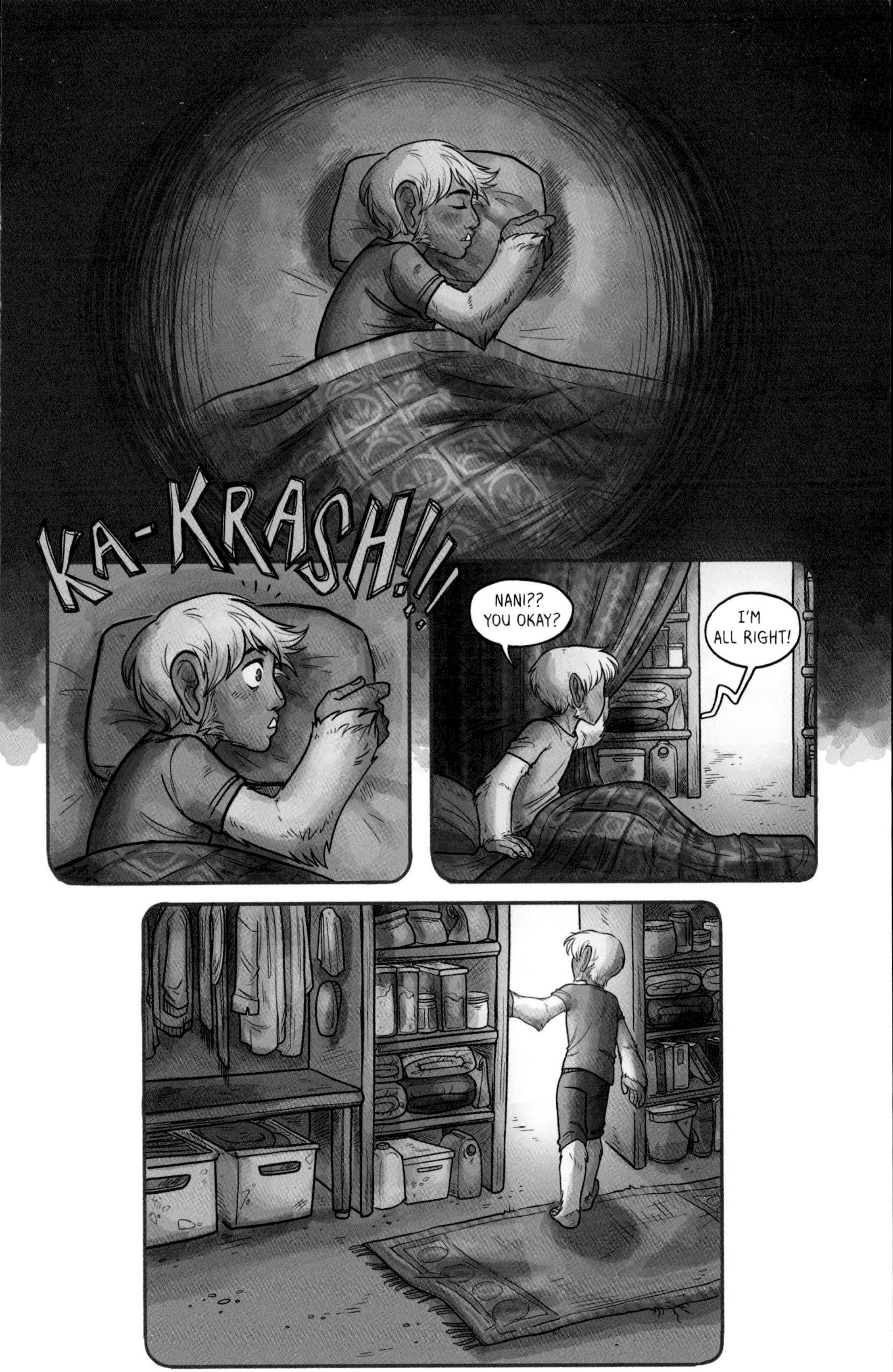
KA-KRASH!!!
NANI?? YOU OKAY?
I'M ALL RIGHT!

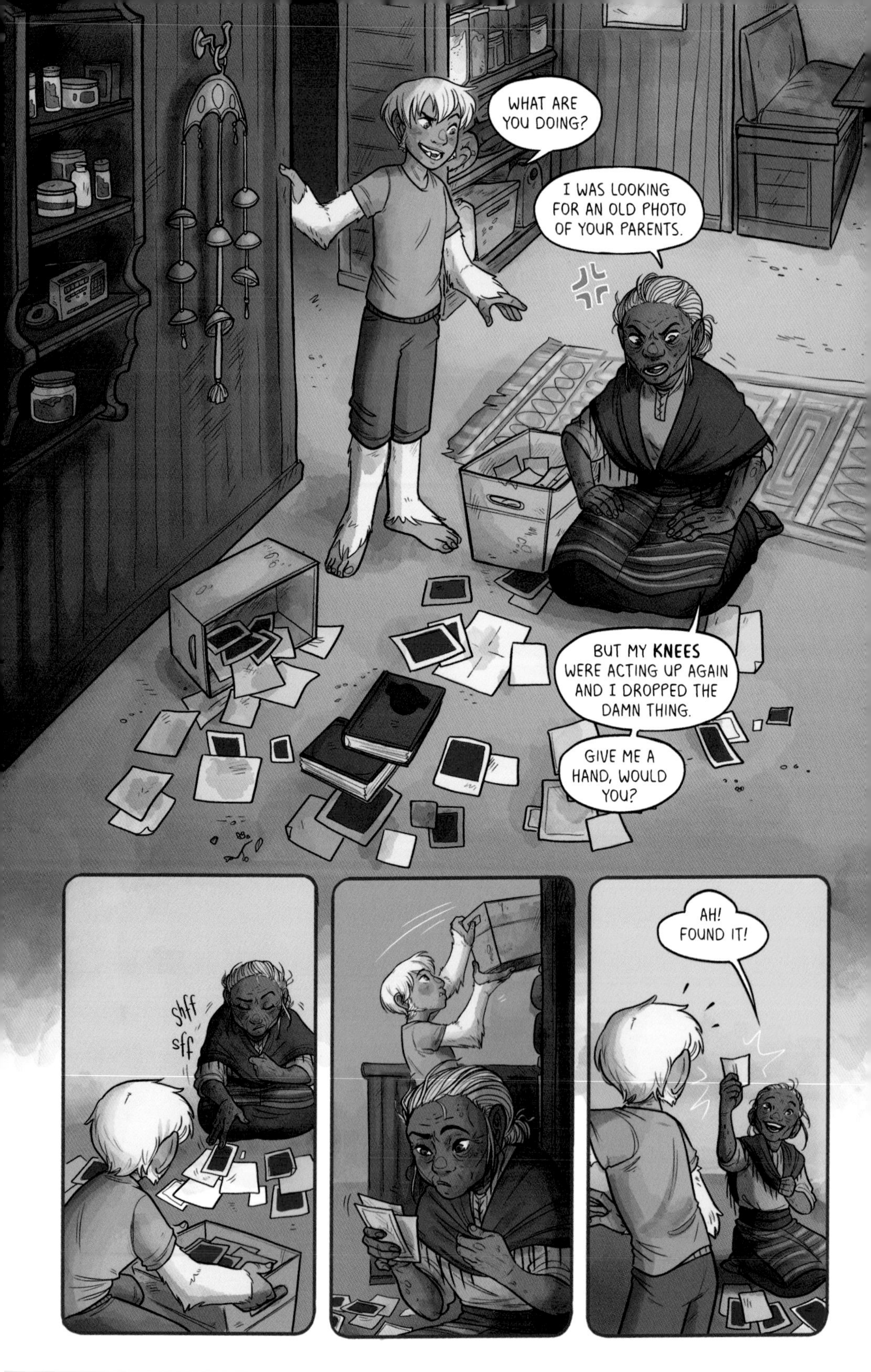
WHAT ARE YOU DOING?
I WAS LOOKING FOR AN OLD PHOTO OF YOUR PARENTS.
BUT MY **KNEES** WERE ACTING UP AGAIN AND I DROPPED THE DAMN THING.
GIVE ME A HAND, WOULD YOU?
SHFF
SFF
AH! FOUND IT!

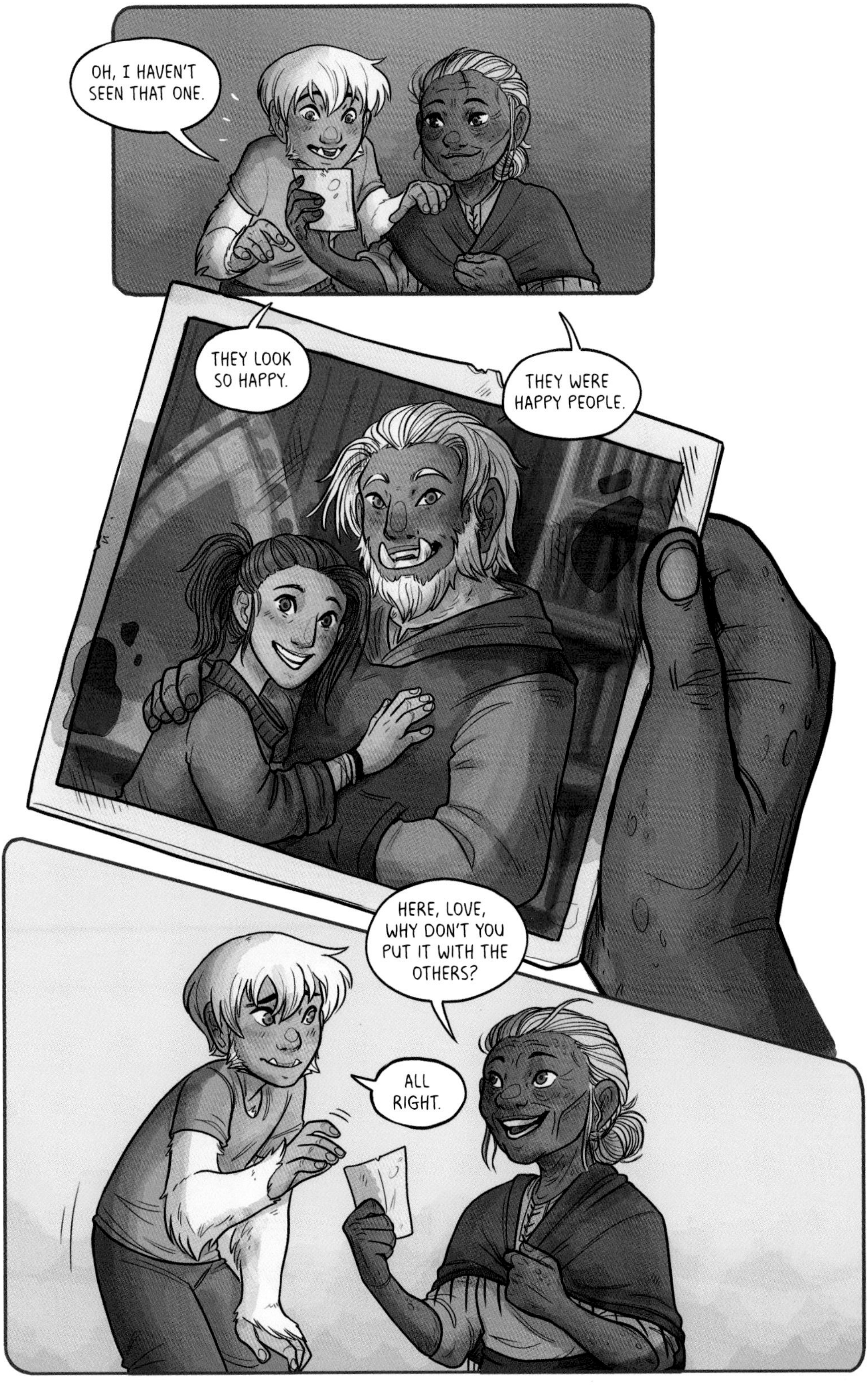
OH, I HAVEN'T SEEN THAT ONE.
THEY LOOK SO HAPPY.
THEY WERE HAPPY PEOPLE.
HERE, LOVE, WHY DON'T YOU PUT IT WITH THE OTHERS?
ALL RIGHT.

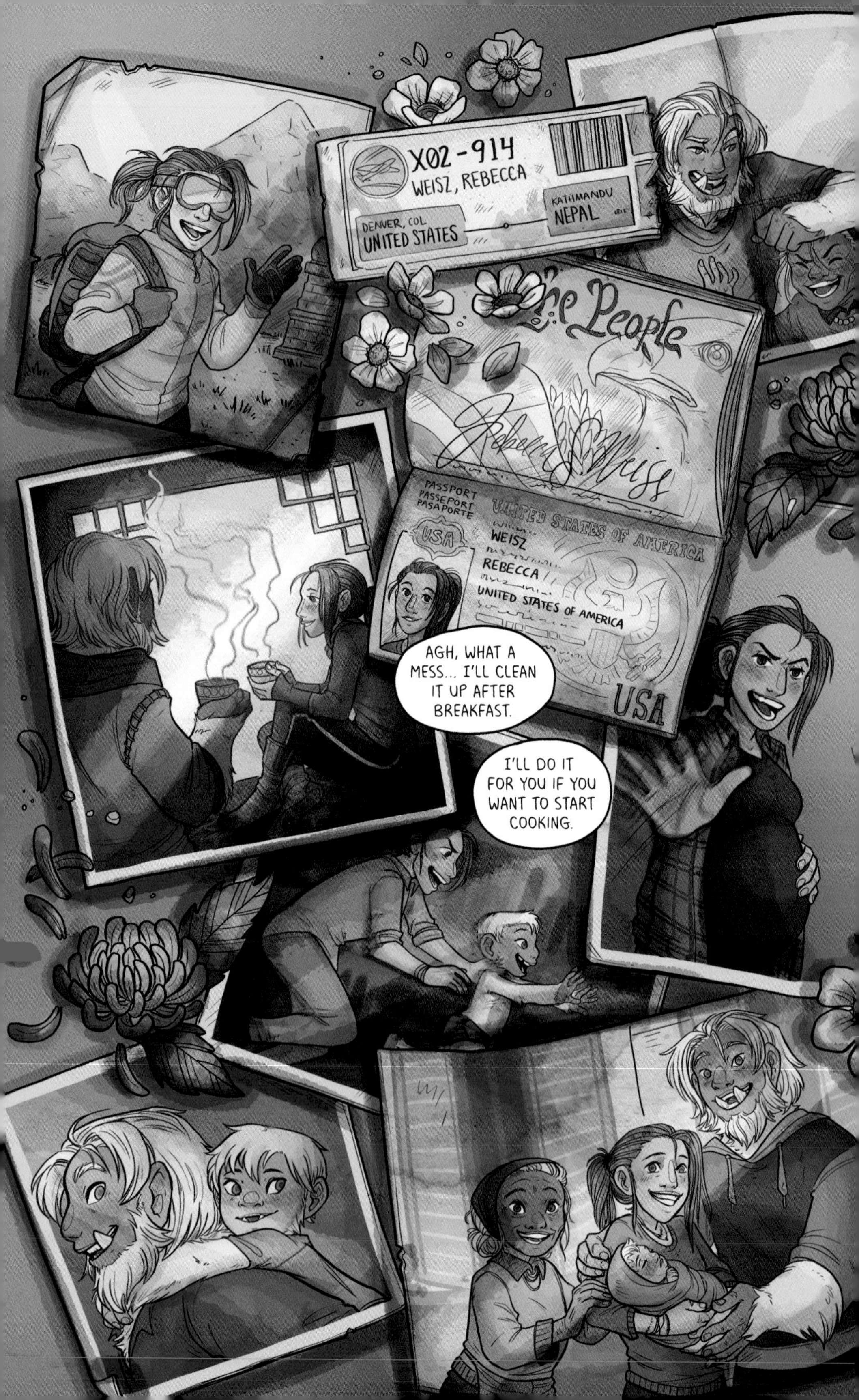
X02-914
WEISZ, REBECCA
DENVER, COL
UNITED STATES
KATHMANDU
NEPAL
PASSPORT
PASSEPORT
PASAPORTE
USA
UNITED STATES OF AMERICA
WEISZ
REBECCA
UNITED STATES OF AMERICA
USA
AGH, WHAT A MESS... I'LL CLEAN IT UP AFTER BREAKFAST.
I'LL DO IT FOR YOU IF YOU WANT TO START COOKING.

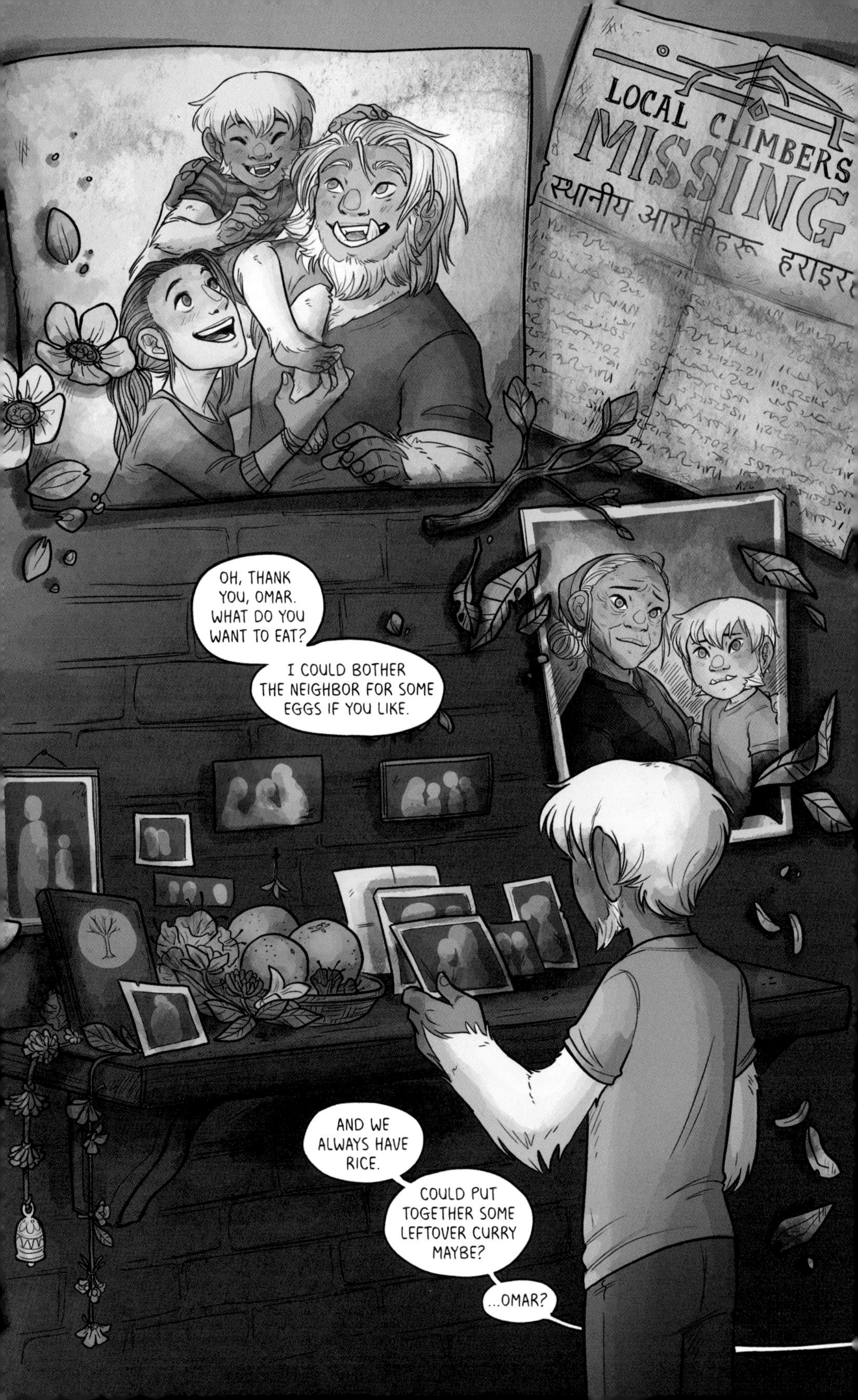
LOCAL CLIMBERS MISSING
स्थानीय आरोहीहरू
OH, THANK YOU, OMAR. WHAT DO YOU WANT TO EAT?
I COULD BOTHER THE NEIGHBOR FOR SOME EGGS IF YOU LIKE.
AND WE ALWAYS HAVE RICE.
COULD PUT TOGETHER SOME LEFTOVER CURRY MAYBE?
...OMAR?

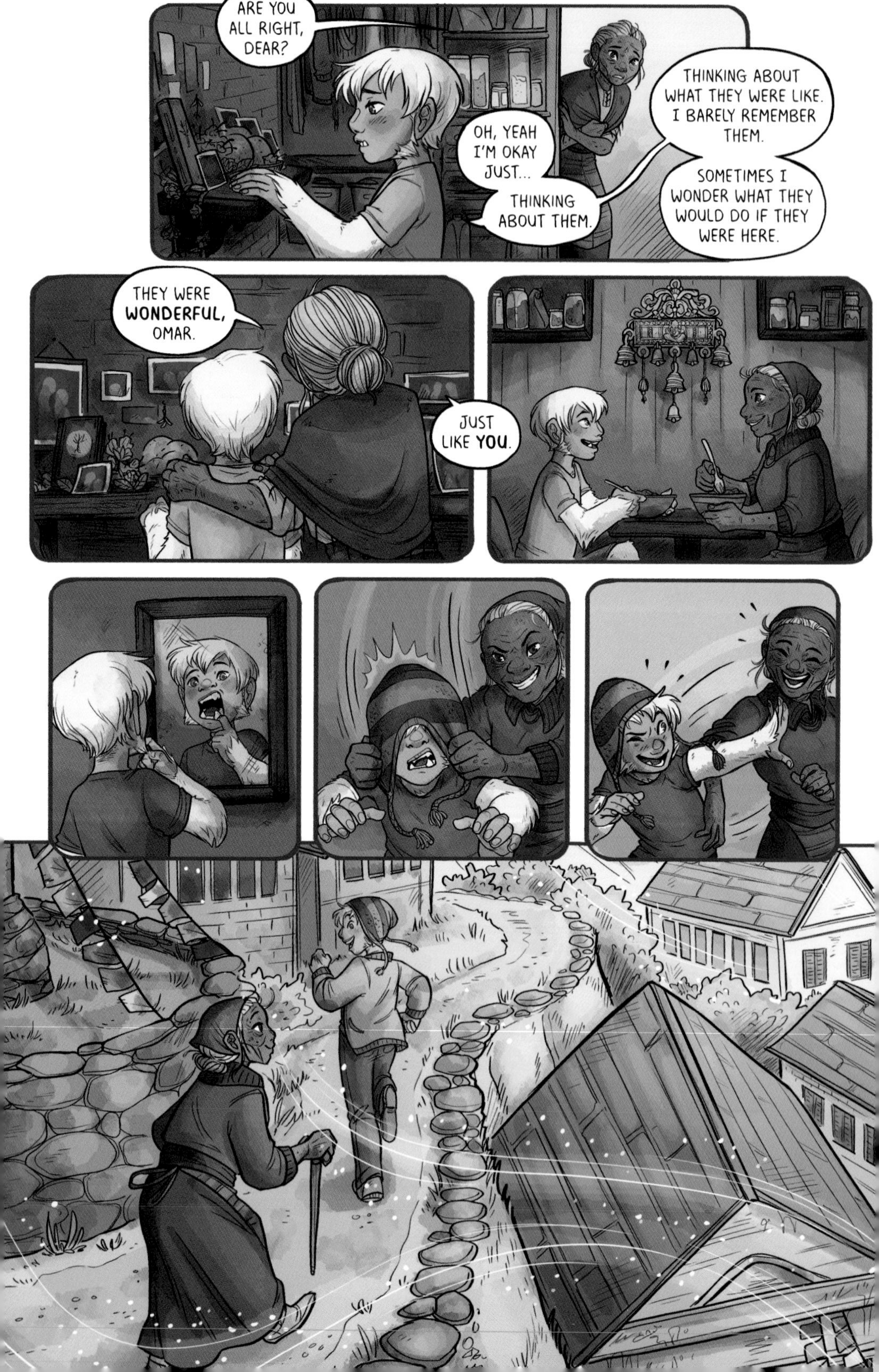
ARE YOU ALL RIGHT, DEAR?
OH, YEAH I'M OKAY JUST...
THINKING ABOUT THEM.
THINKING ABOUT WHAT THEY WERE LIKE. I BARELY REMEMBER THEM.
SOMETIMES I WONDER WHAT THEY WOULD DO IF THEY WERE HERE.
THEY WERE **WONDERFUL,** OMAR.
JUST LIKE **YOU**.

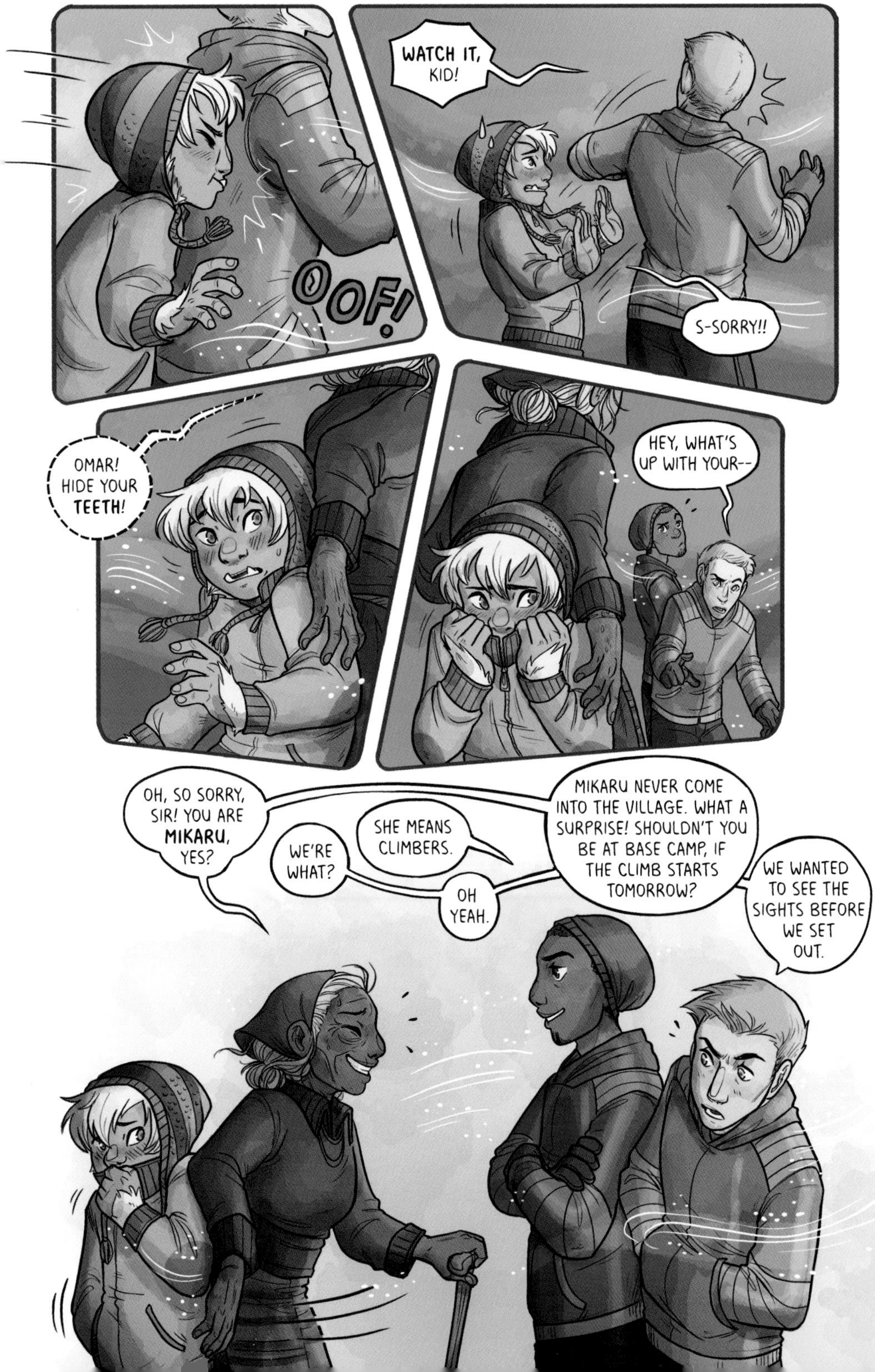
OOF!
WATCH IT, KID!
S-SORRY!!
OMAR! HIDE YOUR TEETH!
HEY, WHAT'S UP WITH YOUR--
OH, SO SORRY, SIR! YOU ARE MIKARU, YES?
WE'RE WHAT?
SHE MEANS CLIMBERS.
OH YEAH.
MIKARU NEVER COME INTO THE VILLAGE. WHAT A SURPRISE! SHOULDN'T YOU BE AT BASE CAMP, IF THE CLIMB STARTS TOMORROW?
WE WANTED TO SEE THE SIGHTS BEFORE WE SET OUT.

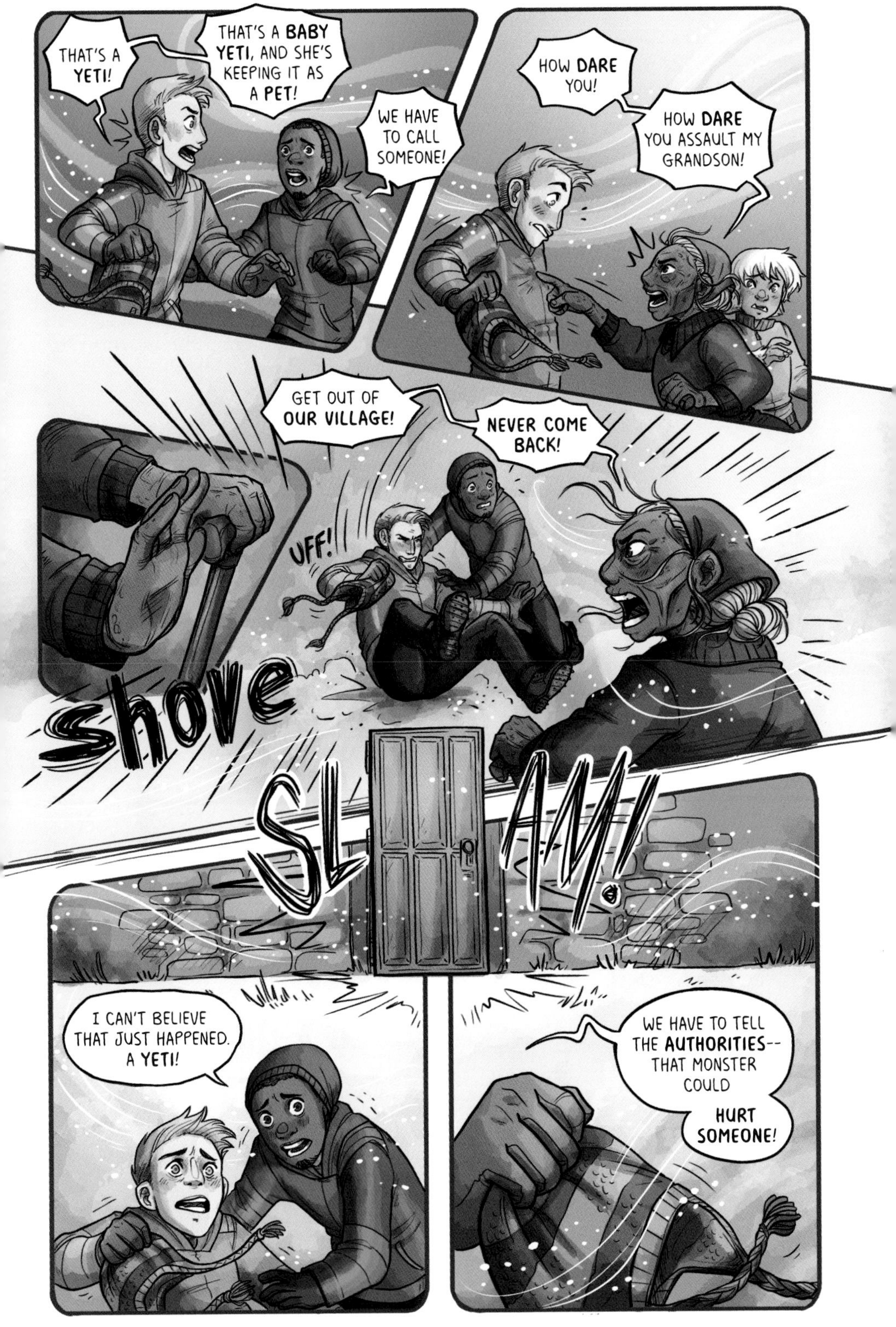
THAT'S A YETI!
THAT'S A BABY YETI, AND SHE'S KEEPING IT AS A PET!
WE HAVE TO CALL SOMEONE!
HOW DARE YOU!
HOW DARE YOU ASSAULT MY GRANDSON!
GET OUT OF OUR VILLAGE!
NEVER COME BACK!
UFF!
SHOVE
SLAM!
I CAN'T BELIEVE THAT JUST HAPPENED. A YETI!
WE HAVE TO TELL THE AUTHORITIES--THAT MONSTER COULD
HURT SOMEONE!

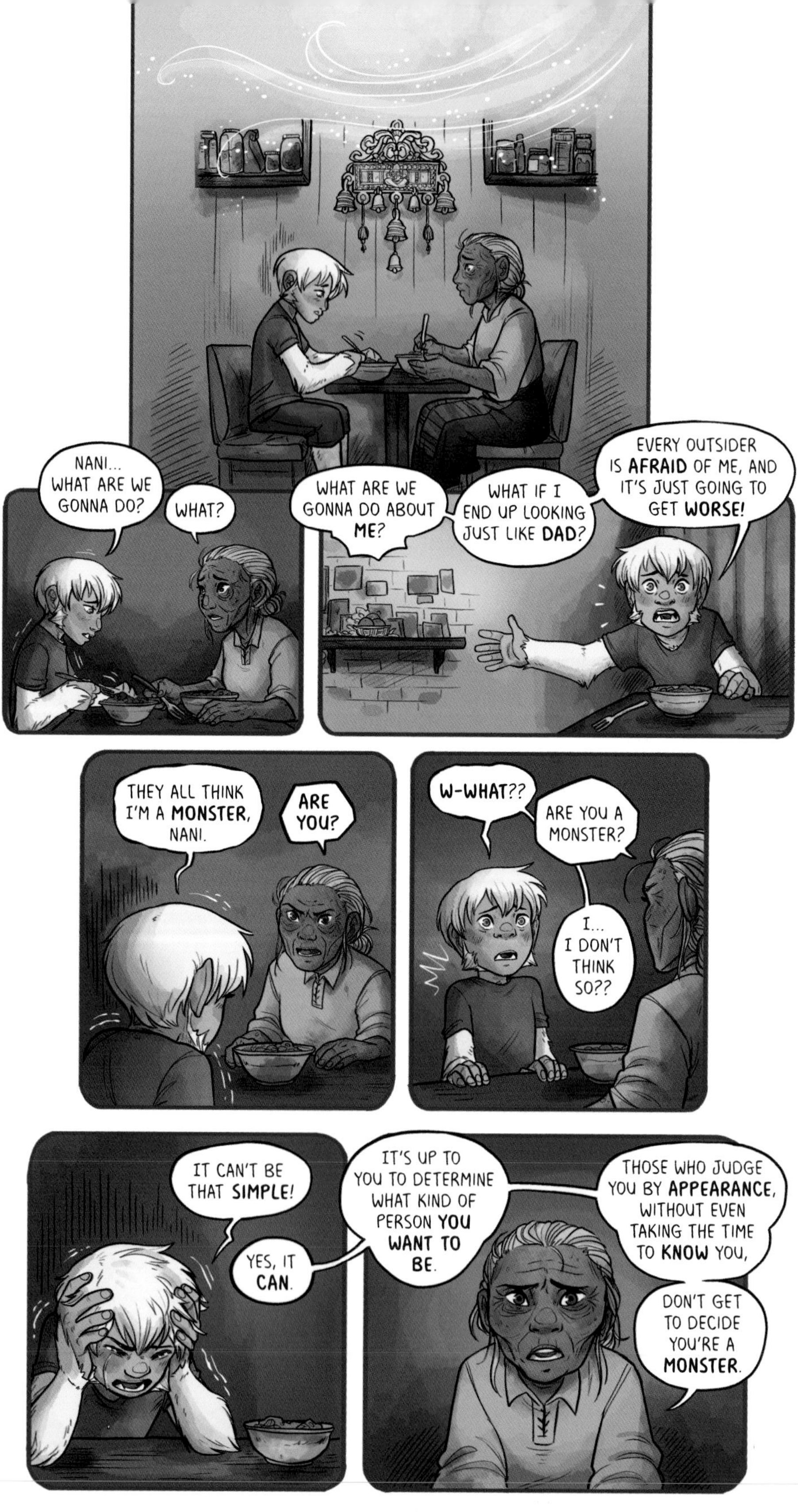
NANI... WHAT ARE WE GONNA DO?
WHAT?
WHAT ARE WE GONNA DO ABOUT ME?
WHAT IF I END UP LOOKING JUST LIKE DAD?
EVERY OUTSIDER IS AFRAID OF ME, AND IT'S JUST GOING TO GET WORSE!
THEY ALL THINK I'M A MONSTER, NANI.
ARE YOU?
W-WHAT??
ARE YOU A MONSTER?
I... I DON'T THINK SO??
IT CAN'T BE THAT SIMPLE!
YES, IT CAN.
IT'S UP TO YOU TO DETERMINE WHAT KIND OF PERSON YOU WANT TO BE.
THOSE WHO JUDGE YOU BY APPEARANCE, WITHOUT EVEN TAKING THE TIME TO KNOW YOU,
DON'T GET TO DECIDE YOU'RE A MONSTER.

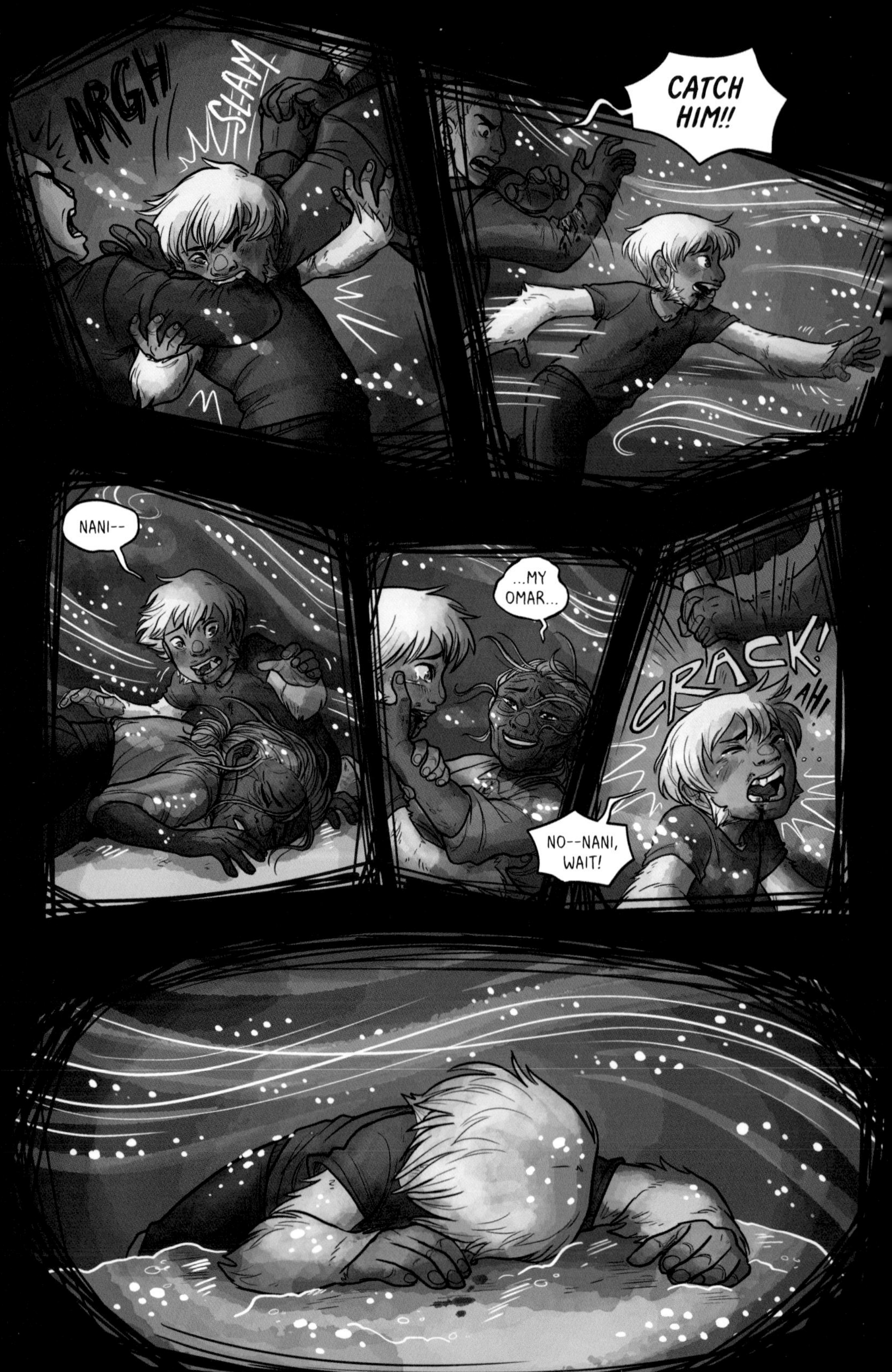
ARGH
SLAM
CATCH HIM!!
NANI--
...MY OMAR...
CRACK!
AH!
NO--NANI, WAIT!

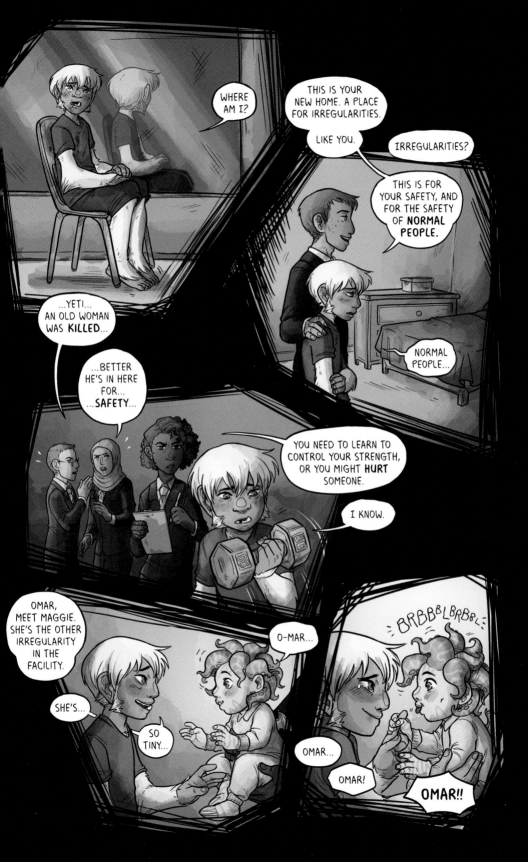

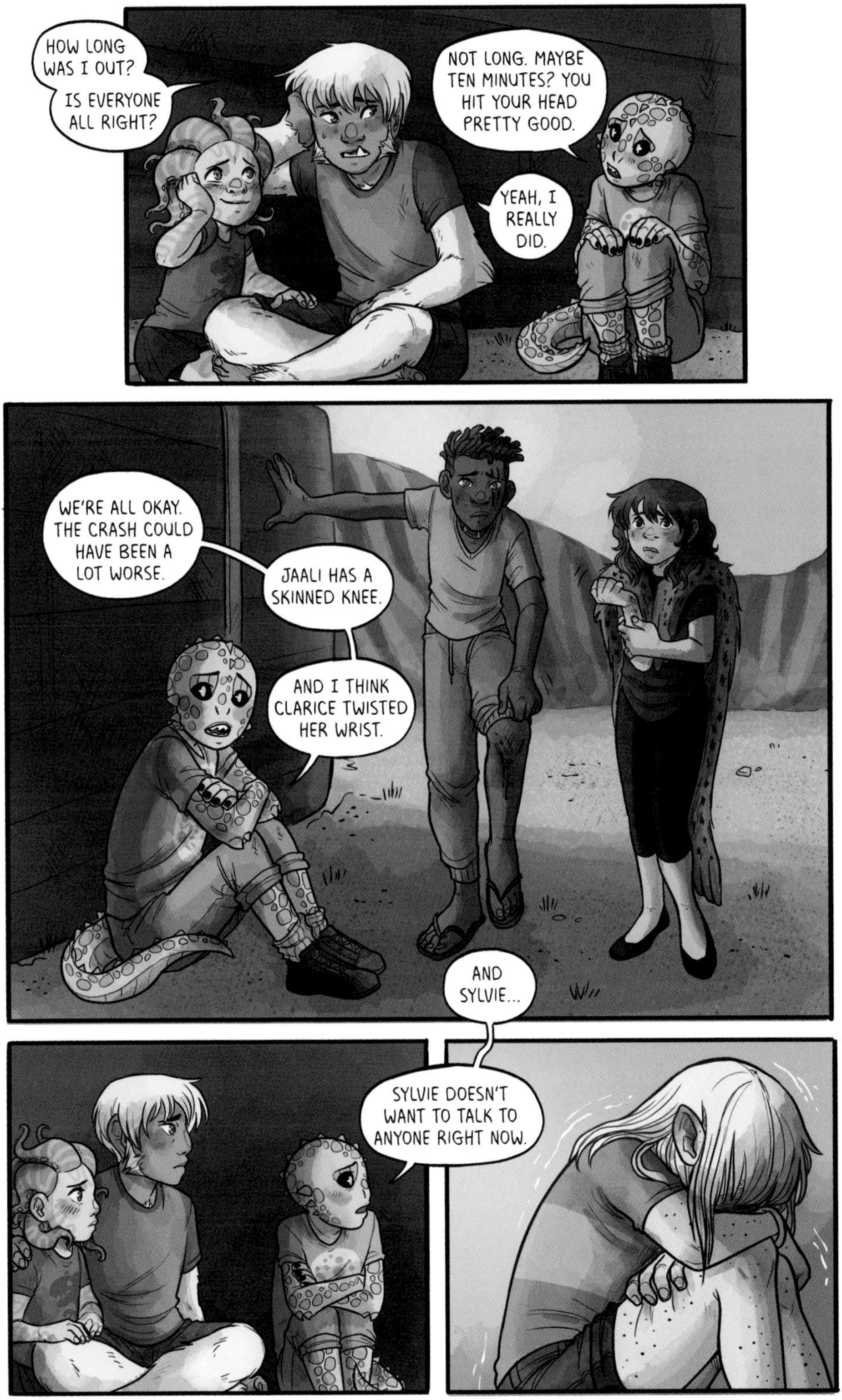

HOW LONG WAS I OUT?
IS EVERYONE ALL RIGHT?
NOT LONG. MAYBE TEN MINUTES? YOU HIT YOUR HEAD PRETTY GOOD.
YEAH, I REALLY DID.
WE'RE ALL OKAY. THE CRASH COULD HAVE BEEN A LOT WORSE.
JAALI HAS A SKINNED KNEE.
AND I THINK CLARICE TWISTED HER WRIST.
AND SYLVIE...
SYLVIE DOESN'T WANT TO TALK TO ANYONE RIGHT NOW.

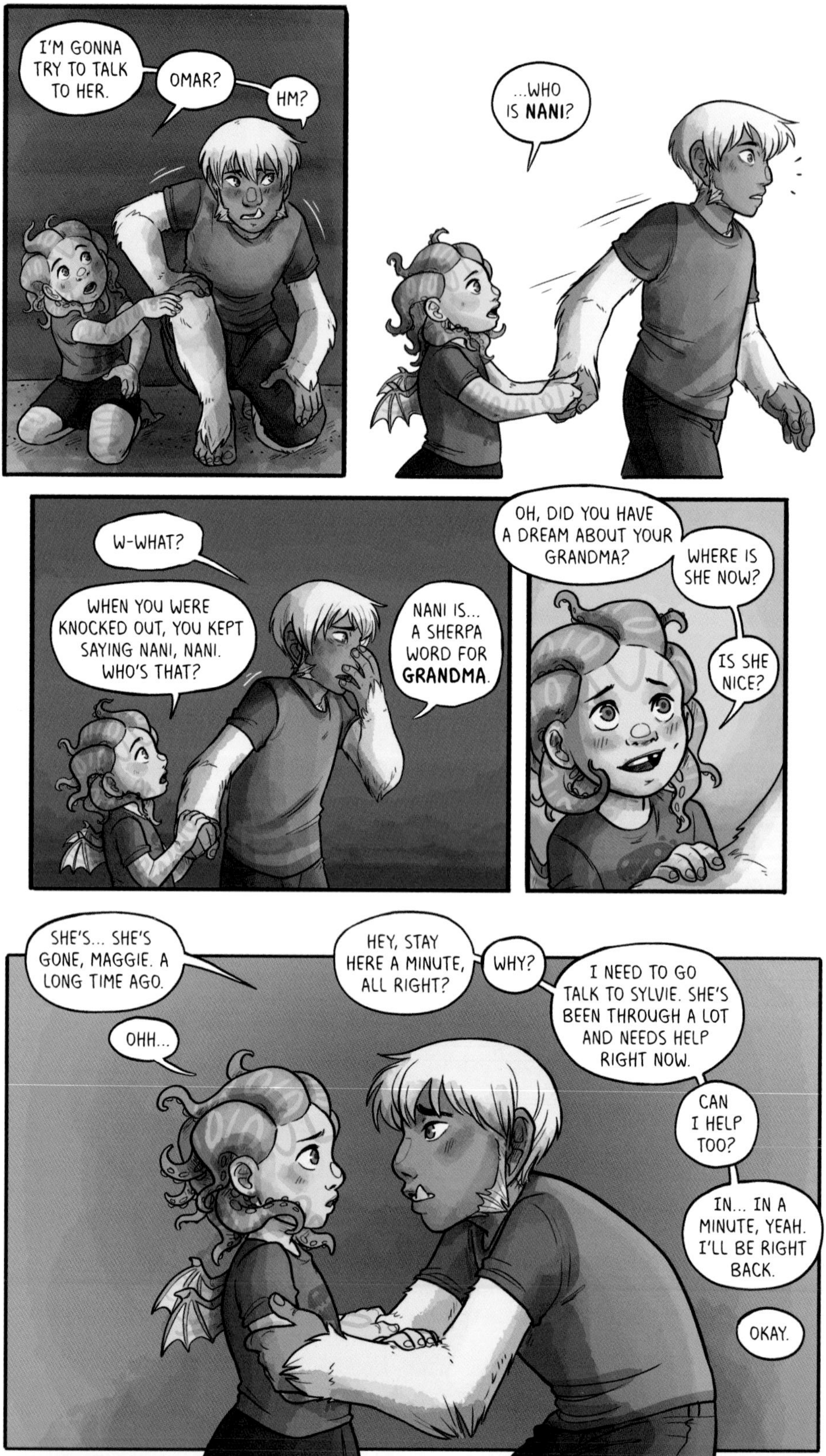
I'M GONNA TRY TO TALK TO HER.
OMAR?
HM?
...WHO IS **NANI**?
W-WHAT?
WHEN YOU WERE KNOCKED OUT, YOU KEPT SAYING NANI, NANI. WHO'S THAT?
NANI IS... A SHERPA WORD FOR **GRANDMA**.
OH, DID YOU HAVE A DREAM ABOUT YOUR GRANDMA?
WHERE IS SHE NOW?
IS SHE NICE?
SHE'S... SHE'S GONE, MAGGIE. A LONG TIME AGO.
OHH...
HEY, STAY HERE A MINUTE, ALL RIGHT?
WHY?
I NEED TO GO TALK TO SYLVIE. SHE'S BEEN THROUGH A LOT AND NEEDS HELP RIGHT NOW.
CAN I HELP TOO?
IN... IN A MINUTE, YEAH. I'LL BE RIGHT BACK.
OKAY.

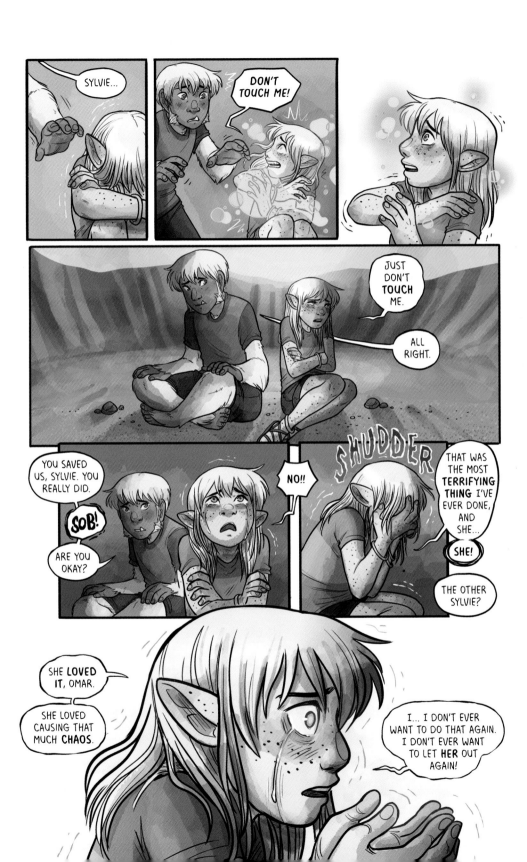

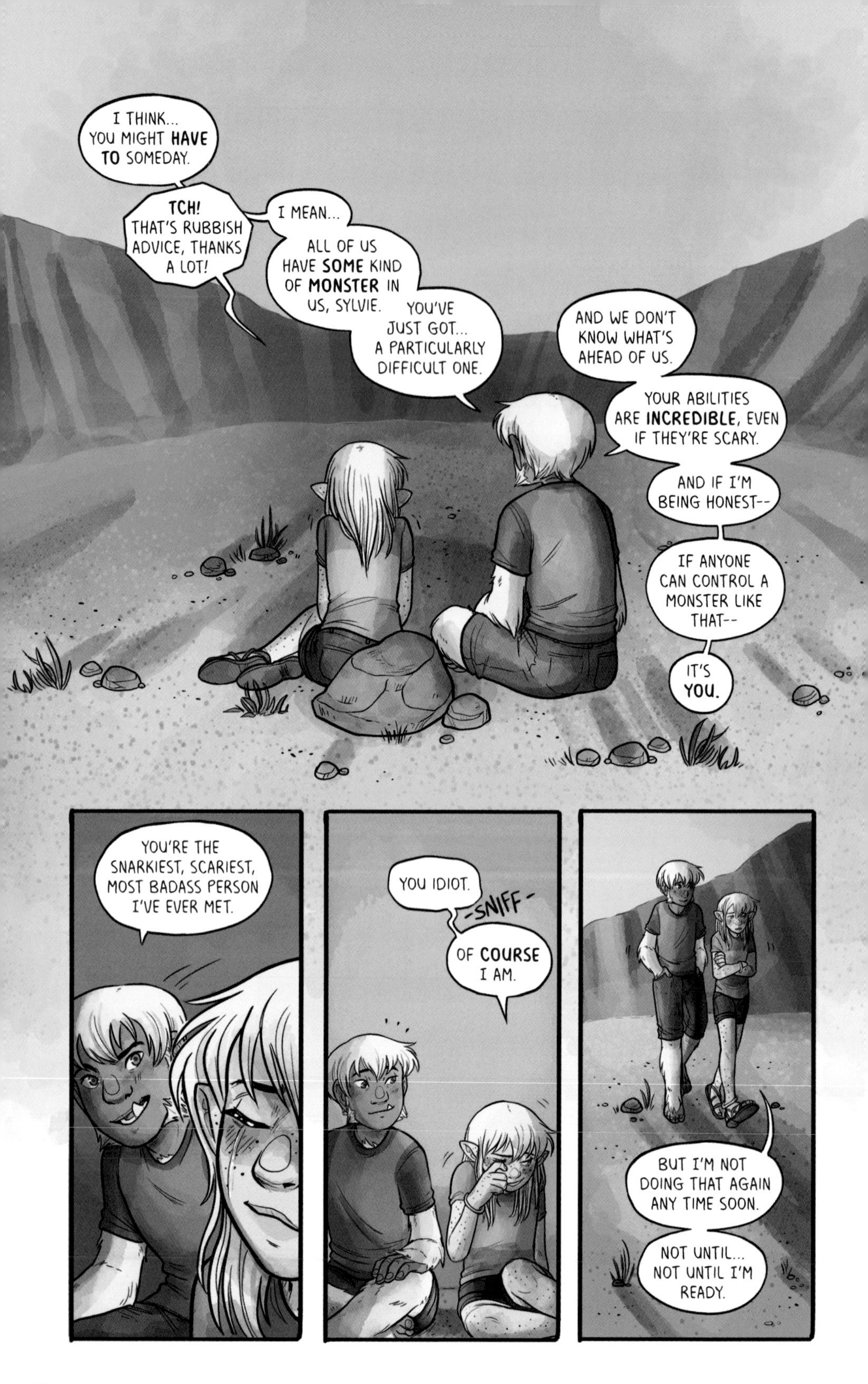
I THINK... YOU MIGHT **HAVE TO** SOMEDAY.
TCH! THAT'S RUBBISH ADVICE, THANKS A LOT!
I MEAN...
ALL OF US HAVE **SOME** KIND OF **MONSTER** IN US, SYLVIE.
YOU'VE JUST GOT... A PARTICULARLY DIFFICULT ONE.
AND WE DON'T KNOW WHAT'S AHEAD OF US.
YOUR ABILITIES ARE **INCREDIBLE**, EVEN IF THEY'RE SCARY.
AND IF I'M BEING HONEST--
IF ANYONE CAN CONTROL A MONSTER LIKE THAT--
IT'S **YOU.**
YOU'RE THE SNARKIEST, SCARIEST, MOST BADASS PERSON I'VE EVER MET.
YOU IDIOT.
-SNIFF-
OF **COURSE** I AM.
BUT I'M NOT DOING THAT AGAIN ANY TIME SOON.
NOT UNTIL... NOT UNTIL I'M READY.

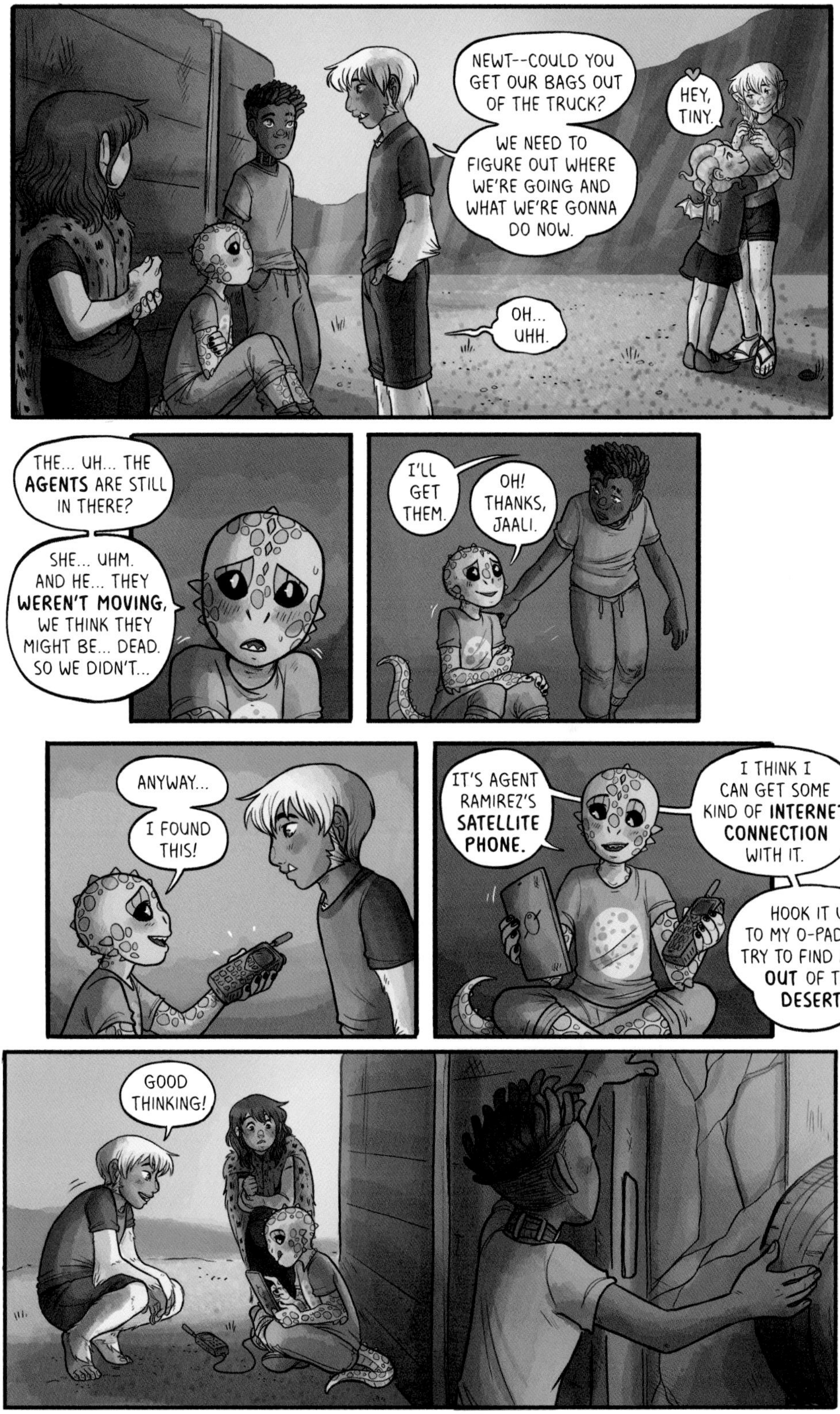
NEWT--COULD YOU GET OUR BAGS OUT OF THE TRUCK?
WE NEED TO FIGURE OUT WHERE WE'RE GOING AND WHAT WE'RE GONNA DO NOW.
HEY, TINY.
OH... UHH.
THE... UH... THE AGENTS ARE STILL IN THERE?
SHE... UHM. AND HE... THEY WEREN'T MOVING, WE THINK THEY MIGHT BE... DEAD. SO WE DIDN'T...
I'LL GET THEM.
OH! THANKS, JAALI.
ANYWAY...
I FOUND THIS!
IT'S AGENT RAMIREZ'S SATELLITE PHONE.
I THINK I CAN GET SOME KIND OF INTERNET CONNECTION WITH IT.
HOOK IT UP TO MY O-PAD AND TRY TO FIND A WAY OUT OF THIS DESERT!
GOOD THINKING!

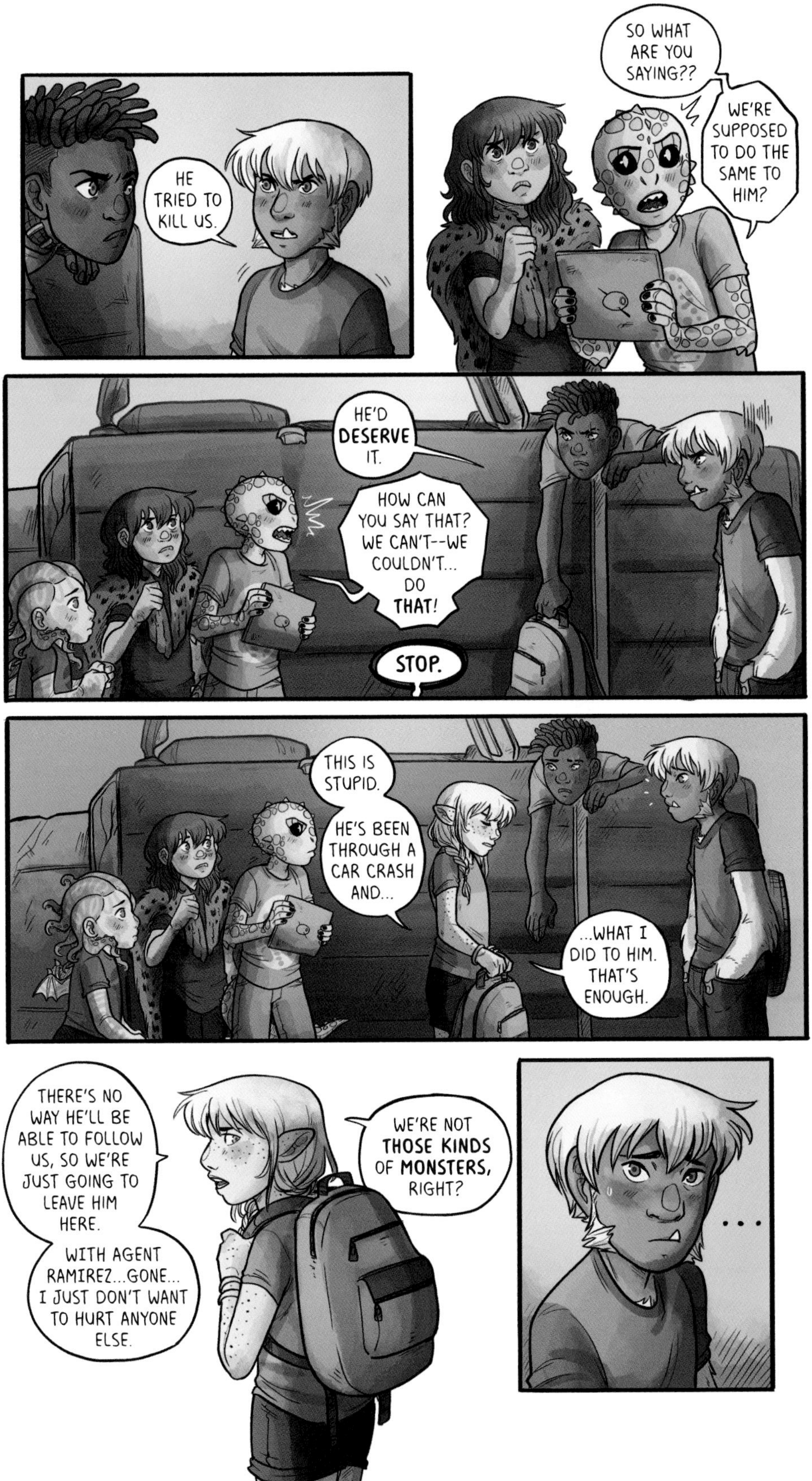
HE TRIED TO KILL US.
SO WHAT ARE YOU SAYING??
WE'RE SUPPOSED TO DO THE SAME TO HIM?
HE'D **DESERVE** IT.
HOW CAN YOU SAY THAT? WE CAN'T--WE COULDN'T... DO **THAT**!
STOP.
THIS IS STUPID.
HE'S BEEN THROUGH A CAR CRASH AND...
...WHAT I DID TO HIM. THAT'S ENOUGH.
THERE'S NO WAY HE'LL BE ABLE TO FOLLOW US, SO WE'RE JUST GOING TO LEAVE HIM HERE.
WITH AGENT RAMIREZ...GONE... I JUST DON'T WANT TO HURT ANYONE ELSE.
WE'RE NOT **THOSE KINDS** OF **MONSTERS,** RIGHT?
...

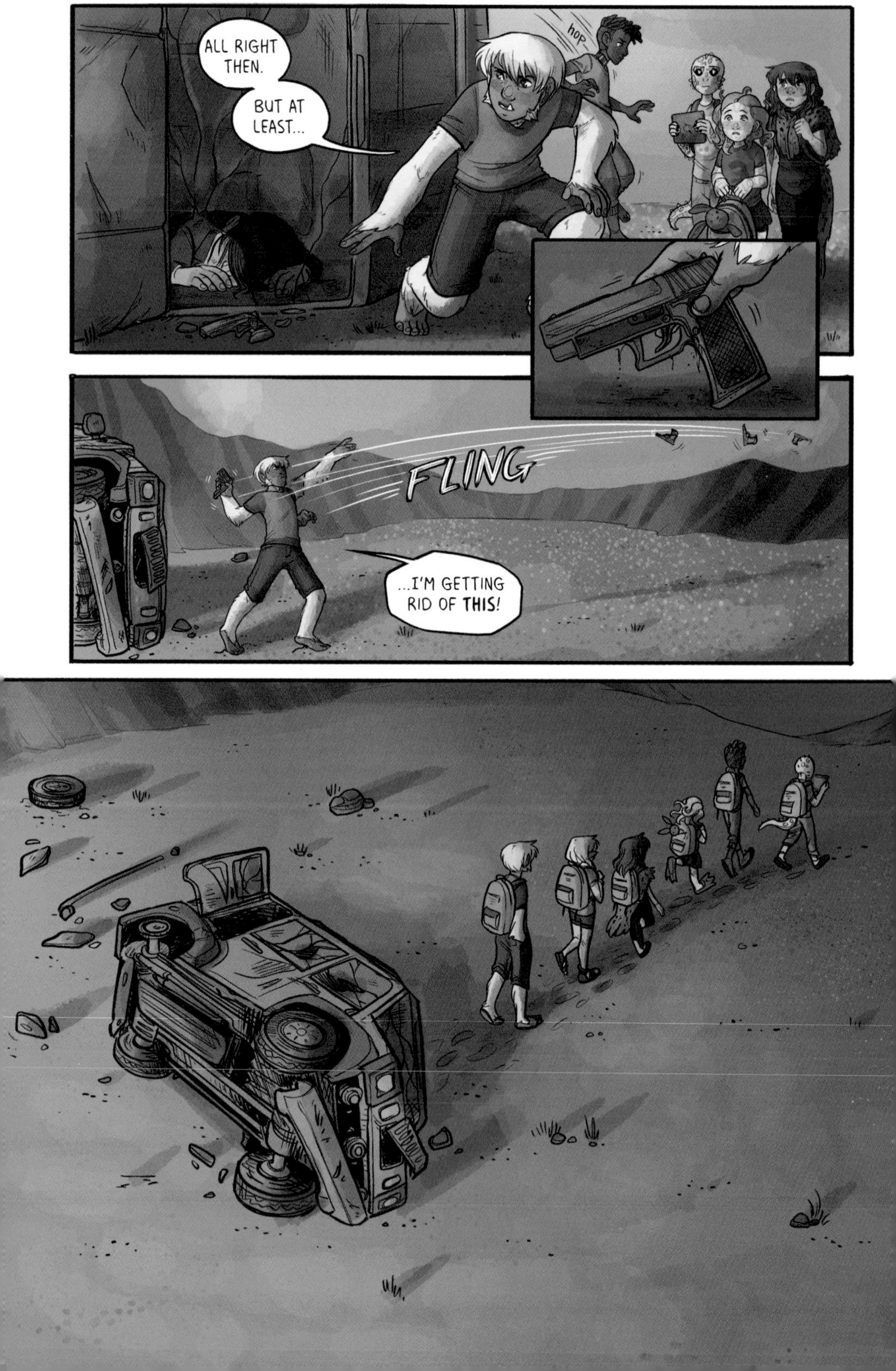

ALL RIGHT THEN.
BUT AT LEAST...
hop
FLING
...I'M GETTING RID OF **THIS**!

OKAY... THE R-ROAD SHOULD BE J-JUST UP AHEAD.

S-S-SEE! I KNEW WE'D FIND THE R-ROAD EVENTUALLY!

GOOD JOB, NEWT!

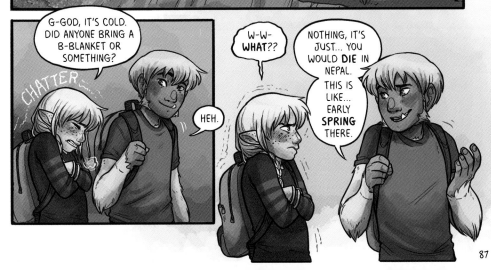

G-GOD, IT'S COLD. DID ANYONE BRING A B-BLANKET OR SOMETHING?

CHATTER

HEH.

W-W-**WHAT??**

NOTHING, IT'S JUST... YOU WOULD **DIE** IN NEPAL. THIS IS LIKE... EARLY **SPRING** THERE.

87

ARE YOU KIDDING ME?? THOSE ARE THE GUYS WHO WERE STALKING THE GATE--

THEY'D DO **EXPERIMENTS** ON US OR SOMETHING!

WHAT IN THE WORLD ARE YOU LAUGHING AT? THEY ALMOST **SAW US!**

I'M SORRY, I CAN'T HELP IT!

WHAT IS SO FUNNY?!

snort

PFFFFT

HEE HEE HEE

THEIR BUMPER STICKER SAID "I'M SQUATCHING YOU"!

HA HA HA HA HA HA HA HA HA HA HA HA HA

PFF

HEH.

HA HA HA HA HA HA HA HA

HA HA HA HA HA HA HA HA HA HA

I DIDN'T KNOW YOU MADE ANY NOISE!! YOU CAN LAUGH! WOW!

HA HA HA HA HA HA HA HA HA HA HA HA HA HA

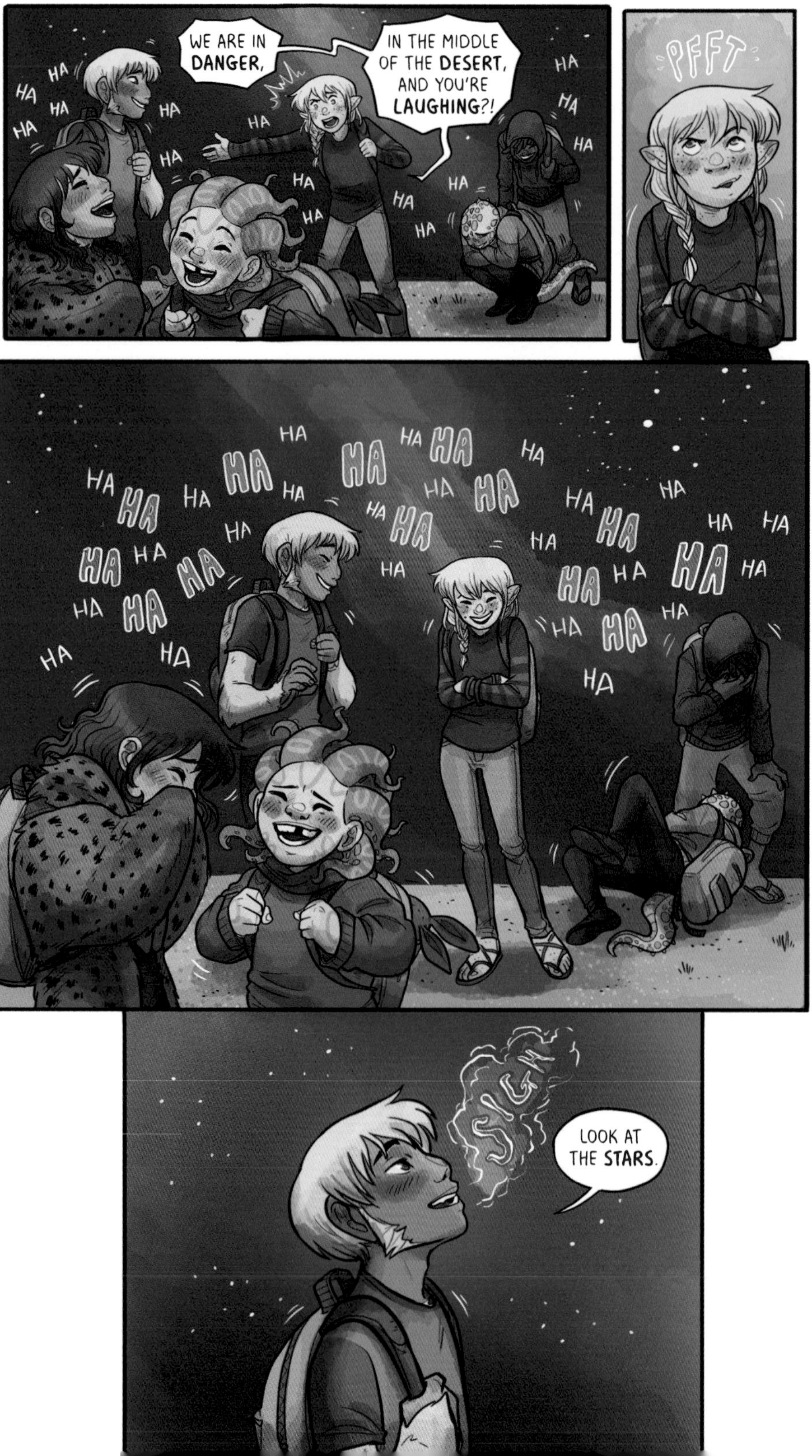
HA HA HA HA
WE ARE IN DANGER,
IN THE MIDDLE OF THE DESERT, AND YOU'RE LAUGHING?!
HA HA HA HA HA HA HA HA HA HA HA HA HA
PFFT
HA HA HA HA HA HA HA HA HA HA HA HA HA HA HA HA HA HA HA HA HA HA HA HA HA HA HA HA HA HA HA HA HA HA HA HA HA HA HA HA
SIGH
LOOK AT THE STARS.

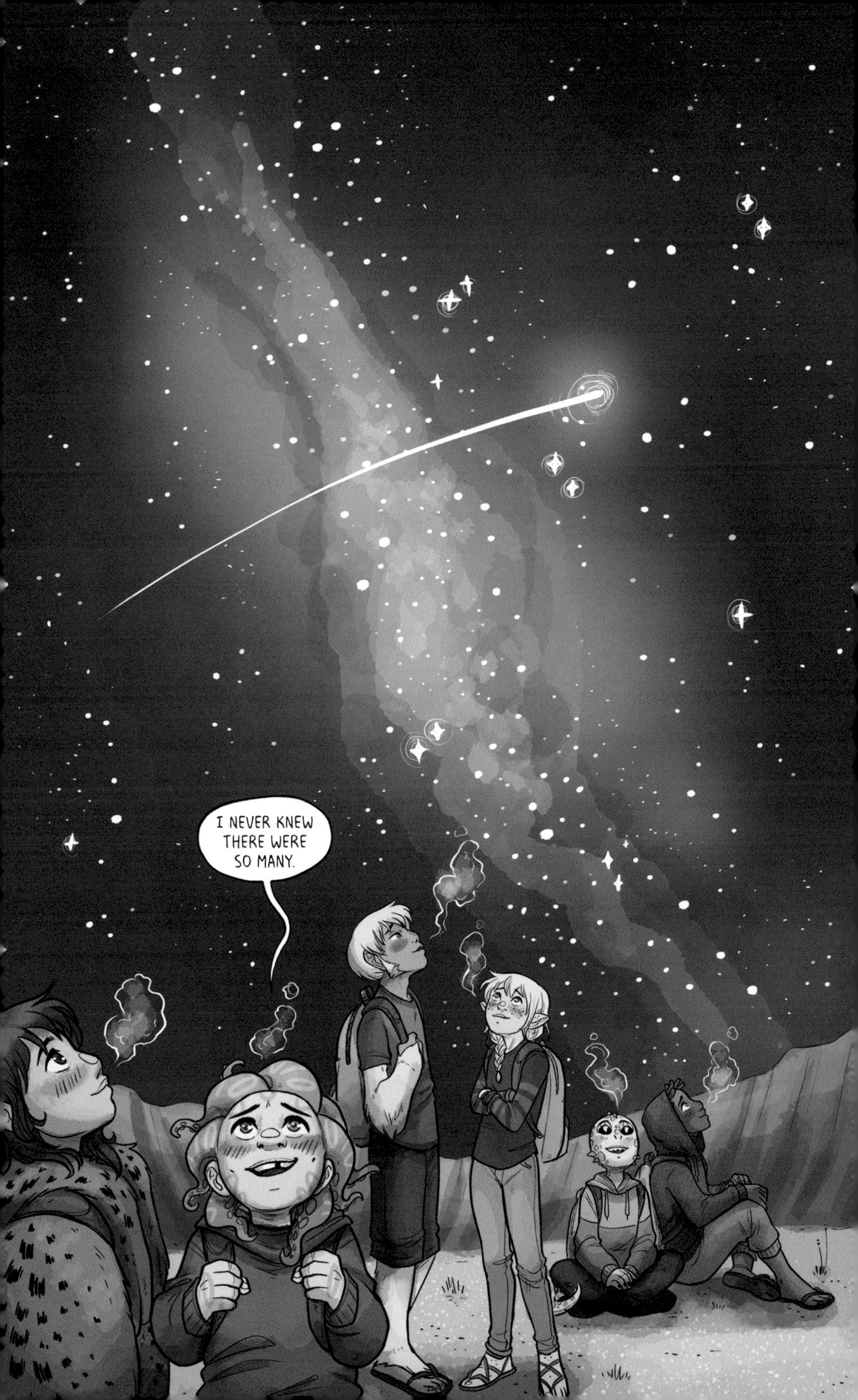
I NEVER KNEW THERE WERE SO MANY.

CHAPTER FOUR

HEAT WAVES

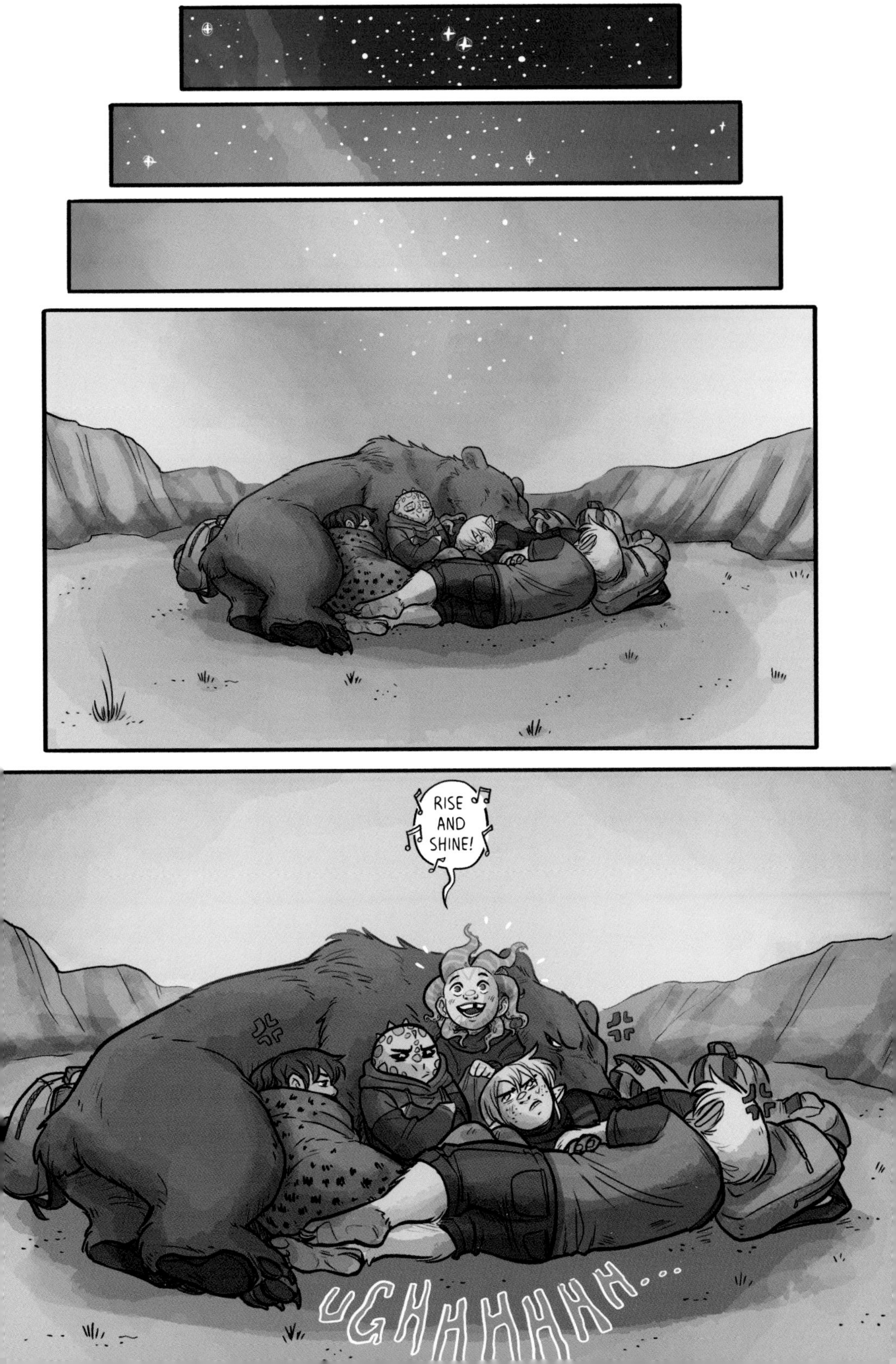
RISE AND SHINE!
UGHHHHHH...

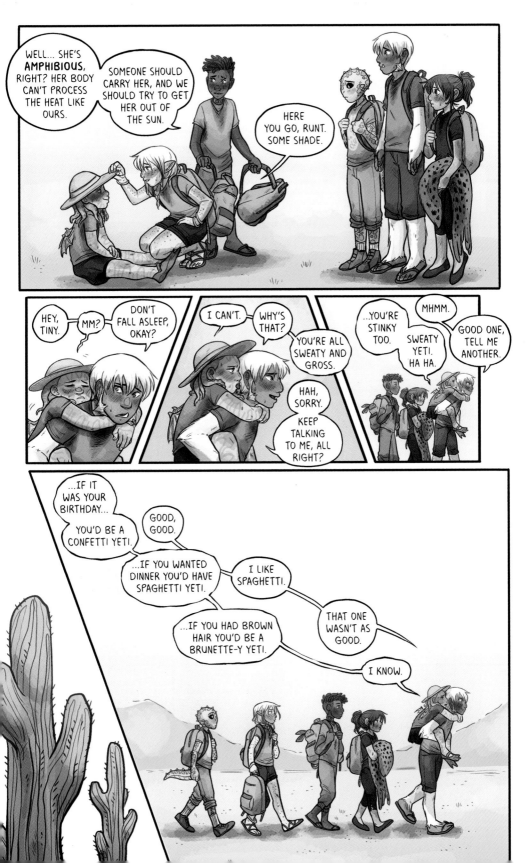

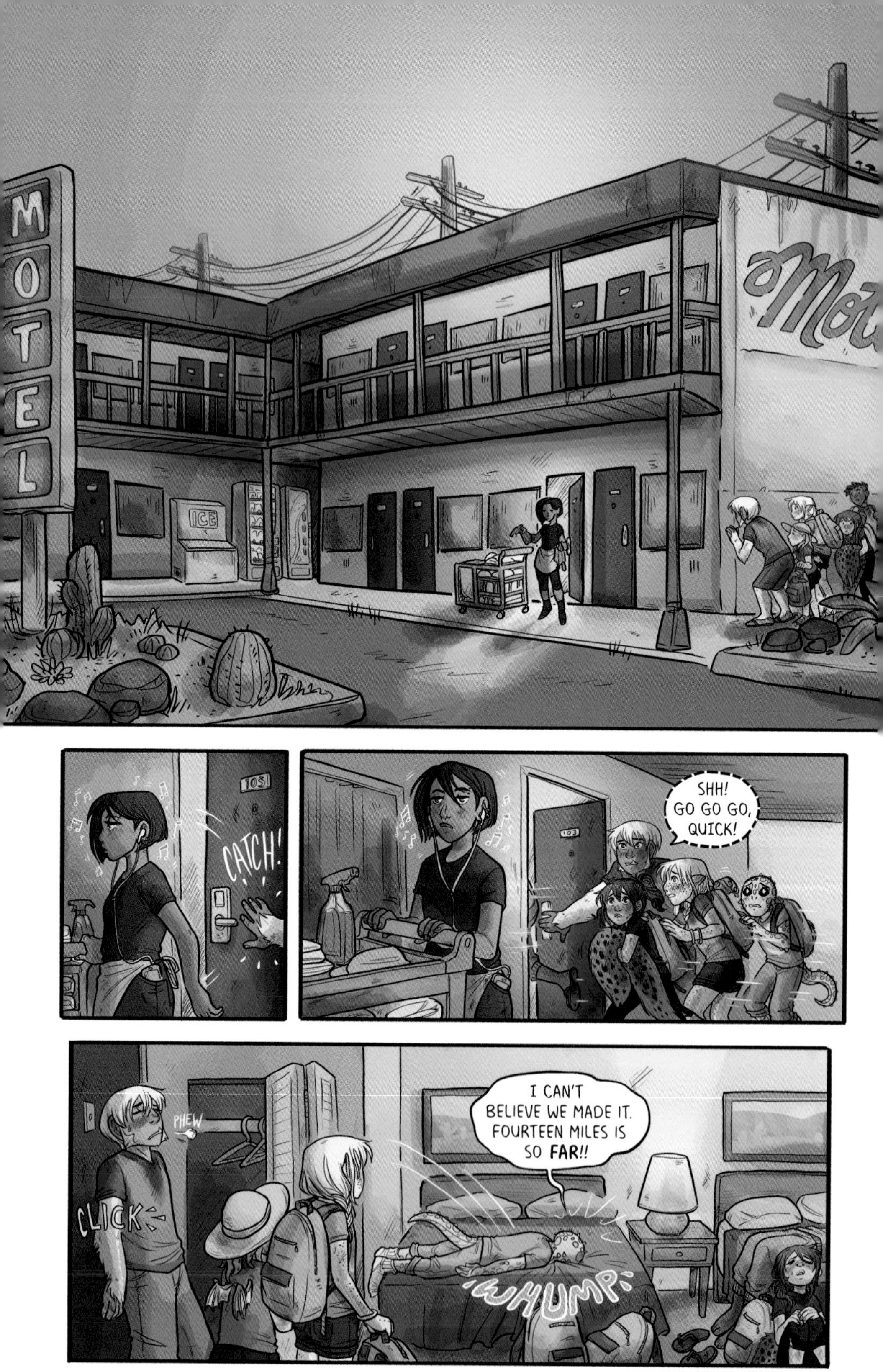
MOTEL
ICE
105
CATCH!
103
SHH! GO GO GO, QUICK!
PHEW
CLICK
I CAN'T BELIEVE WE MADE IT. FOURTEEN MILES IS SO **FAR**!!
WHUMP

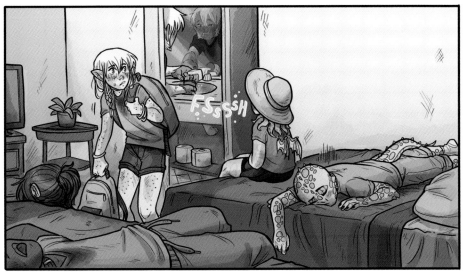

HERE, TINY.

DON'T DRINK TOO FAST, OKAY?

GULP. GULP.

MHM.

HEY... ANYONE NEED THE BATHROOM OR CAN I GO?

NAH.

GO FOR IT.

SO...

WHAT ARE WE GOING TO DO NOW?

WE COULD ORDER ROOM SERVICE!

HAHA, YEAH RIGHT.

I AM HUNGRY THOUGH...

WE ALL ARE.

nod nod

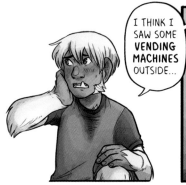

I THINK I SAW SOME **VENDING MACHINES** OUTSIDE...

BUT WE DON'T HAVE ANY **MONEY**.

OH, UH... WHAT, CLARICE?

RUMMAGE

WHERE DID YOU GET THAT?!

$ $ $

CLARICE, YOU'RE AMAZING!

CAN I HAVE CHIPS, PLEASE??

HOW MUCH MONEY IS IT??

Sure was fun......wasn't it?

ha ha ha ha ha ha ha ha

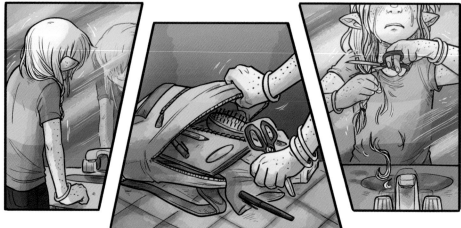

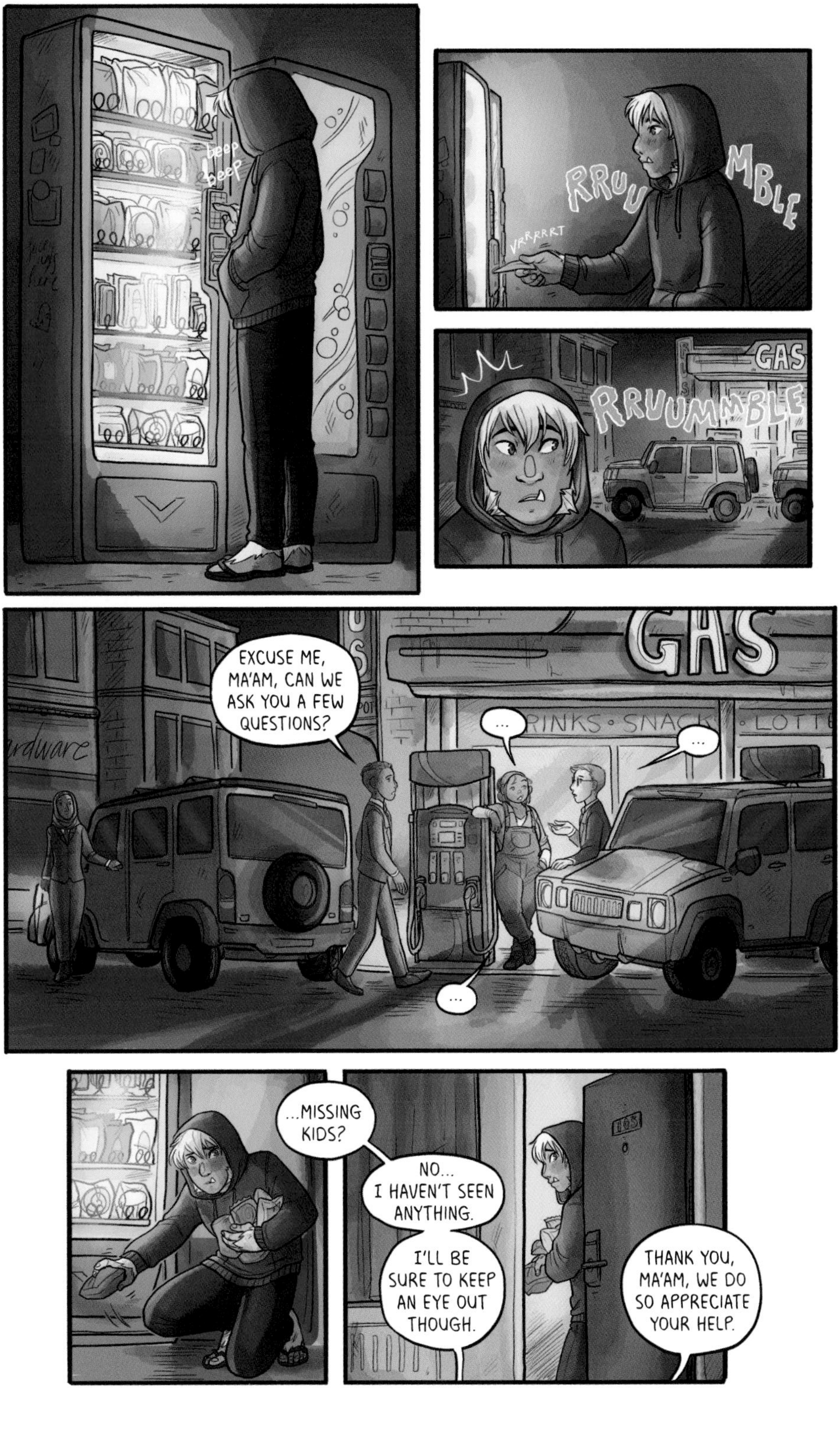

beep beep
VRRRRRT
RRUUMBLE
GAS
RRUUMMBLE
GAS
EXCUSE ME, MA'AM, CAN WE ASK YOU A FEW QUESTIONS?
...
...
...
...MISSING KIDS?
NO... I HAVEN'T SEEN ANYTHING.
I'LL BE SURE TO KEEP AN EYE OUT THOUGH.
THANK YOU, MA'AM, WE DO SO APPRECIATE YOUR HELP.

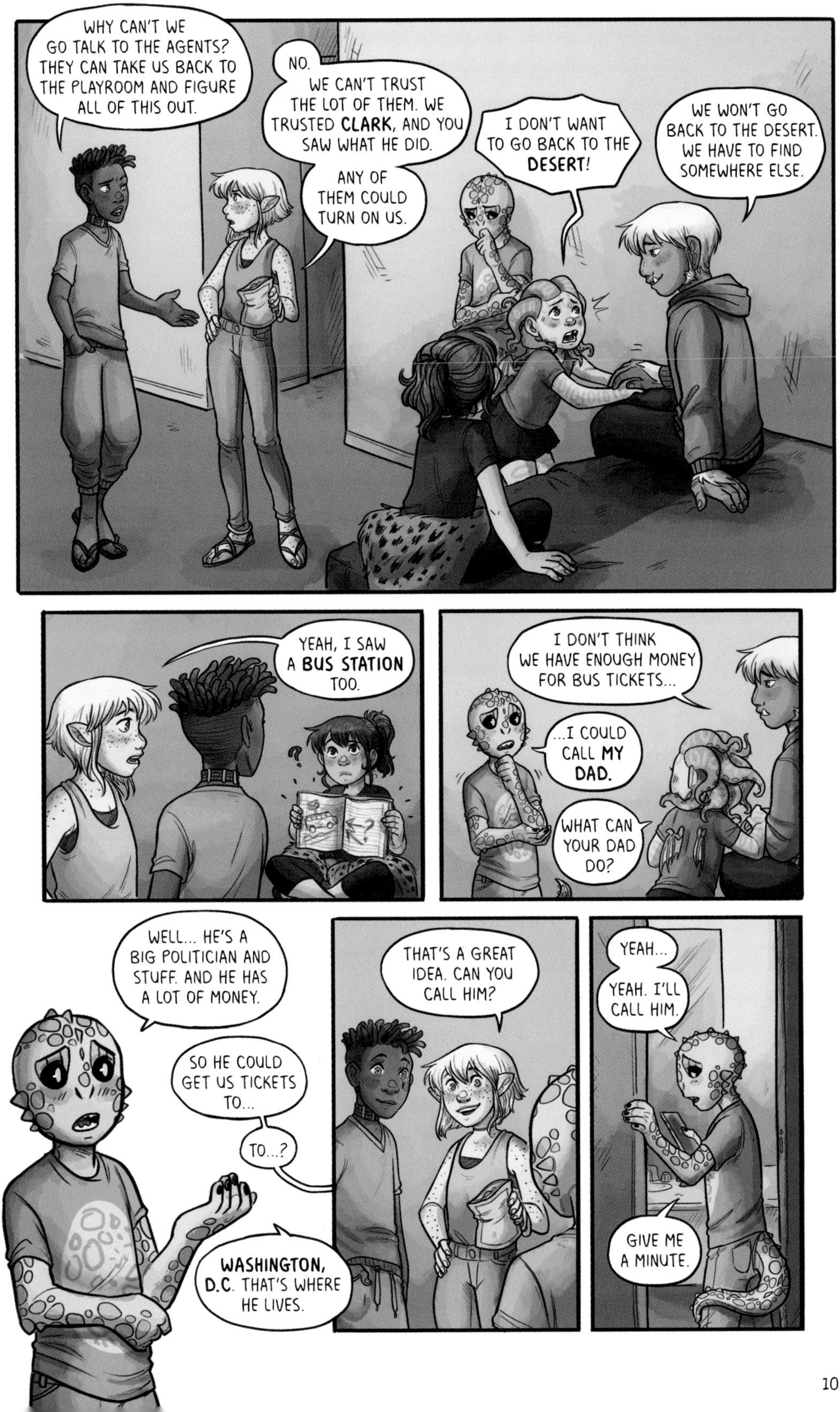

WHY CAN'T WE GO TALK TO THE AGENTS? THEY CAN TAKE US BACK TO THE PLAYROOM AND FIGURE ALL OF THIS OUT.
NO.
WE CAN'T TRUST THE LOT OF THEM. WE TRUSTED **CLARK**, AND YOU SAW WHAT HE DID.
ANY OF THEM COULD TURN ON US.
I DON'T WANT TO GO BACK TO THE **DESERT**!
WE WON'T GO BACK TO THE DESERT. WE HAVE TO FIND SOMEWHERE ELSE.
YEAH, I SAW A **BUS STATION** TOO.
I DON'T THINK WE HAVE ENOUGH MONEY FOR BUS TICKETS...
...I COULD CALL **MY DAD.**
WHAT CAN YOUR DAD DO?
WELL... HE'S A BIG POLITICIAN AND STUFF. AND HE HAS A LOT OF MONEY.
SO HE COULD GET US TICKETS TO...
TO...?
WASHINGTON, D.C. THAT'S WHERE HE LIVES.
THAT'S A GREAT IDEA. CAN YOU CALL HIM?
YEAH...
YEAH. I'LL CALL HIM.
GIVE ME A MINUTE.

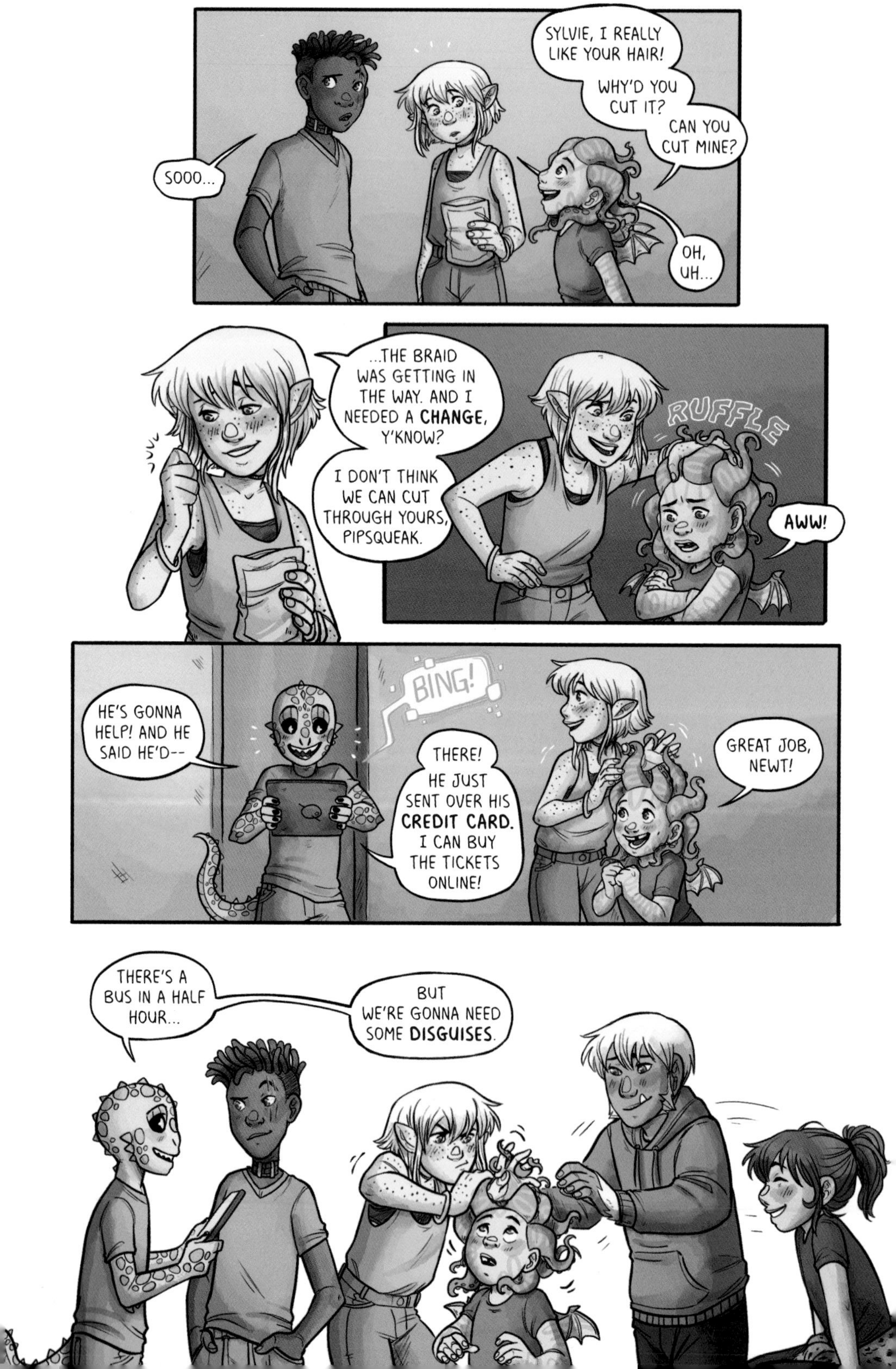
SOOO...
SYLVIE, I REALLY LIKE YOUR HAIR!
WHY'D YOU CUT IT?
CAN YOU CUT MINE?
OH, UH...
...THE BRAID WAS GETTING IN THE WAY. AND I NEEDED A **CHANGE**, Y'KNOW?
I DON'T THINK WE CAN CUT THROUGH YOURS, PIPSQUEAK.
RUFFLE
AWW!
HE'S GONNA HELP! AND HE SAID HE'D--
BING!
THERE! HE JUST SENT OVER HIS **CREDIT CARD.** I CAN BUY THE TICKETS ONLINE!
GREAT JOB, NEWT!
THERE'S A BUS IN A HALF HOUR...
BUT WE'RE GONNA NEED SOME **DISGUISES**.

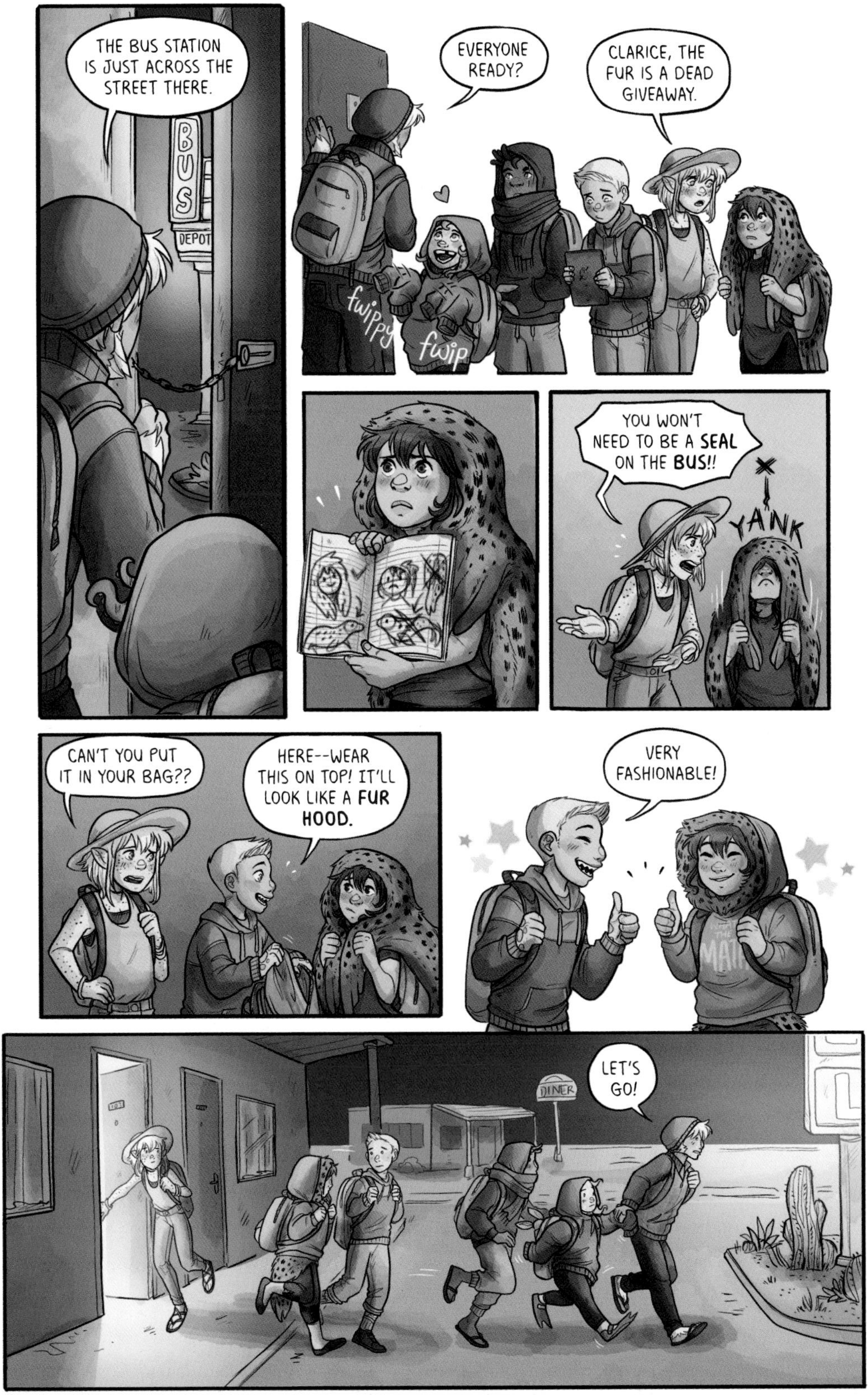
THE BUS STATION IS JUST ACROSS THE STREET THERE.
BUS
DEPOT
EVERYONE READY?
CLARICE, THE FUR IS A DEAD GIVEAWAY.
fwippy
fwip
YOU WON'T NEED TO BE A **SEAL** ON THE **BUS**!!
YANK
CAN'T YOU PUT IT IN YOUR BAG??
HERE--WEAR THIS ON TOP! IT'LL LOOK LIKE A **FUR HOOD.**
VERY FASHIONABLE!
DINER
LET'S GO!

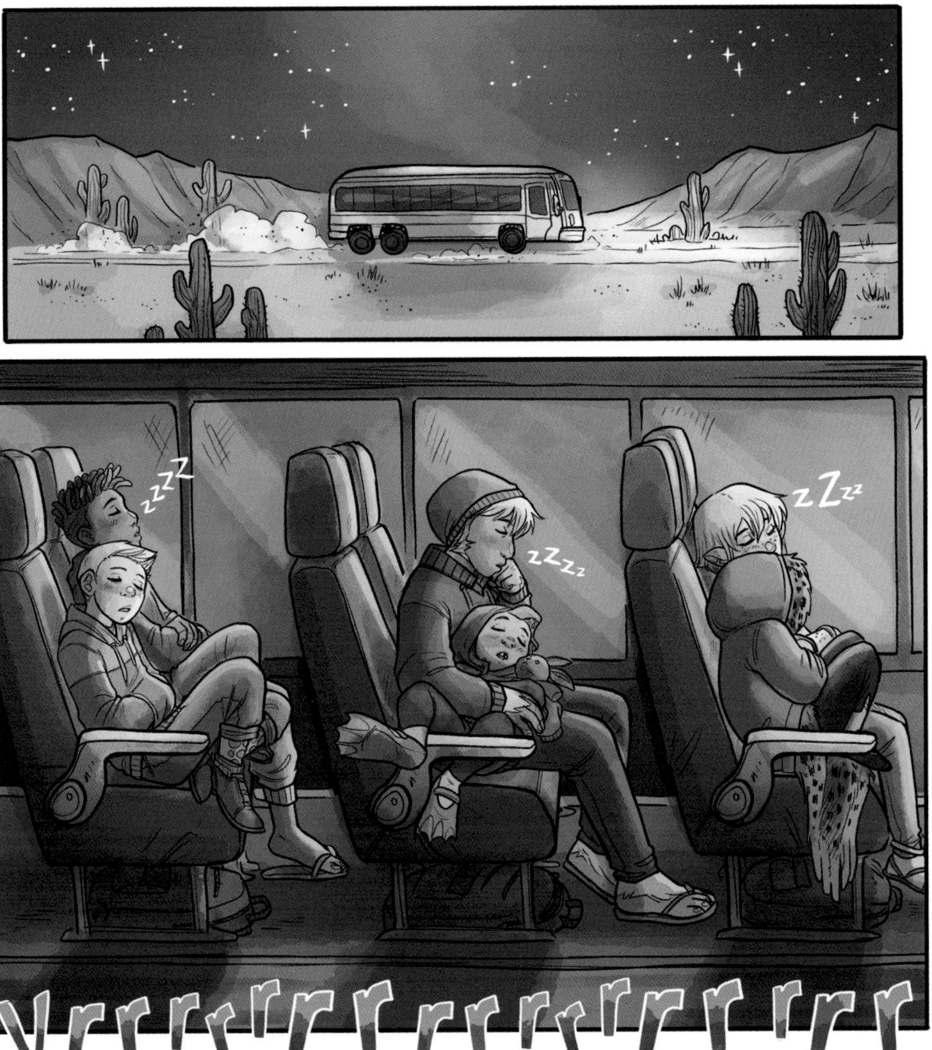
zzZZ
zZZzz
zZZzz
Vrrrrrrrrrrrrrrrrrr

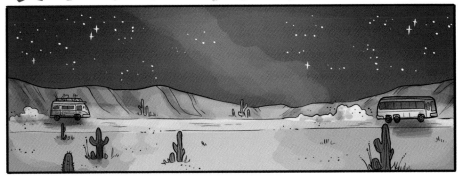

CHAPTER FIVE

HIGHLY IRREGULAR

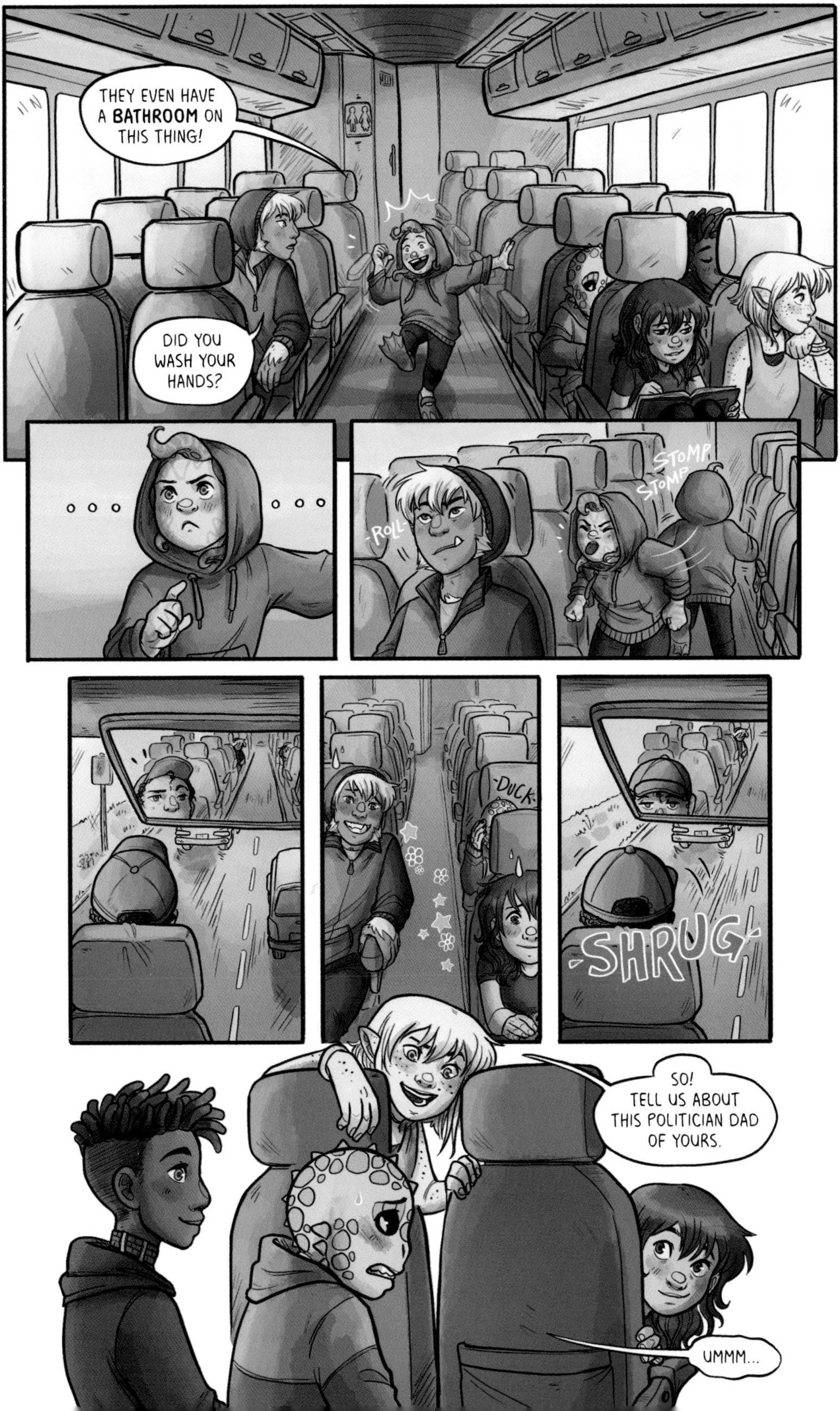
THEY EVEN HAVE A BATHROOM ON THIS THING!
DID YOU WASH YOUR HANDS?
...
...
ROLL
STOMP
STOMP
DUCK
SHRUG
SO! TELL US ABOUT THIS POLITICIAN DAD OF YOURS.
UMMM...

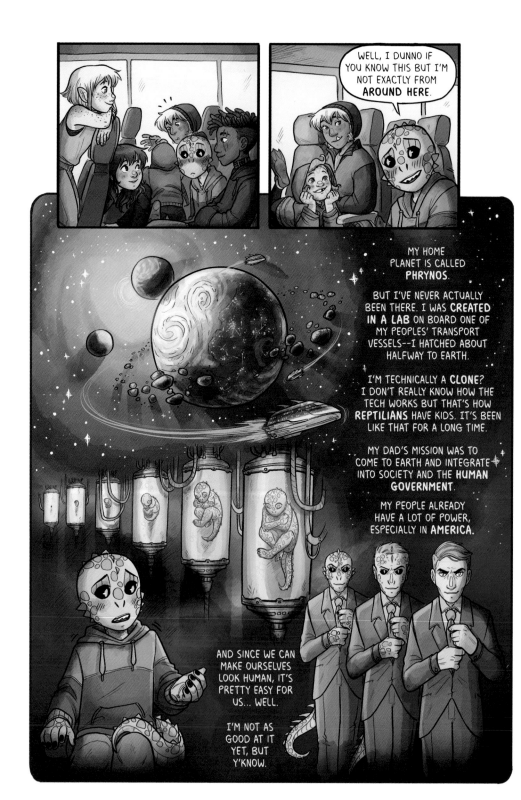

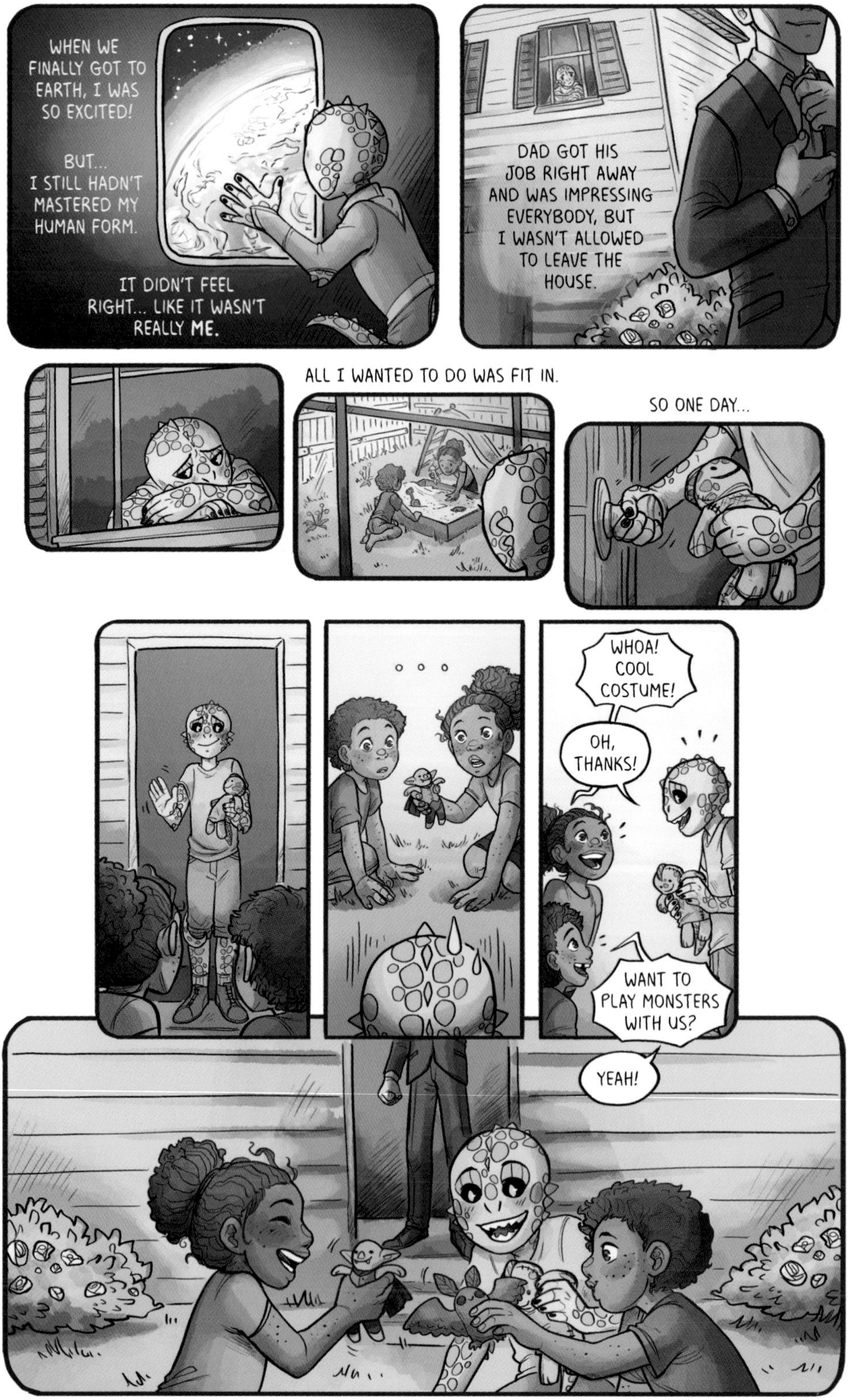
WHEN WE FINALLY GOT TO EARTH, I WAS SO EXCITED!
BUT... I STILL HADN'T MASTERED MY HUMAN FORM.
IT DIDN'T FEEL RIGHT... LIKE IT WASN'T REALLY **ME.**
DAD GOT HIS JOB RIGHT AWAY AND WAS IMPRESSING EVERYBODY, BUT I WASN'T ALLOWED TO LEAVE THE HOUSE.
ALL I WANTED TO DO WAS FIT IN.
SO ONE DAY...
WHOA! COOL COSTUME!
OH, THANKS!
WANT TO PLAY MONSTERS WITH US?
YEAH!

THIS WAY. KEEP UP.

CONFERENCE ROOM 1

GREETINGS, NEWTON.

...HI, DAD.

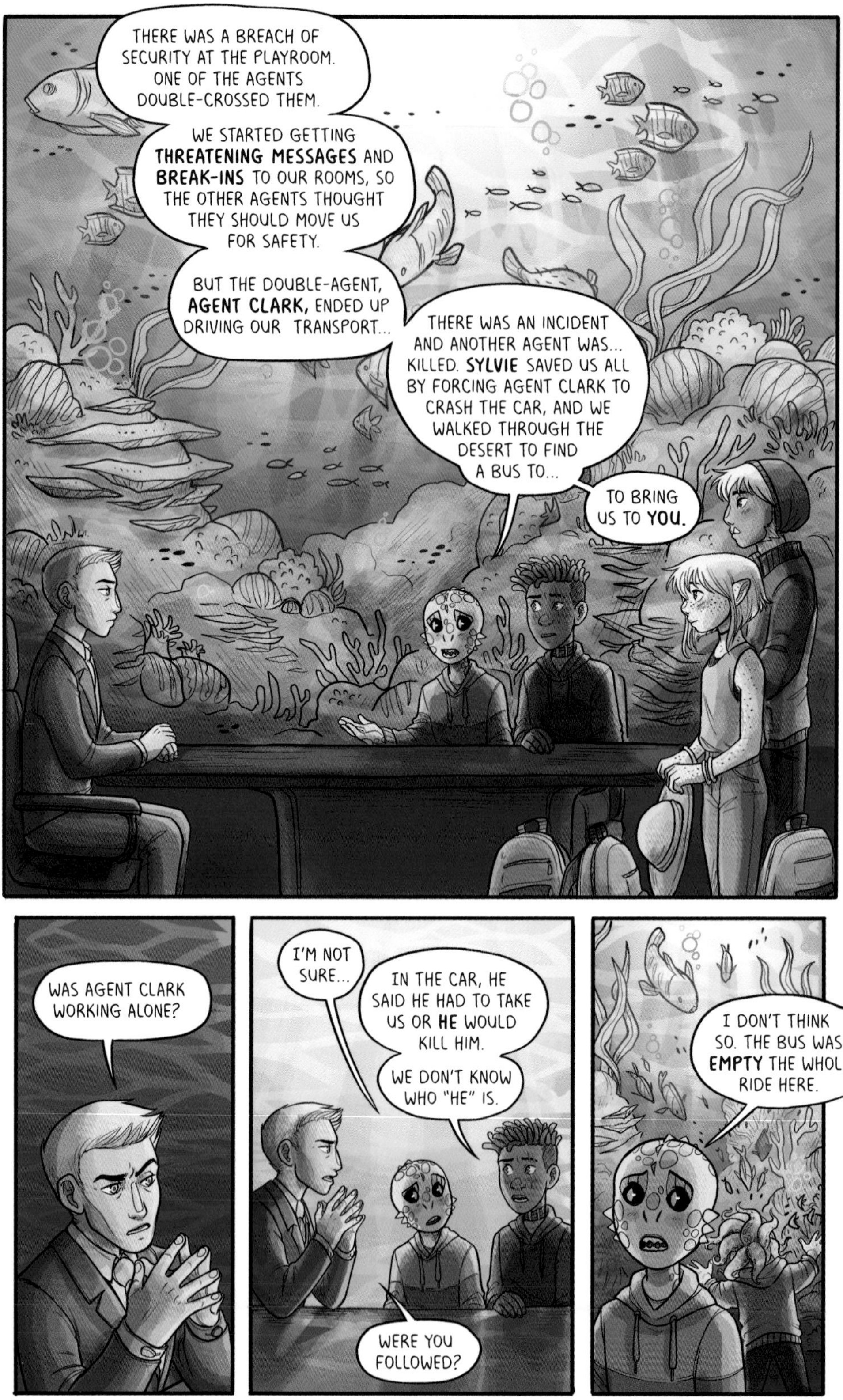
THERE WAS A BREACH OF SECURITY AT THE PLAYROOM. ONE OF THE AGENTS DOUBLE-CROSSED THEM.
WE STARTED GETTING **THREATENING MESSAGES** AND **BREAK-INS** TO OUR ROOMS, SO THE OTHER AGENTS THOUGHT THEY SHOULD MOVE US FOR SAFETY.
BUT THE DOUBLE-AGENT, **AGENT CLARK,** ENDED UP DRIVING OUR TRANSPORT...
THERE WAS AN INCIDENT AND ANOTHER AGENT WAS... KILLED. **SYLVIE** SAVED US ALL BY FORCING AGENT CLARK TO CRASH THE CAR, AND WE WALKED THROUGH THE DESERT TO FIND A BUS TO...
TO BRING US TO **YOU.**
WAS AGENT CLARK WORKING ALONE?
I'M NOT SURE...
IN THE CAR, HE SAID HE HAD TO TAKE US OR **HE** WOULD KILL HIM.
WE DON'T KNOW WHO "HE" IS.
WERE YOU FOLLOWED?
I DON'T THINK SO. THE BUS WAS **EMPTY** THE WHOLE RIDE HERE.

IT SOUNDS LIKE YOU HAVE BEEN THROUGH QUITE THE ORDEAL.

TYPICAL **HUMANS**.

MISHANDLING **DELICATE MATTERS** SEEMS TO BE ONE OF THEIR **SPECIALITIES**.

I JUST KNEW SOMETHING LIKE THIS WOULD HAPPEN.

THOSE **FOOLS** RUNNING THE PLAYROOM NEVER HAD PROPER SECURITY TO BEGIN WITH.

HOW COULD THEY HANDLE SUCH A COMPLICATED ISSUE?

NO MATTER. I KEPT UP **MY END** OF THE **BARGAIN**.

IT IS NO FAULT OF MINE IF THEY COULD NOT KEEP THEIRS.

tp tp tp

B...BARGAIN?

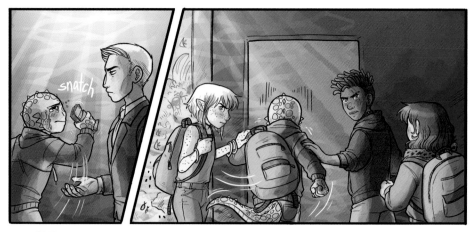

snatch

TIME TO GO, MAGGIE.

OKAY.

fwip

BYE!

STOMP STOMP

...NEWT?

I'M SO SORRY.

I'M SO SORRY I DRAGGED YOU INTO THIS--AND NOW WE HAVE **NOWHERE** TO GO!

IT'S OKAY, WE'LL FIGURE SOMETHING OUT.

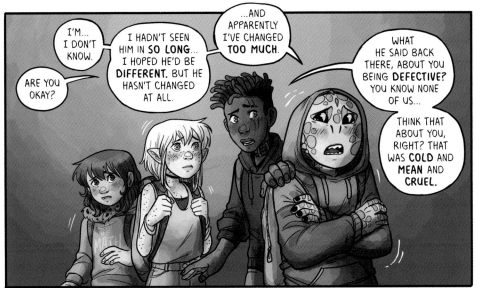

ARE YOU OKAY?

I'M... I DON'T KNOW.

I HADN'T SEEN HIM IN **SO LONG**... I HOPED HE'D BE **DIFFERENT.** BUT HE HASN'T CHANGED AT ALL.

...AND APPARENTLY I'VE CHANGED **TOO MUCH.**

WHAT HE SAID BACK THERE, ABOUT YOU BEING **DEFECTIVE?** YOU KNOW NONE OF US...

THINK THAT ABOUT YOU, RIGHT? THAT WAS **COLD** AND **MEAN** AND **CRUEL.**

WELL, OF COURSE IT WAS COLD, HE'S **COLD-BLOODED!**

HE'S A **REPTILE!**

HA HA HA HA HA HA HA HA HA HA

HA...HA... HEH... *sniff...*

SOB

CHAPTER SIX

TWO HOUSES

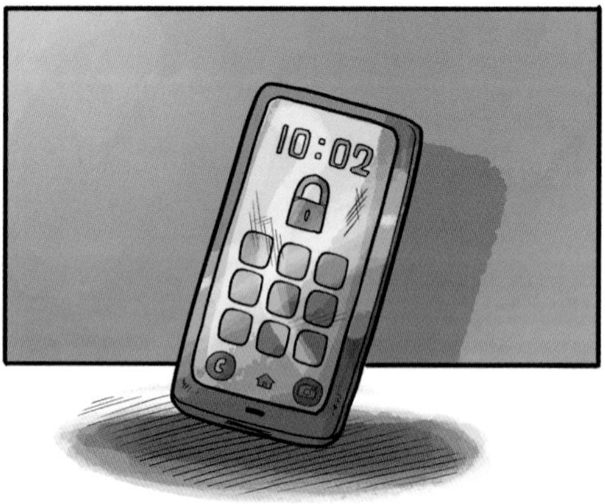
10:02

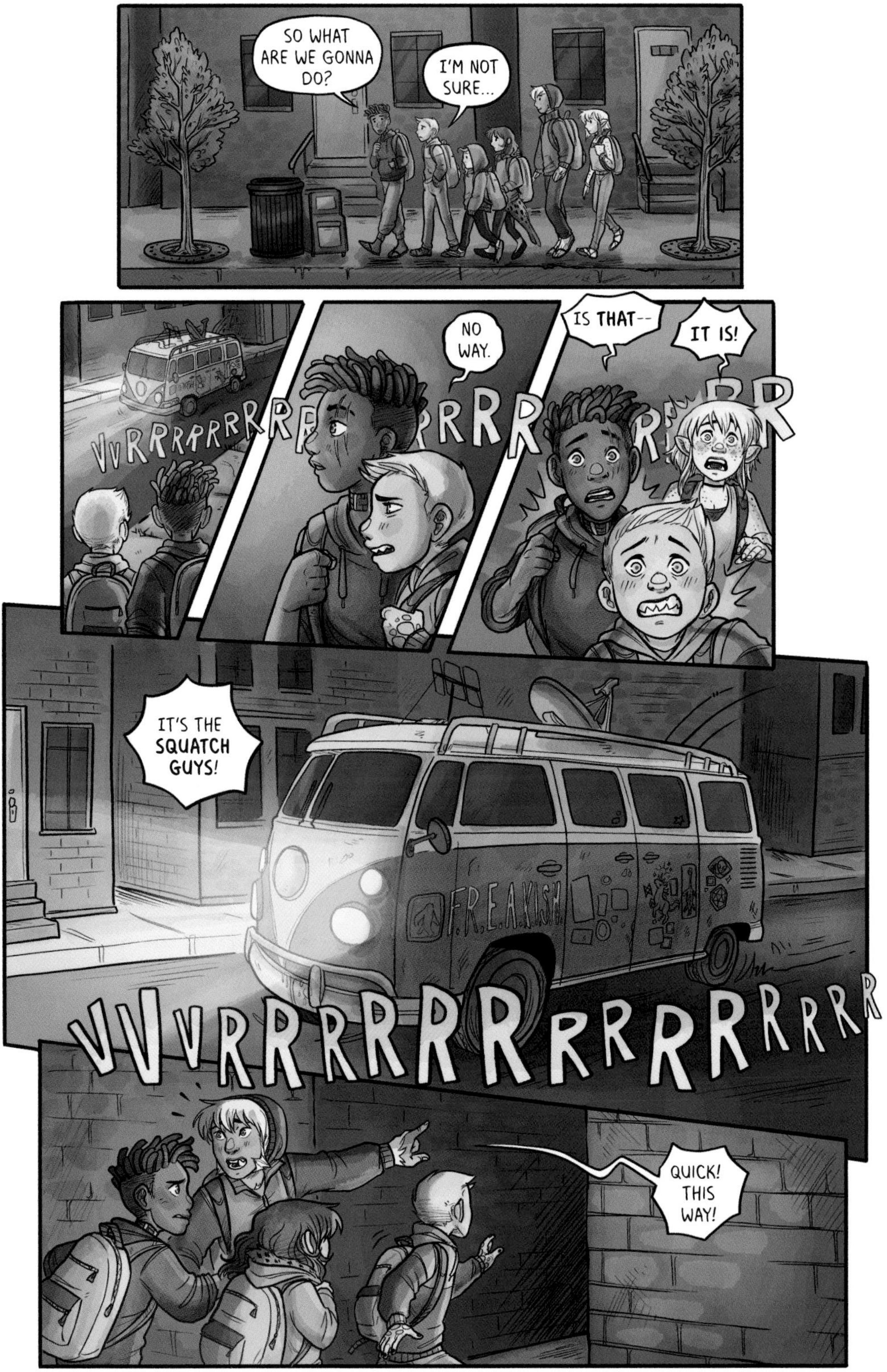
SO WHAT ARE WE GONNA DO?
I'M NOT SURE...
VvRRRRRRRRRRRR
NO WAY.
IS THAT--
IT IS!
IT'S THE SQUATCH GUYS!
VVvRRRRRRRRRRRRR
QUICK! THIS WAY!

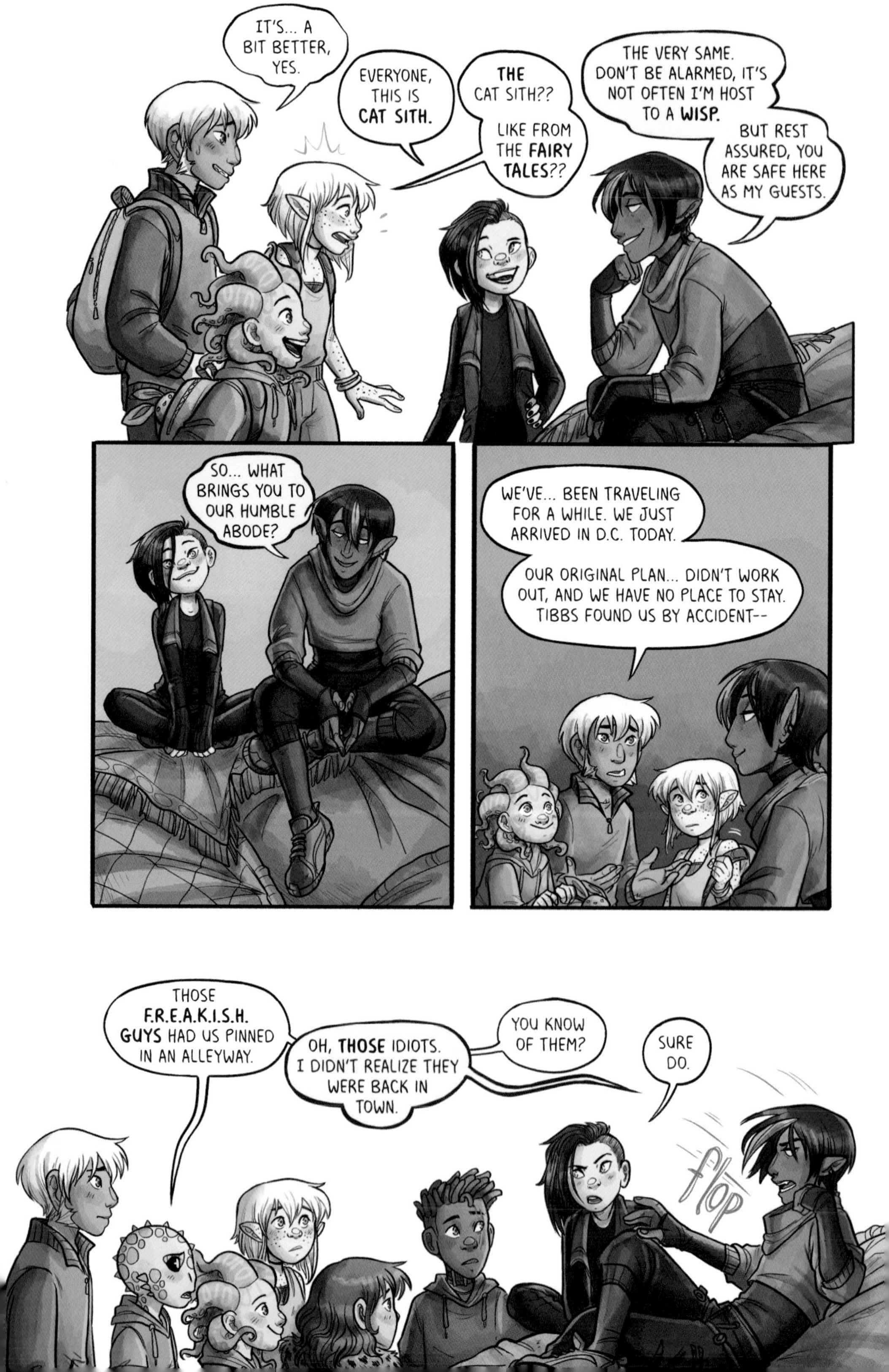
IT'S... A BIT BETTER, YES.
EVERYONE, THIS IS **CAT SITH.**
THE CAT SITH??
LIKE FROM THE **FAIRY TALES**??
THE VERY SAME. DON'T BE ALARMED, IT'S NOT OFTEN I'M HOST TO A **WISP.**
BUT REST ASSURED, YOU ARE SAFE HERE AS MY GUESTS.
SO... WHAT BRINGS YOU TO OUR HUMBLE ABODE?
WE'VE... BEEN TRAVELING FOR A WHILE. WE JUST ARRIVED IN D.C. TODAY.
OUR ORIGINAL PLAN... DIDN'T WORK OUT, AND WE HAVE NO PLACE TO STAY. TIBBS FOUND US BY ACCIDENT--
THOSE **F.R.E.A.K.I.S.H. GUYS** HAD US PINNED IN AN ALLEYWAY.
OH, **THOSE** IDIOTS. I DIDN'T REALIZE THEY WERE BACK IN TOWN.
YOU KNOW OF THEM?
SURE DO.
flop

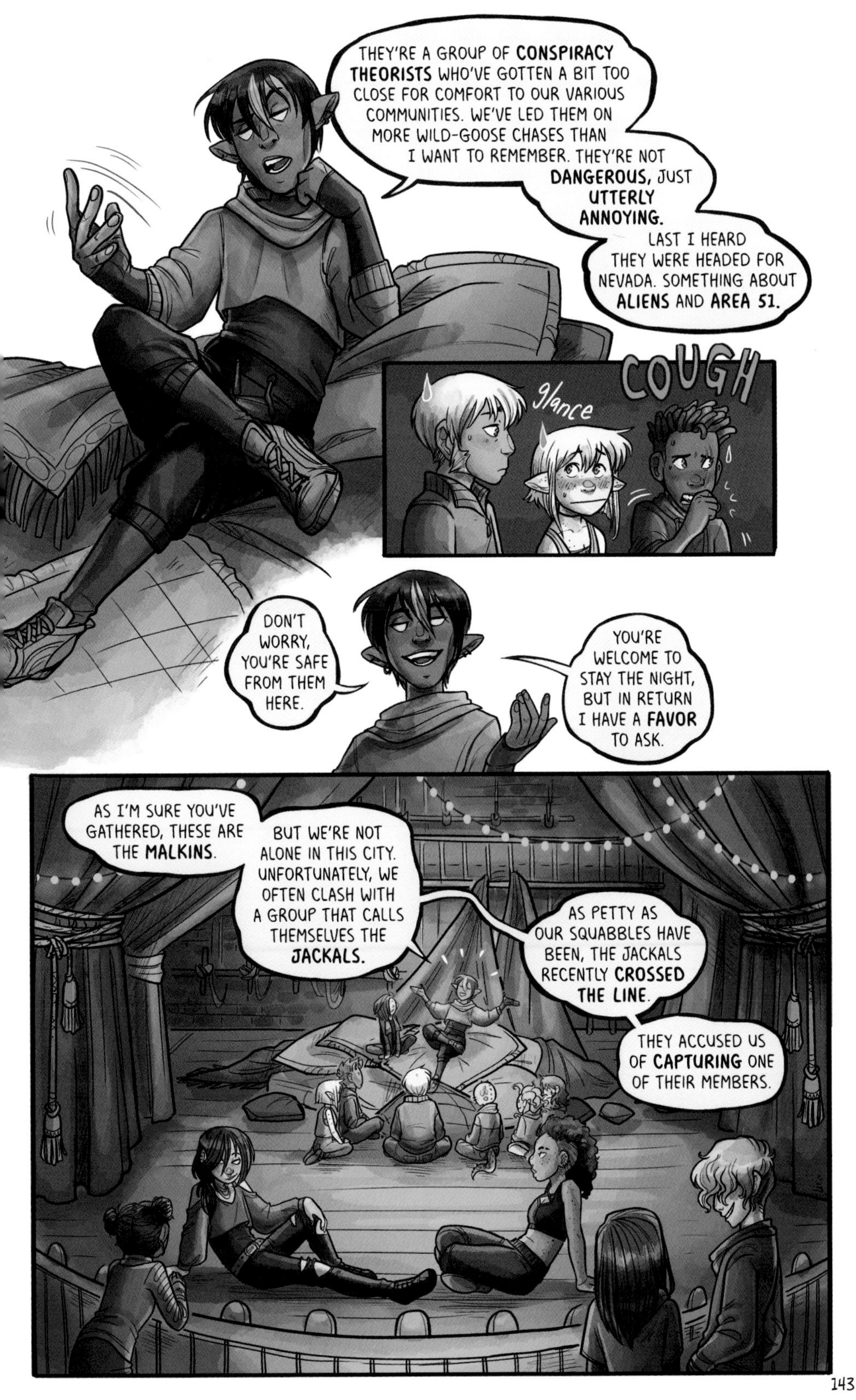

THEY'RE A GROUP OF **CONSPIRACY THEORISTS** WHO'VE GOTTEN A BIT TOO CLOSE FOR COMFORT TO OUR VARIOUS COMMUNITIES. WE'VE LED THEM ON MORE WILD-GOOSE CHASES THAN I WANT TO REMEMBER. THEY'RE NOT **DANGEROUS,** JUST **UTTERLY ANNOYING.**
LAST I HEARD THEY WERE HEADED FOR NEVADA. SOMETHING ABOUT **ALIENS** AND **AREA 51.**
glance
COUGH
DON'T WORRY, YOU'RE SAFE FROM THEM HERE.
YOU'RE WELCOME TO STAY THE NIGHT, BUT IN RETURN I HAVE A **FAVOR** TO ASK.
AS I'M SURE YOU'VE GATHERED, THESE ARE THE **MALKINS**.
BUT WE'RE NOT ALONE IN THIS CITY. UNFORTUNATELY, WE OFTEN CLASH WITH A GROUP THAT CALLS THEMSELVES THE **JACKALS.**
AS PETTY AS OUR SQUABBLES HAVE BEEN, THE JACKALS RECENTLY **CROSSED THE LINE**.
THEY ACCUSED US OF **CAPTURING** ONE OF THEIR MEMBERS.

AND AS **REVENGE**, THEY'VE TAKEN ONE OF OURS. **JAYLA**.

BUT YOU **DIDN'T** KIDNAP THEIR FRIEND?

OF COURSE **NOT**!

WHAT REASON WOULD WE HAVE?

BESIDES, OUR METHODS ARE MUCH **QUIETER** AND **MORE SUBTLE**.

IN RETURN FOR ROOM AND BOARD HERE, I WOULD ASK THAT YOU RESCUE OUR MISSING MALKIN.

THE JACKALS KNOW TO WATCH OUT FOR US, BUT THEY WILL NEVER SEE YOU COMING.

TIBBS CAN GIVE YOU MORE INFORMATION AND LEAD YOU TO THE JACKAL HIDEOUT TOMORROW.

THEY KNOW THIS CITY LIKE THE BACK OF THEIR HAND.

FOR TONIGHT, EAT, SLEEP, REST.

THANK YOU, SIR.

THANKS, MR. KITTY!

YOU'RE WELCOME, MY DEAR.

TOSS

CATCH

THANKS!

ISN'T THIS **AMAZING**?? ALL THESE IRREGULARITIES LIVING RIGHT UNDER THE CITY'S NOSE!

IT IS IMPRESSIVE.

munch munch

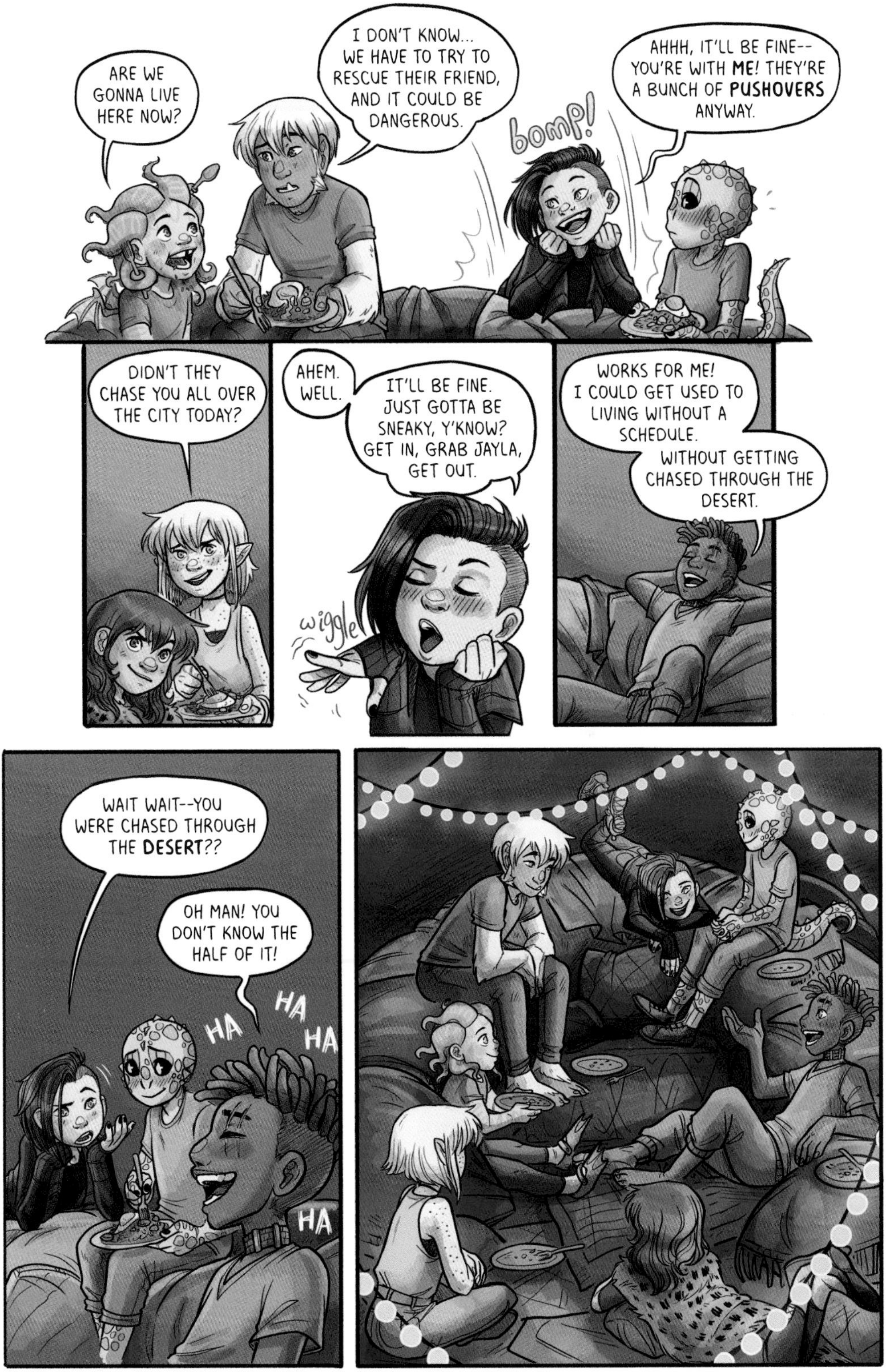
ARE WE GONNA LIVE HERE NOW?
I DON'T KNOW... WE HAVE TO TRY TO RESCUE THEIR FRIEND, AND IT COULD BE DANGEROUS.
bomp!
AHHH, IT'LL BE FINE-- YOU'RE WITH **ME**! THEY'RE A BUNCH OF **PUSHOVERS** ANYWAY.
DIDN'T THEY CHASE YOU ALL OVER THE CITY TODAY?
AHEM. WELL.
IT'LL BE FINE. JUST GOTTA BE SNEAKY, Y'KNOW? GET IN, GRAB JAYLA, GET OUT.
wiggle
WORKS FOR ME! I COULD GET USED TO LIVING WITHOUT A SCHEDULE.
WITHOUT GETTING CHASED THROUGH THE DESERT.
WAIT WAIT--YOU WERE CHASED THROUGH THE **DESERT**??
OH MAN! YOU DON'T KNOW THE HALF OF IT!
HA
HA
HA
HA

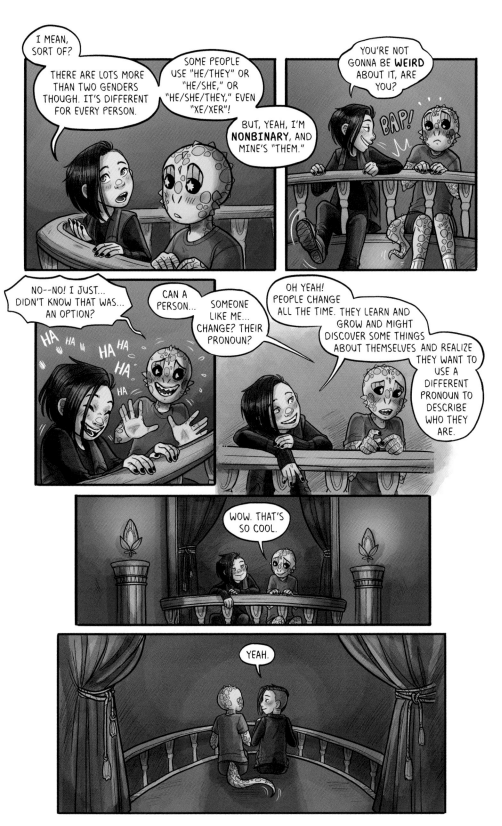

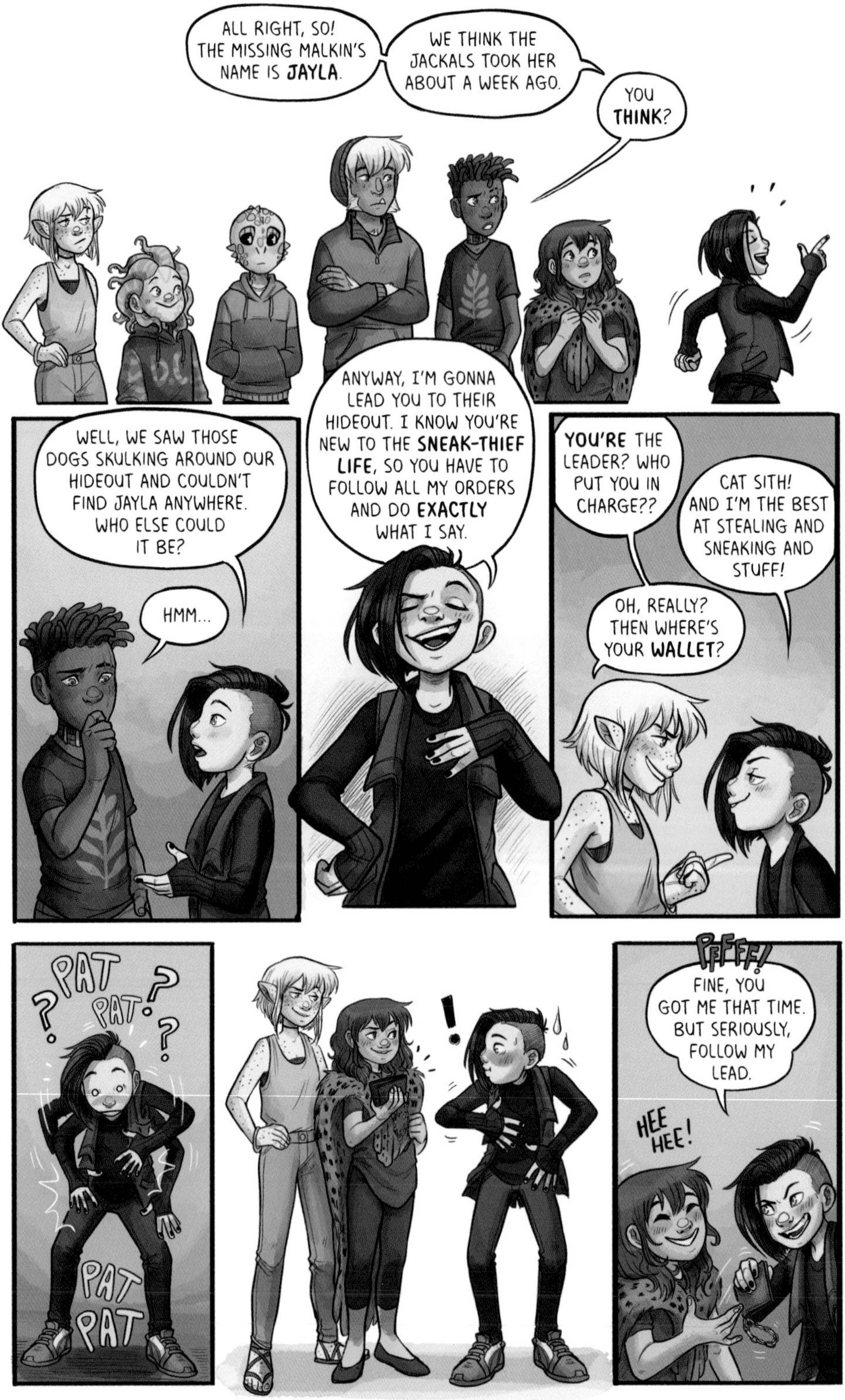
ALL RIGHT, SO! THE MISSING MALKIN'S NAME IS **JAYLA**.
WE THINK THE JACKALS TOOK HER ABOUT A WEEK AGO.
YOU **THINK**?
WELL, WE SAW THOSE DOGS SKULKING AROUND OUR HIDEOUT AND COULDN'T FIND JAYLA ANYWHERE. WHO ELSE COULD IT BE?
HMM...
ANYWAY, I'M GONNA LEAD YOU TO THEIR HIDEOUT. I KNOW YOU'RE NEW TO THE **SNEAK-THIEF LIFE**, SO YOU HAVE TO FOLLOW ALL MY ORDERS AND DO **EXACTLY** WHAT I SAY.
YOU'RE THE LEADER? WHO PUT YOU IN CHARGE??
CAT SITH! AND I'M THE BEST AT STEALING AND SNEAKING AND STUFF!
OH, REALLY? THEN WHERE'S YOUR **WALLET**?
PAT PAT
PAT PAT
PFFFF!
FINE, YOU GOT ME THAT TIME. BUT SERIOUSLY, FOLLOW MY LEAD.
HEE HEE!

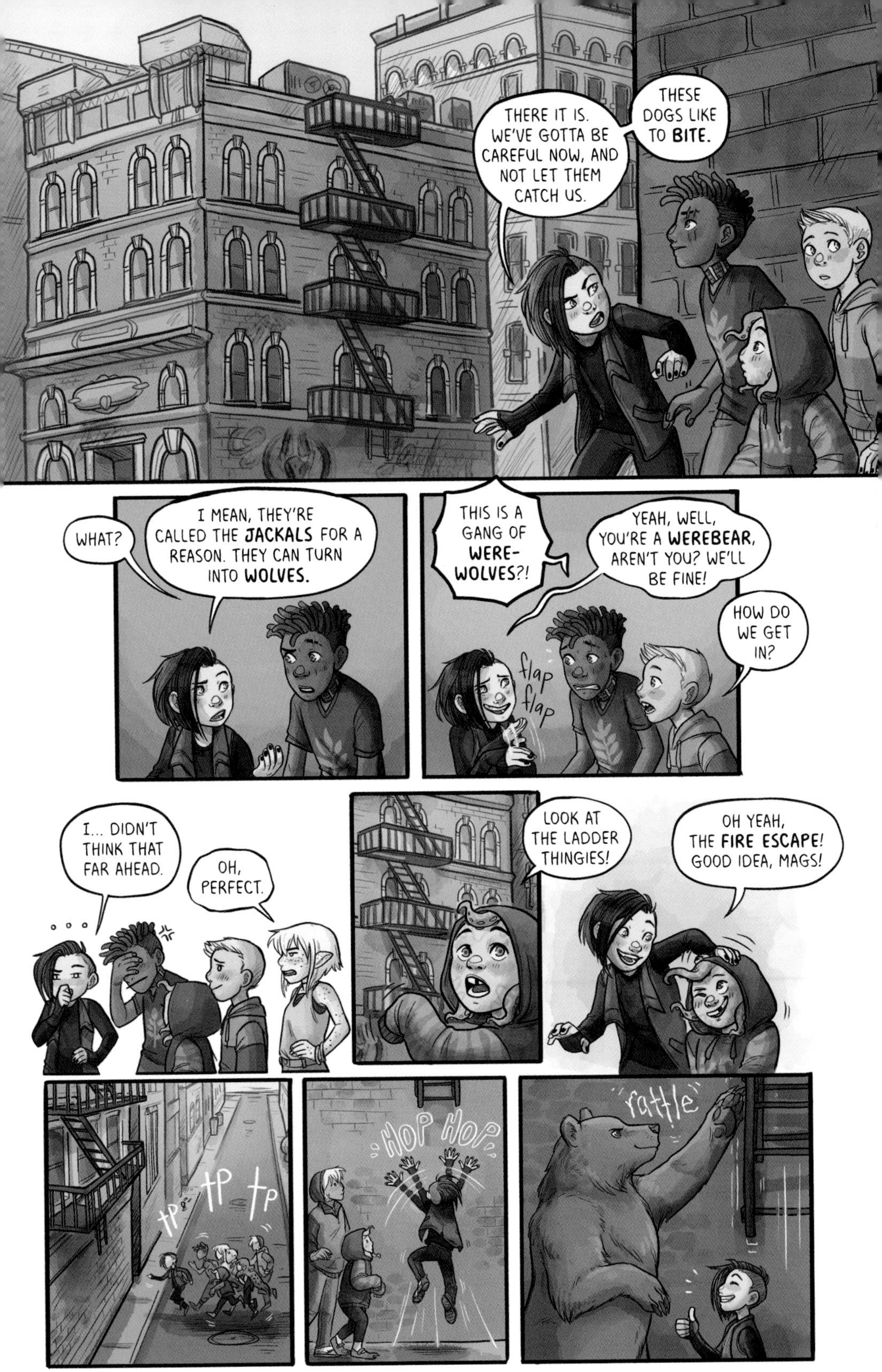
THERE IT IS. WE'VE GOTTA BE CAREFUL NOW, AND NOT LET THEM CATCH US.
THESE DOGS LIKE TO BITE.
WHAT?
I MEAN, THEY'RE CALLED THE JACKALS FOR A REASON. THEY CAN TURN INTO WOLVES.
THIS IS A GANG OF WERE-WOLVES?!
YEAH, WELL, YOU'RE A WEREBEAR, AREN'T YOU? WE'LL BE FINE!
flap flap
HOW DO WE GET IN?
I... DIDN'T THINK THAT FAR AHEAD.
OH, PERFECT.
LOOK AT THE LADDER THINGIES!
OH YEAH, THE FIRE ESCAPE! GOOD IDEA, MAGS!
tp tp tp
HOP HOP
rattle

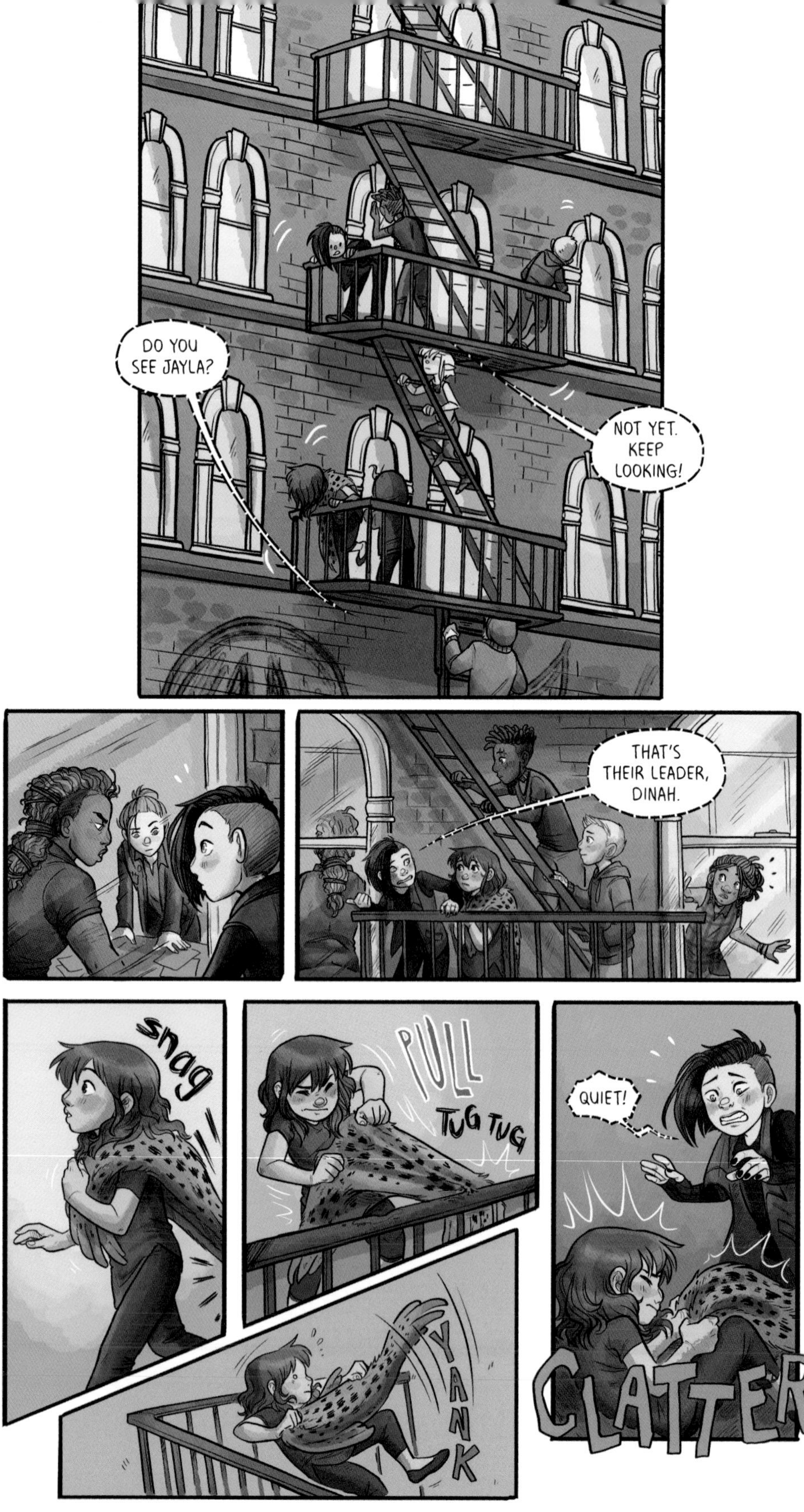
DO YOU SEE JAYLA?
NOT YET. KEEP LOOKING!
THAT'S THEIR LEADER, DINAH.
snag
PULL
TUG TUG
YANK
QUIET!
CLATTER

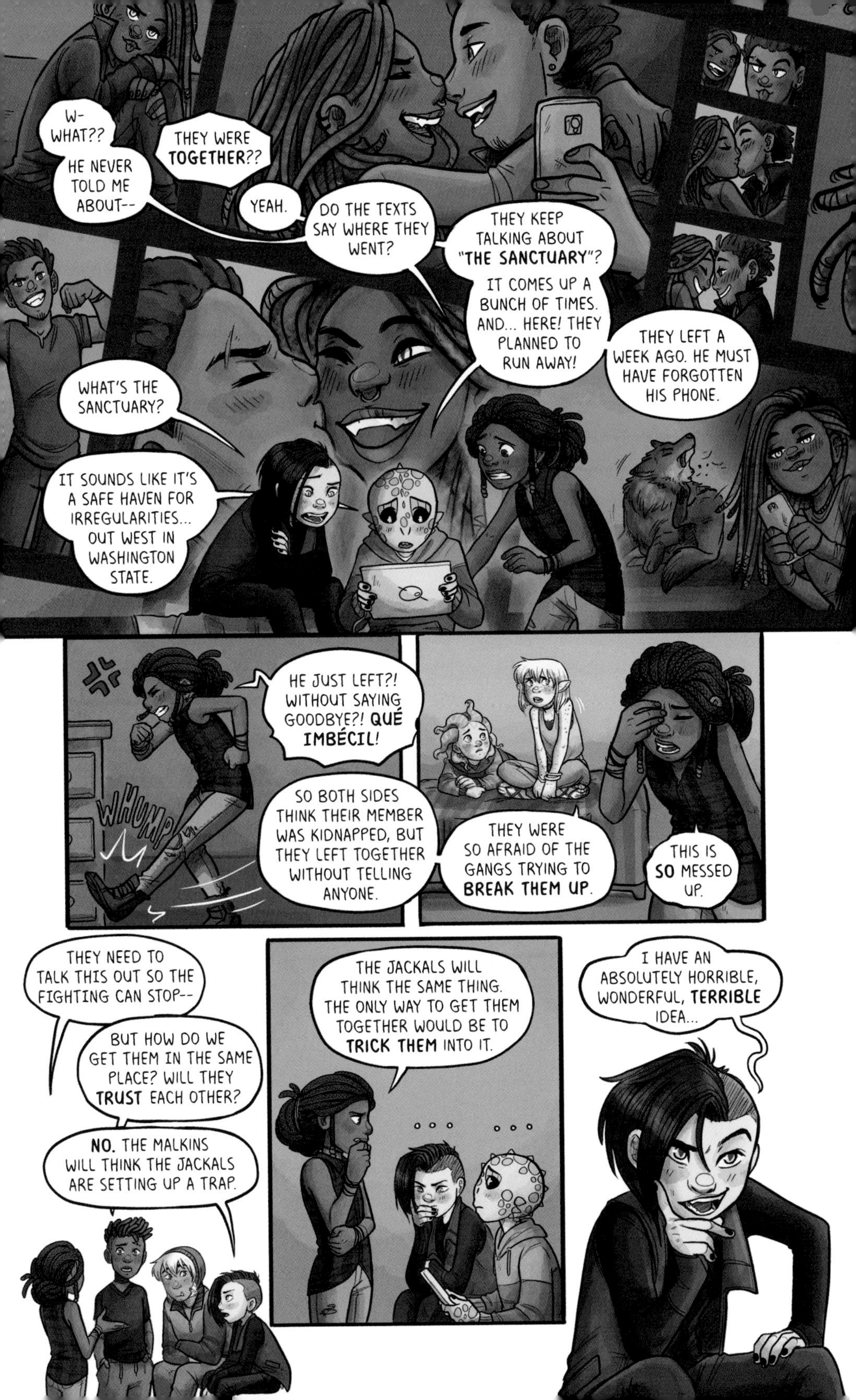
W-
WHAT??
THEY WERE TOGETHER??
HE NEVER TOLD ME ABOUT--
YEAH.
DO THE TEXTS SAY WHERE THEY WENT?
THEY KEEP TALKING ABOUT "THE SANCTUARY"?
IT COMES UP A BUNCH OF TIMES. AND... HERE! THEY PLANNED TO RUN AWAY!
THEY LEFT A WEEK AGO. HE MUST HAVE FORGOTTEN HIS PHONE.
WHAT'S THE SANCTUARY?
IT SOUNDS LIKE IT'S A SAFE HAVEN FOR IRREGULARITIES... OUT WEST IN WASHINGTON STATE.
HE JUST LEFT?! WITHOUT SAYING GOODBYE?! QUÉ IMBÉCIL!
WHUMP
SO BOTH SIDES THINK THEIR MEMBER WAS KIDNAPPED, BUT THEY LEFT TOGETHER WITHOUT TELLING ANYONE.
THEY WERE SO AFRAID OF THE GANGS TRYING TO BREAK THEM UP.
THIS IS SO MESSED UP.
THEY NEED TO TALK THIS OUT SO THE FIGHTING CAN STOP--
BUT HOW DO WE GET THEM IN THE SAME PLACE? WILL THEY TRUST EACH OTHER?
NO. THE MALKINS WILL THINK THE JACKALS ARE SETTING UP A TRAP.
THE JACKALS WILL THINK THE SAME THING. THE ONLY WAY TO GET THEM TOGETHER WOULD BE TO TRICK THEM INTO IT.
...
...
I HAVE AN ABSOLUTELY HORRIBLE, WONDERFUL, TERRIBLE IDEA...

158

-HUFF-
HUFF-

SPEAK
THEN.

THIS IS
RAY'S.

NEWT WAS ABLE
TO UNLOCK IT AND CHECK
THROUGH HIS PHOTOS
AND MESSAGES.

HE AND
JAYLA WERE
TOGETHER.

WHAT?!

THEY FELL IN
LOVE! LOOK AT THEM--
LOOK AT HOW **HAPPY**
THEY ARE!

BUT YOU FOUGHT
SO MUCH AND WERE SO
DIVIDED, THEY KNEW
THAT YOU WOULD TRY
TO END THEIR
RELATIONSHIP.

SO THEY
RAN AWAY
TOGETHER.

YOU **DROVE**
THEM AWAY.

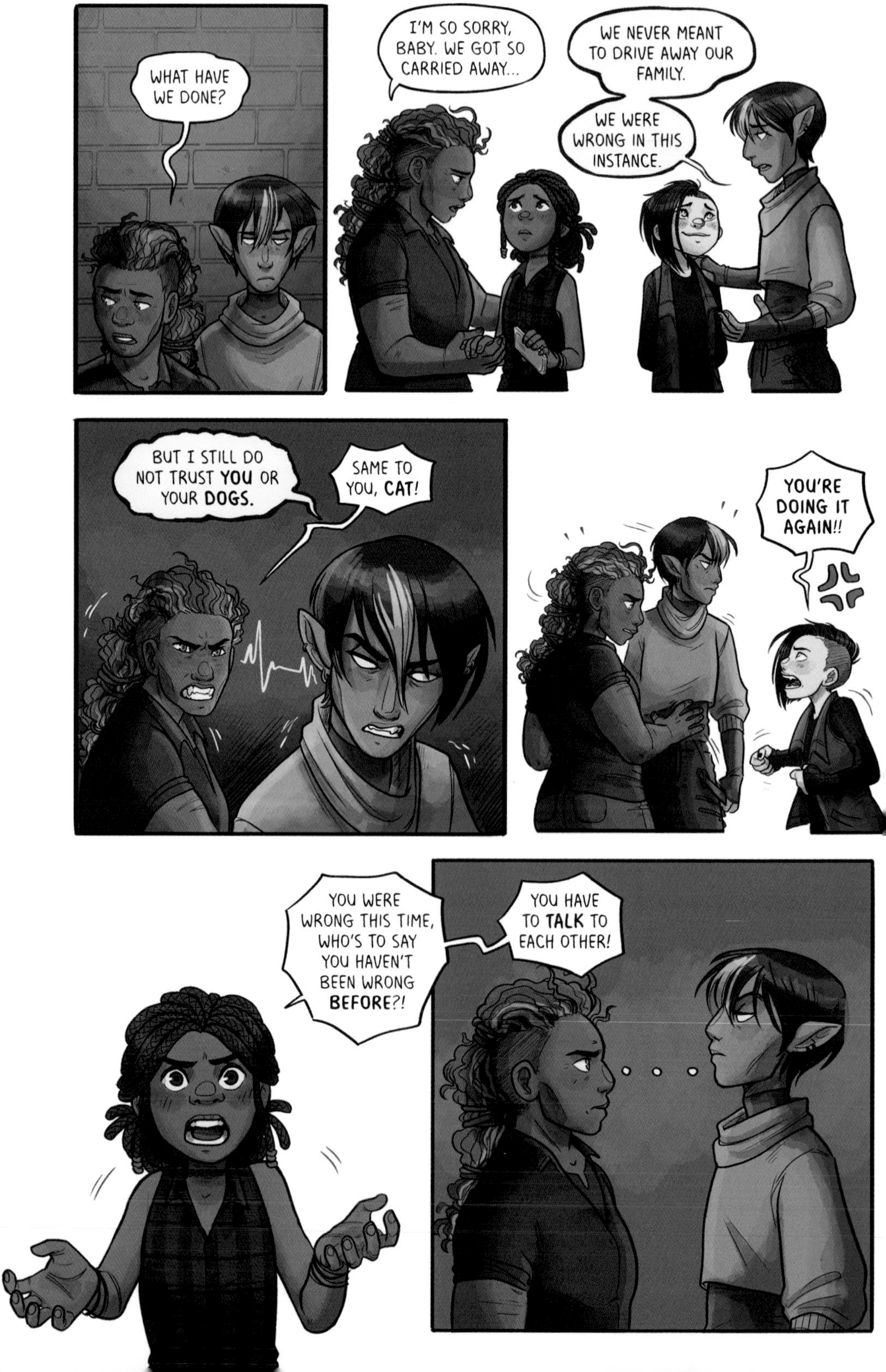
WHAT HAVE WE DONE?
I'M SO SORRY, BABY. WE GOT SO CARRIED AWAY...
WE NEVER MEANT TO DRIVE AWAY OUR FAMILY.
WE WERE WRONG IN THIS INSTANCE.
BUT I STILL DO NOT TRUST **YOU** OR YOUR **DOGS.**
SAME TO YOU, **CAT!**
YOU'RE DOING IT AGAIN!!
YOU WERE WRONG THIS TIME, WHO'S TO SAY YOU HAVEN'T BEEN WRONG **BEFORE**?!
YOU HAVE TO **TALK** TO EACH OTHER!

163

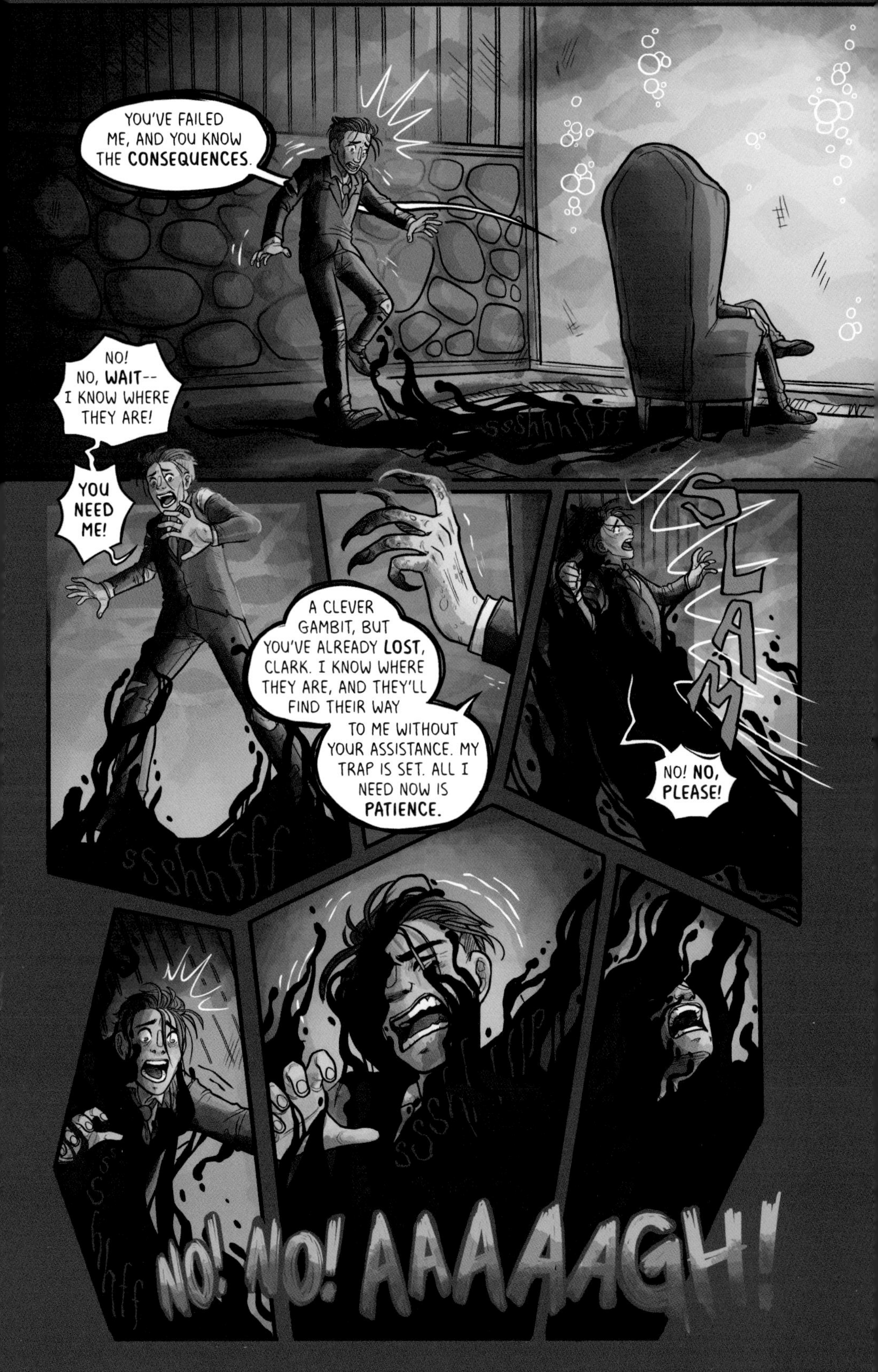

YOU'VE FAILED ME, AND YOU KNOW THE CONSEQUENCES.
NO! NO, WAIT-- I KNOW WHERE THEY ARE!
sssshhhfff
YOU NEED ME!
A CLEVER GAMBIT, BUT YOU'VE ALREADY LOST, CLARK. I KNOW WHERE THEY ARE, AND THEY'LL FIND THEIR WAY TO ME WITHOUT YOUR ASSISTANCE. MY TRAP IS SET. ALL I NEED NOW IS PATIENCE.
sSshhfff
SLAM
NO! NO, PLEASE!
NO! NO! AAAAAGH!

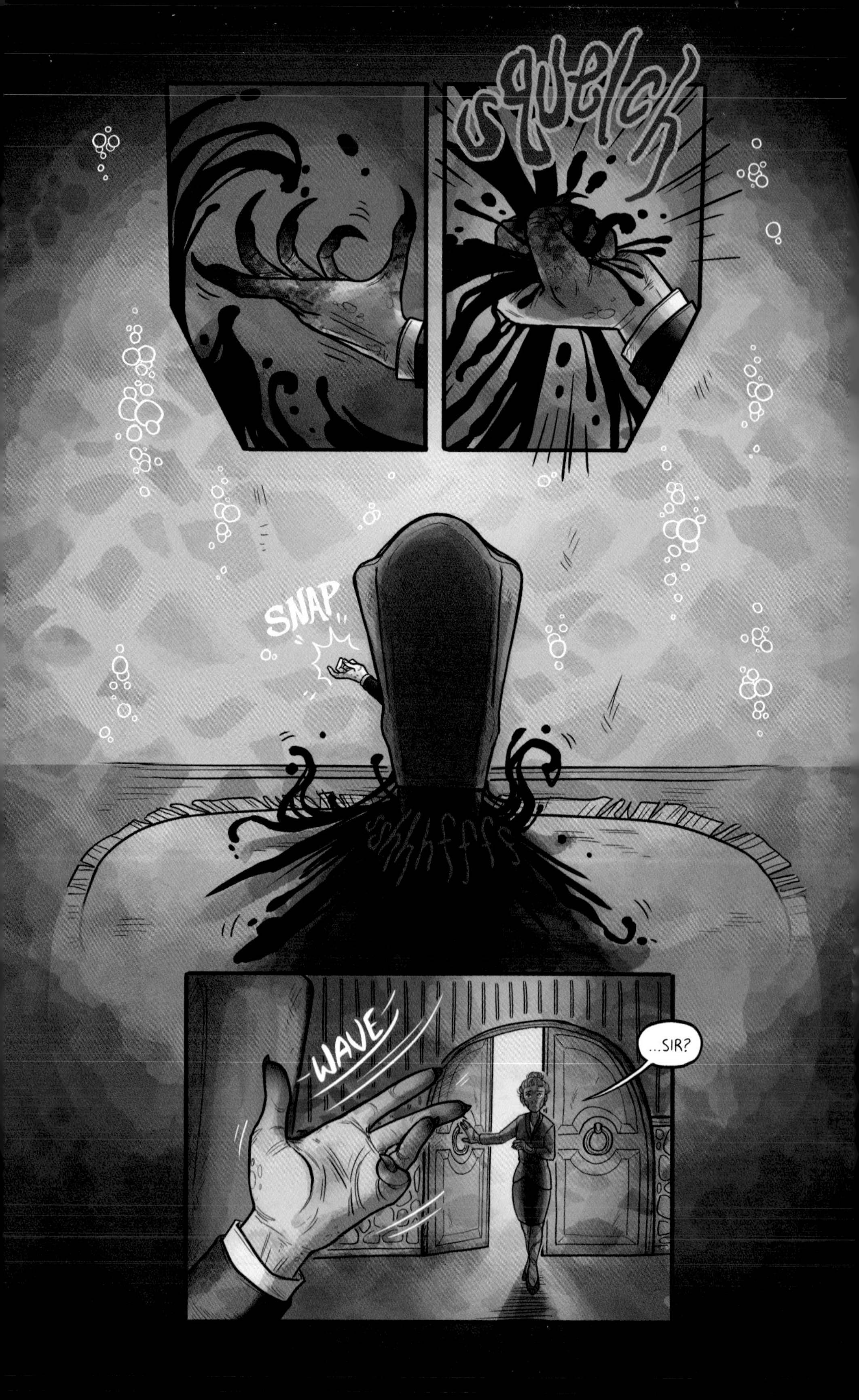
squelch
SNAP
shhfffs
WAVE
...SIR?

CHAPTER SEVEN

CROSS COUNTRY

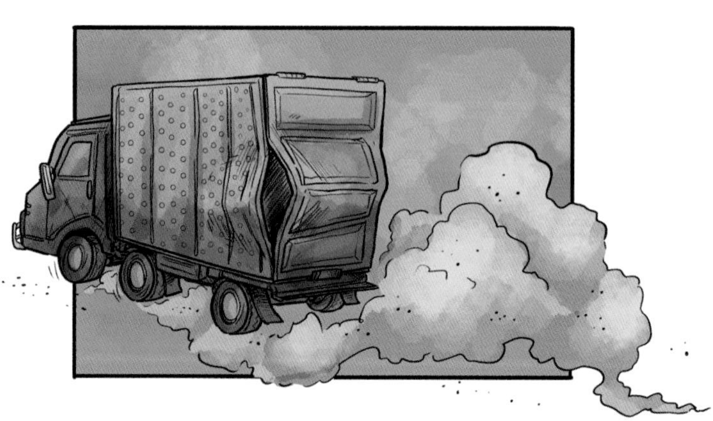

SO I KNOW IT'S IN WASHINGTON STATE-- THAT'S WHERE RAY AND JAYLA WERE HEADED.

THEY HAVE A COUPLE OF MESSAGES BACK AND FORTH ABOUT BUS TICKETS AND STUFF...

BUT NO **ADDRESSES**.

CAN'T YOU JUST... LIKE... **GOOGLE** IT?

OH **SURE**, JUST SEARCH "HI, WHERE CAN A GROUP OF SIX **MONSTERS** THAT MAY OR MAY NOT INCLUDE...

A BEAR, A SELKIE, A YETI, AN ALIEN, A WILL-O-THE-WISP, AND **WHATEVER MAGGIE IS**, GO HIDE BECAUSE THE **GOVERNMENT** IS AFTER THEM?"

I'M SURE THAT WOULD WORK OUT **PERFECTLY**.

169

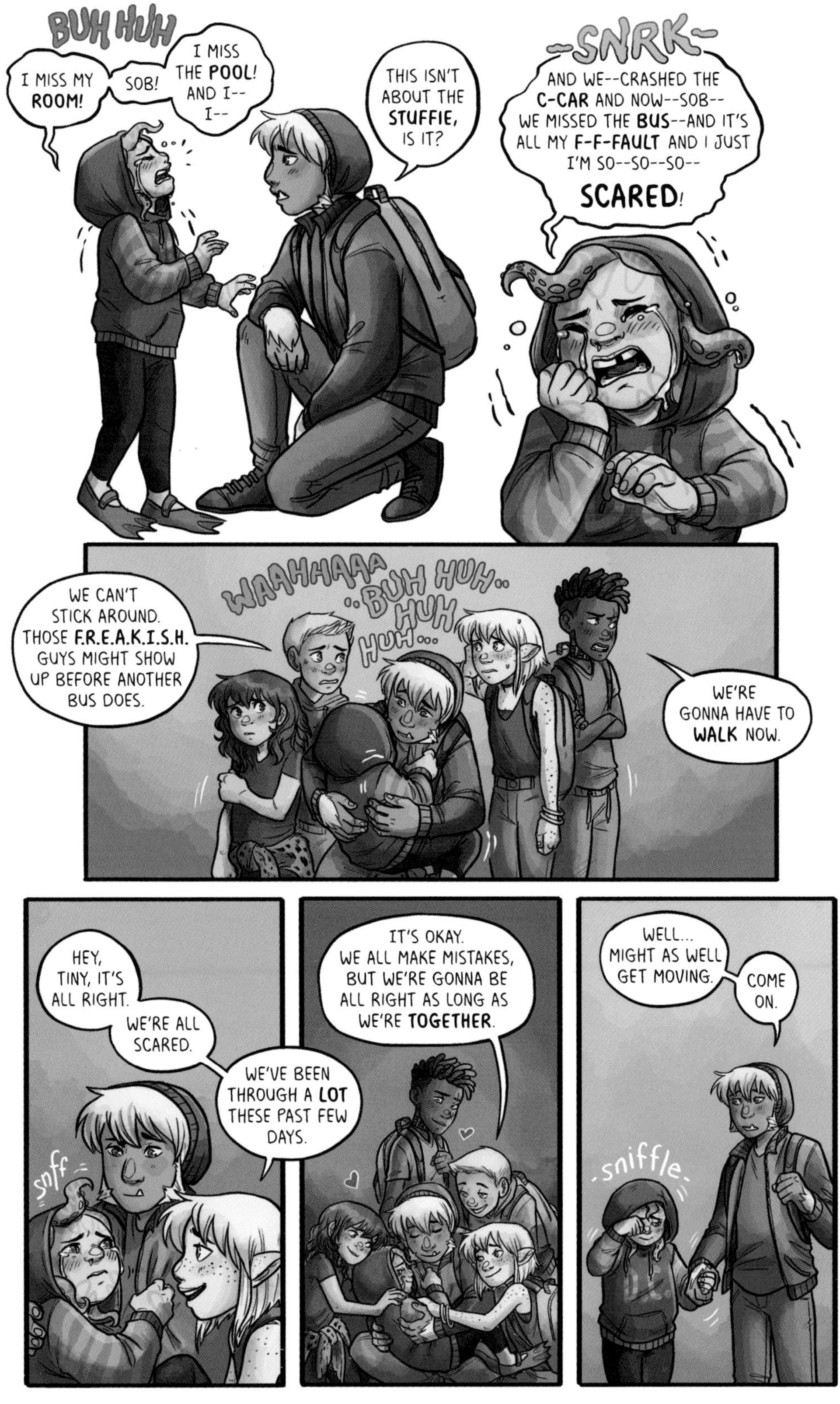
BUH HUH
I MISS MY **ROOM**!
SOB!
I MISS THE **POOL**! AND I-- I--
THIS ISN'T ABOUT THE **STUFFIE**, IS IT?
-SNRK-
AND WE--CRASHED THE **C-CAR** AND NOW--SOB-- WE MISSED THE **BUS**--AND IT'S ALL MY **F-F-FAULT** AND I JUST I'M SO--SO--SO--
SCARED!
WE CAN'T STICK AROUND. THOSE **F.R.E.A.K.I.S.H.** GUYS MIGHT SHOW UP BEFORE ANOTHER BUS DOES.
WAAHHAAA
..BUH HUH.. HUH
HUH...
WE'RE GONNA HAVE TO **WALK** NOW.
HEY, TINY, IT'S ALL RIGHT.
WE'RE ALL SCARED.
WE'VE BEEN THROUGH A **LOT** THESE PAST FEW DAYS.
snff
IT'S OKAY. WE ALL MAKE MISTAKES, BUT WE'RE GONNA BE ALL RIGHT AS LONG AS WE'RE **TOGETHER**.
WELL... MIGHT AS WELL GET MOVING.
COME ON.
sniffle

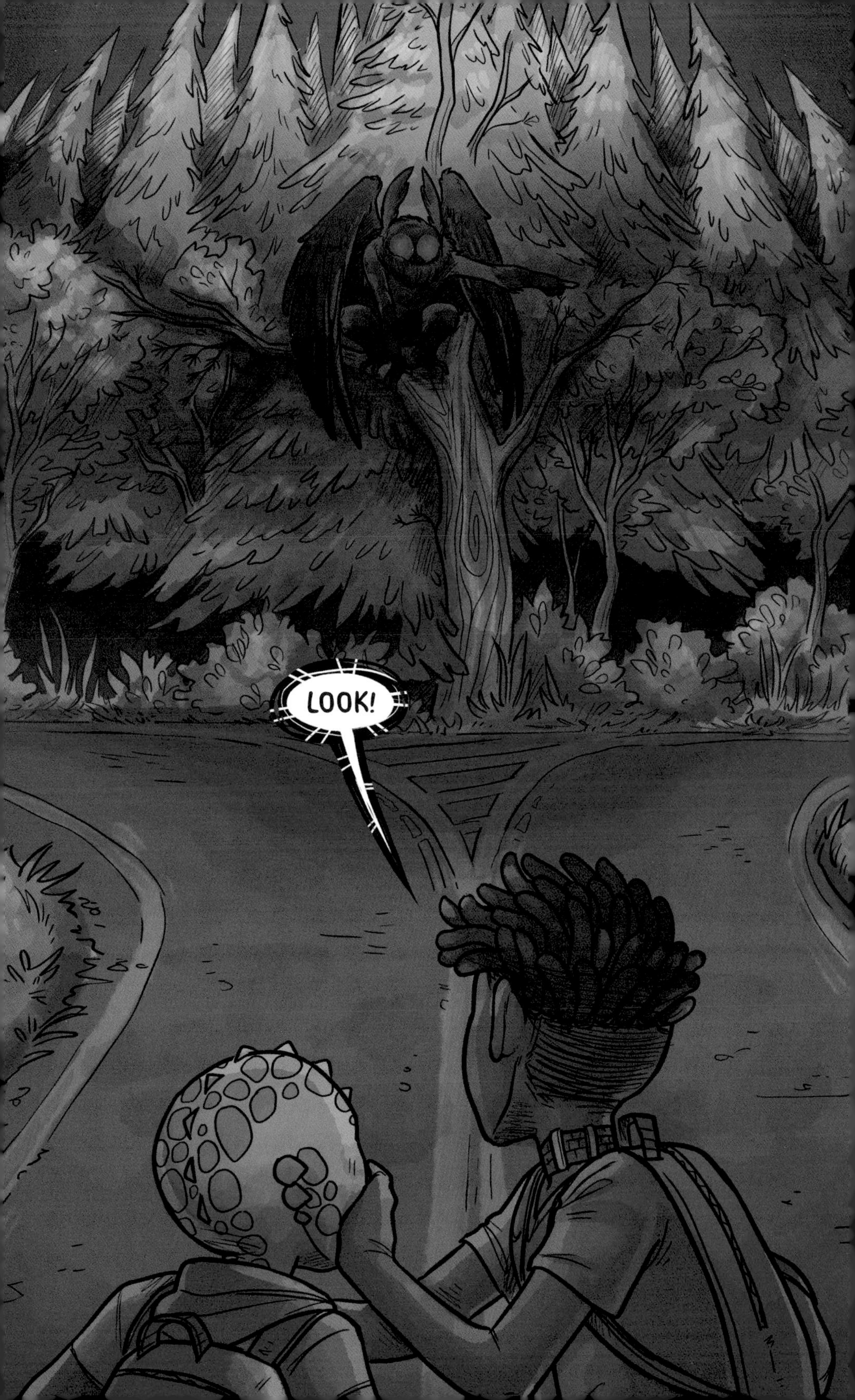
LOOK!

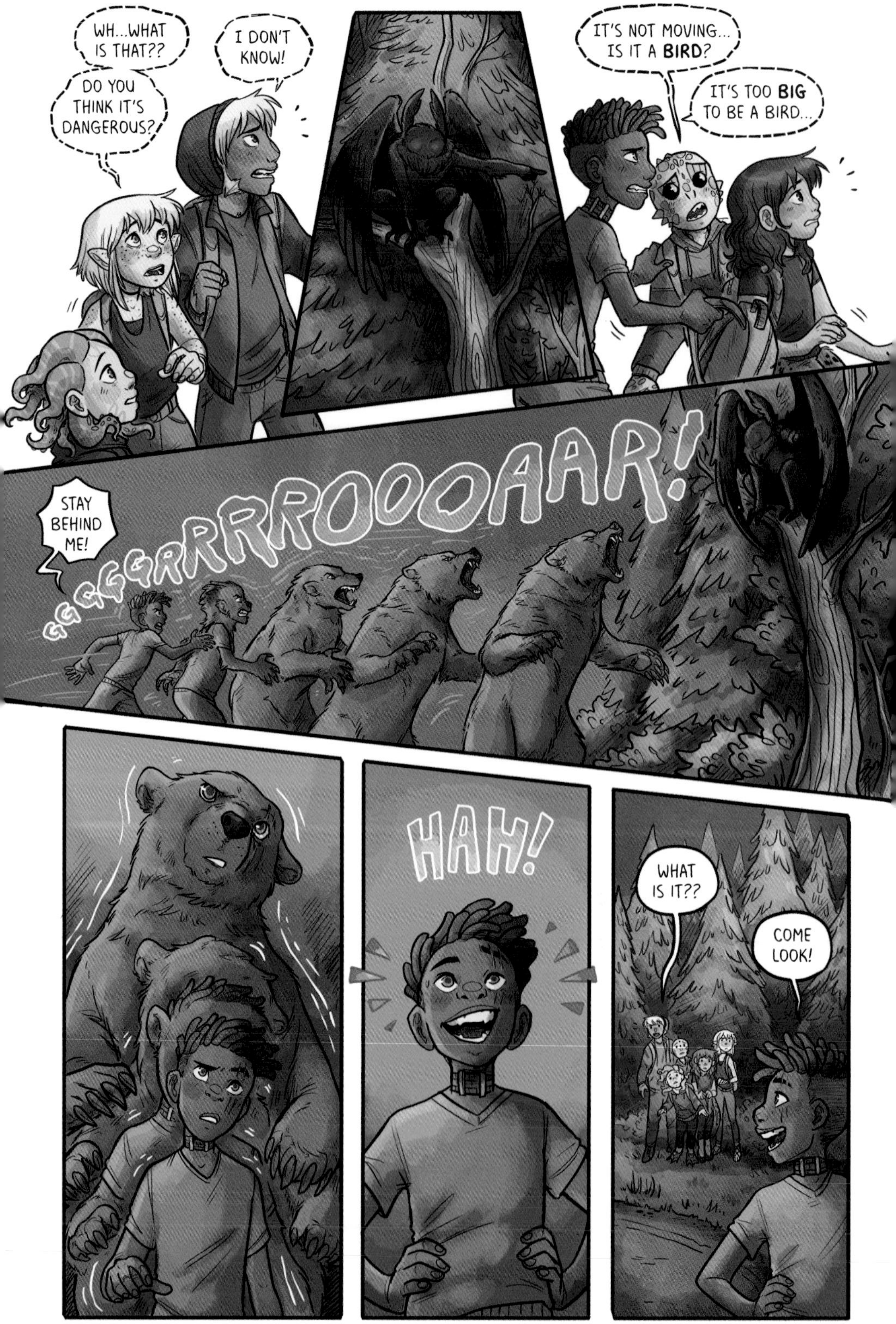
WH...WHAT IS THAT??
I DON'T KNOW!
DO YOU THINK IT'S DANGEROUS?
IT'S NOT MOVING... IS IT A **BIRD**?
IT'S TOO **BIG** TO BE A BIRD...
STAY BEHIND ME!
GGGGGRRRRROOOOAAR!
HAH!
WHAT IS IT??
COME LOOK!

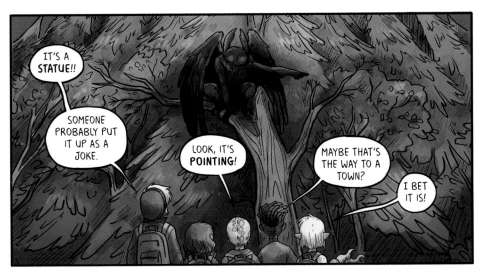

IT'S A **STATUE!!**

SOMEONE PROBABLY PUT IT UP AS A JOKE.

LOOK, IT'S **POINTING!**

MAYBE THAT'S THE WAY TO A TOWN?

I BET IT IS!

THAT THING SCARED THE CRAP OUT OF ME.

ME TOO!

ME THREE.

PHEW

MIGHT AS WELL FOLLOW ITS DIRECTIONS. FIND SOMEPLACE TO CHARGE YOUR O-PAD, NEWT.

YEAH.

LET'S GO!

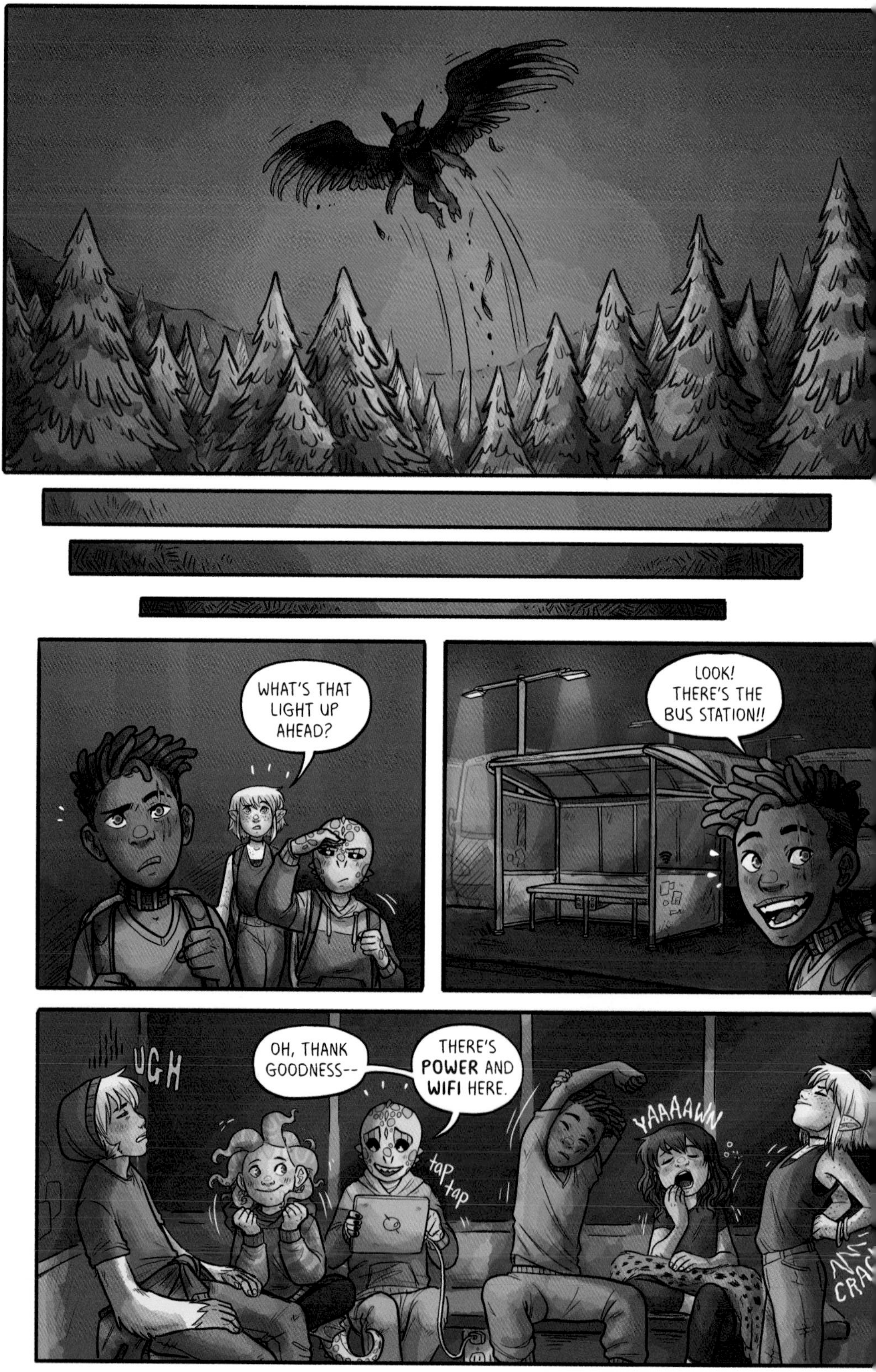
WHAT'S THAT LIGHT UP AHEAD?
LOOK! THERE'S THE BUS STATION!!
UGH
OH, THANK GOODNESS--
THERE'S **POWER** AND **WIFI** HERE.
tap tap
YAAAAWN
CRAC

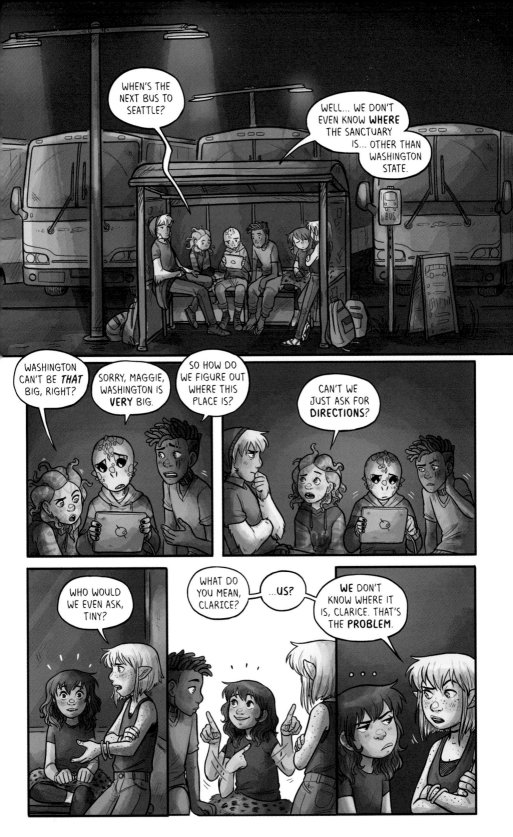

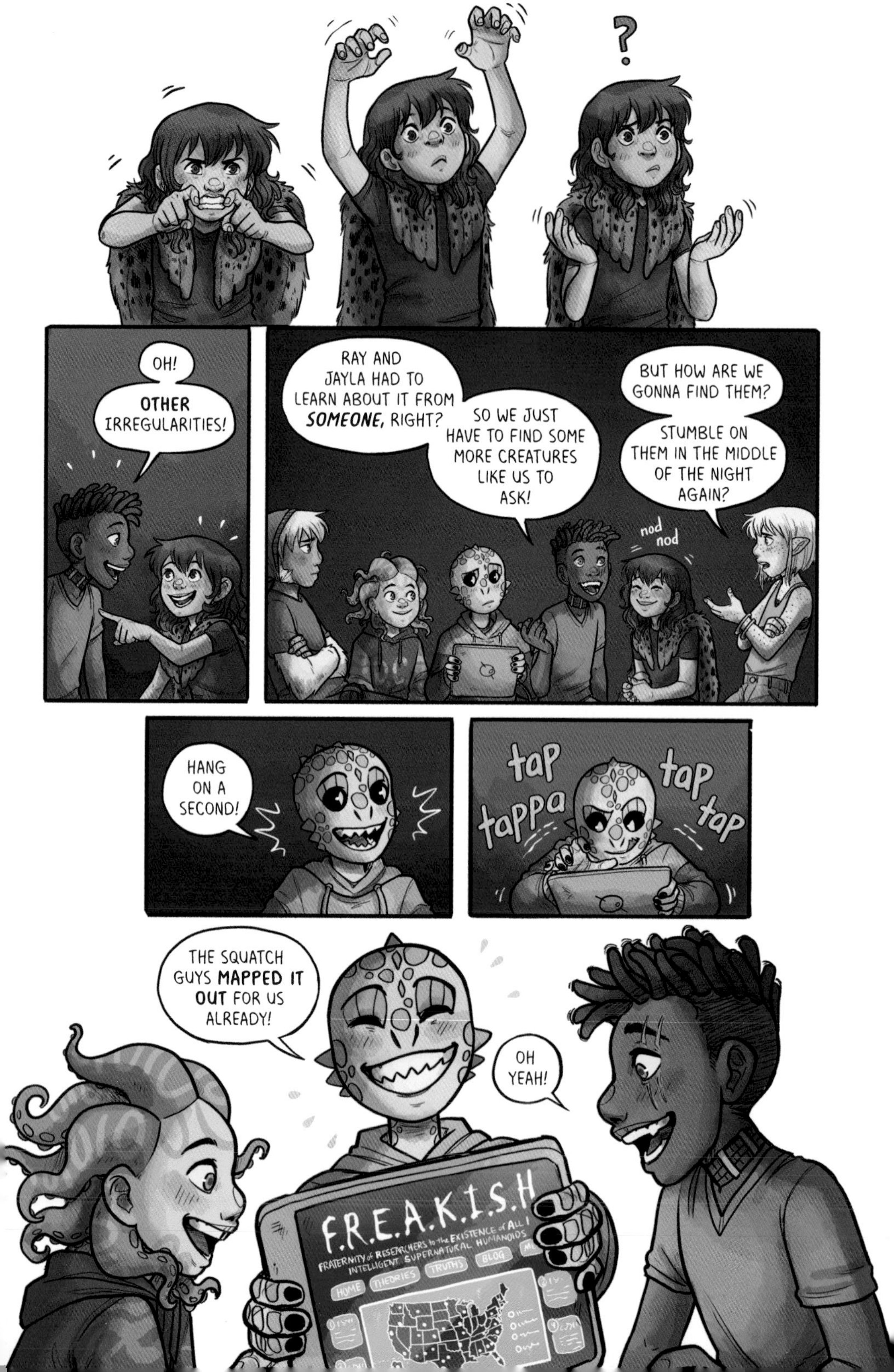
?
OH!
OTHER IRREGULARITIES!
RAY AND JAYLA HAD TO LEARN ABOUT IT FROM *SOMEONE*, RIGHT?
SO WE JUST HAVE TO FIND SOME MORE CREATURES LIKE US TO ASK!
BUT HOW ARE WE GONNA FIND THEM?
STUMBLE ON THEM IN THE MIDDLE OF THE NIGHT AGAIN?
nod nod
HANG ON A SECOND!
tap tappa tap tap
THE SQUATCH GUYS **MAPPED IT OUT** FOR US ALREADY!
OH YEAH!
F.R.E.A.K.I.S.H
FRATERNITY of RESEARCHERS to the EXISTENCE of ALL
INTELLIGENT SUPERNATURAL HUMANOIDS
HOME
THEORIES
TRUTHS
BLOG

F.R.E.A.K.I.S.H.
FRATERNITY of RESEARCHERS to the EXISTENCE of ALL KNOWN INTELLIGENT SUPERNATURAL HUMANOIDS
HOME
THEORIES
TRUTHS
BLOG
MERCH
LOVELAND FROGMAN
Loveland, OH
Seems to enjoy scaring tourists. Likely a hoax.
?
THE MOMO
Mississippi River, LA, MO
Short for "Missouri Monster, it has a terrible odor. Super creepy.
?
N
W
E
S
POPE LICK MONSTER
Pope Lick Creek, KY
Half-man half-goat. Very dangerous rumors from various victims!

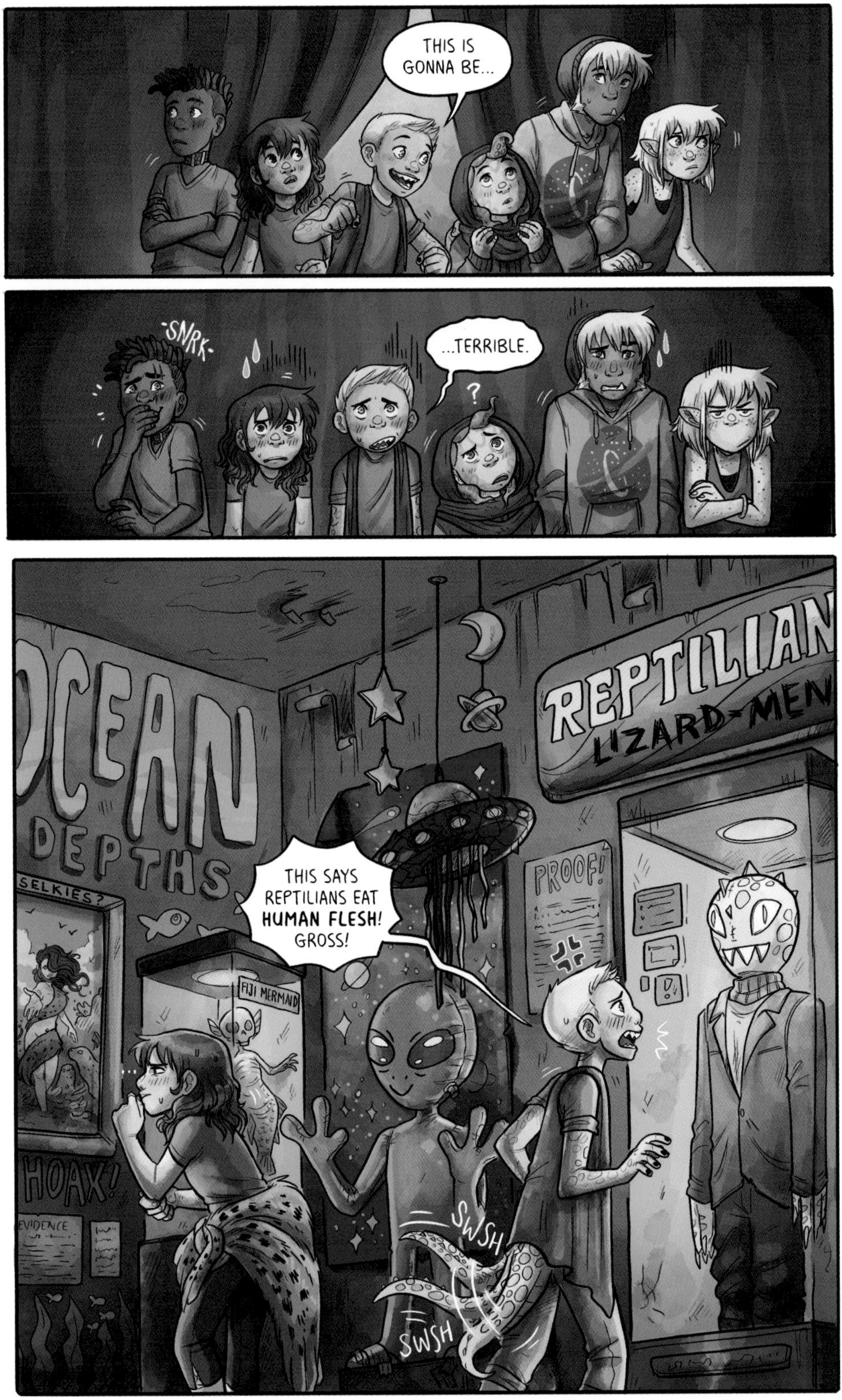
THIS IS GONNA BE...
-SNRK-
...TERRIBLE.
?
OCEAN DEPTHS
SELKIES?
HOAX!
EVIDENCE
FIJI MERMAID
REPTILIAN LIZARD-MEN
PROOF!
THIS SAYS REPTILIANS EAT **HUMAN FLESH!** GROSS!
SWSH
SWSH

WHY ARE THEY ALL **NAKED**??

WHY ARE WHO ALL WHA--

HEY!

I THINK... I THINK I'M OFFENDED.

YUCK!

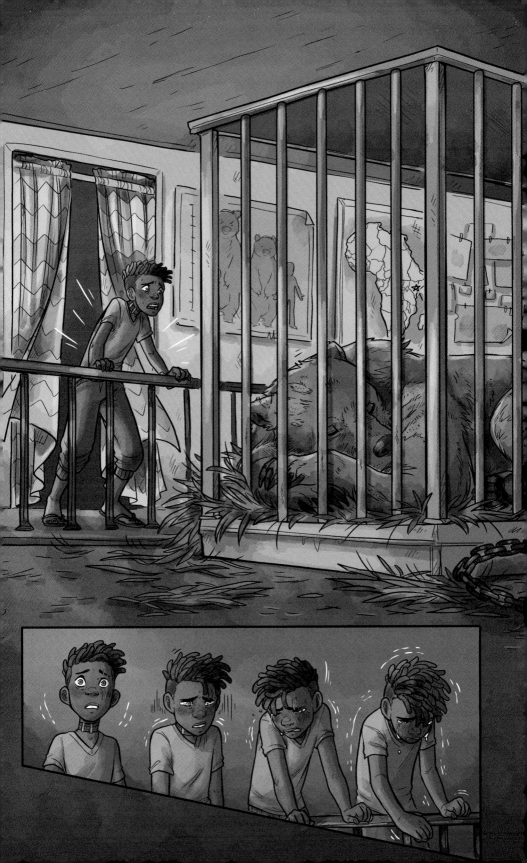

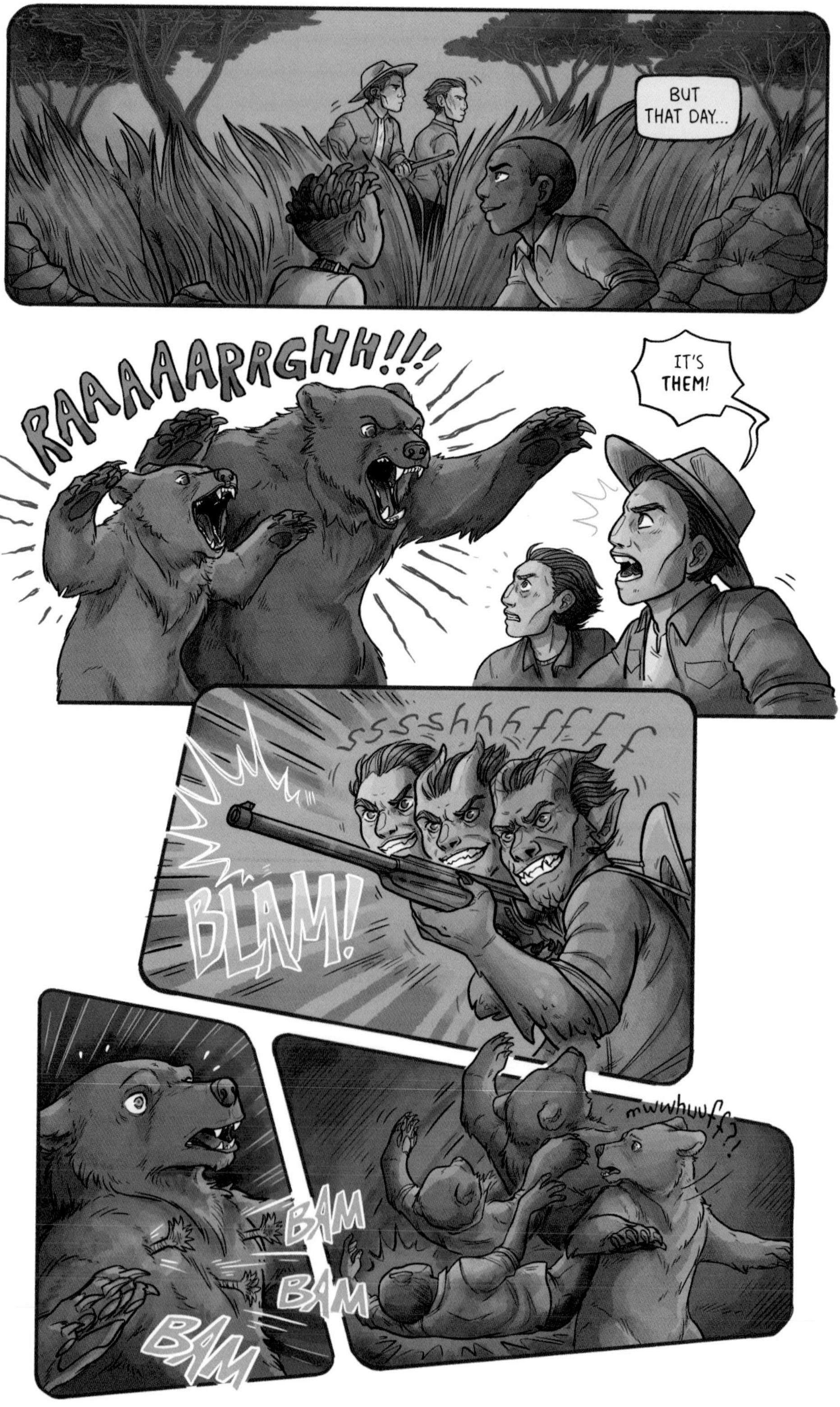
BUT THAT DAY...
RAAAAARRGHH!!!
IT'S THEM!
sssshhhfffff
BLAM!
BAM
BAM
BAM
mwwhuuff?!

191

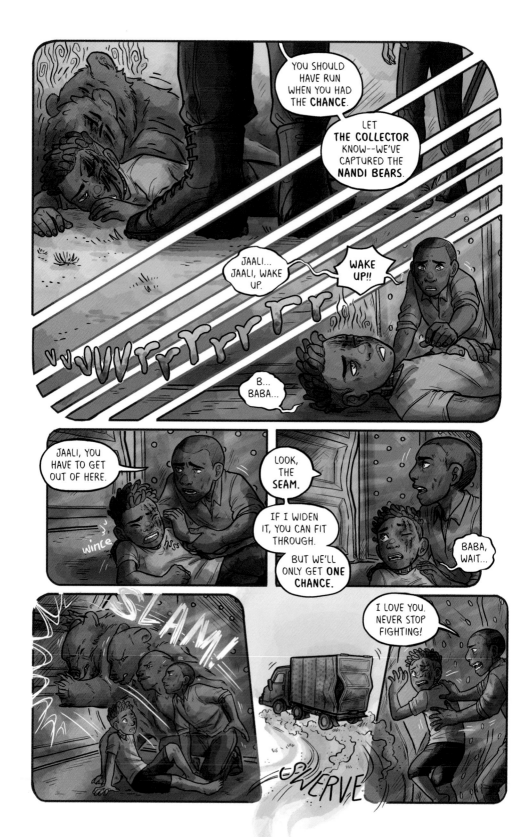

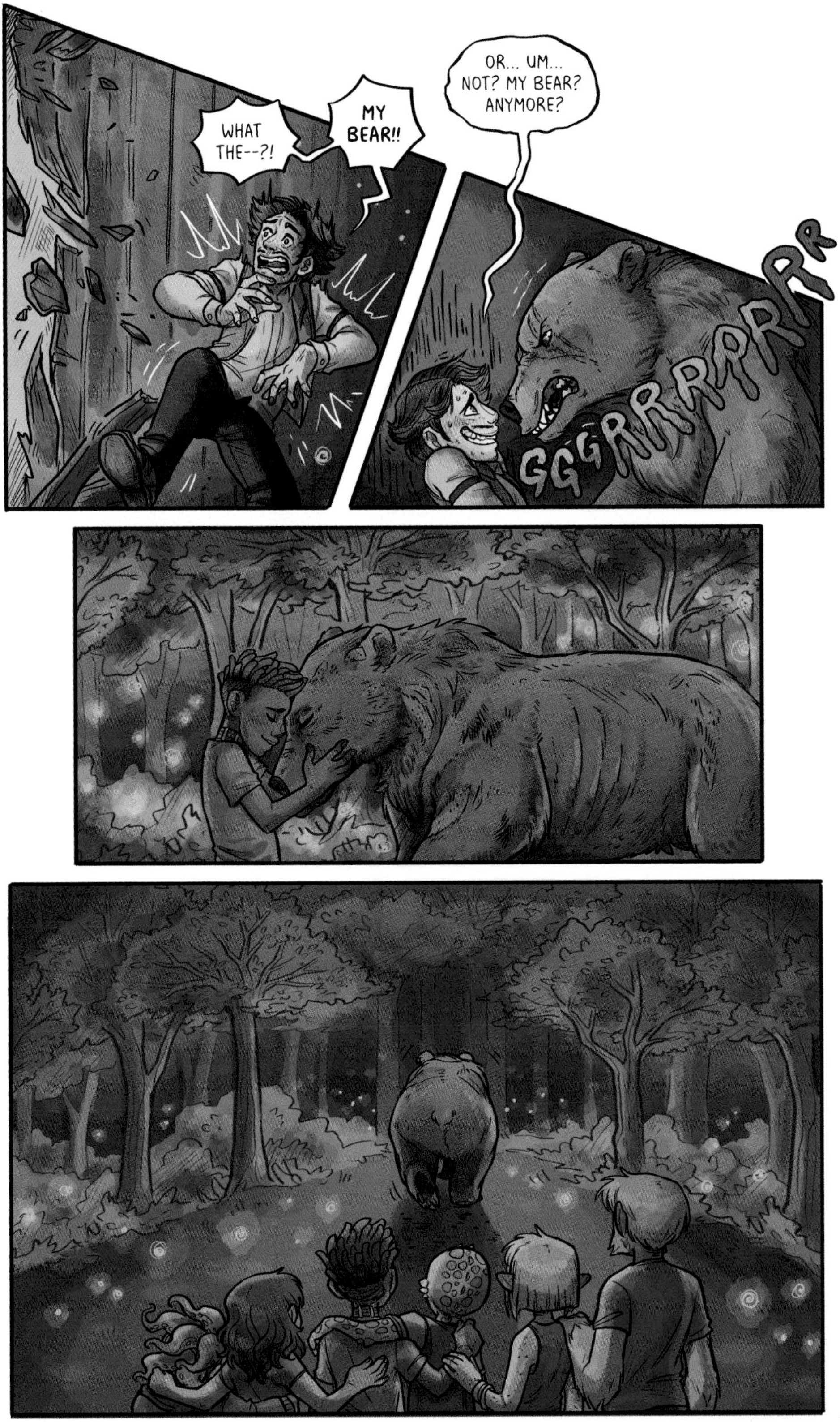
WHAT THE--?!
MY BEAR!!
OR... UM... NOT? MY BEAR? ANYMORE?
GGGRRRRRRRR

CHAPTER EIGHT

BRIEF RESPITE

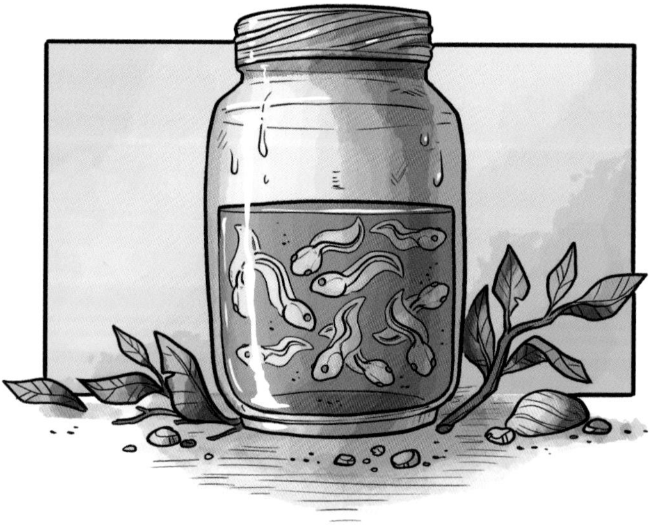

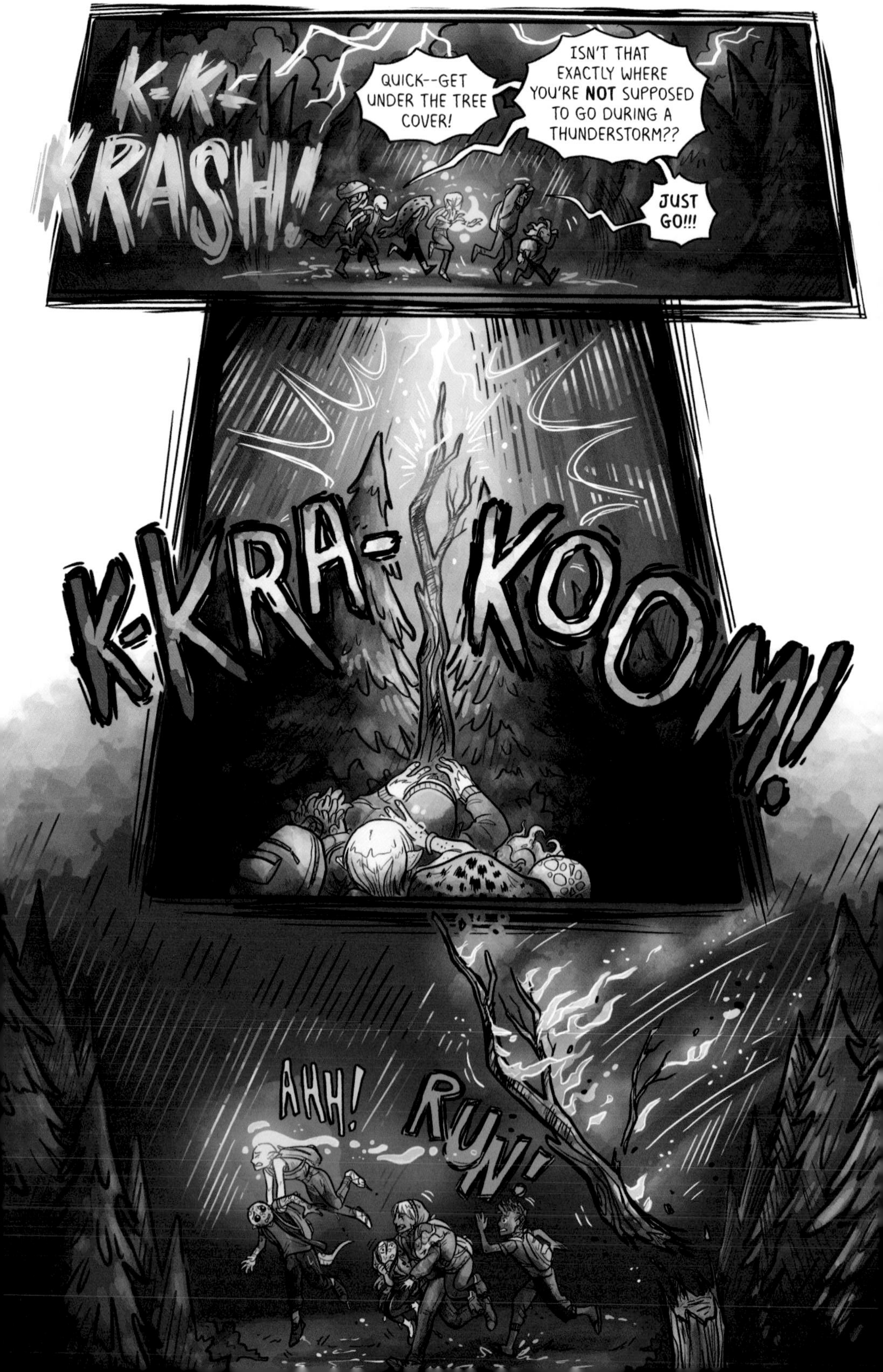
K-K-
KRASH!
QUICK--GET UNDER THE TREE COVER!
ISN'T THAT EXACTLY WHERE YOU'RE NOT SUPPOSED TO GO DURING A THUNDERSTORM??
JUST GO!!!
K-KRA-KOOM!!
AHH!
RUN!

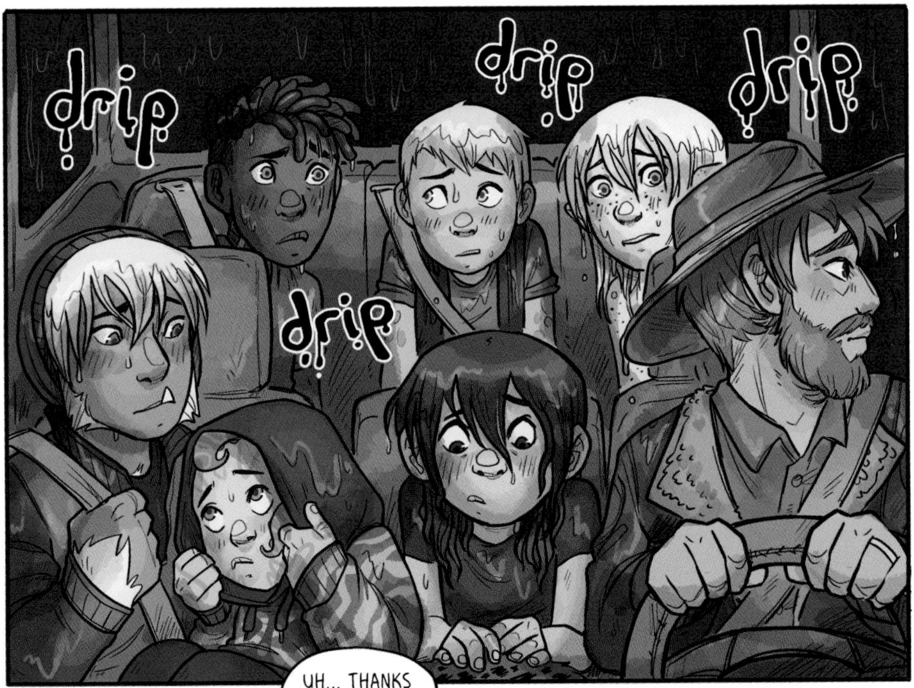
drip
drip
drip
drip

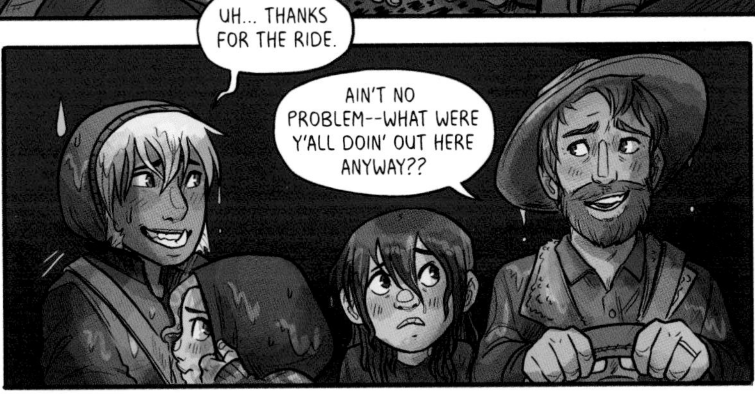
UH... THANKS FOR THE RIDE.
AIN'T NO PROBLEM--WHAT WERE Y'ALL DOIN' OUT HERE ANYWAY??

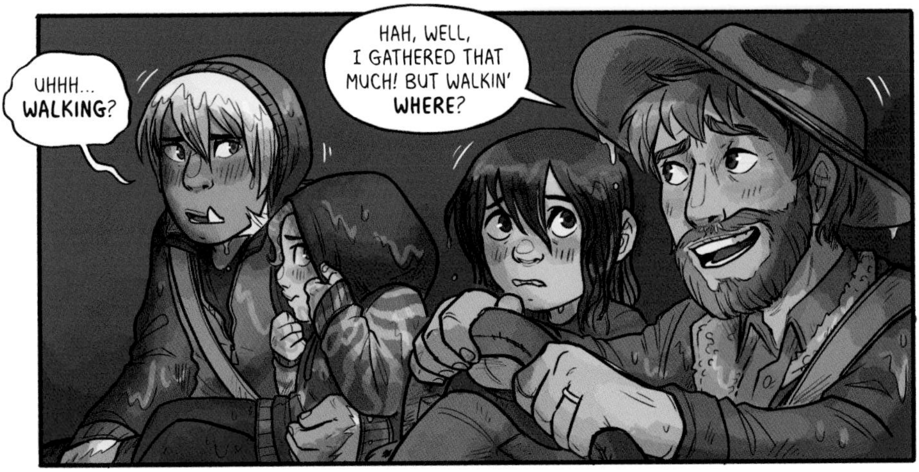
UHHH... **WALKING**?
HAH, WELL, I GATHERED THAT MUCH! BUT WALKIN' **WHERE**?

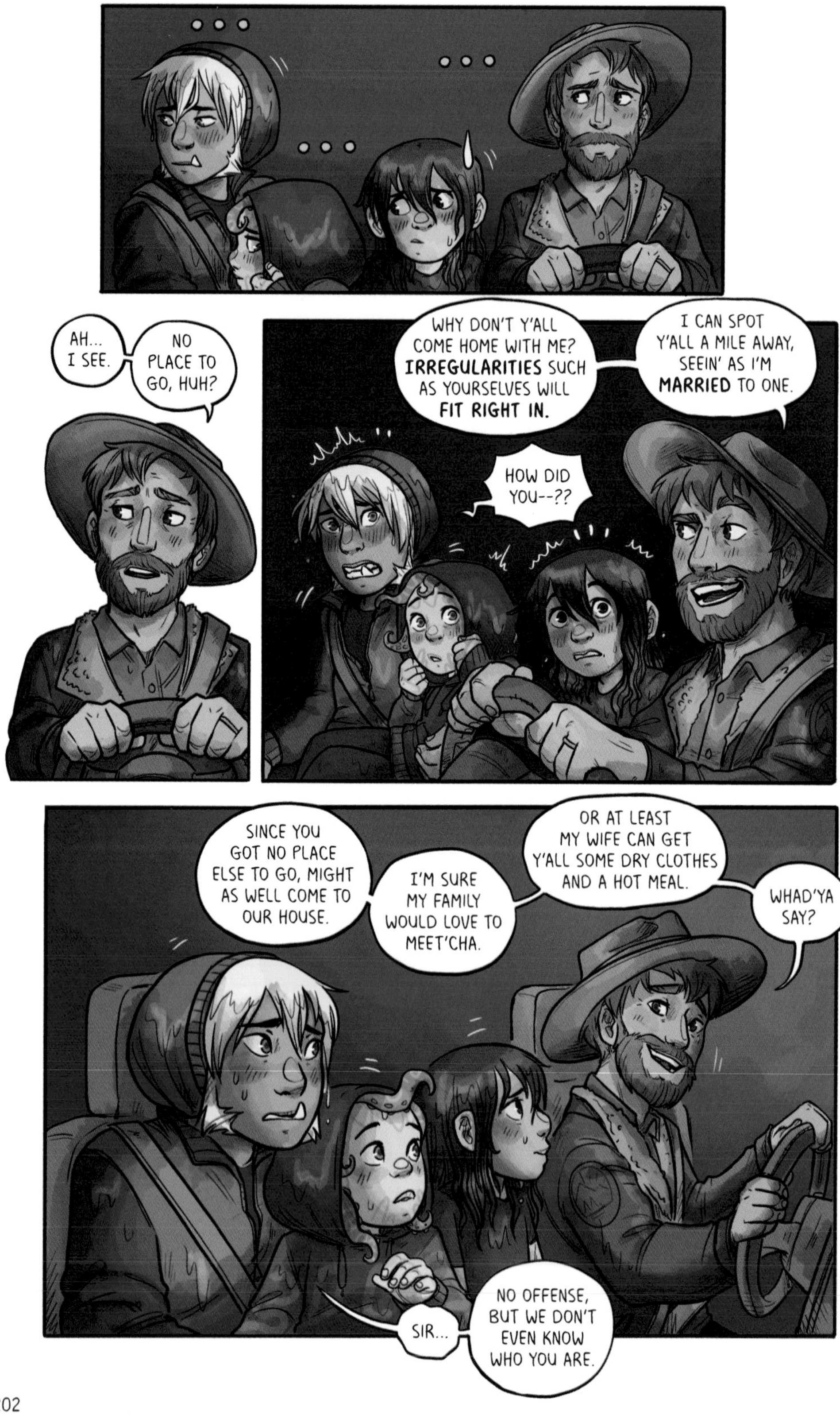
...
...
...
AH... I SEE.
NO PLACE TO GO, HUH?
WHY DON'T Y'ALL COME HOME WITH ME? IRREGULARITIES SUCH AS YOURSELVES WILL FIT RIGHT IN.
I CAN SPOT Y'ALL A MILE AWAY, SEEIN' AS I'M MARRIED TO ONE.
HOW DID YOU--??
SINCE YOU GOT NO PLACE ELSE TO GO, MIGHT AS WELL COME TO OUR HOUSE.
I'M SURE MY FAMILY WOULD LOVE TO MEET'CHA.
OR AT LEAST MY WIFE CAN GET Y'ALL SOME DRY CLOTHES AND A HOT MEAL.
WHAD'YA SAY?
SIR...
NO OFFENSE, BUT WE DON'T EVEN KNOW WHO YOU ARE.

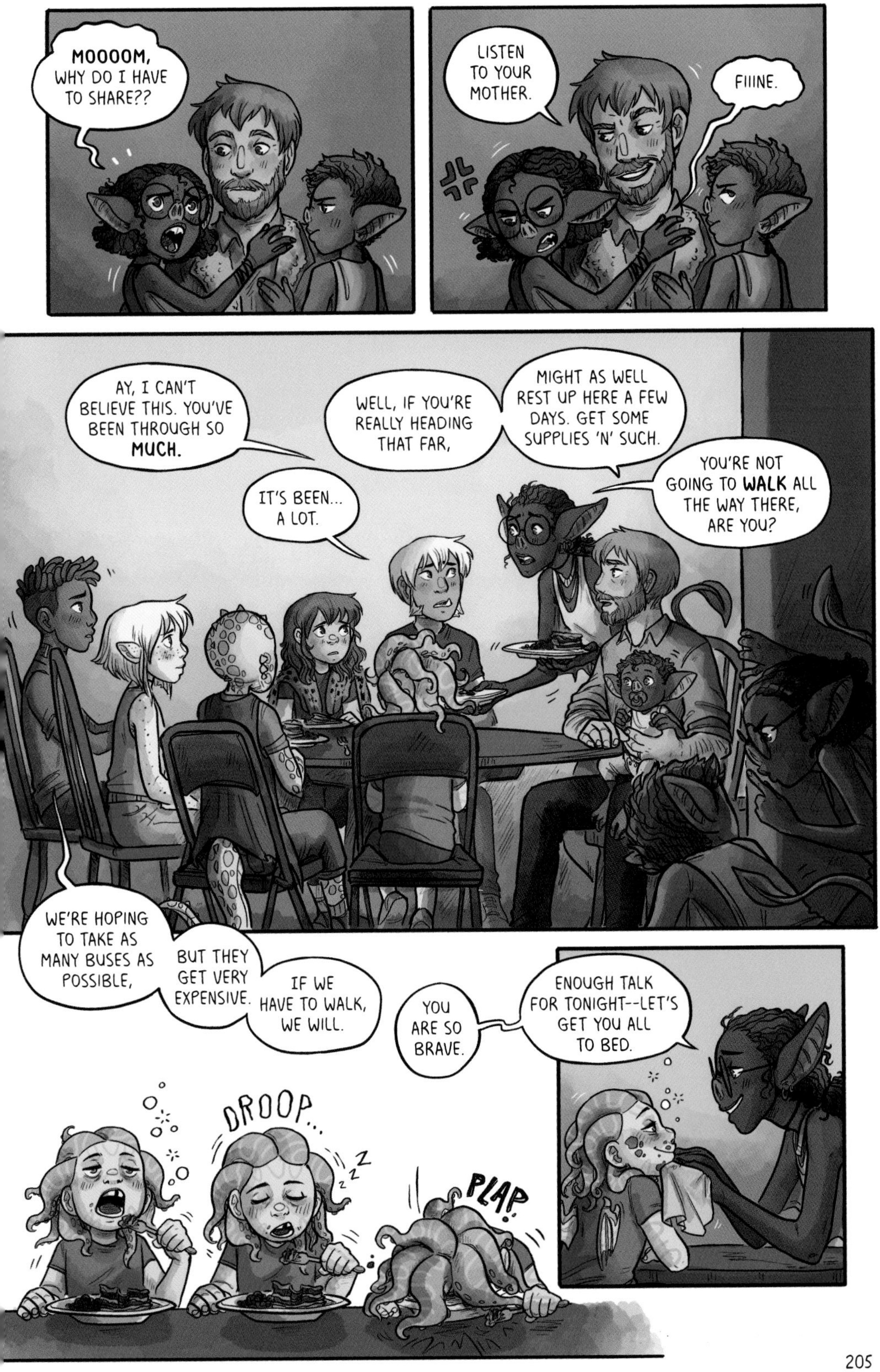
MOOOOM, WHY DO I HAVE TO SHARE??
LISTEN TO YOUR MOTHER.
FIIINE.
AY, I CAN'T BELIEVE THIS. YOU'VE BEEN THROUGH SO MUCH.
IT'S BEEN... A LOT.
WELL, IF YOU'RE REALLY HEADING THAT FAR,
MIGHT AS WELL REST UP HERE A FEW DAYS. GET SOME SUPPLIES 'N' SUCH.
YOU'RE NOT GOING TO WALK ALL THE WAY THERE, ARE YOU?
WE'RE HOPING TO TAKE AS MANY BUSES AS POSSIBLE,
BUT THEY GET VERY EXPENSIVE.
IF WE HAVE TO WALK, WE WILL.
YOU ARE SO BRAVE.
ENOUGH TALK FOR TONIGHT--LET'S GET YOU ALL TO BED.
DROOP...
Z Z Z
PLAP!

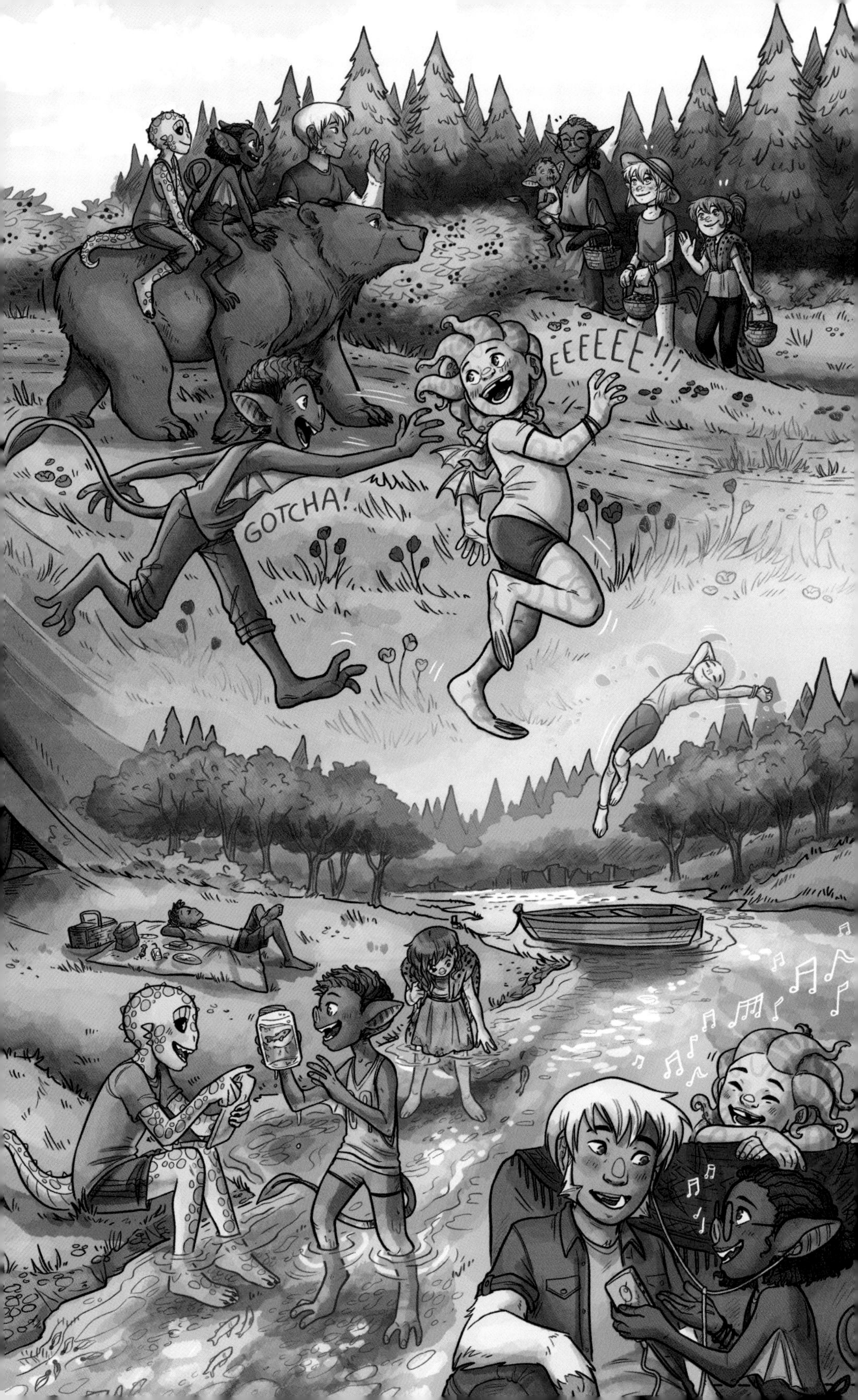

EEEEEE!!!
GOTCHA!

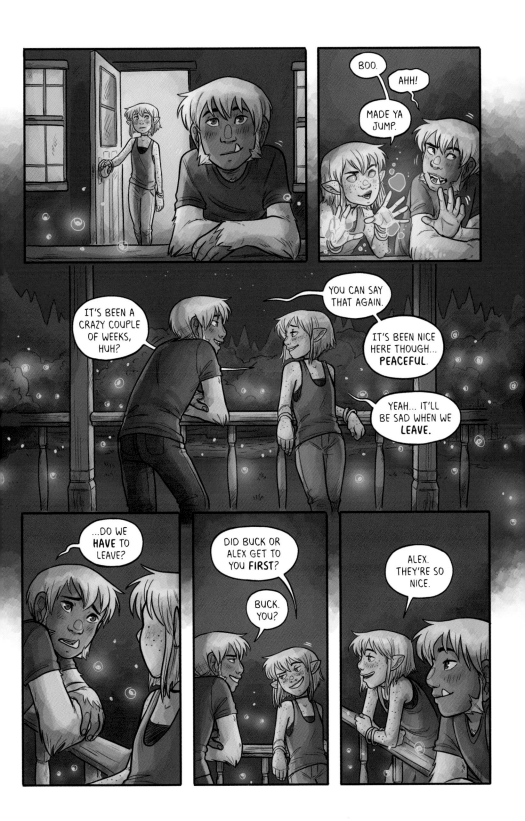

213

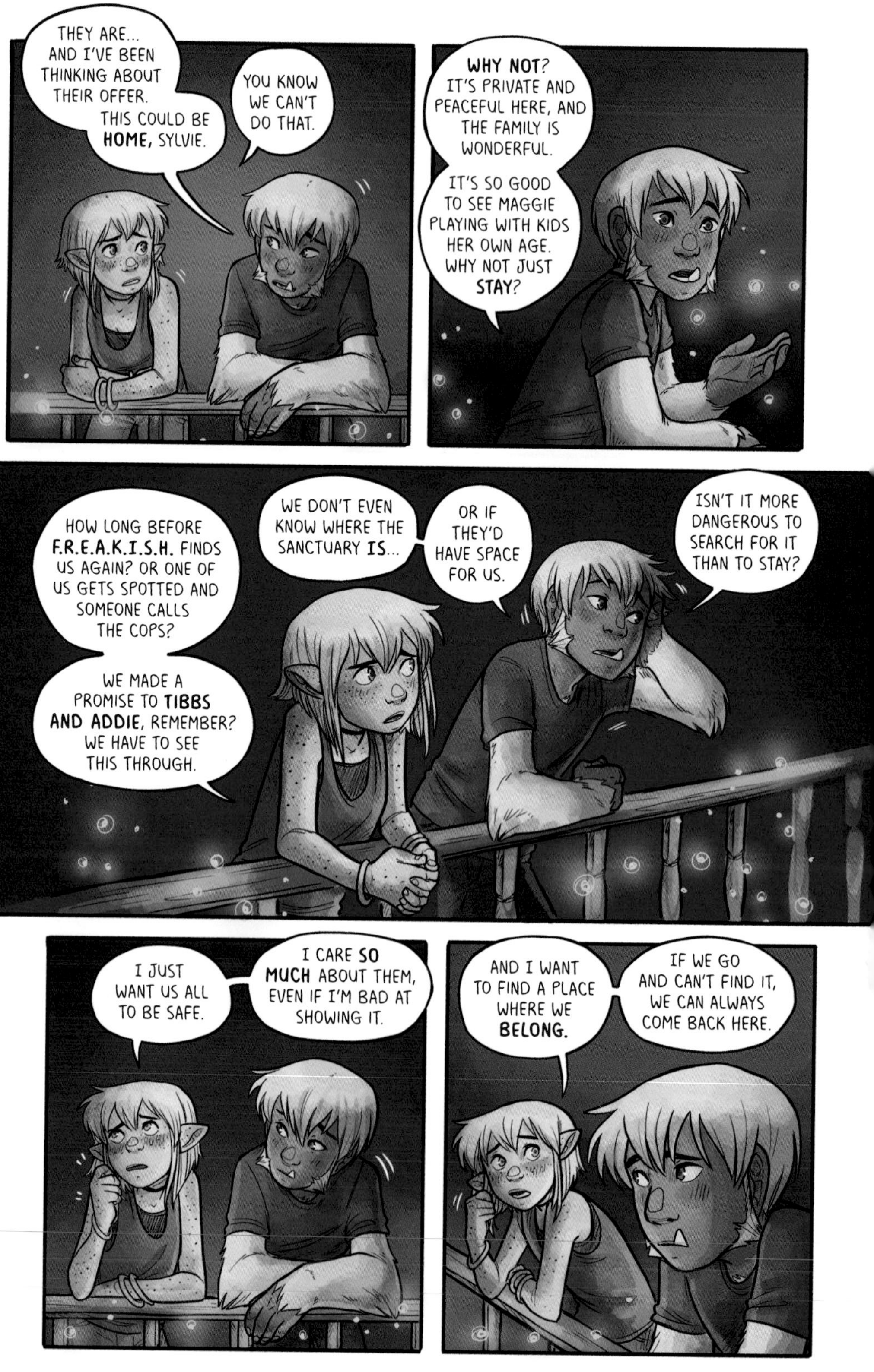
THEY ARE... AND I'VE BEEN THINKING ABOUT THEIR OFFER.
THIS COULD BE **HOME,** SYLVIE.
YOU KNOW WE CAN'T DO THAT.
WHY NOT? IT'S PRIVATE AND PEACEFUL HERE, AND THE FAMILY IS WONDERFUL.
IT'S SO GOOD TO SEE MAGGIE PLAYING WITH KIDS HER OWN AGE. WHY NOT JUST **STAY?**
HOW LONG BEFORE **F.R.E.A.K.I.S.H.** FINDS US AGAIN? OR ONE OF US GETS SPOTTED AND SOMEONE CALLS THE COPS?
WE MADE A PROMISE TO **TIBBS AND ADDIE**, REMEMBER? WE HAVE TO SEE THIS THROUGH.
WE DON'T EVEN KNOW WHERE THE SANCTUARY **IS**...
OR IF THEY'D HAVE SPACE FOR US.
ISN'T IT MORE DANGEROUS TO SEARCH FOR IT THAN TO STAY?
I JUST WANT US ALL TO BE SAFE.
I CARE **SO MUCH** ABOUT THEM, EVEN IF I'M BAD AT SHOWING IT.
AND I WANT TO FIND A PLACE WHERE WE **BELONG.**
IF WE GO AND CAN'T FIND IT, WE CAN ALWAYS COME BACK HERE.

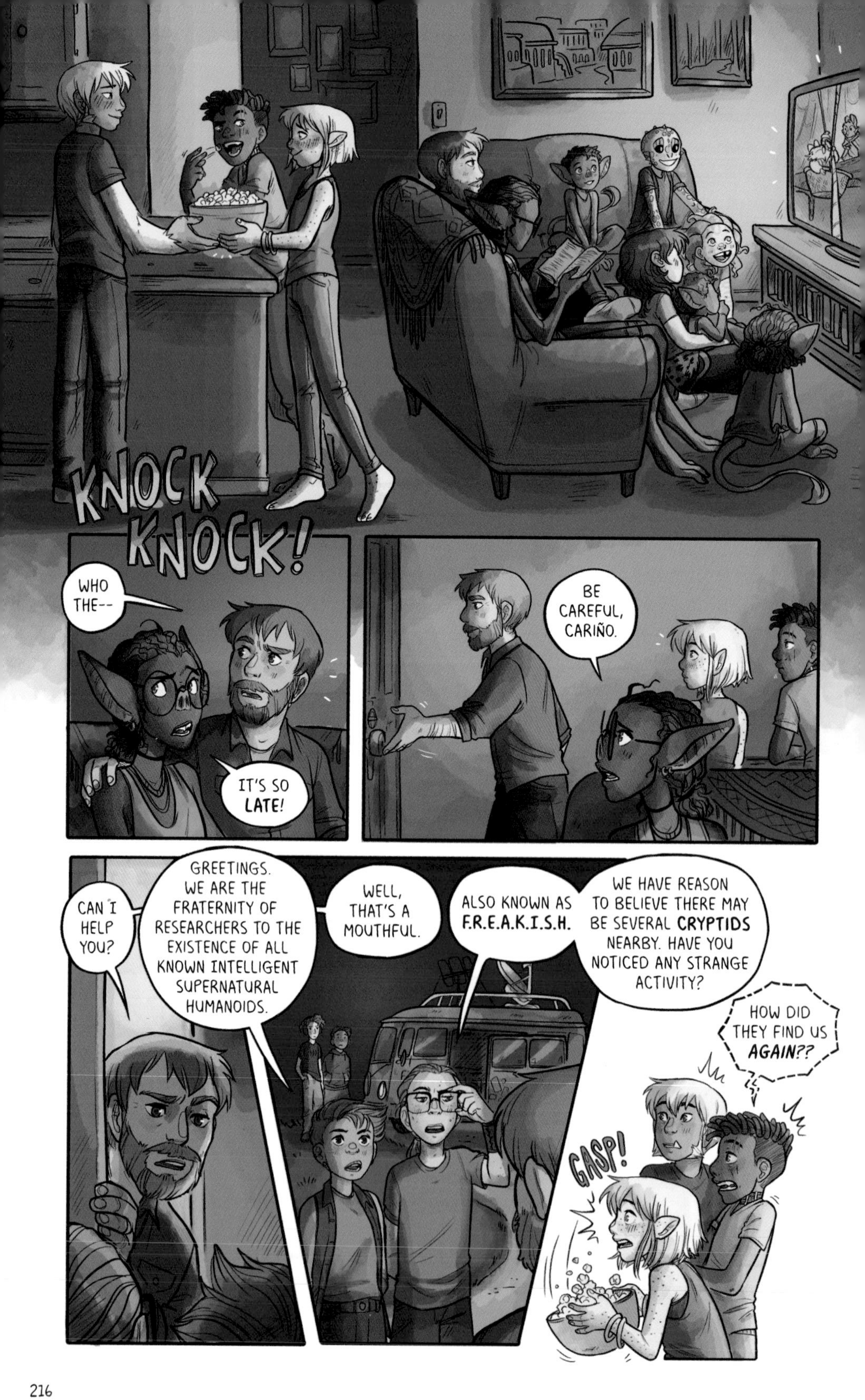
KNOCK KNOCK!
WHO THE--
IT'S SO LATE!
BE CAREFUL, CARIÑO.
CAN I HELP YOU?
GREETINGS. WE ARE THE FRATERNITY OF RESEARCHERS TO THE EXISTENCE OF ALL KNOWN INTELLIGENT SUPERNATURAL HUMANOIDS.
WELL, THAT'S A MOUTHFUL.
ALSO KNOWN AS F.R.E.A.K.I.S.H.
WE HAVE REASON TO BELIEVE THERE MAY BE SEVERAL CRYPTIDS NEARBY. HAVE YOU NOTICED ANY STRANGE ACTIVITY?
HOW DID THEY FIND US AGAIN??
GASP!

217

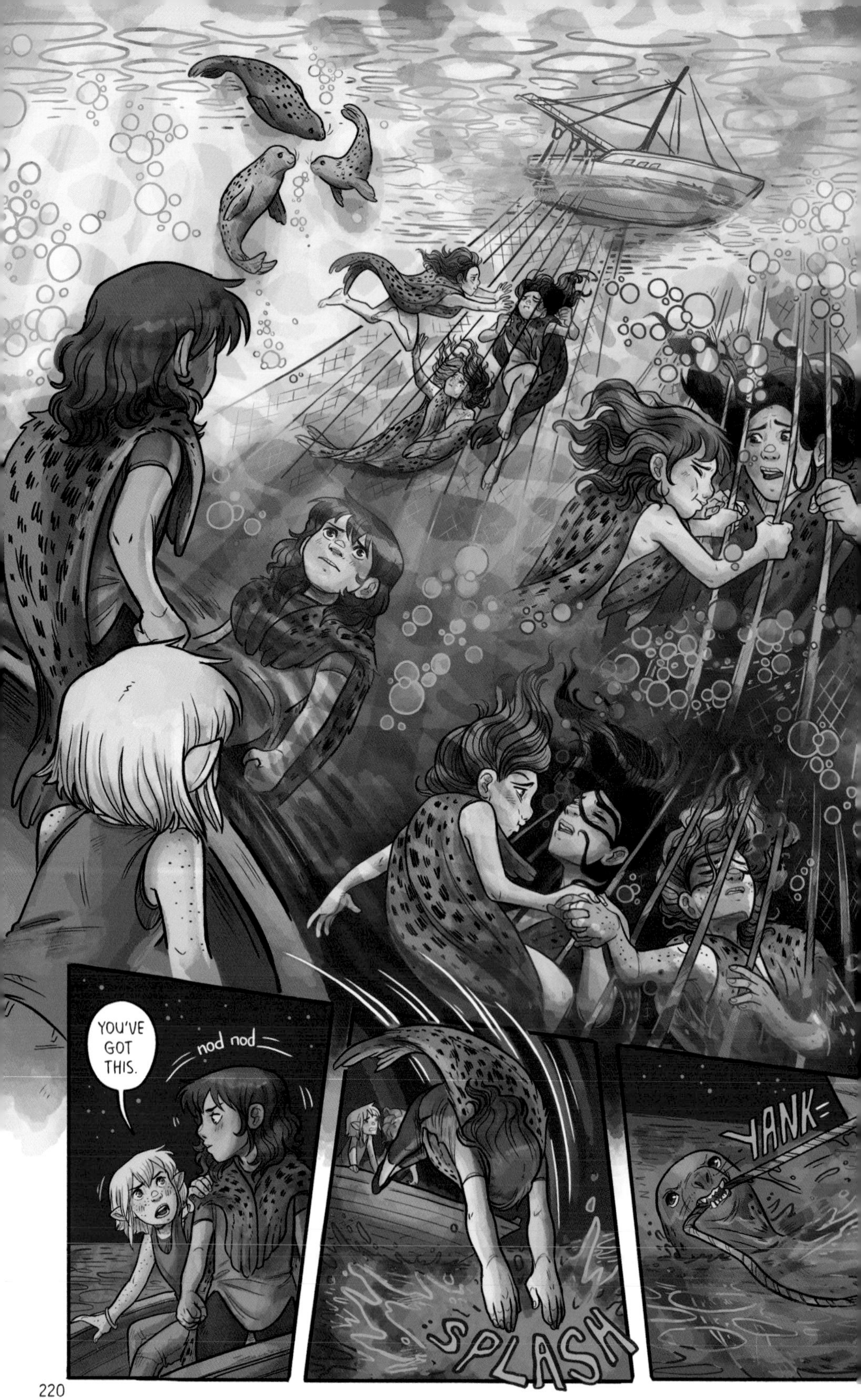
YOU'VE GOT THIS.
nod nod
SPLASH
YANK

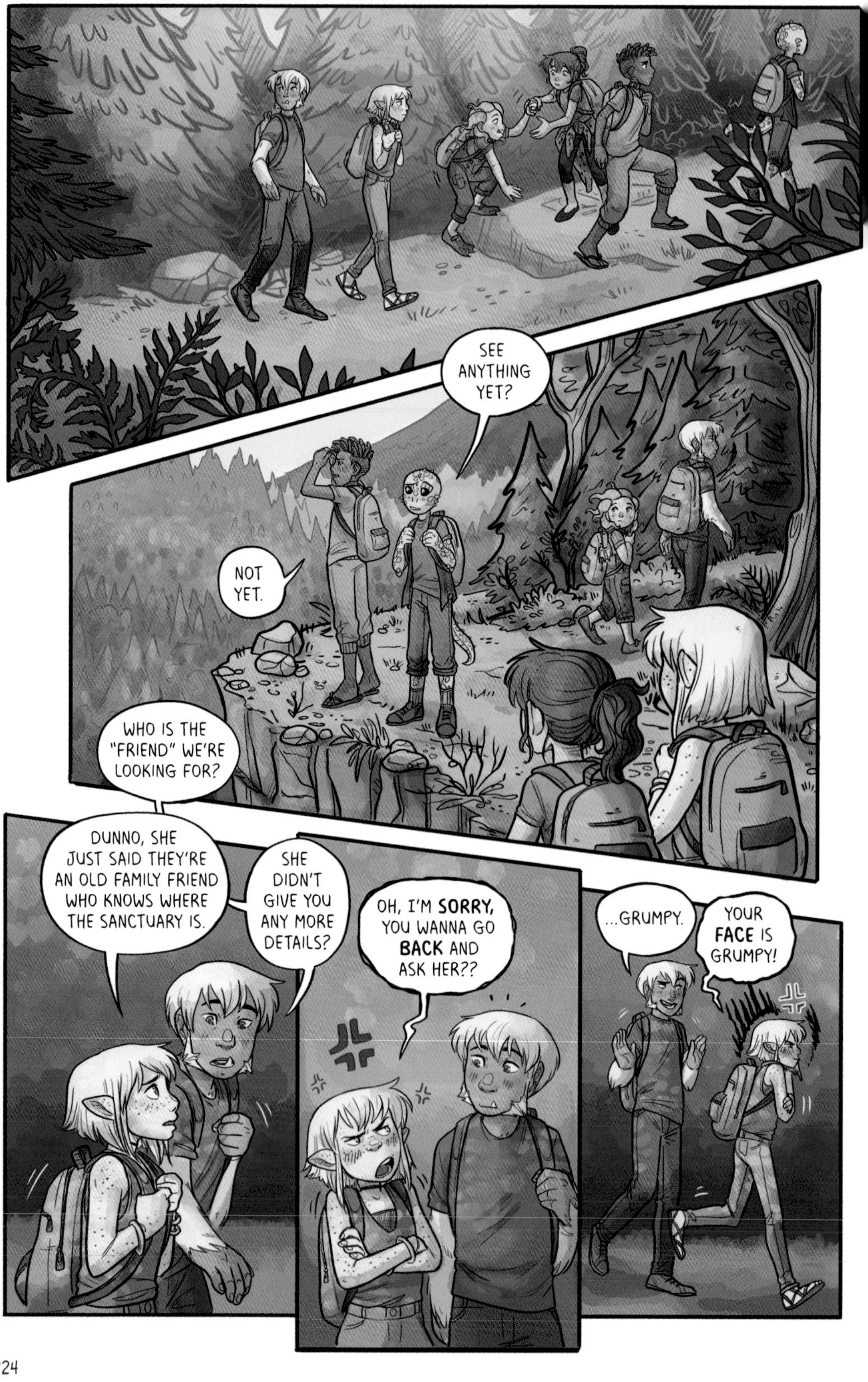
SEE ANYTHING YET?
NOT YET.
WHO IS THE "FRIEND" WE'RE LOOKING FOR?
DUNNO, SHE JUST SAID THEY'RE AN OLD FAMILY FRIEND WHO KNOWS WHERE THE SANCTUARY IS.
SHE DIDN'T GIVE YOU ANY MORE DETAILS?
OH, I'M **SORRY,** YOU WANNA GO **BACK** AND ASK HER??
...GRUMPY.
YOUR **FACE** IS GRUMPY!

SIX IRREGULARITIES, ALL IN MY HOUSE AT ONCE! WHO'DA THUNK, EH?

SO TO WHAT DO I OWE THE PLEASURE?

ALEX ANDERSON SENT US. SHE SAID YOU MIGHT KNOW ABOUT THE SANCTUARY?

WELL UH, MR. BIGFOOT, SIR,

BAH, MORE OF THIS **SANCTUARY** BUSINESS.

EVERYONE COMING THROUGH MY WOODS SEEMS TO WANT TO GET THERE.

YOU KNOW WHERE IT IS?

OH, I KNOW WHERE IT IS, BUT I DON'T TRUST IT FARTHER THAN I COULD THROW IT!

WHY NOT?

IRREGULARITIES GO IN, **NO ONE** EVER COMES OUT!

COULD THAT BE... BECAUSE THEY **LIVE THERE** NOW?

DON'T YOU **SASS** ME, MISSY!

DON'T WORRY, MR. BIGFOOT,

SHE SASSES **EVERYBODY.**

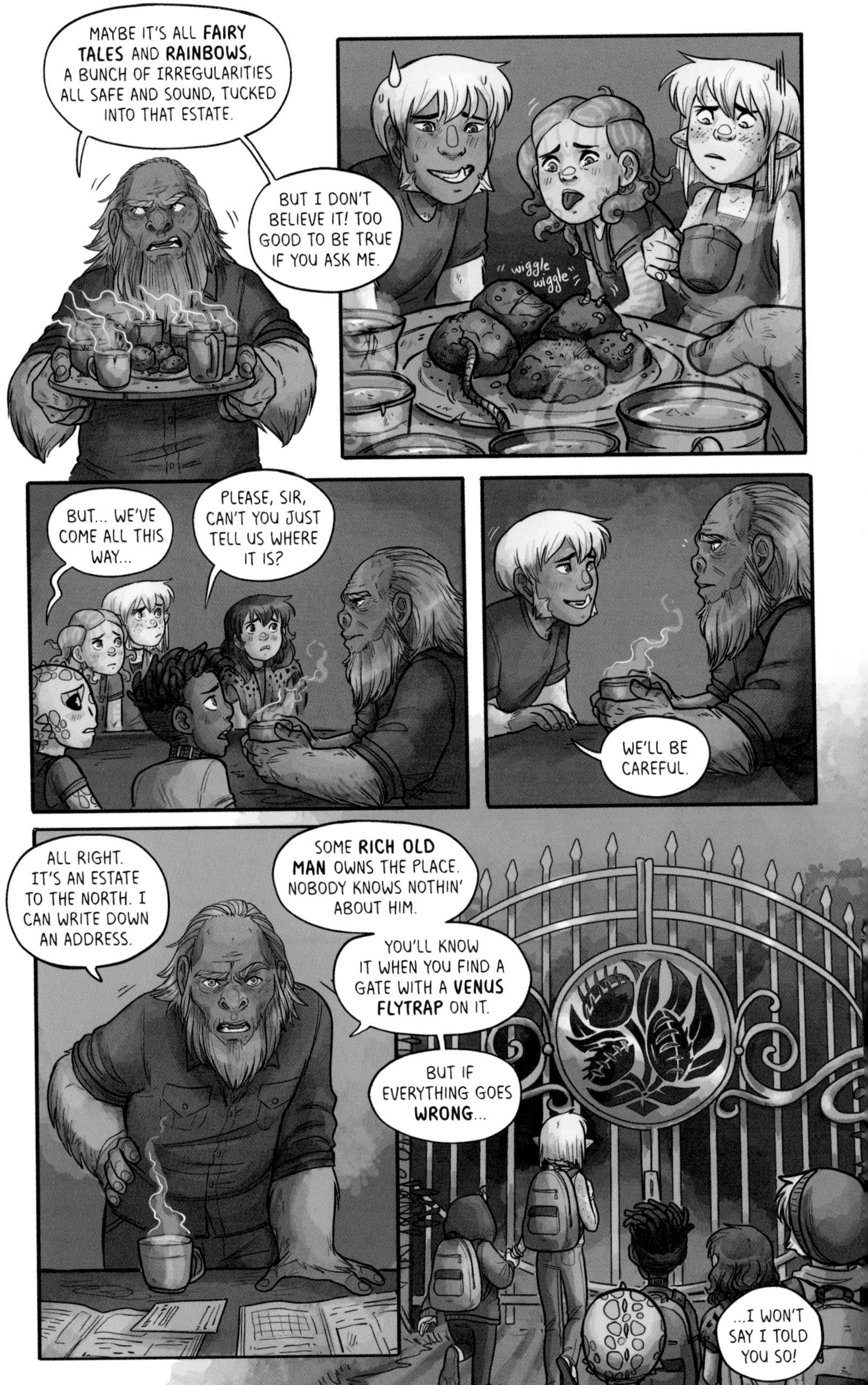
MAYBE IT'S ALL **FAIRY TALES** AND **RAINBOWS**, A BUNCH OF IRREGULARITIES ALL SAFE AND SOUND, TUCKED INTO THAT ESTATE.
BUT I DON'T BELIEVE IT! TOO GOOD TO BE TRUE IF YOU ASK ME.
wiggle wiggle
BUT... WE'VE COME ALL THIS WAY...
PLEASE, SIR, CAN'T YOU JUST TELL US WHERE IT IS?
WE'LL BE CAREFUL.
ALL RIGHT. IT'S AN ESTATE TO THE NORTH. I CAN WRITE DOWN AN ADDRESS.
SOME **RICH OLD MAN** OWNS THE PLACE. NOBODY KNOWS NOTHIN' ABOUT HIM.
YOU'LL KNOW IT WHEN YOU FIND A GATE WITH A **VENUS FLYTRAP** ON IT.
BUT IF EVERYTHING GOES **WRONG**...
...I WON'T SAY I TOLD YOU SO!

CHAPTER NINE

UNRAVELING

GUH! I'M SICK OF WEARING ALL THIS **STUFF**!

IT'S **HOT** AND IT SQUISHES MY **WINGS**!

fumble

WE'VE TALKED ABOUT THIS--NORMAL PEOPLE WOULD **FREAK OUT** IF THEY SAW YOU.

I HAVE TO DO MY HUMAN FACE AND HIDE MY TAIL. WE ALL HAVE TO LOOK HUMAN.

BUT THAT ONE GUY THOUGHT I WAS WEARING A **COSTUME**!

QWIKMART 24/7

I KNOW BUT HE DIDN'T GET A VERY GOOD LOOK AT YOU. WE JUST DON'T WANT TO GET IN TROUBLE OR SENT BACK TO THE PLAYROOM.

BING-BONG

SWIP

SWIP

ONCE WE'RE IN THE SANCTUARY I'M SURE YOU'LL NEVER HAVE TO WEAR IT AGAIN.

...FINE.

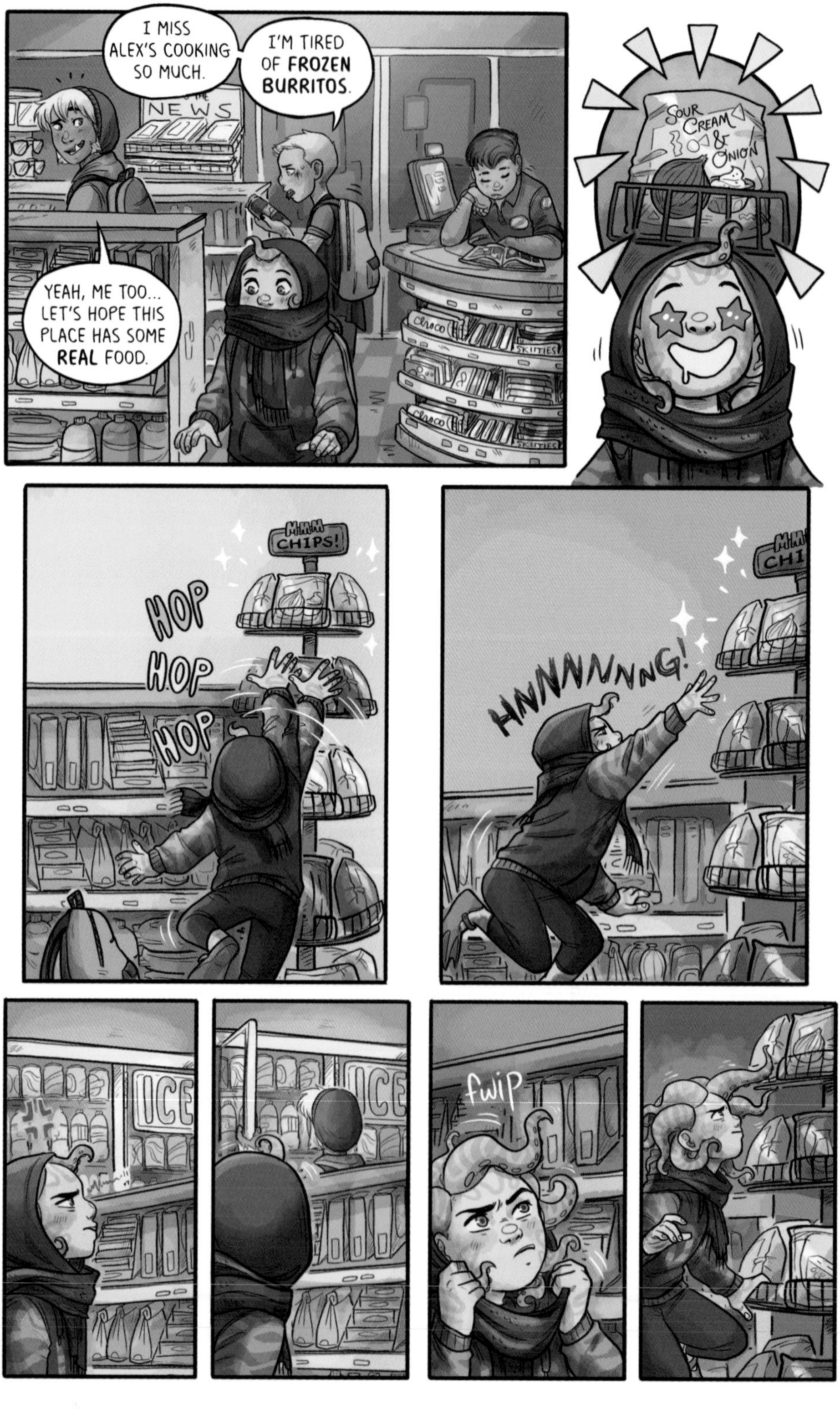
I MISS ALEX'S COOKING SO MUCH.
I'M TIRED OF **FROZEN BURRITOS**.
YEAH, ME TOO... LET'S HOPE THIS PLACE HAS SOME **REAL** FOOD.
NEWS
SOUR CREAM & ONION
CHIPS!
HOP
HOP
HOP
HNNNNNNG!
ICE
fwip

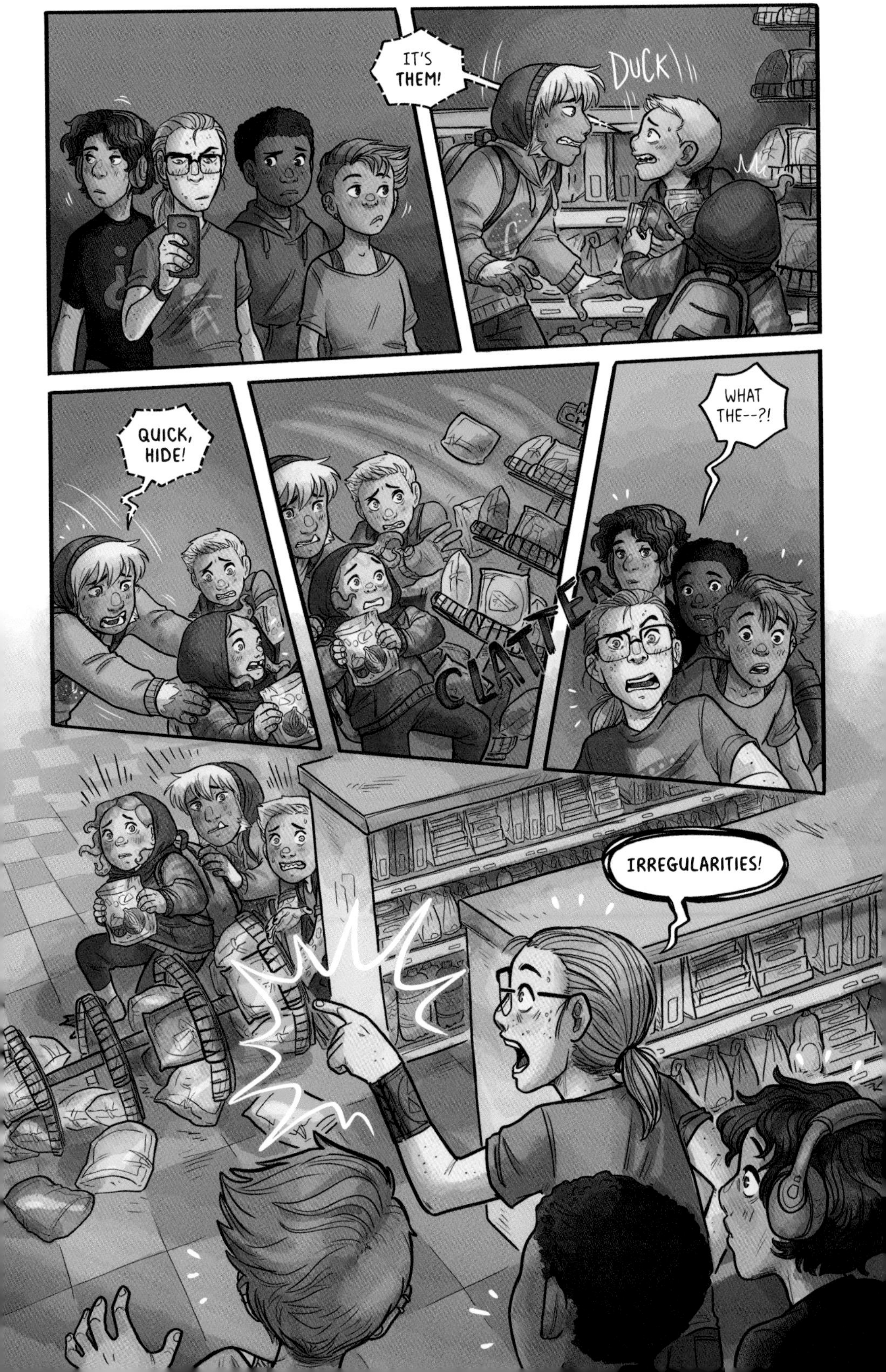
IT'S THEM!
DUCK
QUICK, HIDE!
CLATTER
WHAT THE--?!
IRREGULARITIES!

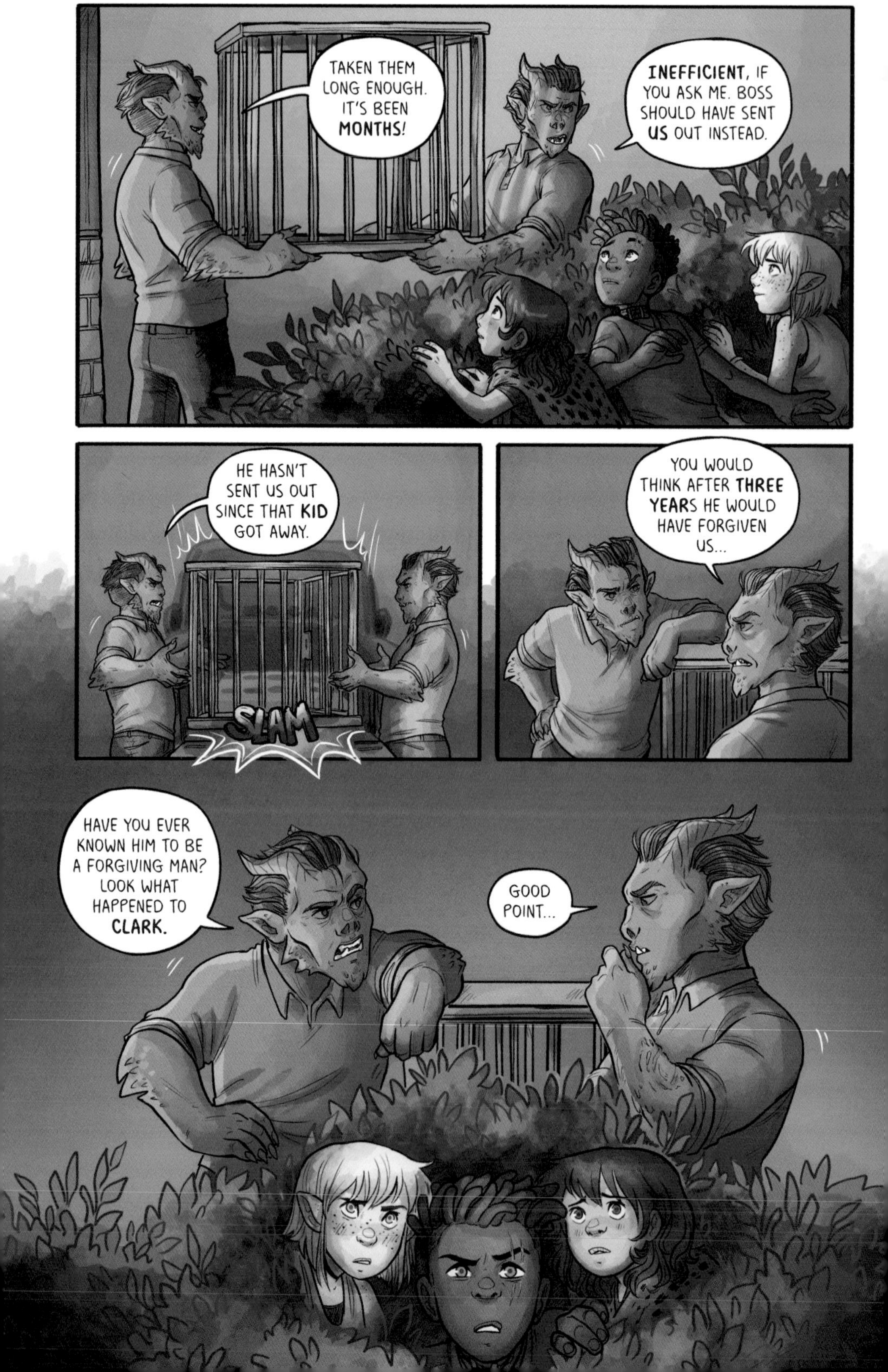
TAKEN THEM LONG ENOUGH. IT'S BEEN **MONTHS**!
INEFFICIENT, IF YOU ASK ME. BOSS SHOULD HAVE SENT **US** OUT INSTEAD.
HE HASN'T SENT US OUT SINCE THAT **KID** GOT AWAY.
SLAM
YOU WOULD THINK AFTER **THREE YEAR**S HE WOULD HAVE FORGIVEN US...
HAVE YOU EVER KNOWN HIM TO BE A FORGIVING MAN? LOOK WHAT HAPPENED TO **CLARK**.
GOOD POINT...

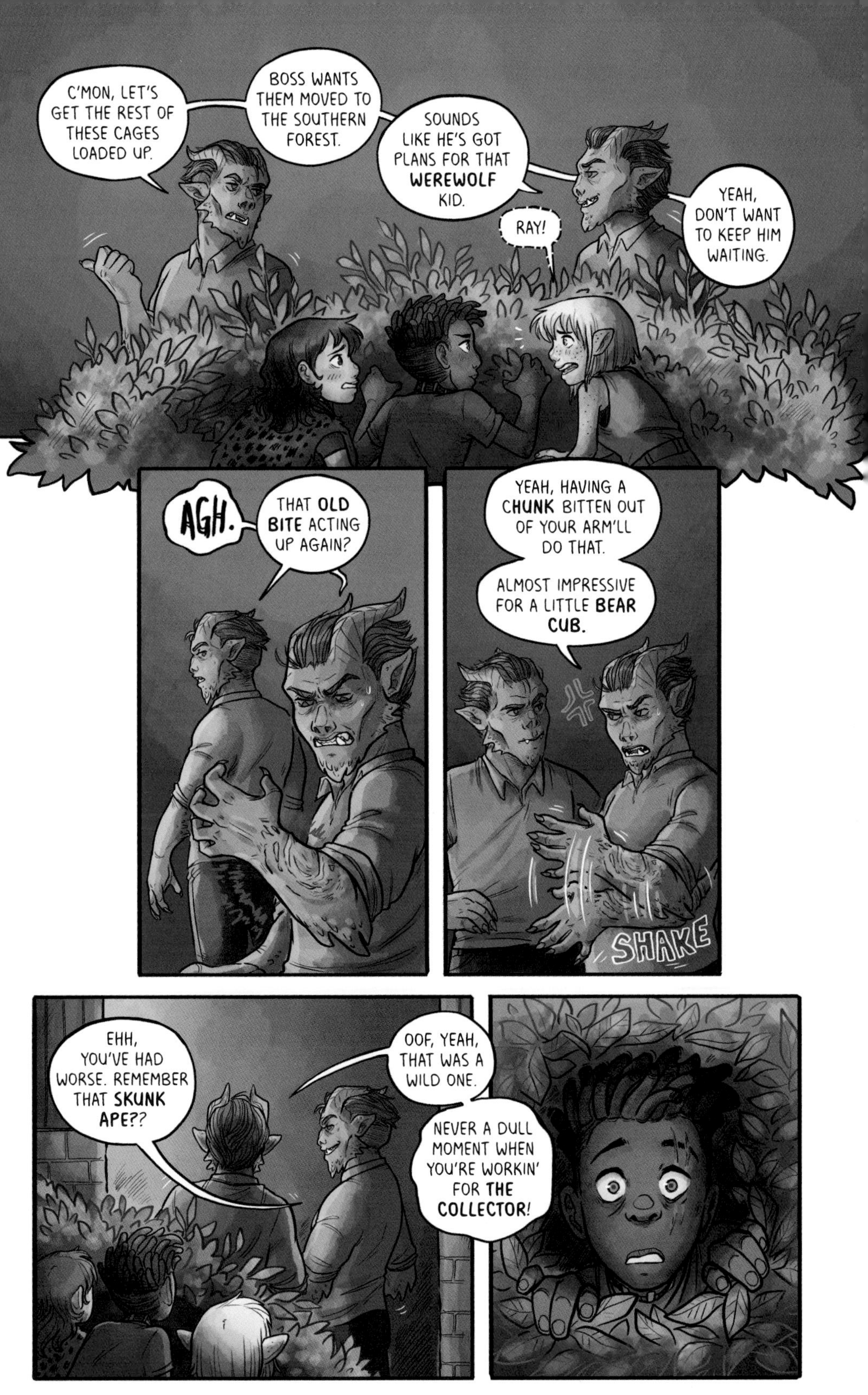
C'MON, LET'S GET THE REST OF THESE CAGES LOADED UP.
BOSS WANTS THEM MOVED TO THE SOUTHERN FOREST.
SOUNDS LIKE HE'S GOT PLANS FOR THAT **WEREWOLF** KID.
YEAH, DON'T WANT TO KEEP HIM WAITING.
RAY!
AGH.
THAT **OLD BITE** ACTING UP AGAIN?
YEAH, HAVING A **CHUNK** BITTEN OUT OF YOUR ARM'LL DO THAT.
ALMOST IMPRESSIVE FOR A LITTLE **BEAR CUB.**
SHAKE
EHH, YOU'VE HAD WORSE. REMEMBER THAT **SKUNK APE**??
OOF, YEAH, THAT WAS A WILD ONE.
NEVER A DULL MOMENT WHEN YOU'RE WORKIN' FOR **THE COLLECTOR**!

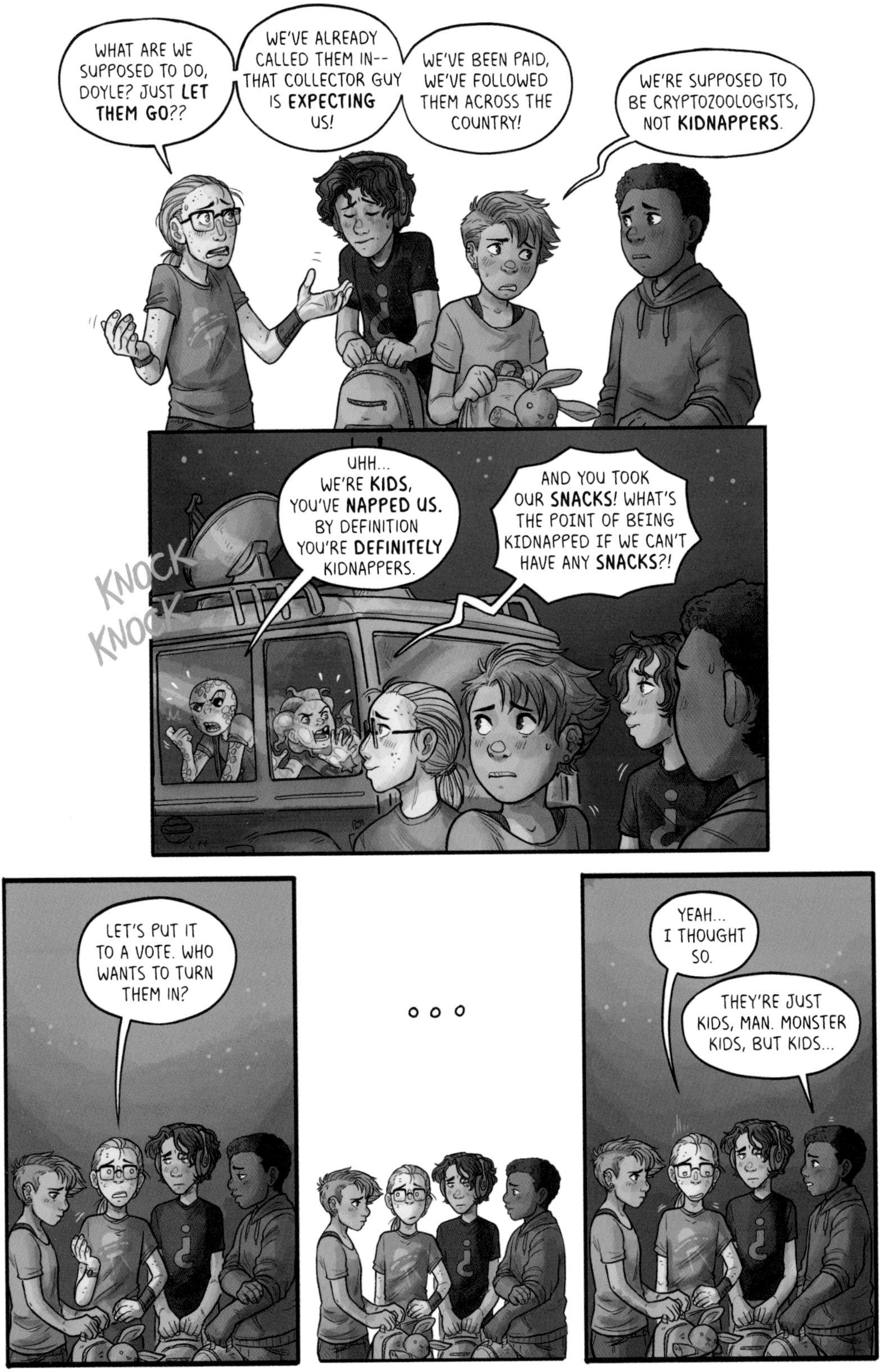
WHAT ARE WE SUPPOSED TO DO, DOYLE? JUST LET THEM GO??
WE'VE ALREADY CALLED THEM IN-- THAT COLLECTOR GUY IS EXPECTING US!
WE'VE BEEN PAID, WE'VE FOLLOWED THEM ACROSS THE COUNTRY!
WE'RE SUPPOSED TO BE CRYPTOZOOLOGISTS, NOT KIDNAPPERS.
KNOCK KNOCK
UHH... WE'RE KIDS, YOU'VE NAPPED US. BY DEFINITION YOU'RE DEFINITELY KIDNAPPERS.
AND YOU TOOK OUR SNACKS! WHAT'S THE POINT OF BEING KIDNAPPED IF WE CAN'T HAVE ANY SNACKS?!
LET'S PUT IT TO A VOTE. WHO WANTS TO TURN THEM IN?
...
YEAH... I THOUGHT SO.
THEY'RE JUST KIDS, MAN. MONSTER KIDS, BUT KIDS...

HEY... WE WANNA TALK.

SLIDE

snatch

ARE YOU GONNA **LET** US GO??

LISTEN, SORRY ABOUT ALL THIS... WE'RE JUST TRYING TO DO WHAT WE WERE **PAID** FOR.

CRONCH

WHO WOULD PAY YOU TO **STALK AND KIDNAP** A BUNCH OF **KIDS**?!

WE DIDN'T **KNOW** YOU WERE KIDS!! WE JUST THOUGHT... I DUNNO. YOU WERE SOME KIND OF **INTELLIGENT HUMANOIDS**? WHICH, UH, YOU **ARE**! I MEAN, YOU'RE **WAY** MORE HUMAN THAN WE THOUGHT YOU'D BE?? OR IS THAT **INSULTING**? CRAP--

WAY TO GO, BEN.

...SORRY.

WE KNEW YOU'D HAVE TO BE **INTELLIGENT**, OBVIOUSLY. YOU COULD USE OUR **TECHNOLOGY**.

WHAT DO YOU MEAN?

WE TRACKED YOU BY **TRIANGULATING** THE SIGNAL FROM AN **O-PAD**.

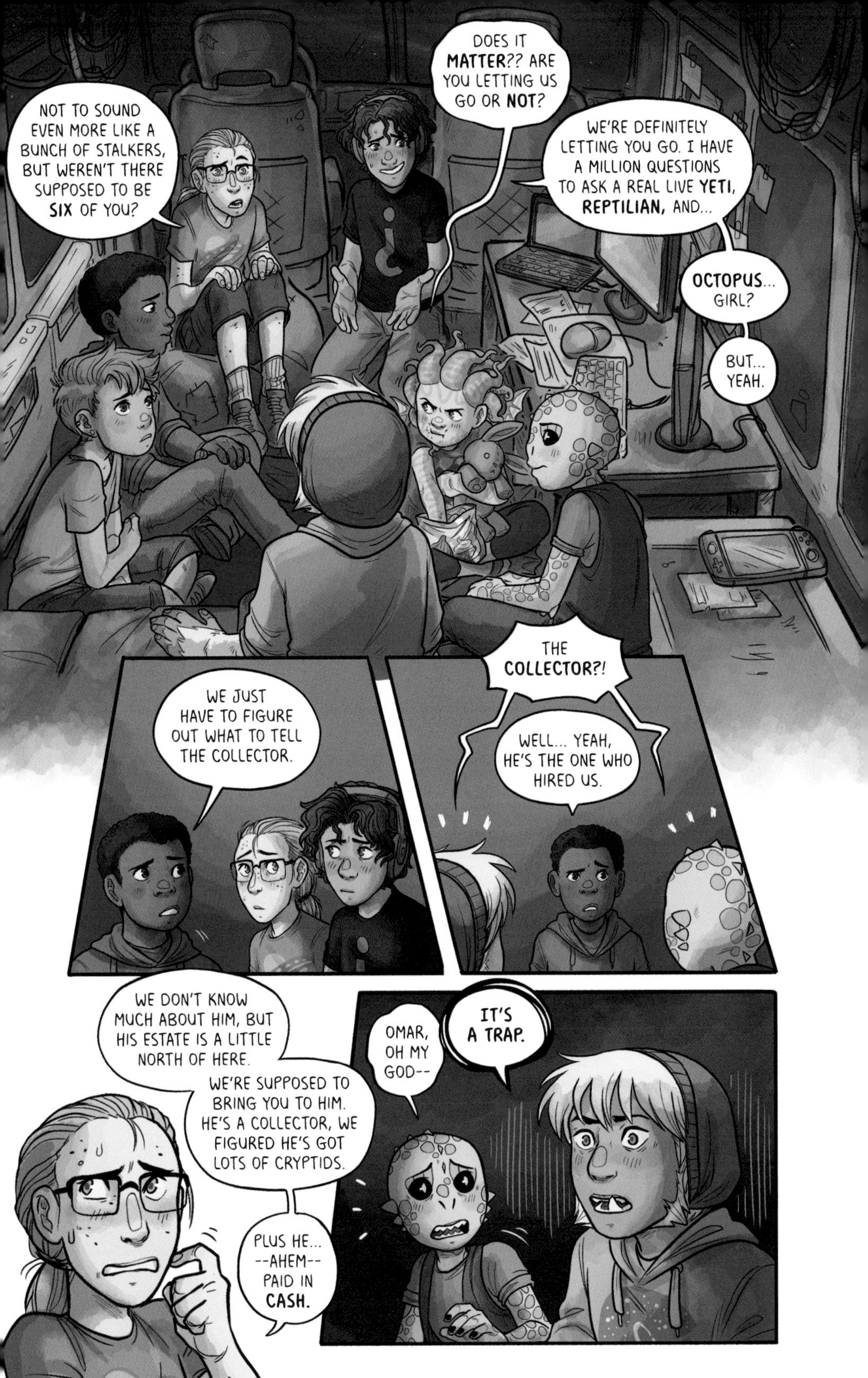

NOT TO SOUND EVEN MORE LIKE A BUNCH OF STALKERS, BUT WEREN'T THERE SUPPOSED TO BE SIX OF YOU?
DOES IT MATTER?? ARE YOU LETTING US GO OR NOT?
WE'RE DEFINITELY LETTING YOU GO. I HAVE A MILLION QUESTIONS TO ASK A REAL LIVE YETI, REPTILIAN, AND...
OCTOPUS... GIRL?
BUT... YEAH.
WE JUST HAVE TO FIGURE OUT WHAT TO TELL THE COLLECTOR.
THE COLLECTOR?!
WELL... YEAH, HE'S THE ONE WHO HIRED US.
WE DON'T KNOW MUCH ABOUT HIM, BUT HIS ESTATE IS A LITTLE NORTH OF HERE.
WE'RE SUPPOSED TO BRING YOU TO HIM. HE'S A COLLECTOR, WE FIGURED HE'S GOT LOTS OF CRYPTIDS.
PLUS HE... --AHEM-- PAID IN CASH.
OMAR, OH MY GOD--
IT'S A TRAP.

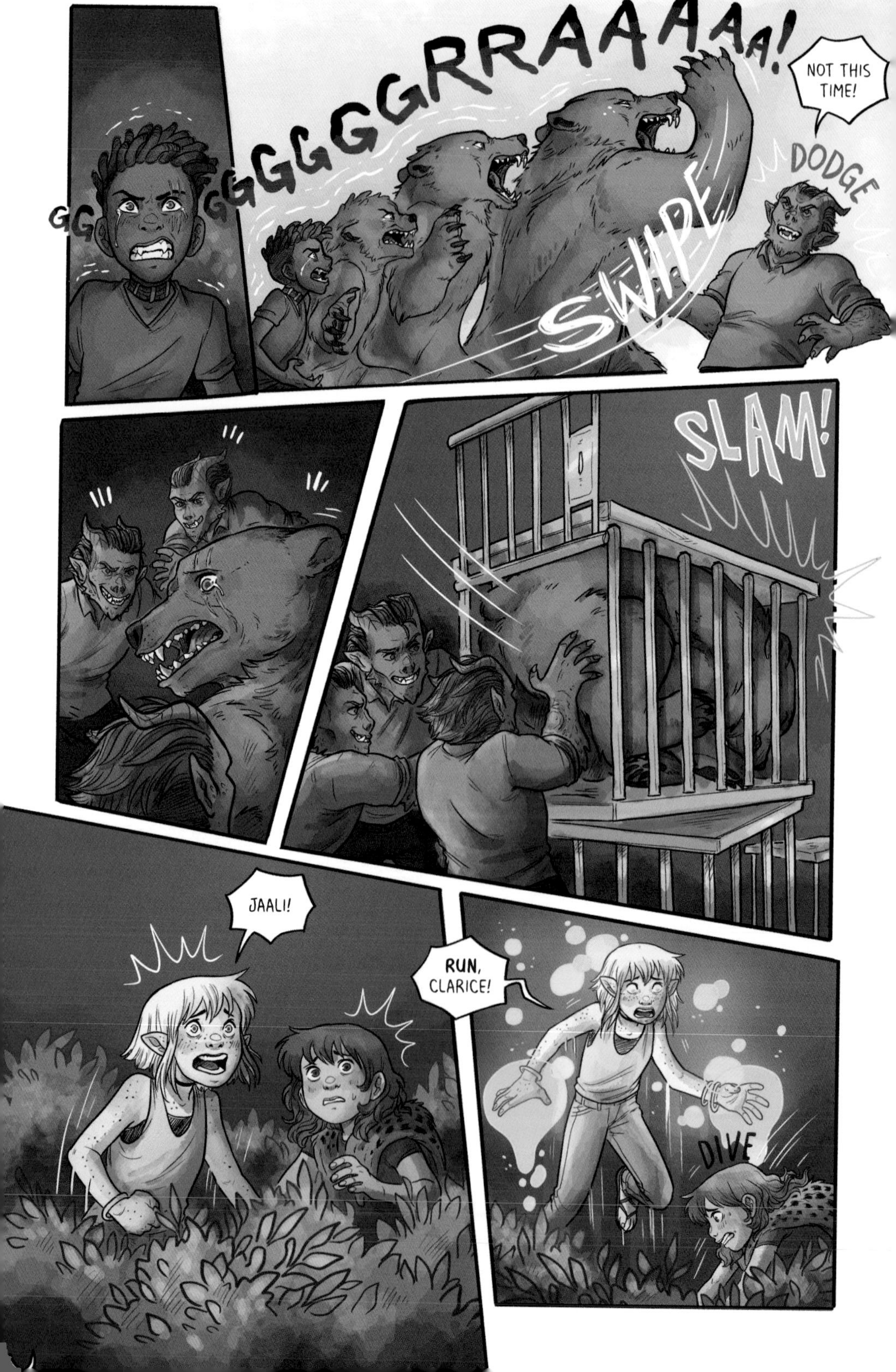
GGGGGGGRRAAAAAA!
NOT THIS TIME!
SWIPE
DODGE
SLAM!
JAALI!
RUN, CLARICE!
DIVE

LET ME GET THIS STRAIGHT.

YOU'VE BEEN ON THE RUN FOR WEEKS BECAUSE YOU ESCAPED **AREA 51**--

CONTAINMENT 9, ACTUALLY, BUT YEAH, IT'S THE SAME THING.

AND YOU HEARD ABOUT THIS SANCTUARY FOR IRREGULARITIES, BUT IT TURNS OUT IT'S A **TRAP**...

...SET BY THE COLLECTOR--**OUR BOSS**--WHO IS ACTUALLY CAPTURING CREATURES LIKE YOU AGAINST THEIR WILL??

AND NOW OUR FRIENDS ARE IN DANGER. THEY LEFT TO SCOUT OUT THE ESTATE.

WHAT THE--?

THAT'S MY O-PAD!

BiNG!

OH.. UH, RIGHT, SORRY.

OH NO...

IT MIGHT ALREADY BE **TOO LATE!**

✉ HELKP; TRAP WERR CAGUHT HFELP

CHAPTER TEN

HOME

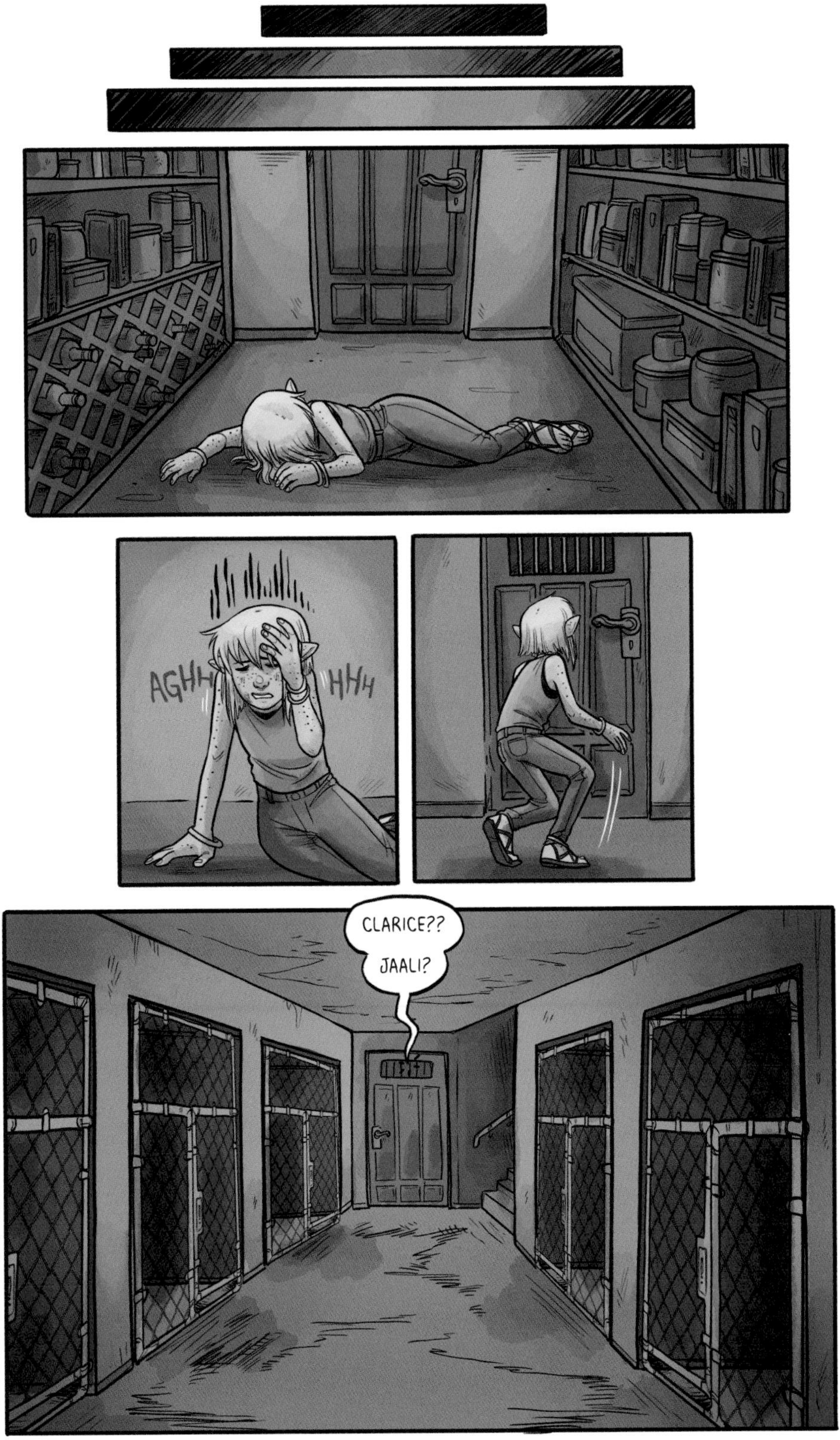
AGHHHHH
CLARICE??
JAALI?

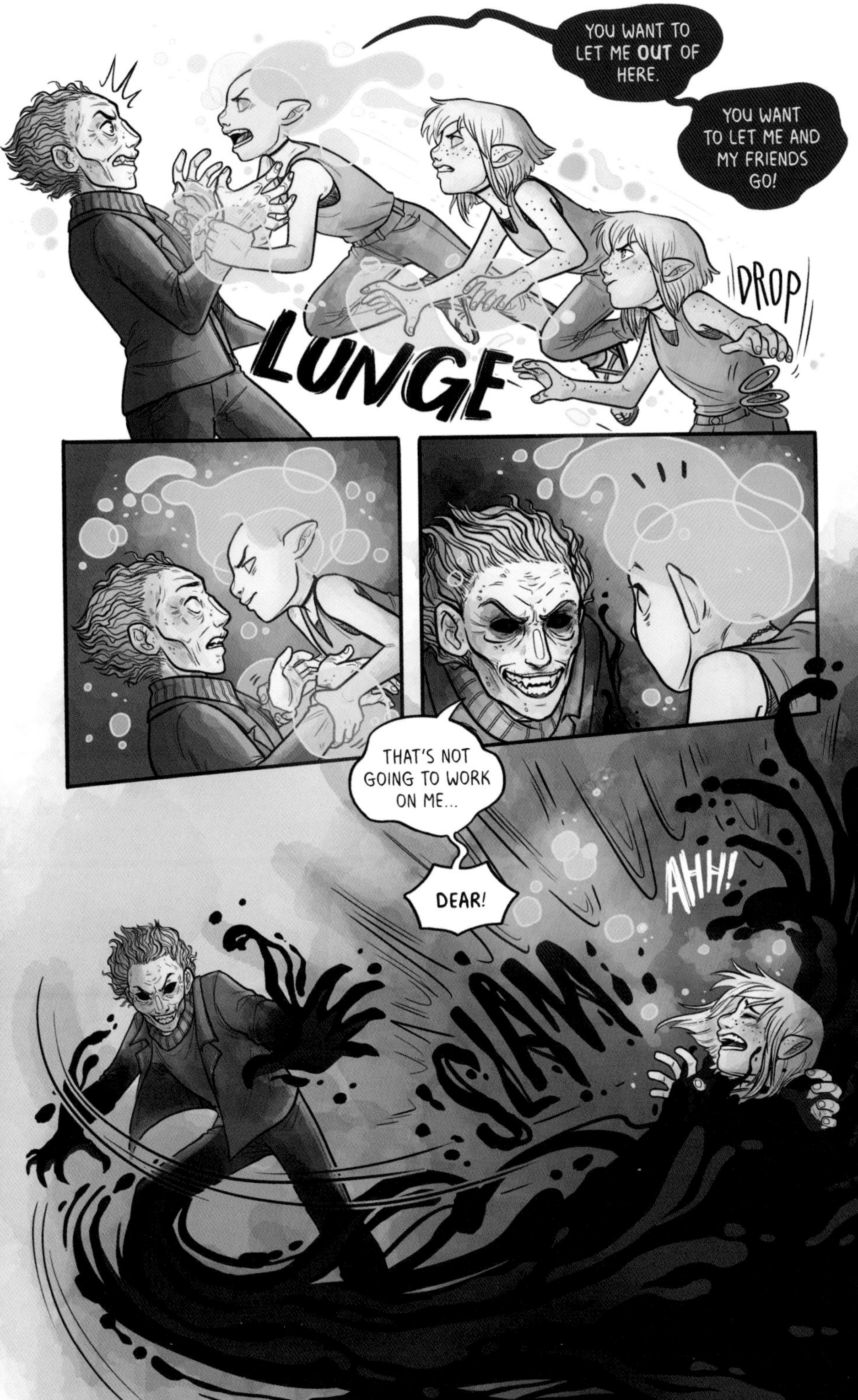
YOU WANT TO LET ME **OUT** OF HERE.
YOU WANT TO LET ME AND MY FRIENDS GO!
LUNGE
DROP
THAT'S NOT GOING TO WORK ON ME...
DEAR!
AHH!
SLAM!

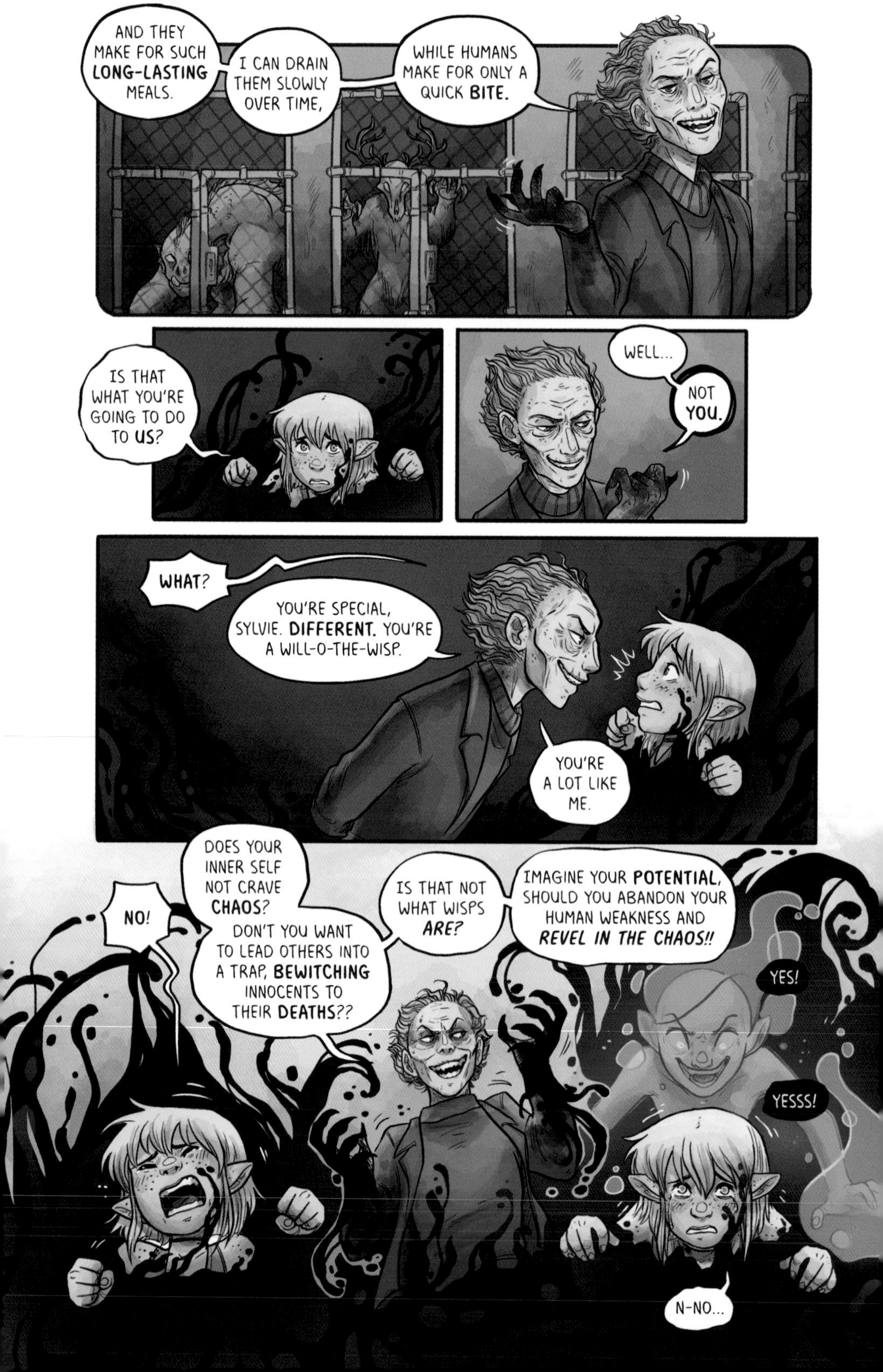
AND THEY MAKE FOR SUCH **LONG-LASTING** MEALS.
I CAN DRAIN THEM SLOWLY OVER TIME,
WHILE HUMANS MAKE FOR ONLY A QUICK **BITE.**
IS THAT WHAT YOU'RE GOING TO DO TO **US**?
WELL...
NOT **YOU.**
WHAT?
YOU'RE SPECIAL, SYLVIE. **DIFFERENT.** YOU'RE A WILL-O-THE-WISP.
YOU'RE A LOT LIKE ME.
NO!
DOES YOUR INNER SELF NOT CRAVE **CHAOS**?
DON'T YOU WANT TO LEAD OTHERS INTO A TRAP, **BEWITCHING** INNOCENTS TO THEIR **DEATHS**??
IS THAT NOT WHAT WISPS ***ARE?***
IMAGINE YOUR **POTENTIAL**, SHOULD YOU ABANDON YOUR HUMAN WEAKNESS AND ***REVEL IN THE CHAOS!!***
YES!
YESSS!
N-NO...

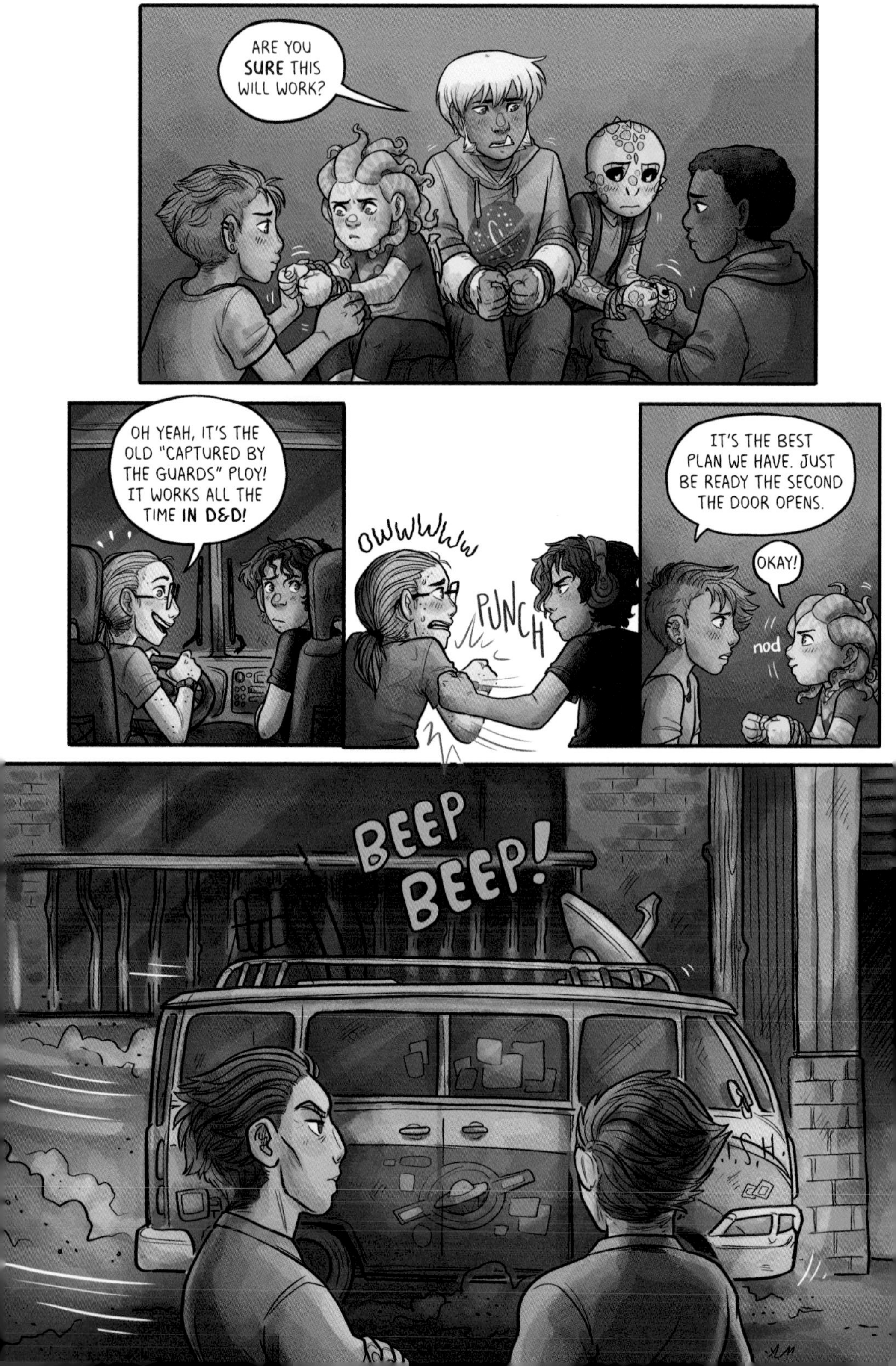
ARE YOU SURE THIS WILL WORK?
OH YEAH, IT'S THE OLD "CAPTURED BY THE GUARDS" PLOY! IT WORKS ALL THE TIME IN D&D!
OWWWWW
PUNCH
IT'S THE BEST PLAN WE HAVE. JUST BE READY THE SECOND THE DOOR OPENS.
OKAY!
nod
BEEP BEEP!

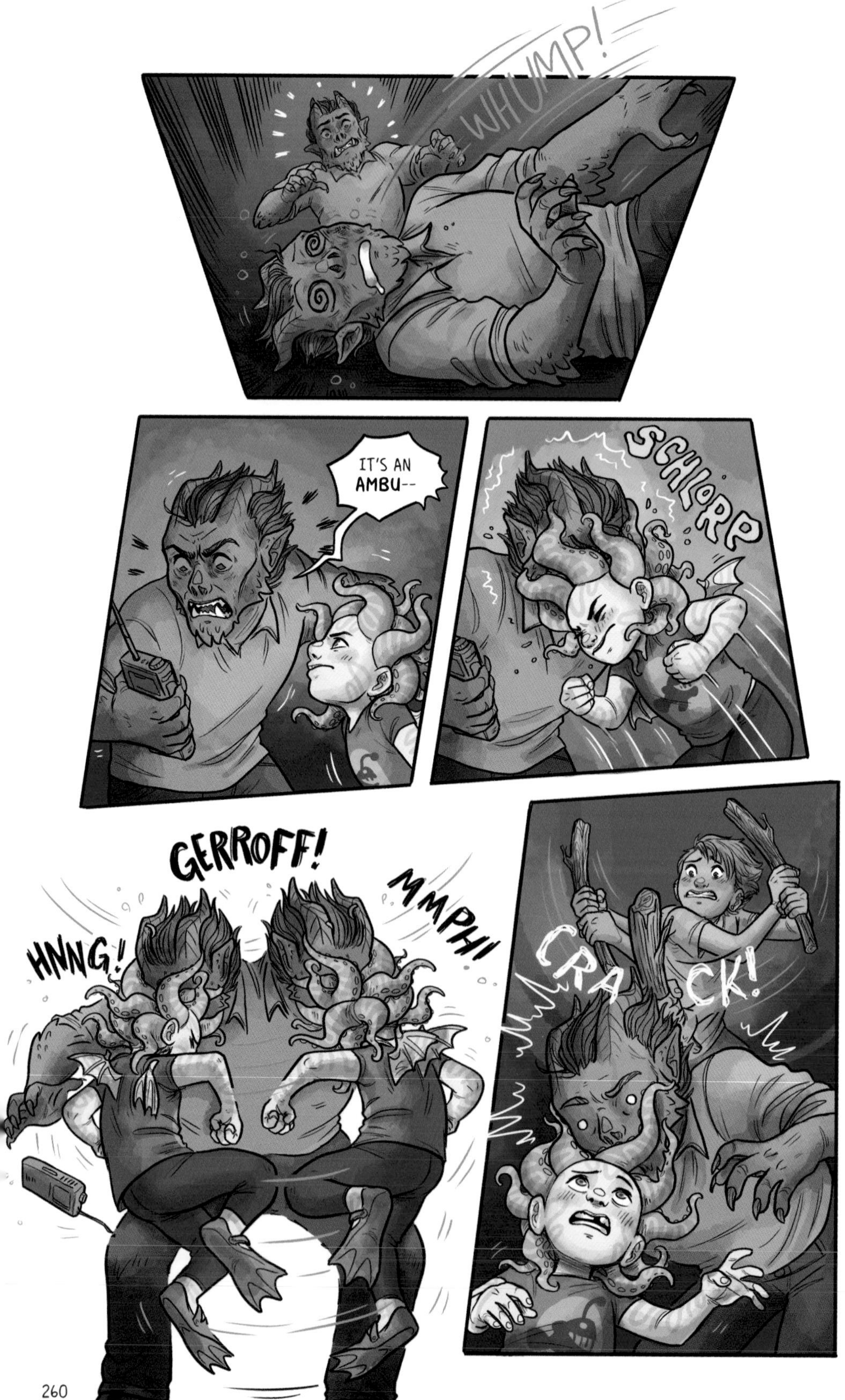
WHUMP!
IT'S AN AMBU--
SCHLORP
GERROFF!
MMPH!
HNNG!
CRACK!

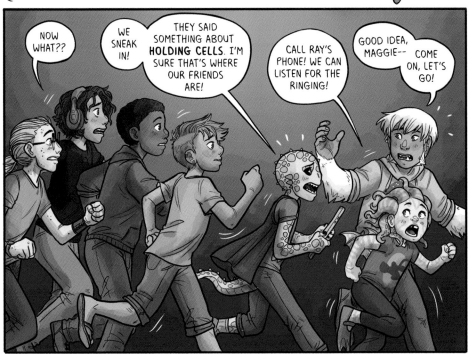

262

HOW DID YOU GUYS GET IN??

WE HAD SOME HELP FROM OUR NEW FRIENDS.

HIIIII...

EH HEH...

IT'S THE SQUATCH GUYS!!

IT'S OKAY! THEY'RE OUR FRIENDS NOW!

SORRY ABOUT THE WHOLE... STALKING... THING...

WAIT, WHERE'S SYLVIE?

SHE'S BETRAYED US.

SHE LEFT TO JOIN THE COLLECTOR.

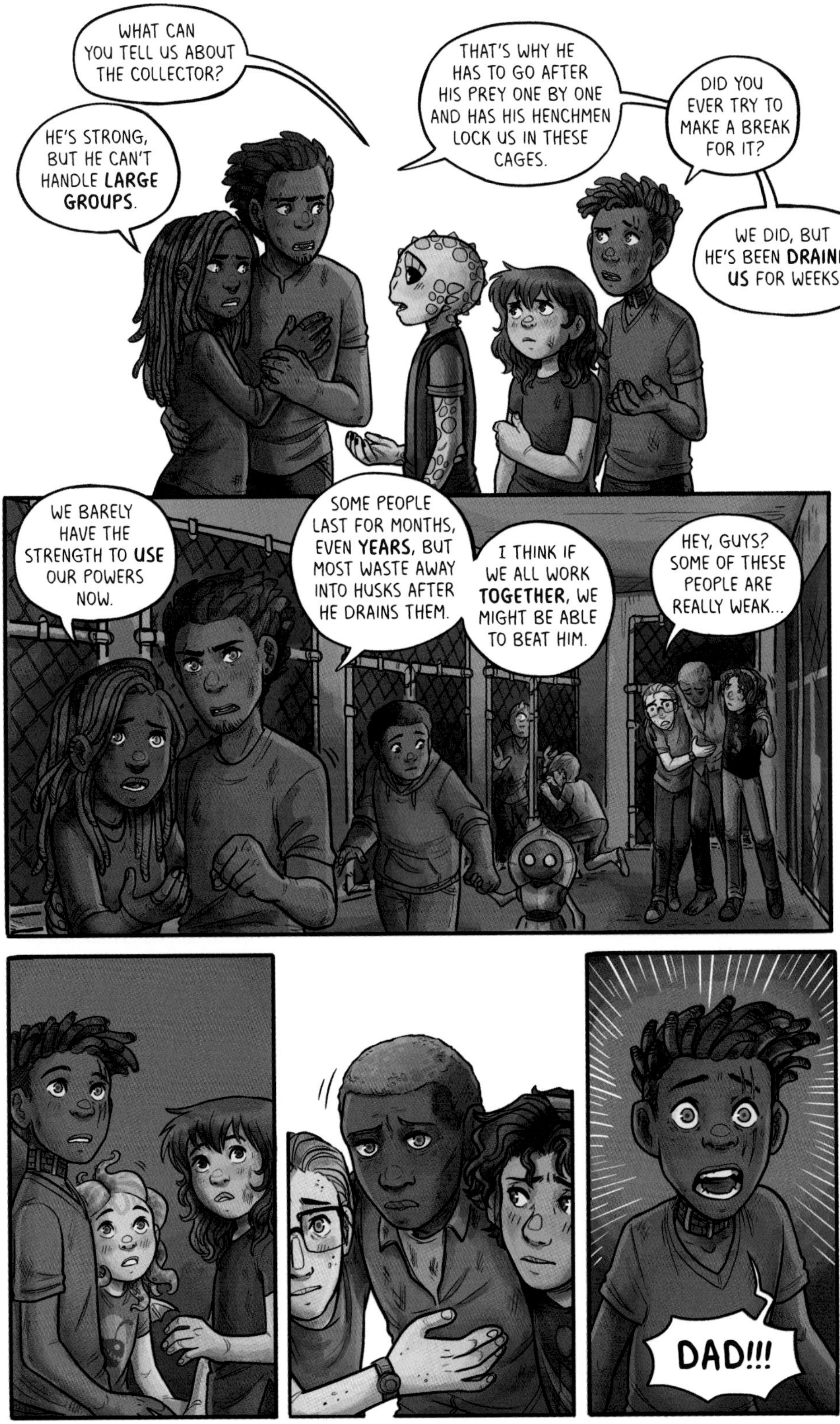
WHAT CAN YOU TELL US ABOUT THE COLLECTOR?
HE'S STRONG, BUT HE CAN'T HANDLE LARGE GROUPS.
THAT'S WHY HE HAS TO GO AFTER HIS PREY ONE BY ONE AND HAS HIS HENCHMEN LOCK US IN THESE CAGES.
DID YOU EVER TRY TO MAKE A BREAK FOR IT?
WE DID, BUT HE'S BEEN DRAINING US FOR WEEKS.
WE BARELY HAVE THE STRENGTH TO USE OUR POWERS NOW.
SOME PEOPLE LAST FOR MONTHS, EVEN YEARS, BUT MOST WASTE AWAY INTO HUSKS AFTER HE DRAINS THEM.
I THINK IF WE ALL WORK TOGETHER, WE MIGHT BE ABLE TO BEAT HIM.
HEY, GUYS? SOME OF THESE PEOPLE ARE REALLY WEAK...
DAD!!!

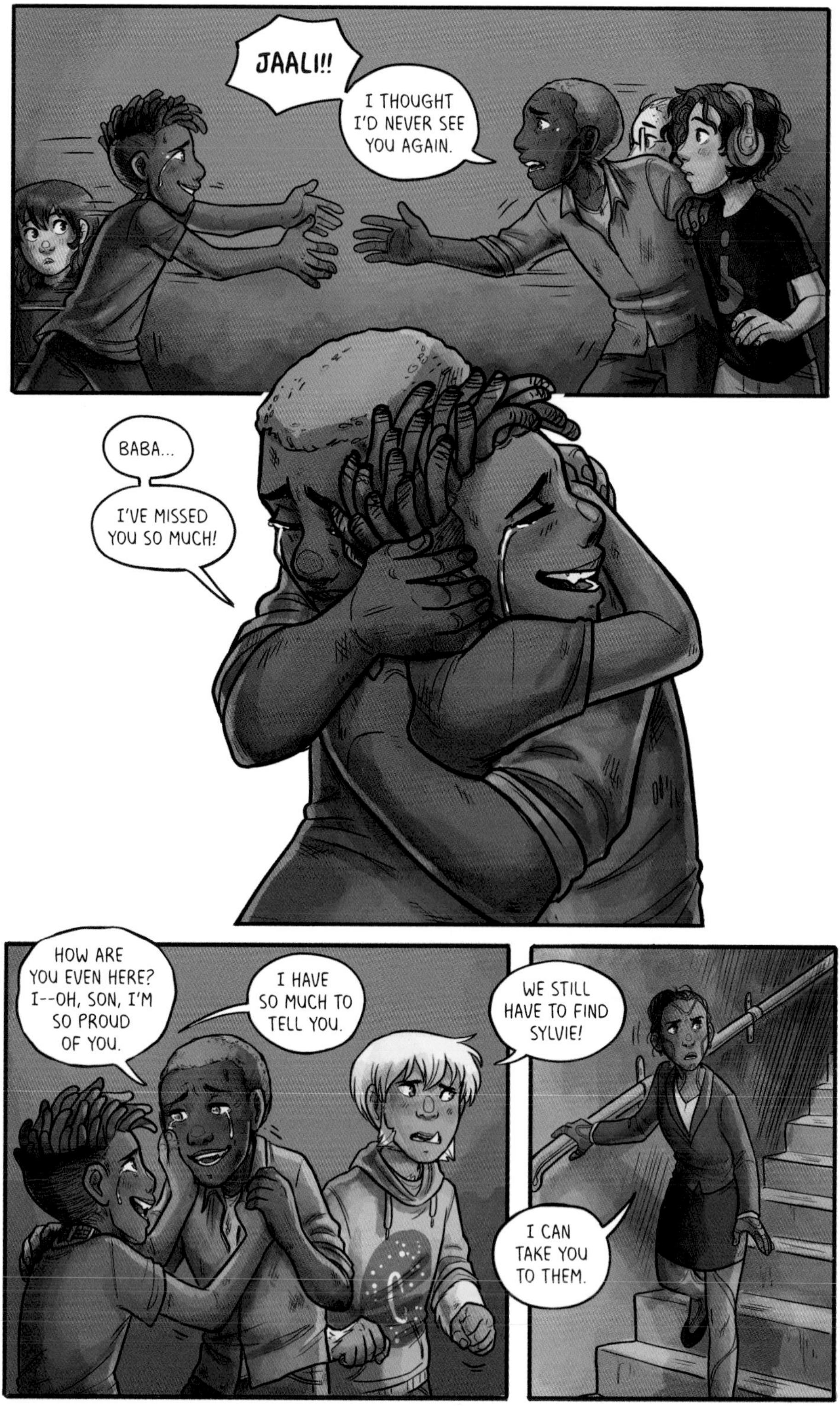
JAALI!!
I THOUGHT I'D NEVER SEE YOU AGAIN.
BABA...
I'VE MISSED YOU SO MUCH!
HOW ARE YOU EVEN HERE? I--OH, SON, I'M SO PROUD OF YOU.
I HAVE SO MUCH TO TELL YOU.
WE STILL HAVE TO FIND SYLVIE!
I CAN TAKE YOU TO THEM.

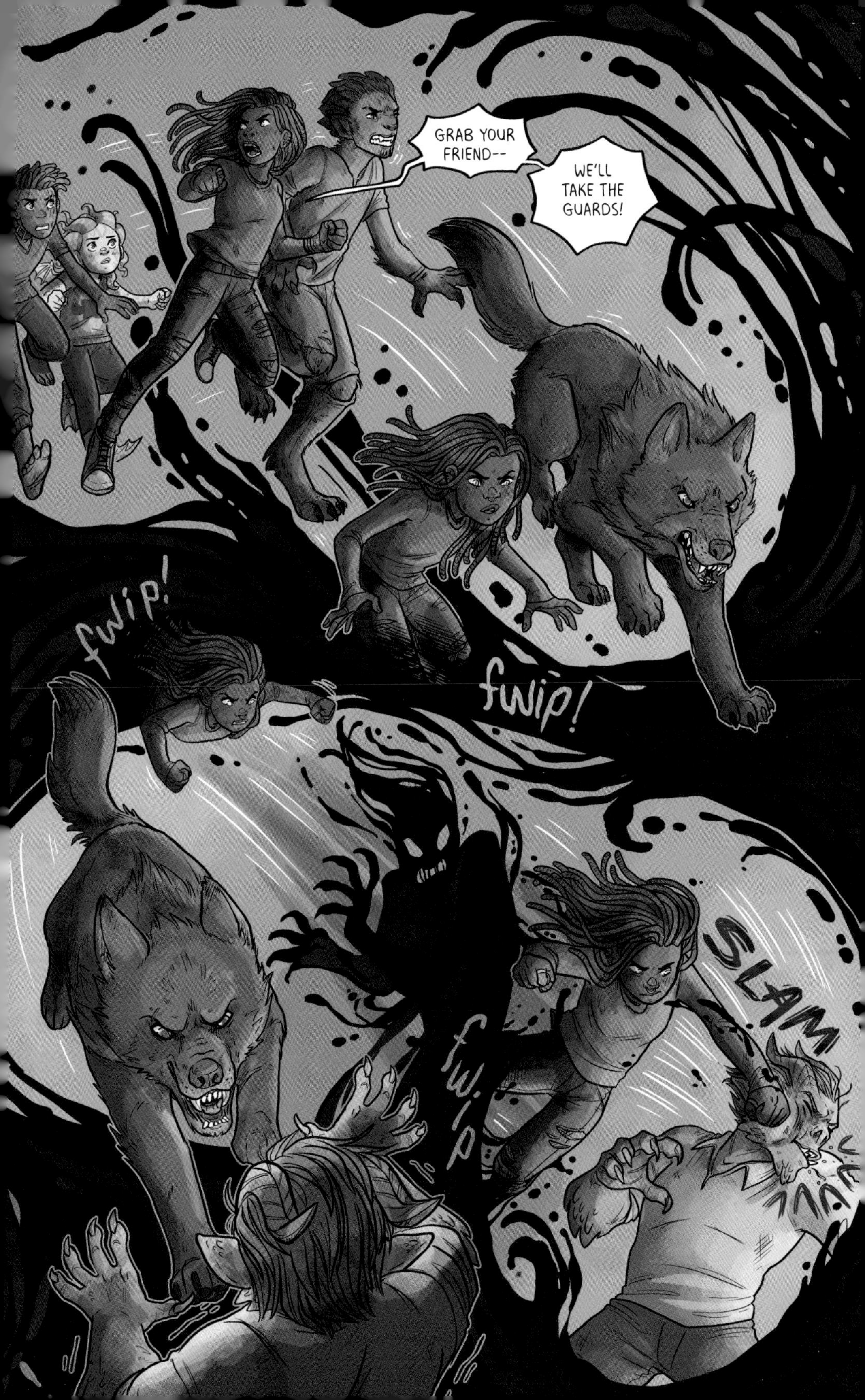
GRAB YOUR FRIEND--
WE'LL TAKE THE GUARDS!
fwip!
fwip!
fwip
SLAM

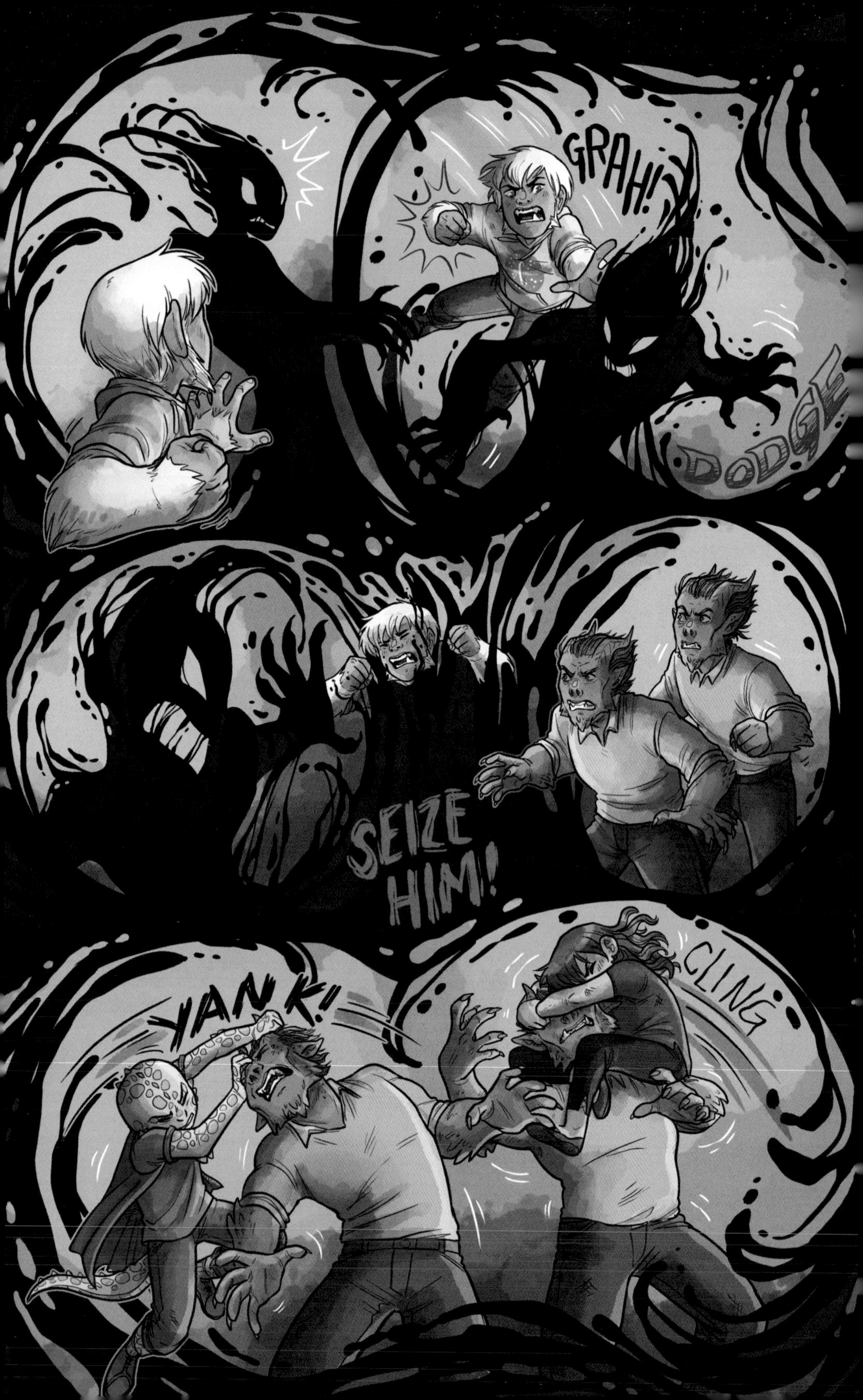
GRAH!
DODGE
SEIZE HIM!
YANK!
CLING

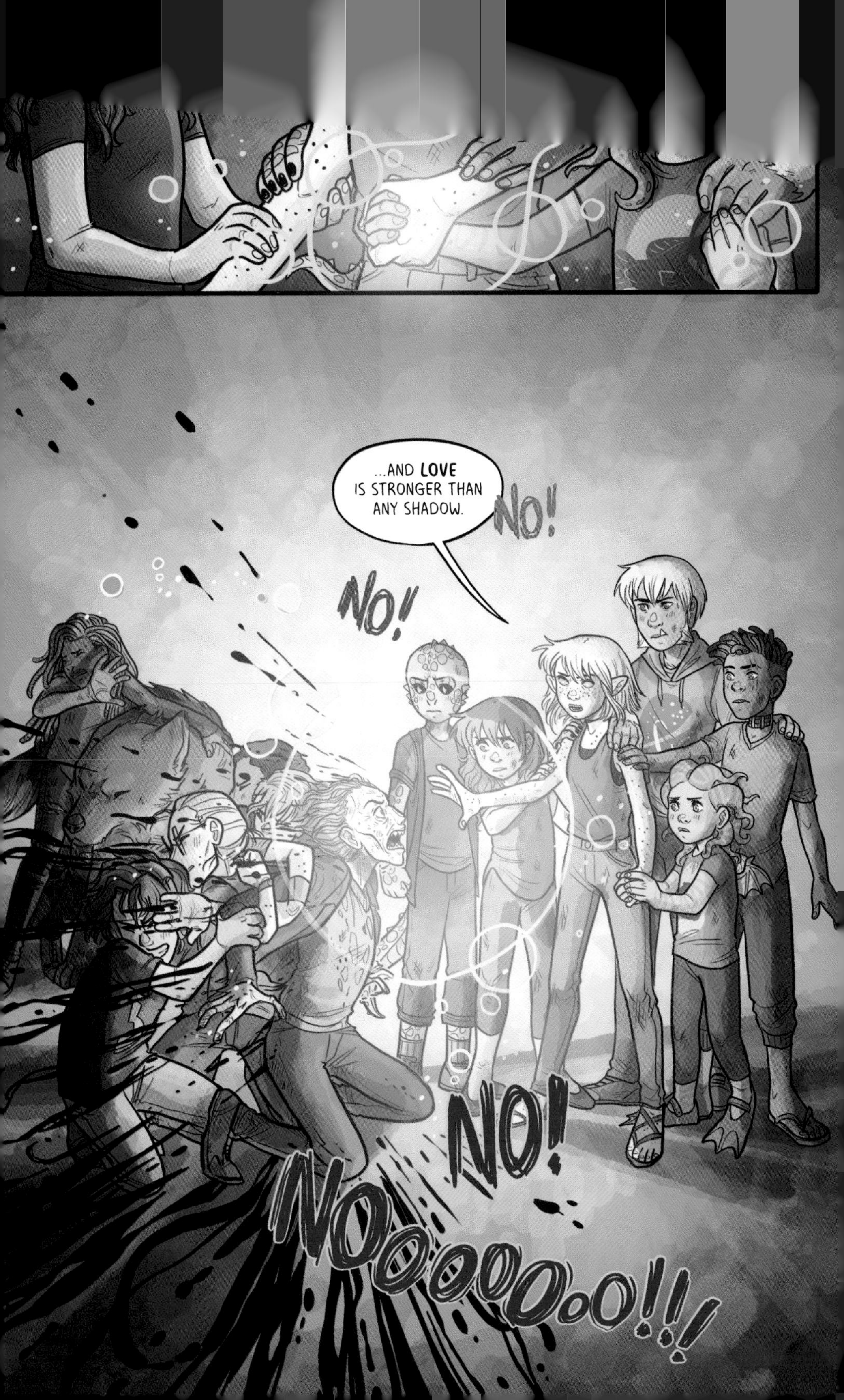
...AND **LOVE** IS STRONGER THAN ANY SHADOW.
NO!
NO!
NO!
NOOOOOOoO!!!

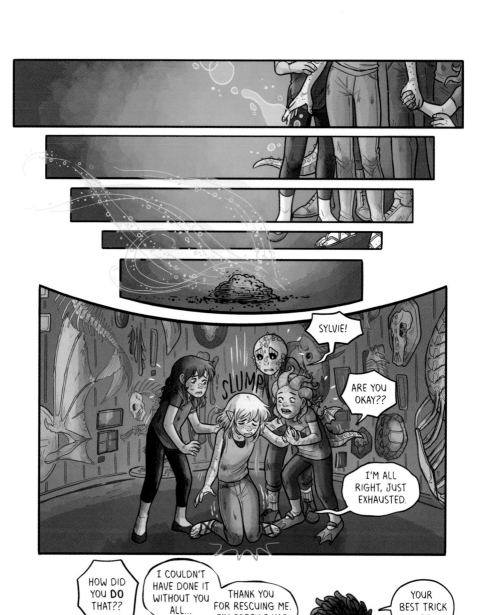

SYLVIE!

ARE YOU OKAY??

SLUMP

I'M ALL RIGHT, JUST EXHAUSTED.

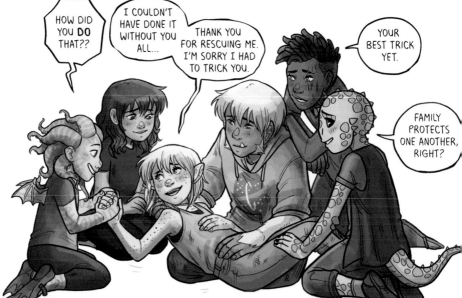

HOW DID YOU **DO** THAT??

I COULDN'T HAVE DONE IT WITHOUT YOU ALL...

THANK YOU FOR RESCUING ME. I'M SORRY I HAD TO TRICK YOU.

YOUR BEST TRICK YET.

FAMILY PROTECTS ONE ANOTHER, RIGHT?

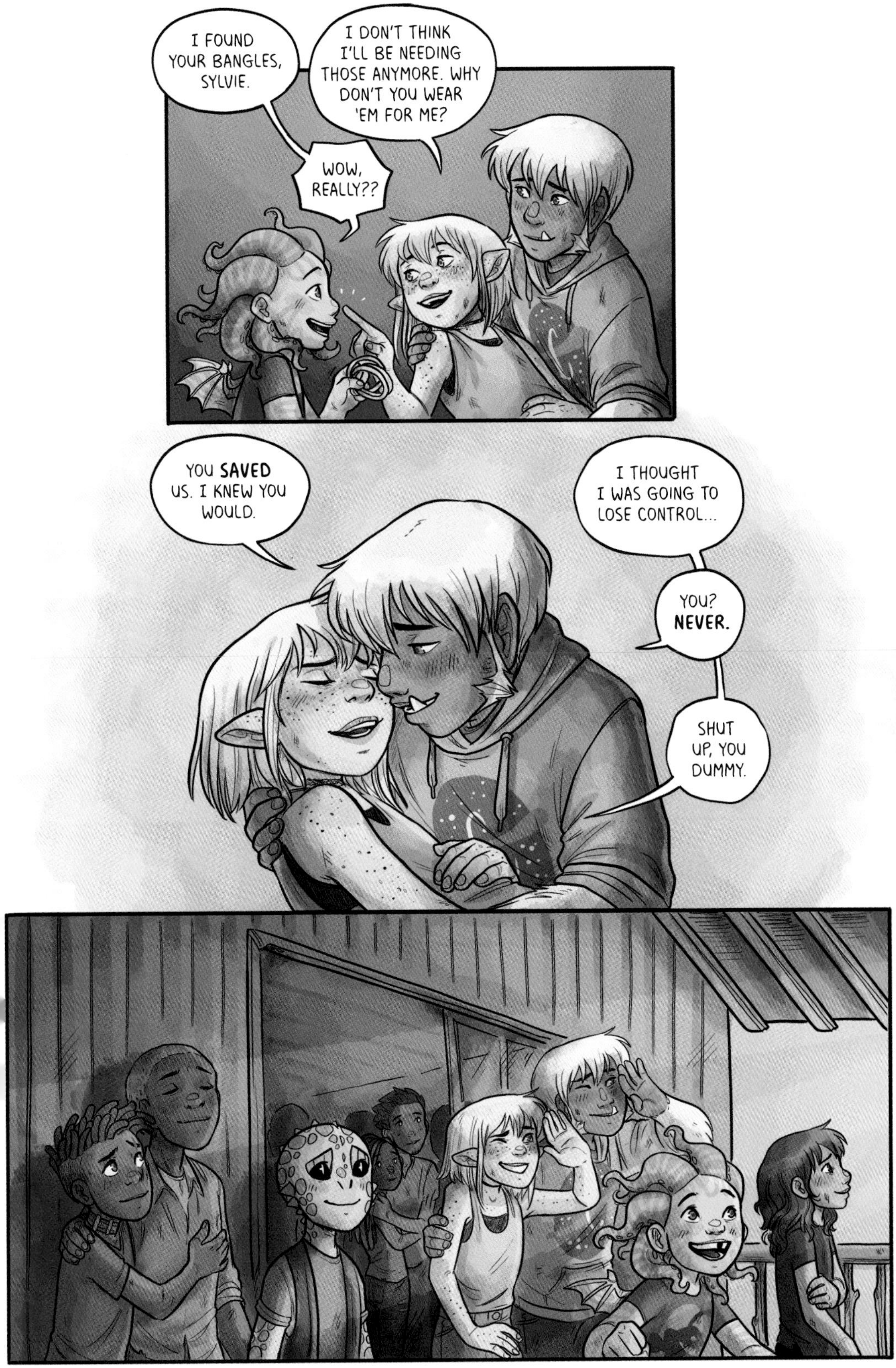
I FOUND YOUR BANGLES, SYLVIE.
I DON'T THINK I'LL BE NEEDING THOSE ANYMORE. WHY DON'T YOU WEAR 'EM FOR ME?
WOW, REALLY??
YOU **SAVED** US. I KNEW YOU WOULD.
I THOUGHT I WAS GOING TO LOSE CONTROL...
YOU? **NEVER.**
SHUT UP, YOU DUMMY.

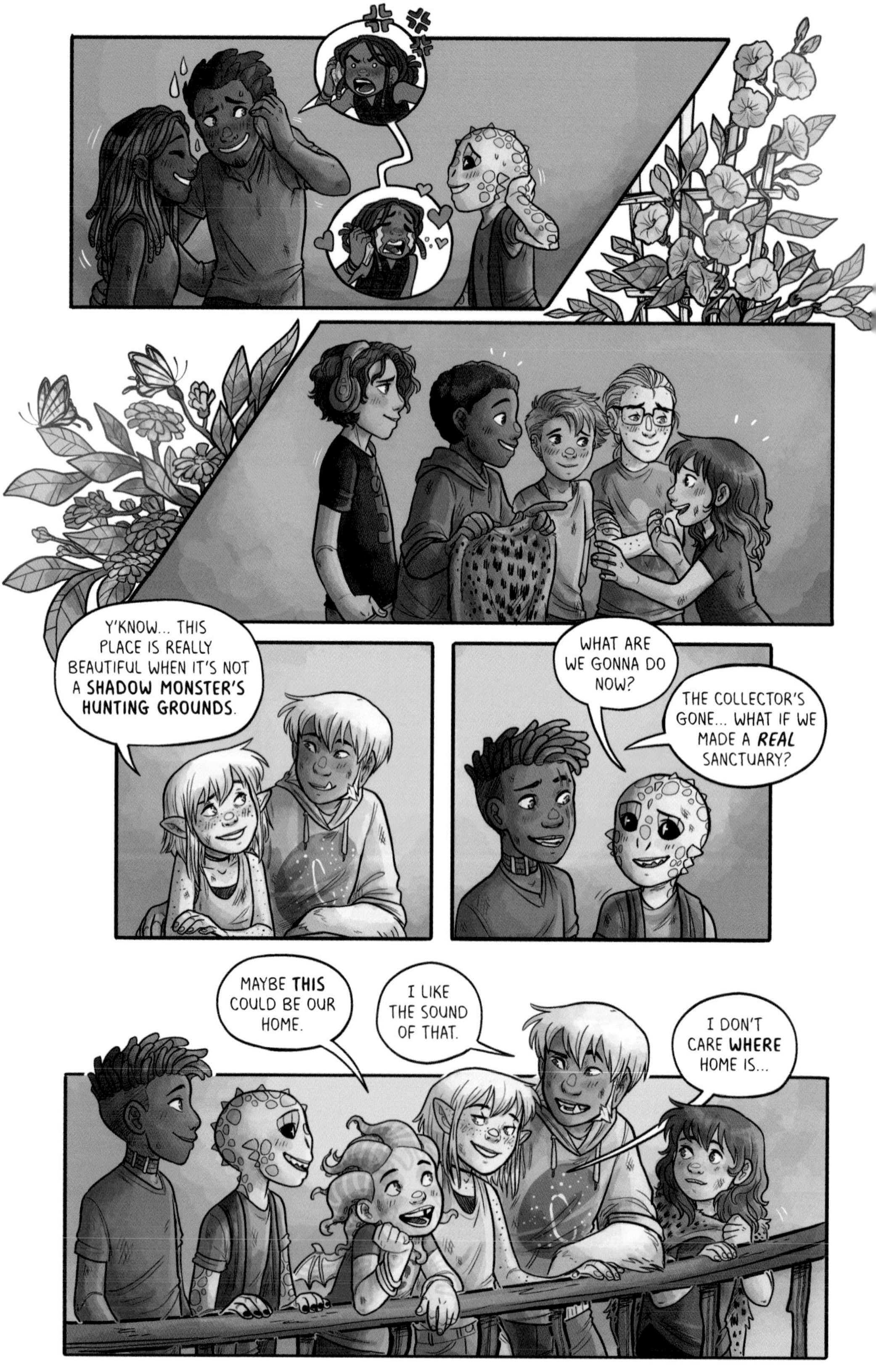
Y'KNOW... THIS PLACE IS REALLY BEAUTIFUL WHEN IT'S NOT A SHADOW MONSTER'S HUNTING GROUNDS.
WHAT ARE WE GONNA DO NOW?
THE COLLECTOR'S GONE... WHAT IF WE MADE A REAL SANCTUARY?
MAYBE THIS COULD BE OUR HOME.
I LIKE THE SOUND OF THAT.
I DON'T CARE WHERE HOME IS...

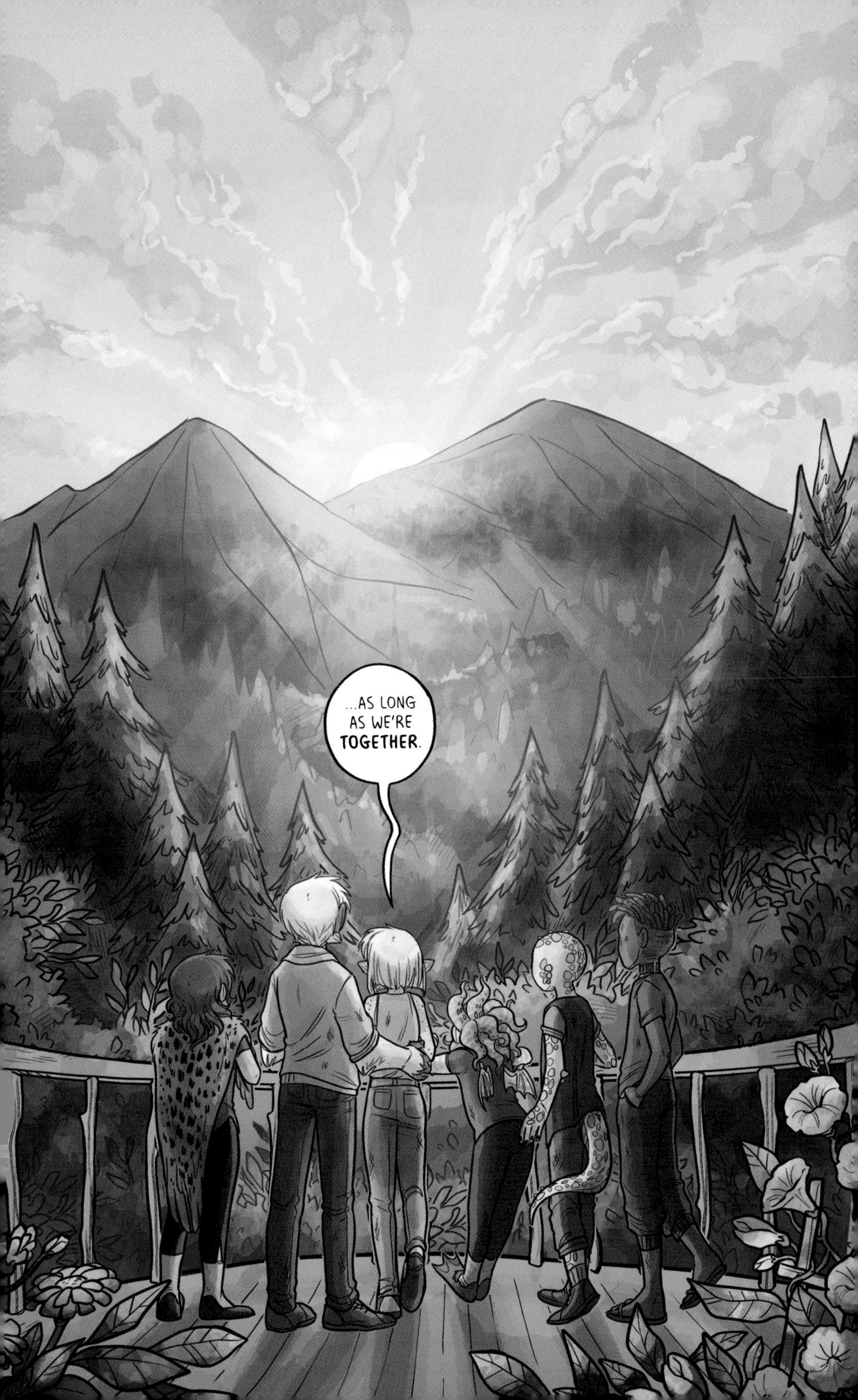
...AS LONG AS WE'RE TOGETHER.

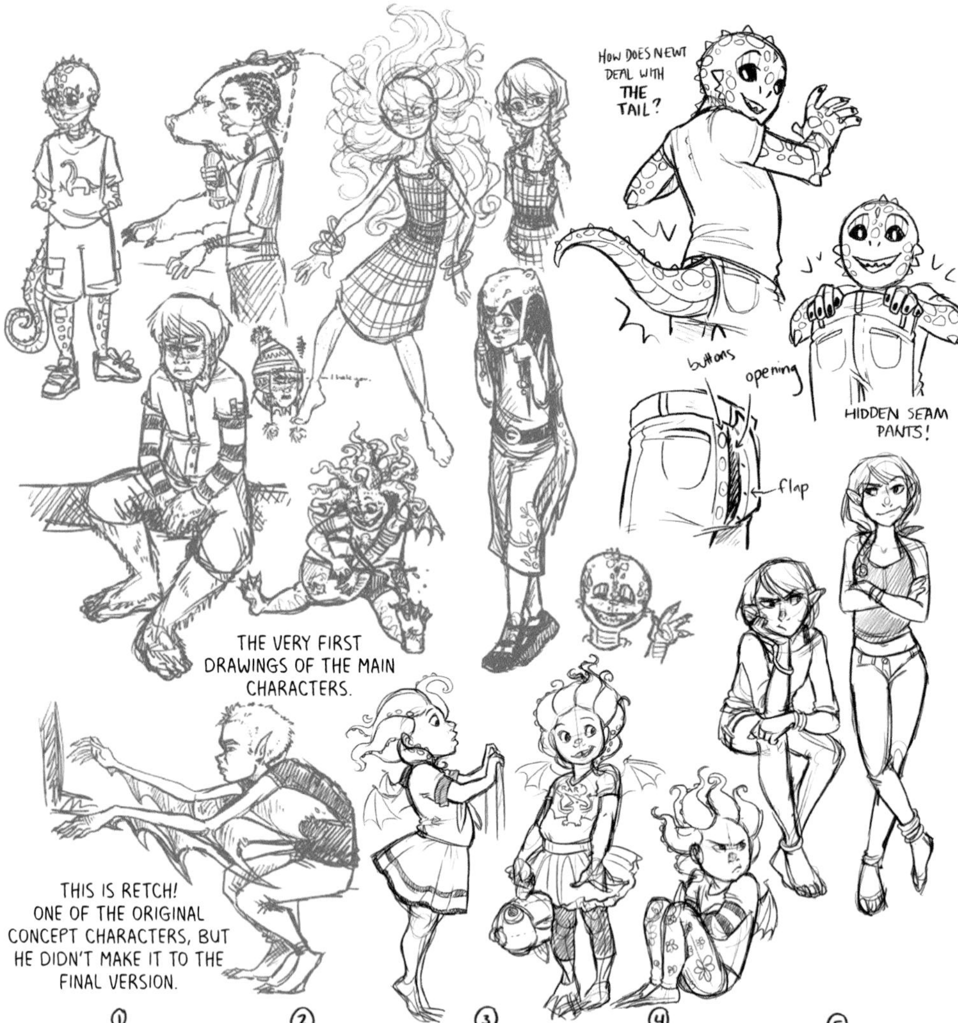
HOW DOES NEWT DEAL WITH THE TAIL?
buttons
opening
flap
HIDDEN SEAM PANTS!

THE VERY FIRST DRAWINGS OF THE MAIN CHARACTERS.

THIS IS RETCH! ONE OF THE ORIGINAL CONCEPT CHARACTERS, BUT HE DIDN'T MAKE IT TO THE FINAL VERSION.

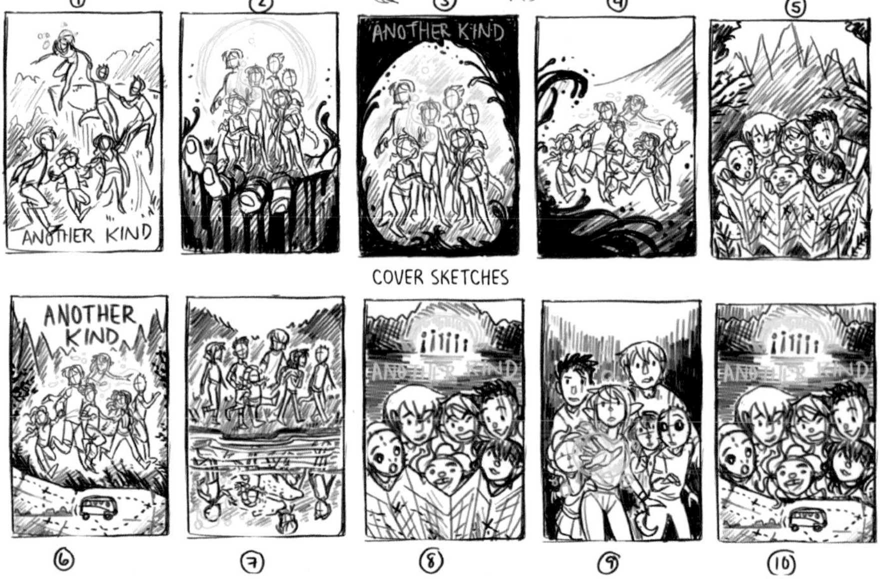
1
2
3
4
5
ANOTHER KIND
ANOTHER KIND
ANOTHER KIND
6
7
8
9
10

COVER SKETCHES

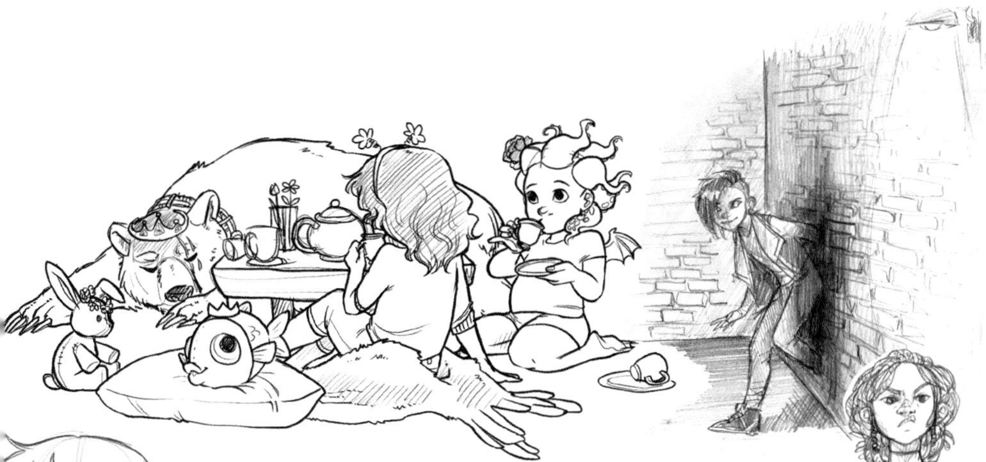

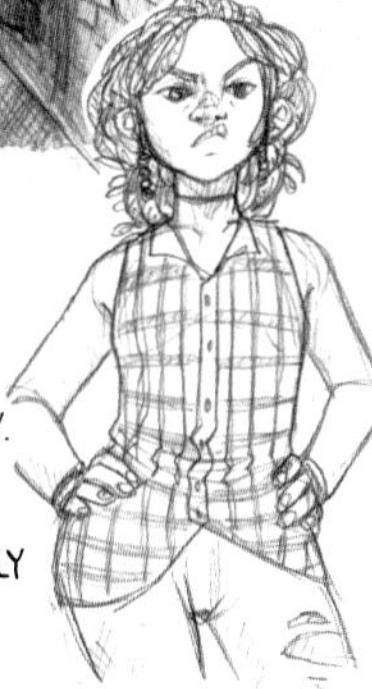

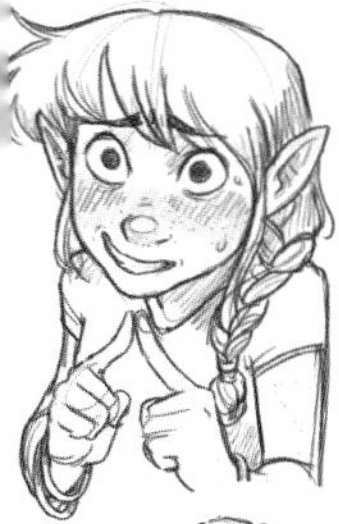

ACKNOWLEDGMENTS

THANK YOU TO OUR FRIENDS AND FAMILY FOR THEIR UNENDING SUPPORT AND ENTHUSIASM THROUGHOUT THE CREATION OF THIS BOOK. YOU KEPT US GOING AND INSPIRED SO MANY OF THE FAMILIES IN THIS STORY. WE LOVE YOU!

THANK YOU A MILLION TIMES OVER TO SAVANNA AND GIGI—OUR UNBELIEVABLY AMAZING FLATTERS WHO MADE THIS BOOK POSSIBLE THROUGH THEIR PATIENCE, PERSERVERENCE, AND DEDICATION TO THE MEME. BDB FOREVER.

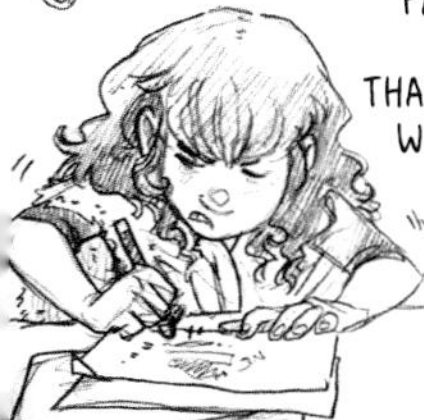

THANK YOU TO CLAIRE, THE AGENT OF OUR DREAMS, WHO GEEKED WITH US THE WHOLE TIME AND IS MAGGIE'S #1 FAN IN THE ENTIRE UNIVERSE. THANK YOU FOR HELPING US MAKE THIS HAPPEN.

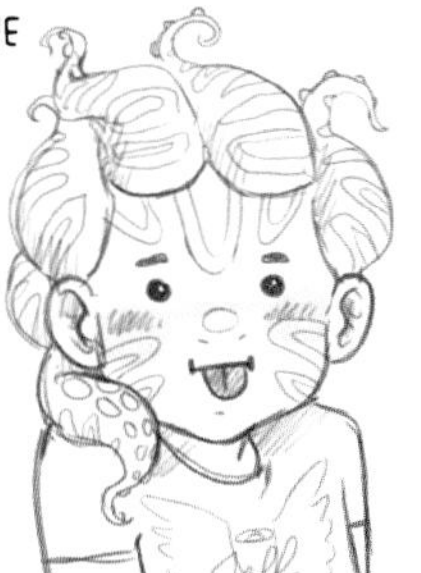

THANK YOU TO ROSE, ANDREW, AND JOE AT HARPER FOR BEING THE BEST TEAM WE COULD ASK FOR! Y'ALL ARE CHAMPIONS AND WE CAN'T WAIT FOR THE NEXT.

THANK YOU TO OUR HOME OFFICE FURRY COWORKERS FOR ALWAYS LAYING ON US WHEN WE WERE TRYING TO GET WORK DONE. MANY SCRITCHES AND PETS FOR YOU.

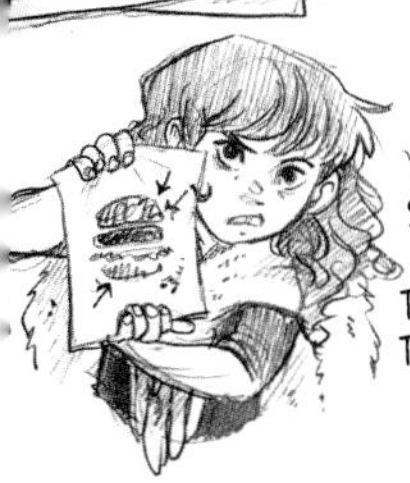

SHOUT-OUTS TO THE DIPPERS—OUR FIRST AND BIGGEST FANS. THANK YOU JOAN HILTY, ALEX FINE, THE ELDRITCH CREW, THE GIRL* GANG, THE PEPPER PAUPERS, LOREN COLEMAN, AND THE CRYPTOZOOLOGY MUSEUM. THANK YOU TO *BUZZFEED UNSOLVED*, *THE ADVENTURE ZONE*, *CRITICAL ROLE*, AND WAY TOO MANY PODCASTS FOR HELPING KEEP OUR MINDS OCCUPIED THROUGH THE TOUGH TIMES.

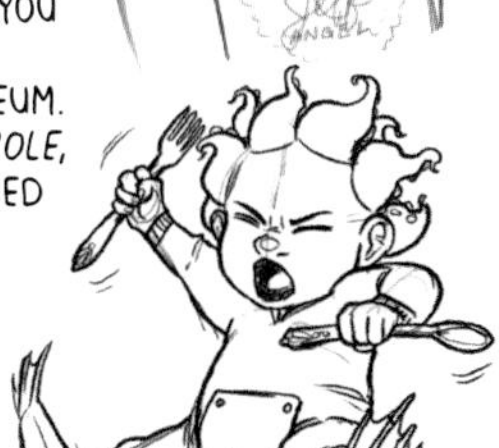

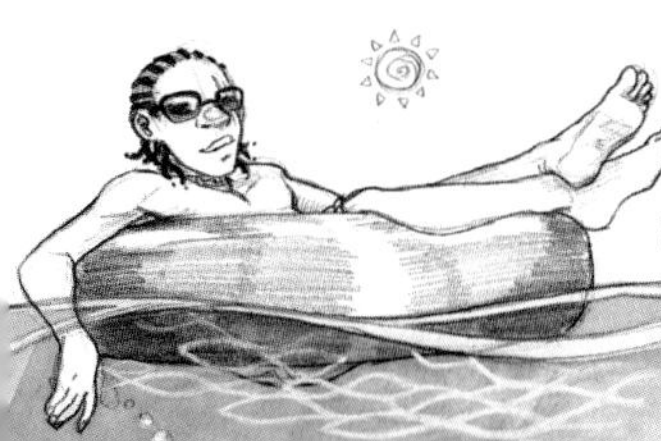

TO ALL THE CRYPTOZOOLOGISTS WHO HAVE COME BEFORE US. WITHOUT YOUR DEDICATION TO THE STUDY OF WEIRD PHENOMENA, WE MIGHT NEVER HAVE LEARNED TO LOVE THEM JUST LIKE YOU DO.

AND FINALLY—
THANK YOU FOR READING!

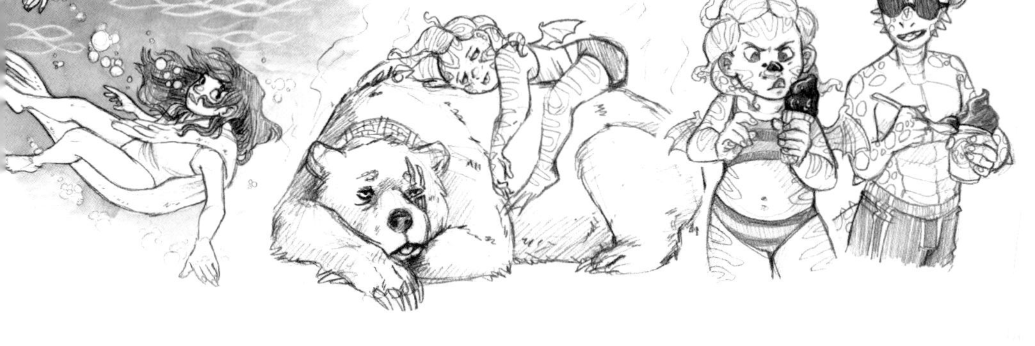

FOR DOYLE
AND FOR OUR FAMILIES,
OF ONE KIND OR
ANOTHER

HARPERALLEY IS AN IMPRINT OF HARPERCOLLINS PUBLISHERS.

ANOTHER KIND
COPYRIGHT © 2021 BY CAIT MAY AND TREVOR BREAM
ALL RIGHTS RESERVED. PRINTED IN BOSNIA AND HERZEGOVINA.
NO PART OF THIS BOOK MAY BE USED OR REPRODUCED IN ANY MANNER WHATSOEVER WITHOUT WRITTEN PERMISSION
EXCEPT IN THE CASE OF BRIEF QUOTATIONS EMBODIED IN CRITICAL ARTICLES AND REVIEWS. FOR INFORMATION ADDRESS
HARPERCOLLINS CHILDREN'S BOOKS, A DIVISION OF HARPERCOLLINS PUBLISHERS, 195 BROADWAY, NEW YORK, NY 10007.
WWW.HARPERALLEY.COM

LIBRARY OF CONGRESS CONTROL NUMBER: 2021939648
ISBN 978-0-06-304353-4 (PBK.) — ISBN 978-0-06-304354-1

TYPOGRAPHY BY JOE MERKEL

23 24 25 GPS 10 9 8 7 6 5

❖

FIRST EDITION